Satisfaction

THEA DEVINE

Satisfaction

BRAVA

KENSINGTON PUBLISHING CORP.
http://www.kensingtonbooks.com

BRAVA BOOKS are published by

Kensington Publishing Corp.
850 Third Avenue
New York, NY 10022

All Kensington titles, imprints and distributed lines are available at special quantity discounts for bulk purchases for sales promotion, premiums, fund raising, educational or institutional use.

Special book excerpts or customized printings can also be created to fit specific needs. For details, write or phone the office of the Kensington Special Sales Manager: Kensington Publishing Corp., 850 Third Avenue, New York, NY 10022. Attn. Special Sales Department. Phone: 1-800-221-2647.

Brava and the B logo Reg. U.S. Pat. & TM Off.

ISBN 0-7582-0401-9

First Kensington Trade Paperback Printing: May 2004
10 9 8 7 6 5 4 3 2 1

Printed in the United States of America

In memory of our beloved calico, Emily

. . . and, as always, for John . . .

Chapter One

Waybury House, Darfield
Hertfordshire, England
Spring 1894

This could have been mine . . .

Feeling a little curl of bitterness, Jancie shifted forward in her seat in the rumbling dray as it turned into the gate and onto the drive to Waybury House.

This could have been mine . . . all right, Father's—our family's . . .

Everything exuded prosperity: the beautifully tended hedges, the wide swath of emerald green lawn, the crisp crack of oyster shell under the wagon wheels, and as they got closer to the house, the riot of flowers lining the drive and bursting under the windows of the huge stone house that suddenly loomed in front of her.

Dear heaven. And I spent my growing-up years in that mausoleum of a girls' school while Father labored for a government pittance under the hot Indian sun?

Don't think about that.

Don't think about what? All those years peeling potatoes? All those years belowstairs?

All those years she was maligned and disdained because she was a kitchen girl . . . Kitchen girl. Working for her bread and board. Lower than vermin. Not To Be Associated With. To be teased, scorned, and mocked and looked down upon by the full-tuition girls.

The kitchen girls ate scraps and soup. Sneaked a treat now and again. Banded together like ferrets. Lived on the topmost floors in the garrets and attics. Sat in the very last row in classes.

And as the wealthier girls advanced in years, in grade, and in station, things got considerably worse. The kitchen girls now took their classes apart from the tuition girls. And there were lessons to which the kitchen girls had no access: dancing, deportment, art, music, French, and all the elegant things that young ladies of society needed to know—how to dress, flirt, arrange flowers, set a perfect table.

All the extras for which kitchen girls had no money.

They were called "dirty girls" then, the maids and kitchen girls who earned their room and tuition by dint of hard, honest work. They were to be pitied, used, derided, made fun of, treated like—well, dirt, and made to do onerous, malicious things, and never to be raised from the gutter.

And on the horizon, there were social events during which the polished and finished young women from St. Boniface would mix and mingle with the top-notch and top-drawer young gentlemen of the Eccles and Bristowe Schools.

Boys who lived in houses like this, boys whose fathers had money from commerce, inheritance, or perhaps from the diamond fields in South Africa.

Boys like Hugo Galliard's sons, who had grown up with all the privileges that she had not.

No place on the dance floor, or even the sidelines, for a kitchen girl. No dirty girls allowed. No money anywhere for anything.

Nothing but servitude, and knowing that, but for fate—or Hugo Galliard—her own father could have been every bit as wealthy as those boys' fathers . . .

How many times, in her childhood, her youth, her young

womanhood, had Jancie heard the story of Edmund Renbrook and Hugo Galliard, handshake partners and rogue miners? They had been in South Africa, seeking that one elusive, wealthy-beyond-all-measure, earth-shattering diamond strike—beyond even the strike at Kimberley, so crowded with dreamers and die-hards, and laddered with delegations and deals by the fortunate few who had gotten one of the 500 claim stakes, that there was no room for hope or day pay. And that didn't even include those who went and sold their stakes for thousands of pounds profit.

But that was not for Hugo, and thus not for Edmund, who had been perfectly willing to do the work. Instead, they followed a hunch, a year-long search, for a kimberlitic vein that played out into an unlikely and already abandoned pit in a field in the middle of nowhere, south of the Kimberley fields. Just the two of them, eking out the pith and pebbles of precious diamonds one by one from the yellow soil, until the disastrous day of the explosion that left Edmund unconscious and alone in the veldt and Hugo at the mercy of murderers and thieves.

This had been Jancie's bedtime story almost from the time she had any memory at all. She could recite it by heart. Her father awakened with no memory of what had happened, no memory of Hugo Galliard, or of why he was even there, blast-singed, in the rubble of . . . of what? And how many years it had taken her father to walk and work his way back to Capetown, living on scrub and maggots; how many years more to earn the money to book passage to England?

And then he met her mother, got married, went into the Indian service to support his new wife, all the while his memory slowly returning in bits and pieces, like the pebbles and rocks he had eked from the abandoned pit at Kaamberoo.

Slowly, he remembered. Slowly, his memory returned, honing in on his truth, and one day, he put it all together: the partnership, the mine, the woman whom he and Hugo both loved, Hugo's first betrayal—marrying Olivia before they even left for South Africa. All of it, he remembered. The work. The pit. The strike. The blast.

And then Edmund's wife had died in childbirth, and he simmered with a fine, keen rage that Jancie had to spend her first years in India with him, subject to rampant diseases and even death, while Hugo's sons were being raised in luxury someplace in the English countryside.

Jancie, on whom he pinned all his hopes and dreams.

What hopes and dreams?

She must be educated. She must take her place in that society as if Edmund had returned to England with that fortune in diamonds all those years ago.

Edmund remembered that. All those little pebbles of diamonds they had pulled from the soil.

A fortune in diamonds that instead had bought for Hugo Galliard and his family all of what Jancie saw before her, as the dray lumbered down the drive.

All of this could have been her father's . . . hers. She could have been a tuition girl. She could have had everything that the wealthy girls had. She could have learned etiquette, drawing, dance, French. She could have had suitors, could have made a suitable match.

Instead, she was exchanging one servitude for another.

And she must suppress her welling anger besides. But she prided herself on being pragmatic. Another lesson from the kitchen. She must look at what *was*. The deed was done, after all. Life was unfair, and all she could do was continue on as her father wished— and this he did wish, most emphatically: that she repay Hugo's kindness by coming to Waybury House for as long as Olivia might need her.

She never could comprehend what her father was thinking, and his insistence on her acceptance of this mission only added to her confusion. She would have thought Edmund would want her in India, with him, instead of waiting on his enemy's wife.

And, in fact, when Edmund finally traced Hugo all those years ago, he hadn't gone off on a tear about the past; rather, he had asked but one favor: Hugo's help in keeping his motherless daughter far from the risks of living in India, and his assistance in sending Jancie to a suitable boarding school until she came of age.

Jancie never did understand why her father didn't demand more. After all, Hugo had survived the blast, had returned to England, was living comfortably with his family in Hertfordshire.

So if Hugo could afford to pay her tuition, surely he could honor the terms of the partnership, and write Edmund a check.

But Edmund had no contracts, no promissory notes, no signatures, no partnership papers, nothing in writing or anything binding. They had made a partnership on a handshake, on their honor. And so there was just the knowledge between himself and Hugo about what had been done.

Hugo had an answer for all of Edmund's questions before they were even asked, and he was perfectly willing to explain the circumstances of having seemingly left Edmund in such dire straits—the murderers and thieves part—and he was only too happy to do a signal service in reparation for his old and valued friend.

Olivia (did Edmund remember Olivia?) made the arrangements for Jancie's admission to St. Boniface's School for Young Ladies, and Hugo had arranged to pay her tuition and board until Jancie was old enough to earn her keep.

He hadn't long to wait: the headmistress put her in the kitchen peeling potatoes not two years later.

Edmund happily left her there. And nobody cared.

And now, all these years later, her *oh-so-kind benefactor*, Mr. Hugo Galliard, had need of a companion for the same said Olivia, Olivia whom her father had loved all that long time ago, who was ill with some debilitating disease, and Hugo had the passing thought that perhaps Miss Renbrook might consider returning the favor he had done her father, in keeping her at St. Boniface for the last eleven years, by coming to Waybury House and helping him with his wife.

No, she had thought furiously at first, *I have no obligation to this man in this life to make restitution for all those years of peeling vegetables and being a maid. That was no kindness. That was Hugo Galliard's guilty conscience. He owes my father too much, and I owe him no consideration whatsoever. I have paid my way on every level. I will not wait another year, another moment. I am not going from one servitude to another. I am going to India.*

The India of her childhood memories. The impossibly hot and exotic India, where one could do what one wished, live like a queen, and forever be free . . .

Not to go to India? That dream of going back to India had kept her going all those years at St. Boniface.

That—and Emily. Emily was her family, her cat.

And so instead she and Emily came to Hertfordshire.

India. Hertfordshire.

Somehow, they didn't connect, there wasn't a straight line from one to the other that she could tell, but nevertheless, here she was, at her father's behest, feeling a grinding anger that she must repay this debt at all when Hugo Galliard owed herself and her father so much more.

I could have lived here; my mother might still be alive. I could have grown up here instead of that hellhole of a school. I could have been a tuition girl . . .

And then the wagon ground to a stop beside the shallow front steps of Waybury House.

And Emily leapt out of her basket.

And . . . "No cats."

The voice was like the crack of a whip, from the thin lips of a tall, desiccated-looking man with paper-thin skin and formal dress who stood at the partially open door.

Jancie climbed out of the wagon, and reached in for her one overstuffed suitcase. There ought to have been a servant for that, she thought grimly. Which just immediately put her in her place. And this old fossil had ought to be more respectful, no matter who she was.

She lifted her chin. "Of course there's a cat. I'm Jancie Renbrook. I believe Mr. Galliard is expecting me. And the cat," she added boldly.

"Not the cat."

"Absolutely the cat." She had decided that the moment she had agreed to come, and this family *retainer* had no business telling her what she could or couldn't do in this house that might have been her father's.

She felt a constriction in her vitals. Emily stayed—there was no question. Emily was her playmate, her family, her companion, her best friend, and her confidant—who never scolded, teased, or said no to her. The most practical cat with uncommon good sense. She couldn't live without Emily's companionship—anywhere. And especially *here*.

Of course, the cat, and they had best get used to it—to her.

"Otherwise, I cannot be of service here as Mr. Galliard expected," Jancie added firmly. "Kindly convey my regrets to him and Mrs. Galliard."

"You'll have to walk. The wagon's gone and left . . ."

She knew that, and she ought to have thought to ask the driver to stay. But who could have predicted this impasse over a cat? Well, it was too late now.

She thinned her lips and bent down to scoop up Emily, who made a protesting *owww*. "Then I'll walk." This was a major bluff—the bag was far too heavy, being packed with everything she owned, and carrying Emily in the basket would be awkward—but she would do it, just to show this nasty old man, no matter how many miles she had to walk back to the village.

Wherever the village was.

To reinforce that decision, she thrust Emily into the basket, picked up her bag, and turned from the door.

Down the steps, onto the oyster shell drive . . . with the desiccated old butler watching her with an eagle eye . . . and the dray already out the gate—and too far away to call it back.

This was the life other people lived, with carriages and cabs and footmen to carry their bags. But not her, not her.

Ah—no matter, she had done harder work than this, and her determination was rock-solid once she made up her mind.

Of course, where she would go from here was also debatable. Hugo had paid for her ticket out, and it had only been one-way, and she had no appreciable money to pay her way back to London. She hadn't thought it would be necessary.

No cats, indeed.

Well, she would just find work in the village for a day if she had to—just enough for train fare—or stay long enough to pay her passage to India. How many years would that take? It reeked of her father's experience—and Hugo Galliard having the upper hand and the power, once again.

She felt the anger unfurling in her belly. Always Hugo, always winning somehow . . .

Don't be silly.

Wise, wise Emily, looking at her with those knowing golden eyes.

You'll find a way.

She would. She always did.

She started walking, one foot after the other, her mind blank; she didn't want to think, didn't want to try to figure out how to breach this impasse. No cats. Inconceivable, when it was *they* who needed *her.*

The truth was, she had no idea what she was getting into, whether she stayed or left. And with every crunching step, she felt her anger mounting. She could hardly make the gate at this rate, let alone the village.

"Well, what do I do?" she murmured, looking at Emily so she wouldn't have to look at the long distance between where she was and the gate.

Don't trust the butler.

That hadn't occurred to her. Of course. He was so old. So paper-thin. So disapproving—probably of *everything.*

Of course he didn't want a cat upsetting things. Or a stranger from far away. And he didn't know Emily, so he couldn't know she would be most useful, especially if he needed an excellent mouser.

Emily, a kitchen girl . . .

That was a funny thought, imagining Emily in a ragged apron chasing mice, and so, distracted by that image, she didn't hear the thudding hoofbeats pounding relentlessly toward her until the rider was almost upon her, fighting for control of the horse, and veering wildly off to her right to avoid crashing into her altogether.

And then, with consummate skill, he pulled up and slid off his panting mount, and strode toward her in a most menacing way.

"What flower nearly tripped me up in this misbegotten Eden?"

But she never heard the question. She saw only the raw beauty of his face, the firmness of his lips, his intimidating height, his stormy gray eyes, and the wildness in his soul that matched her own. And an arrogance that could only be met with a profligate defiance in kind.

She was only sixteen, but she knew what that look was about, she knew how the gentry were, if only from overheard gossip, and she knew her response was wholly inappropriate. He scared her to death and she couldn't stop looking at him.

Don't . . .

The ever-pragmatic Emily. But it was too late. She knew it already.

"Oh God—you're . . . that girl—the family cross . . ."

"Jancie," she whispered, mesmerized.

But he didn't hear her.

"Oh, hell. A cat? They won't let her in, you know." He took her bag, took her arm, and forcibly turned her back to the house. His voice was as burnished as cognac. She thought she might drown in it.

"They must. I've had her forever." She noted abstractly that he was very much older than she. She was amazed she could even string two words together, he was that magnetic, and so very powerful.

"Then they will," he said, his brow furrowed. And then he remembered it all. "Right. You're Renbrook. The long-lost partner's daughter. The one for whom he's been paying out guilt money all these years."

He doesn't want you here.

Emily was too perceptive by half.

It would pay to remember that by the grace of God, it could have been her home, her horses, her butler, her attitude . . . *Guilt money . . .*

Belatedly, she digested what he had said. "Guilt money?"

He brushed it off. "Did I say that? You must have misunderstood me."

She knew she hadn't. She knew what he meant. And he meant to be unkind. "He asked me to—"

But he knew that already and interrupted her. "Why wouldn't he? You come virtually free, my dear girl. You'll pay for every shilling he ever laid out for you, trust me."

And feel no guilt nor shame, either, Jancie thought angrily. "And what about you?" she asked bluntly. They were at the steps now, and he was hauling her up to the front door.

"Oh, hell—me? I'm spending every cent in the family coffers as fast as I can. I'm Lujan, by the way."

Lujan, the heir. As opposed to Kyger, the younger brother. Yes, her father had written of both, of him particularly. Perpetually in trouble, always raising hell, perennially in debt, and no doubt down from London right now for that very reason.

But still, for all the dissipation in his face and the weariness etched around his mouth and eyes, he was a force of nature. The minute he erupted into the room, all attention focused on him. Emily, sensing an opportunity, jumped from the basket and scooted under the sofa where Olivia Galliard reclined, smelling salts to the ready at Lujan's unexpected appearance.

"What now?" Hugo demanded.

It was a blunt initiation into the family dynamic; they didn't even notice Jancie was there—or they didn't care. Lujan had the right of it: she would be a servant, a piece of furniture, part of the wall.

The elegant, *opulent* walls and furniture, paid for by the sweat of her father's brow and Hugo's perfidy. She could calculate to the shilling what kind of money had been spent on that room.

But that was beside the point, now she was here. Or was it?

And Lujan, taunting Hugo and Olivia—what to make of him? He was reckless, ruthless, and blunt, and he'd totally forgotten she was there.

Or—in the face of Hugo's wrath, his manners went out the window as well.

She preferred to think that, but no—

"How much?" Hugo asked, a tinge of sarcasm lacing the question.

Lujan shrugged. "The usual. Hello, Mother."

"I'm ill," Olivia whispered.

"She can't take these disruptions," Hugo said. "You have to leave."

That didn't even bother Lujan. Rather, it reminded him that he'd brought a piece of flotsam in the house with him. "Oh— Mother. This is the Renbrook girl—and her cat—where's the cat?— come to . . . what exactly is she going to be doing for you?"

Was there a malicious note in his question?

Olivia levered herself up onto her elbow. "Come here, Jancie. Let me look at you."

Jancie shot a look at Lujan, who shrugged, and then she moved so that Olivia could see her more clearly.

"You look like you could hardly lift a fly."

"Well, she was about to carry that heavy suitcase, and the cat, back to the village, Mother," Lujan said lazily, "so I'm fairly sure she can cope with anything you might need her to do."

Olivia fell back on the couch, and then popped back up again.

"A cat, did you say? I don't like cats. You'll have to relegate it to the barn."

"But she's a very good cat," Jancie said, holding on to her temper. "She's been my companion for years, and I wouldn't dream of—"

"If you want to stay—and I assume you do—you must send the cat to the barn," Olivia said. "There can be no argument about it. From you."

That fired Jancie's temper. "Then perhaps I should go, because I will not tolerate anyone being so cruel to my cat."

Olivia looked taken aback, and Jancie felt a prick of conscience. Olivia really was ill—it showed in her face, in her pallor, in the effort she was making to defuse her son and welcome Jancie.

So she added, "I'm very pleased to be of whatever service to you that I can, but I will have my cat, and if that isn't satisfactory, I will find work in the village until I can join my father in India."

"That's the way, Jancie," Lujan interposed, amused. "And face it, Mother, you're paying this poor child no recompense at all compared to the value of what she will be doing for you. You can at least let her have the damned cat. Or she'll be on the boat to India in no time."

A note of derision in his voice for sure, given all the exigencies before that could happen, so Jancie ignored him.

"I'm too tired to argue." Olivia eased herself down again. "The cat stays out of my sight until I decide what is best."

"Yes, ma'am."

"You won," Lujan whispered loud enough for Olivia to hear. "Good for you for standing up to her. You must, you know."

But Jancie didn't know anything except she didn't think she liked Olivia all that much. And she knew she disliked Hugo just because of what had happened to her father.

And the house, so lovely on the outside, was a veritable mausoleum within, judging just by the parlor, and it depressed her, even with its expensive, elegant furniture. And then Emily had utterly disappeared, and might well be eaten by the butler by now, and that terrified her.

And Lujan was too cavalier about everything, and cared about absolutely nothing. Not one to depend on. Not an ally. Not an enemy, even. He was a cipher, not to be parsed out by the likes of her.

So much for her boarding school education.

She saw a movement under Olivia's sofa. Emily!

I'm here . . .

Cornered. And no way Jancie could get her out.

"This is—" Hugo's voice, bringing her attention back to him. "This is Bingham, Jancie." She turned to find the paper-thin man with the disapproving lips. "He'll take you to your room so you can get settled in."

Emily!

She threw a backward glance over her shoulder. No sign of Emily—just Lujan's dark, mocking gaze following her progress out, and the distinct impression he knew everything she was feeling and thinking.

It was a commodious room, adjacent to Olivia Galliard's bedroom, but since it was at the back the house, it was also dark and gloomy. The windows faced west, which meant she would have the waning light of day, at which time she would probably be busy with Olivia.

No sunshine in this house, in this room, in her life—ever.

The furniture looked to be castoffs that had come to the extra room when they had been replaced elsewhere. Good enough for a dirty girl. Better than she had a right to expect, some might say. But still, it was a large room with comfortable furniture, a beautiful fireplace, and a utilitarian desk by the window where she could write to her father.

She wasn't sure she wanted to write to Edmund yet. She didn't know yet what to make of Hugo and Olivia, so what would she tell him?

Hugo lives in a quite luxurious house deep in the countryside with a butler and servants and periodical visits from his rakehell son. The younger one has yet to put in an appearance. Perhaps he hides when Lujan is around? The rooms are beautifully appointed with furniture and decorations that anyone would admire, and if it hadn't been for Hugo's greed, this might have been our house . . .

She hated everything about it. *Everything.* Including the fact that she and her father were so beholden to him because Edmund had no proof that they were anything more than his charity cases now.

And she would be Olivia's companion until . . . Hugo had never specified just how long she was expected to stay.

Until Olivia—no, don't think that way. Yes, Olivia had looked pale and weak and ill, but that didn't mean that with some judicious care, she might not recover.

Until forever—trapped at Waybury House until she was old and decrepit, and they buried her in the woods . . .

Stop it!

She had no idea what was expected of her. At the least, she would be feeling her way through the minefield of this family's relationships, expectations, and her father's and Hugo's mutual past. Things she couldn't know about, and Hugo did. Things, perhaps, he hoped that Edmund had forgotten.

And maybe her father had. Maybe not every memory had come back cleanly and clearly. Maybe he hadn't remembered correctly, maybe the true story was dimmed by time, and that perspective held sway. Maybe it had been blasted out of his consciousness altogether, and everything he remembered was a fable that he had invented to explain his failures.

No matter. Every step of the way, every minute she was here, she knew she would feel those tentacles of resentment that it could have been her, her father, and her mother, alive, living this life and enjoying these comforts. And it would take every ounce of willpower not to be strangled by those thoughts.

She wondered if Hugo had suggested she come here to rub her and Edmund's noses in it. Oh but, no—that was the most uncharitable thing she had thought yet . . .

She caught a movement out of the corner of her eye, a flick of black and white.

And there came comfort . . . Emily. Somehow Emily had found her way upstairs and found her, just like Emily had found her all those years ago, when she had been a scruffy, scraggly cat who had wandered into the school's kitchen alley one day and attracted her attention.

And once she was bathed and her patchy black, tan, and white coloration was revealed, she had proved to be a most elegant cat, and her slanty golden eyes were ageless and wise.

She looked like an Emily, but Jancie couldn't say why she thought so. It didn't take a day for Emily to become her companion, playmate, and confidant, the one with whom she had conversations and commiserations, who mirrored back and agreed with everything she thought and felt.

If the headmistress had ever got wind of Emily . . .

It didn't bear thinking about, even after the fact. She'd come too close to being turned out here on account of Emily.

But this was the thing: Emily was her family, and she knew instantly, the first day, that she needed Emily as much as Emily needed her.

As Emily sensed Jancie needed her now.

She hopped up onto the bed and prowled up and down its length in her elegantly measured way. *Owww.*

Emily was hungry.

Jancie rubbed her ears, gave her a body-enveloping hug which she wriggled out of, and then Jancie began unpacking her sorry wardrobe. Black bombazine dresses, two. Brown dress trimmed with velvet, one. Two pairs of shoes. Three sets of undergarments. A half-dozen very well mended pairs of stockings. No frills. No trims. No jewelry. A dirty girl's wardrobe, made for practicality and work, but at least she was not consigned to the garret here.

Yet.

How different things might have been, had Edmund not been blown to the sky that day in Kaamberoo . . .

She must stop thinking like this.

Mrrrow, Emily said, curling up on the bed.

"I will get you something to eat, I promise," Jancie told her. "But you must stay here." She hoped the cat would stay there. A little dish of milk would do for now, though the last thing she wanted to do was explore the house.

But she supposed she must learn her way around sooner than later.

Black bombazine . . . she stared at herself in the mirrored door of the armoire. It could have been lace and pearls. Satin and gold. Diamonds and . . .

...diamonds...

Her heartbeat accelerated. Where did that thought come from?

She shook it away.

But—it was only natural to think of the diamonds, after all. Especially now she was here.

She had never allowed herself to think about it. In all the years and all the times Edmund had recounted the story, she had never voiced out loud the thing that tiptoed around the back of her mind...

What if there were more diamonds? What if Hugo could never have spent what he took from the Kaamberoo pipes? What if there were enough diamonds even now for Edmund, for her?

God—what was she thinking?

Ungrateful! Greedy! Edmund did not want this... this wasn't why she had come, this wasn't what she was here for. She had to stop resenting that a share in all this had not come to her father and her by the grace of everything that was fair and holy.

No one could change the past. And if a man did not have the morality to make amends to the partner he had exploited, then he would get his just reward in the next life.

It wasn't for her to say, to judge, to take revenge.

Owwww.

She looked up abruptly, jolted from her thoughts.

I'm hungry.

And wasn't that the most important point? Repining would get her nothing. She should be grateful, satisfied—she had a roof over her head, a decent education, a father still alive, and a job to do.

It was enough. Enough for any girl in her circumstances.

She looked at Emily, curled up on the bed, as she went out the door.

Wasn't it?

Enough?

Chapter Two

"So there you are, finally," Olivia said fretfully. She was still reclined on the sofa, but with a cloth draped over her forehead. "I needed you an hour ago."

Jancie immediately felt herself prickle up. "Surely it hasn't been an hour, ma'am. I was only unpacking and seeing to . . ." Better not to mention Emily, come to that. "Unpacking my clothes, ma'am. Now tell me what I can do for you."

"Rinse out the cloth, for one thing."

There was a porcelain basin on a nearby table. "The water is cold, ma'am. Would you prefer warm water?"

Olivia raised herself slightly off the sofa. "Cold? Cold? It was just brought to me. How could it already be cold? Oh, very well, ring for some warm water . . ." She sank back onto the sofa and, noting Jancie's confused look, waved her hand in the direction of the fireplace. "Over there. Quick, my girl."

Bingham duly appeared.

"We need warm water," Jancie said.

"And be quick about it," Olivia added. She looked at Jancie. Jancie looked at her. "Sit down where I can see you," Olivia said.

That would be at the foot of the sofa, Jancie surmised, and she pulled a chair in as close as she could.

"So there you are," Olivia said. "Edmund's child . . ."

"Yes, ma'am."

"And of course you know the whole story."

No, ma'am. I know my father's story . . . "Yes, ma'am." *Dear God—this woman might have been my mother . . .*

"Mr. Galliard did try to find out what happened to your father those many years ago," Olivia said after a moment.

Did he—really? Jancie didn't trust herself to speak.

"Your father said he'd had a concussion, that for a long time he had no memory of the events."

"Yes, ma'am."

"Everything was stolen, you know, by those madmen who kidnapped my husband."

Why did Olivia feel she had to explain? "Yes, ma'am."

Olivia waved her hand. "Waybury comes down to us from my family. We're so fortunate. But for that, Hugo might have entered the Indian service, or some such thing, as well."

"Truly, ma'am." Perspective—everyone had his own perspective. Olivia could pretend all she wanted that Hugo had come back from Kaamberoo penniless, but Jancie didn't believe Olivia's version of their history. Not for one moment.

"Well, then," Olivia continued briskly, "we need to talk about duties."

"Yes, ma'am."

A maid entered the room carrying a bowl of water. Olivia motioned her to set it down on the nearby table, and remove the one there. Then she handed Jancie the cloth, and Jancie rinsed it and gently laid it back across Olivia's brow.

"My duties, ma'am?" she murmured.

"Yes. Yes. Duties. I am very ill, you know. The doctors can do nothing. It only wants that I remain comfortable and without any strain. There are medications, which you will monitor and give to me—Hugo will explain all that. You'll be my companion, you'll write my letters, you'll read to me. Can you play the piano?"

"No, ma'am, I can't." But in fact, she could play some; she loved music, and she had taught herself some rudiments of the piano, deep in the night, dampening the keys so no one could hear her after she slipped into the music room. But that was not for Olivia to know. "There was no money for such niceties in my situation," she added softly, meaning it to be a subtle reproach.

"That's too bad," Olivia said, wholly missing it. Or ignoring it. "I do so like a soft, sweet sonata now and again."

"Perhaps one of your sons plays?"

Olivia laughed; or rather, it was a harsh, huffing sound. "No, my sons are neither of them musically inclined. Lujan is inclined to bad manners, and Kyger is ever angry, and always working. No, forget I said that. Where were we?"

"Going over my duties," Jancie said, ticking them off in precise order. "I am to monitor your medicine, write your letters, read to you, and generally be your companion, and make sure that you are comfortable at all times."

Olivia sent her a sharp glance. "Yes, exactly. I do expect your loyalty, Jancie, after all we have done for you."

All? All? Stuck me in an attic for eleven years and made me work in the school kitchen from the time I was five years old? ALL they did for me?

Jancie swallowed hard, clenched her fists, and kept her expression as impassive as she could. *All. But that was Olivia's perspective.* "Am I to act as your maid as well, ma'am?" She tried to keep her tone even, but something in the way she asked the question made Olivia look at her again.

"No. I have someone to tend my clothes and help me bathe and dress. Your duties will be just as we have discussed."

"Thank you, ma'am. What would you like me to do next, then?"

"Play with *me*, Cinderella," an insinuating voice said from behind her.

She froze; she knew that voice, and even if she hadn't, Olivia's expression would have told her who was lounging in the doorway.

Don't turn. She didn't have to, she could feel him: he was a pulse and a presence that filled the room, and his footsteps were soft as a panther's as he came up behind her.

He scared her to death. He was too old, and she was too innocent; she didn't know a thing about men like Lujan Galliard, and she had a feeling he liked it that way.

He stood directly behind her, facing his mother, and she felt an unaccustomed heat suffuse her whole body; and she saw the doting expression in Olivia's eyes.

But Olivia missed nothing, and Olivia knew her son, and she said sharply, "Jancie's charge is to amuse *me.*"

The comment sat hard in the air. Olivia was serious; Lujan was not. He couldn't be. Jancie said, "Is there anything else, ma'am?"

Olivia thought for a moment. "Yes. The cat. The cat is outside, I trust?"

She almost said, *no—the cat is with me.* And then she thought better of it. "Yes, ma'am—exactly as you wish."

"Good. Then you need to see Mr. Galliard about my medications—you'll find him in the library—and Lujan will keep me company until you return."

"Thank you, ma'am." She couldn't wait to get out of that room. But she had to pass Lujan first, Lujan with his radiating heat, his muscular body, his gleaming eyes, and that sardonic expression.

Lujan knew everything. He knew about the cat, he knew her heart, he knew her soul. She could hide nothing from him. And that scared her even more.

But she knew from experience, the hard experience of being a dirty girl, that you didn't back down from challenges, you never let a bully ride you, and you most especially did not let anyone *male* get the upper hand.

Because boys thought dirty girls were free, didn't count, had no morals, no feelings, and existed solely for their amusement when they demanded it. And all of them always had the same expression on their faces as Lujan Galliard—that right of the titled and wealthy.

Half of which was her father's, to which, if she could prove it, he was NOT entitled. And she'd do well to keep that in mind every minute in all her dealings with the Galliards.

Lujan's knowing way held no charm for her. He was just like every man, ready to take what was easily given, and just as ready to relinquish it in the end.

And her own best course was just to keep out of his way.

* * *

But how was that possible when somehow he was with Hugo Galliard now in the library and she had just left him with Olivia not three minutes before . . . ? She heard his voice distinctly beyond the imposing walnut door, which Bingham had haughtily pointed out to her, and she hesitated another long minute before knocking, because the last thing she wanted to do was look into those knowing eyes again.

"Come." Hugo, decisive, in command of all he surveyed.

Jancie slid open the pocket door and stepped into a room crammed full of books, floor to ceiling. *All those books . . .* She couldn't stop staring at the books, even to look at Hugo, who sat at his imposing desk in the center of the room.

"Jancie."

She swung her startled gaze back to him, and noticed then, seated beside him in a worn leather chair, a younger version of Lujan, who had to be Kyger—whose face was more angular, more focused, more fully defined.

The same eyes, the same hair, taller, his body whip-thin and ready to blast from his seat, and eerily, the same voice. Hugo introduced him, his younger son, manager of the estate, and Kyger said a perfunctory, "Pleased to meet you."

He was just as magnetic, in a different way, a contained man whose emotions were not easily discerned, one whose secrets you wanted to unearth, if only to unleash the furies within.

Jancie tore her eyes away from him as the silence lengthened, and pulled her wits together.

"Mrs. Galliard sent me to . . ."

"Yes. Yes. Mrs. Galliard's medications." He had a tray on the side table with a small brown bottle and a phial of pills. "The liquid—laudanum—twice a day, in the morning, before she starts her day, and at night before she sleeps. The pills, once a day at noon. They are solely to keep her comfortable. Nothing more can be done for her. You understand."

"Yes, sir."

"I was loath to bring in a stranger who might not have her welfare at heart. You are connected."

Jancie shivered as he said that. *Connected. By lies and betray-*

als, and yet he expected the utmost loyalty from her. What had her father been thinking?

"I know you will take excellent care of her in the time that remains."

"Yes, sir." In fact, he was counting on it, on her gratitude, on Edmund's desire for her to reside at Waybury rather than endure the harsh Indian climate that always wreaked havoc with expatriate English roses. Edmund had never wanted her to come to India, and in her heart, despite all her yearning to do so, she still wanted to please him.

But what was here for her, except the drudgery of the sickroom? And why had he not talked of some kind of recompense for the time and the energy she would expend on Olivia?

All those diamonds... When—and if—the end came, she would have nothing, she thought suddenly. And Hugo and his sons would have everything, still. Nor would they hesitate to push her out into the world with nothing, a dirty girl once more.

No. She was being too compliant. They had already taken too much. And if her father wouldn't fight for his portion, then she would. It was time to show some mettle.

She wished beyond measure that she had thought of it, and had made it a requirement before she had agreed to come. But she'd been thinking only of her father's wishes, and suddenly it seemed imperative that she think of her own.

"If I may, sir—?"

"Yes, Jancie?"

In for a penny, in for a diamond... "My stipend, sir?"

Hugo shook his head as if he hadn't heard her. "I'm sorry?"

"My stipend, sir. For caring for your wife."

Hugo bristled. "What do mean, your stipend? You've had eleven years of free tuition at that school."

"Indeed, and how grateful am I to have a gentlewoman's education. I am the best at peeling vegetables and declining Latin verbs, and I truly owe all that to you. However, when my stay here is at an end, I will have nothing. And I will not put in the hours, the days, and the emotional drain it will take caring for your wife without some monthly amount that I can put by for when I must leave."

"Nonsense. We'll take care of you—you have my word."

"Yes, sir." And he meant it, she had no doubt of that—he meant it this day, face-to-face with her, when he needed her so desperately. Just like he had meant it when he and her father shook hands on their agreements.

And she knew he needed her. He was not a man at ease in a sickroom with a demanding wife, and she had no doubt Olivia was as demanding as any preening tuition girl. Hugo needed her, she needed money, and she did not want his charity anymore.

So now what? Take a stand? Make a threat? Coerce him somehow?

What was the thing that would move Hugo Galliard, the thing she could barter?

She knew all about bartering. The dirty girls did it all the time—take a note to a boy for a trinket; help a girl sneak out at night for a few shillings; get in bed and pretend to *be* that girl for the nightly check for a bit of silk cloth.

But an exchange with Hugo was not quite that simple. She had nothing he wanted except her time and sensitivity to his wife's illness. And he knew, *really*, he had no claim on her.

"You *have* kept your word," she began, "and I am all gratitude for that, but—" But what? She grasped at a straw—". . . my father assured me that there would be some kind of allowance that I could set aside for myself for when—my usefulness is at an end."

She watched him cannily, aware that Kyger's attention was wholly focused on her. And she saw immediately that Hugo did not like her bringing her father into the discussion, not at all.

Why?

"You must trust my good will, my girl."

No. She trusted nothing about him except that he needed to foist his wife off into more capable hands for as long as she had left on earth. Very well. This was where you played truth when you bartered, and you never backed down.

"I could just as soon get a post in the village and earn that money without the kind of commitment I must make to your family," she said, keeping her voice cool.

"That's hardly a way to repay all we've done for you, my girl."

He believed his own story. He really, truly believed that he had done his best for her by making her a charity case at St. Boniface while he raised his family in luxury and wealth with all he'd stolen from her father.

Fine, that only strengthened her resolve. "In other circumstances, of course. But I have nothing. *Father* has nothing." She could twist that knife, too, not that his conscience would think to make any kind of reparation. That he could have done years ago.

"None of that changes the fact that I need to work for my living. I cannot take on charity cases myself. I must have money put by for later . . ."

None of this moved him at all. Not at all. So she must bring Edmund back into it again.

". . . but more important than that, *Father* assured me that my time and hard work would be fairly compensated if I came to you."

Yes, that was it—every time she mentioned Edmund, Hugo's expression went sour. *Why?*

"Did he?"

Perfect. What was a pebble's worth of diamond to him, with all he had taken from her father?

"Yes, sir." She knew when to relinquish the ball.

"Even with my housing and feeding you? And,"—he sent her a scathing look—"possibly clothing you? Because that dress is impossible."

"Even so, sir."

He needed her, that was the thing. He had no time to seek and interview a reliable companion for Olivia who met his exacting standards of dress. She had the upper hand, just for the moment, because Hugo was not going to let some sixteen-year-old dirty girl get the best of *him.*

Yet . . . her references to her father put him on edge. *Why?*

"All that costs money, you know."

"Yes, sir."

"Let me think on it."

She couldn't give him that time. He'd disappear and she would never come face-to-face with him again. And here, today, she had a witness. He couldn't renege with his own son having heard his promise.

"Then I must pack and leave for the village, sir."

"Miss *Renbrook* . . ." he roared.

"Sir?"

"What do you want?" he asked her through gritted teeth.

"Just what my father told me I should expect—a fair wage for taking care of your wife."

"And what does *Edmund* think is a fair wage?" His tone was dangerous now, his temper explosive, his whole being resentful of her pushing, her demands. He could tell her to go, but he would be stranded. And if he agreed, she would have won.

This was the moment. They both needed to save face in this confrontation—and it seemed to her that he should name the price. Whatever it would be, it was more than she had counted on having in the first place.

"My father said you would set the amount, and that you would be fair, and it would be generous. Sir."

He seemed to deflate slightly, as if he were relieved she was not going to ask some exorbitant amount. "There is the food."

"Yes, sir."

"And a maid who will take care of your clothes and such. Some new dresses—you must be presentable if you are to be my wife's companion. You may be escorting her to social functions or to church. We have a certain status here that you as well must maintain . . ." He was speaking almost to himself, as if he were talking himself into the notion that she must have some money—maybe some *pin* money, and if he thought of it like that, he wouldn't feel so manipulated into giving it to her.

And he wouldn't feel so unmanned in front of his solemn-faced younger son or embarrassed that he had been outfoxed by a slip of a sixteen-year-old girl with more kitchen alley wisdom in her grasp than he would ever know in a lifetime.

But what did Kyger know? Young whelp. He wished Kyger would give a howl sometimes, but Kyger played everything close, from his opinions to his emotions. Even now, he was pretending to be a piece of furniture, and he'd never say a word about this incident after, to anyone. Only they two—and Jancie—would know it had even transpired. And perhaps that was to the good.

He made some marks on a piece of paper . . . "—Let me do

some calculations—" He jotted some numbers down, as if he had to figure out what kind of money he could offer her. But of course, he knew to the penny already. He just hadn't expected he would have to spend it.

Clever girl. Too clever for her own good, perhaps, because she knew he was not going to put an appreciable sum on the table for her consideration.

But she was going to get something, so her gamble had paid off, damn her; there was nothing he could do to forestall that. He saw immediately she had an iron will and she *would* leave if that was what it was necessary to do.

And then damned Kyger or Lujan would save her, and doom them all to hell.

"All right, Miss Renbrook. Five pounds per year and found."

"Fifteen," she said instantly. Dirty girls knew to the ha'penny what household help was worth.

"Miss Renbrook . . ." A dire note in his voice now, but how could he stop her from leaving? And she would leave. There was no doubt of that in his mind.

She turned toward the door.

"Ten, then."

She turned back. "And a new wardrobe."

"Miss Renbrook—"

"Appearances, Mr. Galliard. You said so yourself. Or you could begin interviewing tomorrow. You might find a girl up to your social standards within a month—or two. Or three."

He was down and done. Not that he'd lost that much in the bargain. "I hope your *father* will be satisfied with the terms," he said caustically.

Oh dear heaven, she'd won. Money and a wardrobe. Bless her iron soul. She moistened her mouth. There was nothing more to say.

"Yes, sir."

"Then you'll excuse me."

"Yes, sir." She stood still as a statue as he crossed the room and exited. Only then did she look at Kyger Galliard's impassive face. He held her gaze for a long minute, so like Lujan, too much like himself, and then he levered himself out of the chair.

He picked up the tray full of medicines, walked slowly across the room, and handed it to her.

"Nicely done—Jancie Renbrook. I think we're going to be great friends."

"Damned girl," Hugo cursed. "A chit I made into a lady out of the goodness of my heart, and she holds me up like a highwayman. Damned Edmund."

"She's fine," Olivia said, summoning up the strength to make him feel better about what had transpired. "She's polite, deferential. She has a sweet voice. She's intelligent. She's happy to have a little money and a few new dresses. It's nothing more than that."

"She bargained like a fishmonger."

"Well, face it, my dear. She's been among fishmongers for years. What do you think kitchen work is all about?"

"I never thought about it at all."

"I shouldn't think so. Nor were you paying out thousands of pounds for her schooling. She'll do fine. She's very gentle. I'm happy with her. When Lujan goes away, everything will be perfect."

"Damned Lujan. Why is he back here, anyway? I ought to cut his portion. I ought to rescind his allowance. I should leave everything to Kyger. Serve the boy right. Damned profligate. Why can't anybody do what they're supposed to do?"

"Kyger has done more than he's supposed to do, my dear. Calm down, will you? It's hardly any money to keep Jancie here, and that's really why you're so testy."

"She wormed her way in here, and then struck out at me. I don't like turncoats."

"You expected a beaten-down little maid who would kiss the ground you walk on for the opportunity to have such a prestigious position. You expected overwhelming gratitude for your kindness, your generosity. You expected a lot for so little, Hugo. She's not stupid. She's resourceful. She's had to be. Besides which, she has a valid point: she ought not be sent away with nothing to her name after this is over. You couldn't be that mean-spirited."

"I hadn't intended to be," Hugo said gruffly, when actually he hadn't given it any thought at all. "Just keep her busy enough to earn that money, Olivia. That's all I care about."

"I know exactly what you care about," Olivia said. "Just be forewarned that *I* intend to spend the rest of your money in the remainder of the time I have left."

Jancie . . . he rolled her name around on his tongue the way he would roll a tongue over a nipple. *Jancie*. Wand-thin, a mop of curly, dark hair, big, dark, lash-fringed eyes, luscious, plump lips, lush breasts that would spill out like pillows in his hands, porcelain skin, calloused hands that had done too much drudge work, backbone of steel.

A package of contradictions. Raised in penury on blood money from Hugo . . . not even Hugo could sell the bedtime story that she had lived with the privileged princesses in the towers at St. Bonny's. The chit had very well had to take care of herself, had had to defend herself, and work at the lowliest of back-door tasks. It was ever the way, though a benefactor like his father would never acknowledge that. It was cleaner that way. And his conscience was salved to boot.

But the chit had gotten a prime kitchen alley education; he'd wager she knew things that the wealthy bad girls at St. Boniface could only guess at. Who would have thought to find such a *diamond in the rough* in his very home? She was deferential, brassy, beautiful, *and* a survivor, just ripe for handling by a master.

That was his function and her purpose. She would be his toy, his plaything. What did his mother need her for, after all? Nothing Olivia wanted could take up a whole day of the chit's time. She could earn her money other ways. She could come to him when Olivia was taking her afternoon nap, after those pills which were meant to restore and revivify her, and never did.

She could come to him then, and he would make her come, over and over, as he pumped his heat, his length, and his seed into her.

He didn't need much time. Though he liked to prolong things as much as possible. Ten minutes, perhaps, for a good, hard first fuck.

God, he was like a rock, planning it, imagining it.

He'd teach her what to wear to please him—no undergarments to get in the way. No narrow skirts to prevent his lifting them above her waist to get at her slit.

Stockings, garters—they were arousing. No shifts, no union

suits, no corsets. Nothing to impede his feeling and touching any part of her nakedness that he wanted.

And he wanted. She was the ripest piece ever to come to Waybury in years.

He was stiff as a poker thinking about it. And she ought to be right there, ready, willing, enticing him into her body. That was what a companion was for: sex, and sympathy. Sympathy for his aching penis because he couldn't just push her up against the wall and mount her right there and then.

And when she got these new dresses that his father so stupidly promised her, he'd have to make certain that they were easy to unbutton, because he wanted to gorge himself on her rosy, hard nipples whenever he felt like it. While he was pumping away between her legs. Up against the wall. Deep in her honey pot.

Where the hell was she? If she kept out of sight like this, he'd have to take one of the tween maids. Not that either of the tweenies would mind. There was one, just waiting, biding her time, salivating for the moment he would catch her on a stairwell, shove up her skirt, and plant himself between her legs.

All alike, those tweens, thinking to catch a gentleman with their willingness to hump and grind. Not him. Tupping a tween was as good as eating leftovers. And just as distasteful. A man gave in to it only to ease the ache, not to nourish his penis.

No. He couldn't think of it. He'd save his spew for the companion. Seduce her, like. Suck her nipples. Make her lick his cream. Make her love it, beg for it, cry for it.

Then she'd find reasons to spread her legs; she'd find hidey-holes all over the house for them where they could meet in secret, find all the time he wanted for a good suck and fuck. That was how it was, how it probably had been in the kitchens of St. Boniface with the delivery boys, and the milkman, milking her breasts, sucking her nipple tips, making her come . . .

This was why he'd come back home: somehow he'd known there was a ripe, young cock-tease right on his very doorstep just waiting for him. A fresh, young body, already accustomed to a man's groping hands and grueling needs, but still, a body not too used up to be mounted and fucked thoroughly by his penis at his desire.

She had just the right amount of experience, knowledge, and

innocence. He'd wager she wasn't a virgin, but she wasn't a tart yet. Not a repository for indiscriminate semen. Just the two or a half-dozen or so who knocked on the kitchen door who needed a quick trick for which they'd give a shilling.

For someone like her, that was so much money; and really, he couldn't blame her—and yet, if it were true, she'd sold her worth for virtually no money at all.

Not only that, but it didn't seem to have jaded her. Rather, she exuded a certain confidence; there was a faint undercurrent of anger in her, and dignity, and a backbone you could gnaw on.

Admirable in the temple of Venus he had chosen to occupy.

All in all, an excellent choice, his companion. To be.

And she had no choice at all about being fucked by him.

Olivia was napping. Jancie had given her the pill and read to her for a good fifteen minutes until she nodded off. So far, her duties were not onerous. She suspected that as time went on, the hardest thing would be to keep up conversation and a semblance of good spirits.

Hugo would now stay out of her way. Kyger, she was finding out, was always out on the property, seeing to repairs, taking the complaints of the tenant farmers, solving problems, trying to improve yields, and generally staying out of sight of his father, and as far away from Lujan as he could get.

She got another bowl of milk for Emily before she made her way back to her room. Emily, thank goodness, was still there, still curled up on the bed.

She slanted a look at Jancie. *Mrow.*

"Aren't you perceptive, dear Emily. Yes, indeed—they're going to pay me. Isn't that something? I went toe-to-toe with Mr. Hugo Galliard and I came away a winner. Oh my God . . ."

She was suddenly dumbstruck by what she had done. Money. Clothes. A solid place to live and a way to earn her living for however long it lasted. No more kitchen, no more dirty girl.

Hugo Galliard was paying up. Paying something for his lies and betrayals, even if it was paying *her* for services rendered.

She sank onto the bed and looked into Emily's golden gaze.

He might have given you more if you'd dug in your heels.

Greedy, greedy cat. "This is more than enough." Jancie said it out loud. She wanted it to be true. Olivia was truly not well. She doubted that she would even be there more than three or four months. Money to her name and some good dresses was not a bad barter for that.

Except if there are more diamonds. Except if—

. . . if . . . ?

DON'T . . .

If . . .

If—what if . . . no, don't think it, don't even let one thought of it into your head—

. . . it's true . . . Emily's gaze never wavered. Emily was thinking exactly what Jancie had been trying not to think.

It's true. That's why your father was adamant about your coming here. That's why Hugo reacted every time you brought up his name.

No! Nooooooo!!!

Emily stared at her.

No!

But—

What if there are more diamonds? Enough for everyone. A fortune ten times over that Hugo could never spend. That's why you're here, you know—your father didn't want to tell you directly, but that's why he wanted you here. That's what he wants you to find out . . .

Chapter Three

But then again, Jancie sometimes thought, perhaps there were some things her father didn't remember clearly, like the breadth of the strike, or how much he and Hugo had actually taken out of the pipes before the explosion. And whether they had planted the explosives to shake loose a kimberlitic layer, or whether it had been those thieves and murderers who had abducted Hugo who set off the blast.

Why hadn't they tried to kill Hugo, too?

The answer to that was simple as Simon. Because there were no thieves. Hugo had lied. Hugo had stolen everything and left her father for dead.

Of course, Edmund needed to find out what had been taken from him all those years ago. Of course, she was the logical conduit through which that knowledge would come—when she was old enough to comprehend what was wanted.

Her father must have planned it so, waiting until she was old enough to find a way to insinuate her into Hugo's life.

Had her father gone as far as to have suggested to Hugo somehow that she would make an ideal companion for Olivia just to get her in the house?

She was shaking. It was not inconceivable. Her father had said

over and over that Hugo would pay; that his not making demands on Hugo all those years ago didn't mean that Hugo wouldn't
pay for what he'd done. Had vowed that Hugo would not have
the satisfaction of a clear victory or the luxury of living a life
without conscience.

Was she to be Hugo's conscience?

If any of her suppositions were even remotely true, she had
bartered for far too little this afternoon.

No—she must not assume . . .

Yet—it made so much sense—it answered all her questions, all
the reasons her father had always been so adamant that she stay
in England.

My dear, he would write, *you cannot imagine the hardships
here.*

*You are as yet too young to take on the burdens of maintain-
ing my household for me. You are so much better off where you
are, onerous as it may be. There are things to learn, an education
to be had; you are so young, too young. All your adventures can
wait . . .*

Every letter she'd written to her father in return, begging to
come to him, was met with some excuse—it was the rainy season, it was too risky, there was rampant fever, it was too hot;
there were too many men, not enough chaperones; not a place
for a young girl; she must be eighteen at least before he would
even consider bringing her out. And above all that, she must
complete her education, if only to repay Hugo Galliard for his
generosity.

She had thought her father meant that sincerely; now she was
aware of the irony and the double edge. For all she knew, there
was a cache of diamonds not yet converted somewhere in the
house. Diamonds whose value, in all fairness, ought to be split
with her father.

This was the next step. She was her father's instrument. He
had waited all these years—and finally the time was here. She was
in place. She owed him everything. The story was told. And now
Hugo must be made to pay.

*   *   *

The idea of outfitting Jancie presentably gave Olivia something new on which to concentrate for the next few days.

"We'll send for my dressmaker," she directed after breakfast, which she took with Jancie in the morning room. She seemed more energetic this morning, more spirited. Her appetite was stronger—she managed to eat some toast, eggs, and tea, as well as swallowing the foul-tasting tablespoon of laudanum, while Jancie entered the date and time of its dispensation in a small pocket diary.

"This is much too cautious, Jancie."

"I want to be certain no mistakes are made," Jancie said. "It's a small thing, easily tucked away. I won't bother you with it again."

"So thoughtful of our little companion." The voice was unmistakable—Lujan—and Jancie barely had time to look away as he sauntered into the room. "She'll do everything by the book, Mother." He pulled out a chair opposite Jancie and grinned at her. "I'm certain she couldn't be in better hands."

Olivia poured him some tea, oblivious of the slip—or was it a slip?—but then he added, "Except mine."

"Up to your tricks again, are you?" Olivia asked him, as she rose to give him the teacup and a plate of eggs and toast.

She must do this every morning, Jancie thought. It was the only thing she could do for him—he was that slippery, that detached.

"Ignore him, Jancie,"

"Oh, don't," Lujan begged.

Olivia shot him a quelling look. "If you hadn't noticed, he's too cocky by half and too used to getting his own way in all things. Half the women in London are in love with him, and the other half don't bear mentioning. His sole entertainment is wielding his . . . his cockiness . . . to the detriment of all who care about him. But he will not bludgeon you with it. I'll make certain of that. So let us go think about clothes, shall we, and leave him to having his way with breakfast."

Lujan watched them over the rim of his cup. Mother had some vinegar flowing this morning, in spite of her illness, and the companion was like a little black crow, obediently trailing behind her. Except she was hardly little. And those awful clothes only begged the question of what the body beneath them looked like naked.

He had passed half the night wondering, spending himself while he imagined what she would look like, how she would feel.

He would know soon enough, but he was of a mind to prolong things a little—anticipation was a wonderful aphrodisiac. Made a man's penis like iron. Made his whole body tight and trim with a seething lust that was like a living heat consuming his vitals. Made him ache to be naked and embedded in something tight, wet, hot, and deep.

He could wait, because the more he waited, the longer and tighter he got, the tauter his balls, the deeper the pleasure, the more satisfaction he would have.

He knew a dozen women, *not* prostitutes, any one of whom would already be under the table licking his balls and sucking him off right now, if she were even aware of his desire. Hell, *three* of them would be under the table between his legs, one at his balls, one rubbing his penis, and the other swallowing his come.

Shit.

His imagination was too powerful—it made his body feel too explosive. Now he really needed surcease. Maybe he'd just spend himself under the table . . . Or maybe the companion sensed his need—he heard footsteps—maybe she was coming to take care of him. . . .

Damn. Hugo.

"Lujan."

"Father." His voice sounded thick, curdled, to his own ears.

Hugo poured tea, took a plate of eggs and toast, and sat himself down across from Lujan. "Has Olivia come down yet?"

"She just left." God, he was rock-hard and he couldn't stop thinking about three tongues, three mouths, six hands, licking, sucking, pumping, stroking . . . shit shit shit . . . "The little companion was with her. She's had her morning medication, she ate a little, and they're . . . calling in the dressmaker today." Not prudent, talking more than usual like that; he couldn't fool Hugo, not for long.

"Good," Hugo said. "It will keep her mind off things."

"She did seem more energetic today," Lujan murmured, his

thoughts still thrumming with the throbbing awareness of his ever-elongating and engorged penis. He couldn't even rise from the table at this point without Hugo noticing what was most obvious. Damn damn damn . . .

"So," Hugo continued, "isn't it time for you to go back to London?"

"Is it?"

"You would be wise. You have your eye on Jancie, and she is the one paid servant who ever came into this house who is untouchable. I will not warn you again. She is untouchable. Do you understand me?"

"She's better than a tween? I don't think so, Father."

"She's older and more experienced than a tween. You don't want to fool around with this, Lujan. I promise you, she's no mewling innocent."

"It's quite obvious, Father. That's what makes her so juicy." Oh, yes—that was exactly the right word. Juicy. He got juicier just thinking about it.

"You're going back to London. I don't care how much trouble you get into, how much money you spend—don't come back here. Send me a wire, and I'll fix it so you can keep going your merry way. We'll take care of things here, my beloved heir, and you can go on being reckless and unaccountable, fucking everything that moves, and letting Kyger bear the burden of your responsibilities."

"Well, hell." That wouldn't quite have been *his* story, but then, his father had always been one to rewrite history as he went along. "The point is made, Father—you don't want me to seduce the companion. Maybe you want her for yourself?"

He threw that jab out just to be nasty, but God, he was shocked to see something flicker in his father's eyes. Surely not. Hell, no—he'd imagined it. His father was just being protective of the little companion because he knew what a careless shit his eldest son could be. Still was. Leaving a trail of downtrodden, knocked-up girls from Hertfordshire to London and beyond, and then dashing their every hope, and fucking them over afterwards with the most elite socialites of every season.

What a game. What a lot of meaningless sexual congress. What a reputation to maintain.

Sometimes he got tired—of the faceless women whom he bedded at their own peril, of the need to up the stakes again and again, and coming up drained and dissatisfied when everyone believed he was sated and indifferent.

And he couldn't see a way to end it. He was a legend now, even if he'd never done half the things people thought he had. His course was set. He was the Casanova of the Court, nothing more, nothing less. Charming as a snake, dangerous as an adder. Come close, and he uncoiled and attacked. No one was safe.

That was what they said. And even he believed it now.

Why else was he throbbing and erect when there wasn't even a woman in the room? Because he knew there was one in the house; her scent filled his pores, pulling him, luring him—a Lilith ready, willing to take advantage of his prowess, his stamina, his reputation, his will.

He had no will—he had surrendered it in lust to his drive for sex, thrown it and everything away along with any vestige of morality. If they wanted him, he came, every which way. He had no discretion, no selectivity. An equal exchange, the pleasure of his penis for the pleasure of embedding it in any anonymous woman's hole.

There was no stopping his course now—he craved it, he was addicted to it.

He needed it now.

And his father wanted him back in London. A day's ride. He'd never last.

Hugo's eyes turned frosty. "I—? Want her? Jesus God, that's unconscionable, even for you. I don't want you here another minute with your filthy mind. I really have had enough of your tricks and your attitude. Get out—do you hear me? Get OUT."

Lujan got up, and got out, his trousers bulging, which was not lost on Hugo, who sent him a blistering look and pushed away his food disgustedly.

But it was ever thus with Lujan, and he knew it—there was no controlling him. He'd probably go find an undermaid and empty himself into her. Probably it was best he relieved himself, in any event, rather than leave Waybury with a gnawing thrust like that. The man was dangerous when he was aroused. Dangerous anyway, and at the mercy of any urge, every appetite.

Hugo couldn't conceive of how his eldest child could have become like this. He wondered if Lujan even knew. He pushed himself away from the table angrily.

God, if only Kyger had been the eldest . . . if only Olivia were not dying . . . if only Edmund had not found him . . .

Want Jancie for himself . . . that son of a bitch bastard . . .

He shook his head disbelievingly.

. . . *how the hell had the bastard known . . . ?*

Olivia was napping again. They'd spent the morning looking through Olivia's pattern books, after having summoned the dressmaker, and now Olivia slept while Jancie ran down the hall to wash her face, comb her hair, and check on Emily.

Oh damn—Emily was nowhere around.

Be careful, Emily.

She ought to write to Edmund.

Dear Father—I've negotiated a wage and a new wardrobe, and I've deduced what it is you intended me to do. . . .

No. That would distress her father. Besides, she had nothing to report except Olivia's kindness, Hugo's wariness, the way Lujan made her feel uneasy, how much like him his younger brother was . . . except that Kyger was Lujan as he should have been: responsible, welcoming, kind, and quick with his friendship, even if his emotions were wrapped tight.

Well, she hadn't seen him since yesterday, and she had to assume he was out and about most of the time, doing whatever it was Lujan ought to be doing, and taking the burdens of managing the estate off Hugo's head.

On the other hand, Hugo could afford to hire people. But as she knew from yesterday's tug-of-war, Hugo was tight with a pound note, even though, presumably, he had sequestered away many thousands of them from the proceeds of the Kaamberoo strike.

And so she came back to that again. Everything, every observation, anything anyone in the household did, from now on, would be colored by her comprehension of how much was taken from her family.

To think she'd had only an inkling of it when she had arrived.

But Hugo would keep nothing visible for anyone to find; he would be doubly cautious with *her* in the house. He would be watching her. He *was* watching her. So her father's expectations would never be met.

Probably everything Hugo had was in the bank, in the funds, and there was nothing left of the diamond lode he'd brought out of Kaamberoo. Probably he'd converted everything into cash years ago. Why wouldn't he? There was no one to contest his find, no one to question the number and quality of the gems.

But still and all, putting that many diamonds on the market all at once? It might have looked as if he'd stolen them. So perhaps he had been more prudent, and sold them in small lots.

God, she wished Edmund could have remembered how much, how many they'd taken out of the mine before the blast. At least she would have some idea of what she was looking for. As she envisioned it, Hugo would have kept what was left of that fortune in a cache box, or a pouch, or perhaps in a small, tabletop chest laid out in velvet so he could easily pick and choose among the stones which ones he would next sell.

Maybe he had sold the largest ones first. Or maybe a large, then a small, and so on.

This was crazy. She was groping blindly, making up theories out of whole cloth like a dressmaker working without measurements. Mining someone else's memories as a road map to divine the truth, which, after so many years, had been twisted, turned, and rearranged to suit the wont of whoever was telling the story.

And so, in truth, Hugo had already paid . . . for her schooling, her pittance of a salary, the fifty or so quid for some dresses for her, and done.

Sorry, Father—I can't think of a thing more I could find; I couldn't even think where to look. . . .

A bell rang, the one wired from her room to Olivia's. The bell meant Olivia was awake and wanted to see her. It was lunchtime. Olivia would ring for tea and sandwiches and they would eat while they waited for the dressmaker to arrive.

A desperately ill woman and her companion.

There was no time at all for any further speculation, which was useless at best, and futile altogether.

Sorry, Father—there's just nothing else I can think to do . . .

* * *

For the rest of the afternoon, she was measured, draped, pinned, and tucked, while Olivia directed everything, chose the fabrics, and conferred with the dressmaker over the ornamentation. She was to have two good day dresses, two shirtwaists and two skirts that she could interchange one with the other, and one serviceable evening dress, not too fancy, not too plain.

With that, a new set of undergarments, a half-dozen stockings, and two pairs of shoes—one pair for every day, one pair suitable for day and evening. Oh, and a practical wool coat, because the winter could be hard.

This was beyond generous, and Jancie said so after the dressmaker left.

"Well, you have practically nothing, my girl, so at least you shall have proper clothing. Everything will be ready by next week, and we'll have another fitting then. Now, you may read to me while we have tea."

And it was while she was reading, and Olivia sipped her tea, that Emily tiptoed into the room with her long, elegantly sinuous cat walk.

I'm here.

As if Jancie hadn't seen her out of the corner of her eye. *Dear Lord, don't let Olivia see her . . .*

Owww . . .

Hungry, that meant. Loud enough so that Olivia could not ignore it. Jancie closed her eyes as Olivia jumped up.

"Is that the cat?"

"Yes, ma'am."

Mrrrow.

"The one who is supposed to be outside."

"Yes, ma'am."

"Is now in my room?"

"Yes, ma'am. She must have found her way inside."

Emily was now rubbing against her leg and sent up an indignant *OOWWW* at this comment.

"Get her out of my room and out of the house right now."

Jancie was not of a mind to argue. She picked Emily up and scurried out of the room with a handful of thrashing cat. Immediately she cleared the threshold, Emily bolted from her grasp and tore off down the hallway in the opposite direction from Olivia's room.

Damn . . . Jancie took off after her, past the door to her room, past other doors that she had no idea where they led, down to the other end of the house where Emily suddenly skittered to a stop and sank onto her haunches.

MRRROOWWWW.

A definitive howl, as Emily sat there like a statue, her hairs bristling.

There was nothing there. A window with a chest underneath it. A staircase winding upward to her right—to the attics, she thought. A door on the opposite wall, closed, as were all the doors on this side of the house.

It was still daylight, as she could see through the window, though the sun was low. There was nothing threatening at this end of the hallway, nothing to make Emily so emphatically anxious.

She bent down to pick her up again.

Mmmrrrrooowwwww.

Emily swiped at her hand, hissed, twisted away, and shot down the hallway in the opposite direction, and disappeared down the main staircase a moment later.

Jancie flew down the hall after her, with Olivia's voice calling to her frantically as she raced past her bedroom door, and barreled down the steps, and right into Kyger, almost knocking him over.

He grabbed her around the waist and turned them both in a wobbling waltz step against the banister for balance before they could topple down the steps. "Jancie—"

"My cat . . ."

"Oh lord. Your cat . . . ?" He let her go and raced after her down the steps, with Olivia's voice a Greek chorus behind them. Down to the reception foyer, into the parlor, into the library, the dining room, the morning room . . . Jancie calling frantically and no immediate sign of Emily anywhere.

"Your mother will send me away for certain now," Jancie fretted, "and she's just spent a good lot of pounds on some clothing for me. And now Emily off and gone . . . What am I going to do . . . ?"

"You'd better go to her, then," Kyger said. "Tell her I got the cat outside."

She looked up at him. God, he was so much like Lujan, but without the veneer, the dissolute worldliness, the oily, sexual overtone. At second glance, she liked him even better because he was so sensitive to her distress and what Emily meant to her. But there was no time to think about the ramifications of that. Olivia was agitated, Emily was missing, and she had to go.

"Thank you," she whispered.

"She hates cats."

"Can I know why?"

"There's really no time to tell you now."

She nodded, touched his arm. "Thank you."

Olivia was in a temper. "That cat . . ."

"Yes, ma'am. Kyger caught her—and put her out."

"She's dead if I see her again."

Jancie was horrified—and just when she was thinking that she was coming to like Olivia, a little. "Surely not, ma'am."

"Continue reading, Jancie."

"Yes, ma'am."

"Dead," Olivia muttered, over her teacup, as Jancie picked up where she'd stopped reading.

So vicious. So angry. So unlike Olivia. Why?

She had better not touch Emily, Jancie thought. If Emily went missing, and Olivia was involved—

I'd kill you first, she thought, and she didn't even feel remorseful at the thought, nor did she skip a syllable as she continued reading down the page.

Dinner was quiet. Lujan was gone, and it was obvious: for some reason, his leaving sucked all the air dry. Kyger was a restrained presence across the dinner table, at least tonight, and Olivia was preternaturally quiet because Jancie had just given her her nightly dose of medicine.

The meal was simple, with just the four of them: a clear soup, roast lamb with mint jelly, cucumbers in a piquant sauce, potatoes and sprouts as sides, plain cake topped with fruit and whipped cream, and tea and coffee to finish.

Hugo drank wine. Olivia barely ate. The silence around the

table was thick, deep. No one could think of a thing to say, and it didn't seem like the right moment to ask about Olivia's aversion to cats.

Besides, she seemed rather disoriented—the laudanum, in all probability—and after about twenty minutes at the table, Hugo suggested she go to bed. Jancie helped her upstairs and summoned her maid, and then returned to the table.

"Is there nothing more I could do for her?" she asked Hugo as she seated herself.

"If you keep her occupied, if you take her mind off the progression of the disease, that is more than enough," Hugo said.

Good, he was feeling rather grateful to her. Maybe now was the time to ask about Olivia and cats.

Jancie plunged in. "And why is it that she hates cats so much?"

Kyger looked at Hugo. Hugo looked at Kyger.

"Emily got into her room today," Kyger said. He looked at Jancie and shook his head. "I haven't found her. I assume she knows when to keep out of sight."

"She's probably in *my* room," Jancie said. No reason they shouldn't know, really. Someone would find out eventually—the maid, the paper-thin butler. Olivia, if she were of a mind to snoop.

"I see," Hugo said. "I thought it was clear that the cat was supposed to be outside."

"Well, she's not, and probably she won't be. It isn't something you can *tell* her to do. And she's accustomed to being with me, anyway. She always has been. So I should know why Olivia is so upset about it."

Her question dropped into a dead silence.

She sipped some tea, ate a piece of the plain cake without the embellishments. Waited. Watched with interest the looks passing between Kyger and Hugo, as if they were battling between them who would speak, who would tell.

Hugo, finally. "We were blessed with three sons, not two. Our third child was Gaunt, the baby. We had dogs, we had a cat, we had family close by. It was a happy time, a happy house. And everyone was here for Christmas that year. Gaunt was—four?"

Kyger nodded.

Hugo went on, "They were playing hide-and-seek all over the house with their cousins. Noisy, as only children can be at Christmas. We were at the table in here, the adults, and we'd left them to their own devices. We could hear them running, shrieking, laughing. No one thought anything of it.

"Later, we were gathered in the parlor while we were having wine at the end of the evening—and the cat wandered in and began meowing. Such a nuisance. She wouldn't stop—she was so insistent, and no one could figure out why, or what she wanted. We put her out, and she stood by the doors, howling while we tried to finish up our celebration on a joyful note. It wasn't possible. The cat wouldn't stop that deep-in-the-throat sound they make when they've killed something.

"It put a damper on the rest of the evening. We all decided to go to bed. We weren't halfway up the steps when the children's maid came racing toward us. She couldn't find Gaunt. He wasn't in his room, he wasn't with his cousins or his brothers. He wasn't anywhere, and everyone was still searching—the children, the staff, everyone. They—they had just been hoping to find him before they had to tell us . . ."

He stopped for a moment, blew out a breath, seemed to be quelling his emotions so he could finish the story.

"We didn't find him. We looked everywhere, just everywhere, cellar to attics. No Gaunt. We tried tracking him with the hounds the next day, but there was no scent. They kept coming back to the house, and yet, in the house, they lost the scent.

"There was just the infernal howling of that cat. And my missing son." He looked at Kyger and caught himself. ". . . A missing child."

He closed his eyes as if he could still see, feel, and taste the terror.

"We never found Gaunt. We got rid of the cat."

Deafening silence.

"She says she still hears the cat," Kyger said. "She says that sometimes she can hear Gaunt crying."

Lord almighty . . . What could she say? "I see. Thank you for telling me."

Hugo seemed as if he were having trouble controlling his emotions. "You'll have to excuse me," he muttered finally. "The memory sits very hard."

He left them abruptly, throwing his napkin on his uneaten dessert.

Kyger removed it. "It's a horrible story, a terrible memory. For all of us. You had to know."

"Yes." It went beyond terrible. It was inconceivable, the loss of a child that young all those years ago. Poor Olivia. And the poor cat.

But Emily wasn't *that* cat. And Emily had nothing to do with the loss of Gaunt.

Gaunt. Strange names that Olivia and Hugo had given their sons.

She felt a welling of sympathy for Olivia. Olivia still held that long-lost child close to her heart.

"Did you assume Gaunt had run away?"

"We had no idea. Have no idea to this day."

"Awful."

Kyger took a sip of wine. "There are no words for it. Even after all this time. And now she's dying, and she'll never know."

Jancie felt a rush of anguish.

"She's losing so much so soon . . . and she's lost so much already."

"Yes."

"And that's why no cats."

"Yes." There was hardly anything else to say. She ached for Olivia, for everything she'd gone through. For everything yet to come. There were some things you couldn't bury in the past. Some things that lived with you always.

"It was so absolutely the right thing to do, bringing you here."

Wait—what??

"Why is that?" she asked, her voice laced with wariness at the abrupt change of topic. Why was she looking for shadows and suspicions after the wrenching story she had just heard?

No, he wasn't his brother. There was nothing slick or crafty about him.

He got up from the table and came around to take her hands. She looked up at him, the tall, darkly handsome, tightly controlled Kyger, and she was just a little shocked by her rush of feeling for him.

"You understand," he said, pulling her to her feet, pulling her close to him, so close that she could see the light glimmering in his eyes, could see the deeply etched lines of worry and care in his face that proved that he, too, was affected, he, too, was moved.

But he wasn't Lujan—he wouldn't push anything further than she wanted him to. This much was enough. More than enough. He sensed the free spirit in her; it echoed his own.

"Good night, Jancie."

You understand . . . "Good night," she whispered on a breath. She couldn't move. Her hands still tingled from his warm grip. Her body resonated from just being near him. She had been so wrong about him. He did have the magnetism of his older brother, had even more because he was sensitive, he was respectful, and he was so tightly contained.

He was gone.

What had just happened here?

She moved.

She pulled her wits together as she walked slowly into the hallway. Something else had happened in there. And it had nothing to do with her response to Kyger. It was something else, and she couldn't shake the feeling that her tightrope walk had just gotten trickier.

But just what had happened?

They had told her a tragic story, and with it, her feelings about Olivia had changed radically. Hugo evinced some appreciation that she was there to keep Olivia occupied. Kyger told her she understood.

You understand . . .

Something—what? What did she understand?

Everything was getting in her way. Sympathy. Gratitude. Attraction.

Kyger. She closed her eyes. *Kyger.*

She could just see him in her mind's eye.

And then she could finally breathe.

Chapter Four

Suddenly everything was infused and colored by the story of the devastating loss of the child.

Jancie felt as if she could not do enough for Olivia, who really needed nothing more than light diversions to keep her mind off her illness.

So, within hours of the third day of Jancie's arrival, there emerged a pattern to how they spent their time. Breakfast was at eight, with Olivia's medication. The balance of the morning was spent outdoors—walking, in conversation, sitting in the garden. Noon, medicine again, and a nap. After, tea, a light luncheon, an afternoon of reading, usually with Jancie reading out loud to Olivia. Six o'clock, dinner with Hugo and Kyger, no more than two courses, usually one. After, Jancie was on her own, which gave her time to explore the library, read books of her own choice. She could write letters, if she so desired, though she hadn't—yet.

Time to think.

She didn't know what to think, actually. Maybe it was better *not* to think, with the ground continually shifting under her.

Lujan rode in on the following Saturday. "Well, I can see everyone is overjoyed to have me home," he said in that deprecating tone that was so irritating. "Especially the little companion. How's Mother?"

"Tolerable," Kyger told him. "Could you tolerate going over accounts?"

"God, no."

And Hugo couldn't demand that he leave; it would upset Olivia too much—she was so glad he'd come to visit. Lujan spent hours entertaining her with stories of London life; he'd brought down a parcel of books for her. He'd bought her a beautiful shawl.

"It's so beautiful, Hugo. So warm. He's so thoughtful."

Hugo sent her a baleful look. *Thoughtful* was not a word in Lujan's vocabulary. But how could he demand that Lujan leave with Olivia positively doting on him?

Or was this some nefarious plan? And where was Jancie, the *paid* companion, while Lujan was casting his lures?

Jancie was staying as far away from Lujan as possible, but if she thought she was fooling anyone, she was mistaken. Kyger caught her Sunday morning, hiding in the library.

"You are ever so wise to keep out of his way, Jancie."

"Am I?" Easier to misunderstand what he was inferring, easier still to feel irritated that *he* understood.

Kyger started to say something and thought better of it.

Because *she understood?*

She was still bothered by it—the gnawing sense that there was an undercurrent to everything that had been said that evening, and that there was something she had missed.

"Well, let us just say, I'm happy you're in *my* way today," Kyger said, and the huskiness in his voice made her knees weak. It would be so easy, too easy to make something out of the way he spoke to her, looked at her, made her the center of his interest and concern.

"You've been so good for Mother," he added, as if he discerned her discomfort, and wanted to diffuse the awareness between them.

What was it about these brothers? They were too attractive, too arresting, too magnetic.

Too different, one from the other. Too easy to like for very different reasons. And easy to hate, exactly the same.

"She is no trouble to care for," Jancie said, following his lead.

She could even see objectively, after this short a time, why her own father had loved Olivia; she liked Olivia, too. And comprehending that, she felt even more deeply the obligation that Hugo had placed upon her in bringing her to Waybury. "Olivia is generous, kind, and undemanding. There is no hardship here for me but the knowledge that at some point, there will be an end to it."

"We talk about it with such detachment, but in truth, we don't believe it," Kyger said. "We just don't believe it, even as we watch her slowly fade before our eyes, watch her take the laudanum to dull her pain, watch her try to act as if everything were perfectly normal. She makes us not believe it until we examine her closely under the skin. Then we know, but we still refuse to come to terms with it."

God, how he loves her, Jancie thought. And how he loyally took over Lujan's role just to be here with her. That was the real reason why he remained at Waybury, the real reason why he'd willingly taken Lujan's place. It wasn't to ease Hugo's burden—or Lujan's, for that matter. He was doing it all for his mother.

It made her feel even warmer toward him. It made her feel things she didn't understand. And it made her turn away every time Lujan came in sight, because perceiving that about Kyger, she did not know what conclusion to draw about *him*.

He hadn't gone back to Town. He insisted on popping up around corners when she least expected it. "Ah, it's the little companion. How diligent she is. A scurrying little mouse, afraid of the big, fat cat."

An unfortunate allusion, that. Cats were still a sore point with Olivia, and she did not hesitate to bore the point home to Jancie.

"Humph . . . I comprehend you've heard the whole awful story about Gaunt just by the look on your face every time I talk about that cat."

"Yes, ma'am. Mr. Galliard was kind enough to ease my mind by recounting just the barest details. I'm so very sorry."

"Where is it, your cat?"

"Catching mice, I hope. Cook was very sanguine about the fact there were so many mice to be caught round and about the cellars and garden that Emily could prove very useful to her in that way—out of your sight, of course, ma'am."

Olivia shook her head. "I will not have a cat in this house."

"Yes, ma'am."

This wasn't the first conversation about it, either. But Emily had an instinctive and healthy respect for Olivia's antipathy. She stayed well out of sight, only slinking into Jancie's room deep into the night to sleep on her hip, and never, ever was she seen on the bedroom floor on the opposite side of the house.

Lujan was there quite frequently, however; his bedroom was one of those closed doors just on that end of the house, nearby the back staircase to the attic where Emily had acted so skittery. He invariably emerged from his room just when Jancie was coming out of hers, as if he were deliberately looking for any way to disconcert and discomfit her.

"Whatever did happen to the cat?" he asked the first time, waiting, Jancie thought, to hear that perhaps Olivia had had her drowned or something.

"She's fine," Jancie said. "We worked it out."

Lujan snorted. "You heard the poor, sad story."

Jancie nodded. And instantly she wondered how old he had been at the time, and whether he knew anything about his younger brother's disappearance.

What a wicked, horrible thought! She banished it instantly, but it crept right back into her consciousness. Why? Because Lujan was dissolute and amoral? Because his father was a liar and a thief? Because his mother had dangled two suitors and had *not* chosen her father? Because under the skin, and in spite of all her empathy and sadness for Olivia, she still felt that niggling anger that she had walked into a way of life that should always have been hers?

Still, it was a list of offenses wholly personal only to *her*. She didn't want to think about it again; she had thought she put it all aside for the moment because she felt her obligation to Olivia superseded any personal acrimony.

What was she thinking? It was obvious she wasn't thinking at all; and it was all because of Lujan's prowling around where she least expected him, and turning her head the wrong way around.

But she could not help wondering where Lujan had been when Gaunt disappeared. Where had Kyger been, for that matter?

And why did it even matter to her? It was Olivia's tragedy, and she lived with it fresh in her mind every day. Hugo and Olivia had done everything they could at the time; she believed that, and that they obviously had absolved their sons of any culpability. And there had been other witnesses—aunts, uncles, cousins—in the house.

Who was she to question any of this?

It was all about the cat—and Lujan.

And while she could put Emily out of sight in the cellar, she couldn't as easily make Lujan go away.

So there was dinner every evening following his arrival, with his glinting gaze following her every move, eyeing her like the hungry predator that he was. There were the walks with Olivia in the morning, when he would appear as if by magic from behind a tree or around a corner and jolly Olivia out of her gloomy moods. There were her quiet times when somehow he found and sought her out just to make the euphemistic sexually charged comment.

It was too much for her. All her experiences at St. Boniface had not prepared her for dueling with a man of such verbal skill and fleshly appetites. He'd devour her if she let him—she didn't know how to wriggle away. She couldn't understand what it was about her that fascinated him.

She found herself hiding from him rather than match wits because she knew she must always lose.

Kyger proved her ally.

"Little brother is hiding the companion," Lujan accosted him one afternoon while Olivia was napping.

"I?" Kyger was the soul of innocence. "I think you've outstayed your welcome, big brother. I think London is calling, not our poor, innocent little companion."

"London is boring."

Kyger laughed mirthlessly. "And a week of dancing a quadrille with our father and the companion isn't? This isn't like you, old son."

"I'm thinking it's time I took an interest in what will be my inheritance and my birthright."

If Lujan had meant to shock him, Kyger didn't let it show. "That it is," he said evenly. "The account books are waiting, big brother. I can't wait to hand them over."

Lujan brushed that comment away. "So is the little companion. Waiting for an accounting from me, that is."

"Lord," Kyger groaned. "Have you gotten away with repartee like that all these years? If that is all it takes to go on in society, then it will be easier than ever I thought to make my mark in London, and way past time I tried my mettle among the debutantes and ladies. I couldn't do worse, that's for certain."

"Two Galliards? God, that would be enough to bring any season to a standstill, little brother. I don't think so."

On the other hand, Kyger thought, it should have been exactly so. The two of them, so alike in so many ways, united in their desire to preserve family, to make marriages, to father an heir.

But that wasn't the case. They were as far apart as the sun and the moon. He wondered just what had estranged them, and what had made Lujan so contemptuous of everything. He wondered now, because the issue had been raised again, what the impact of the loss of their brother had been on Lujan; whether that, in some measure, might account for his go-for-hell-and-damn-the-consequences attitude.

He wondered why Lujan had fixed his interest on Jancie.

"So what is it about the companion?" he asked idly.

Lujan shrugged. "It just is."

"That's because you can't have her. It's ever thus with you, brother mine. Dangle a fresh carrot, and you are galloping after it hell for the horizon, ravenous until you get the first bite, which is never as juicy or delicious as you imagine, and then the rest you just cavalierly toss away. No, Lujan, you won't get that bite this time, not with Jancie."

"Really?" Lujan's tone was deceptively offhanded. "Why is that?"

"Why—there are knights errant and benevolent sorceresses among her retinue. Charms and spells to protect her, dear brother. Gallant gentlemen who are willing to do battle for her."

"Fool," Lujan mocked him. "You're the court jester, old son. You wag your arms and flap your mouth and everyone laughs."

"But—consider this, brother mine. Who knows what the court jester is, really? What an ideal disguise for some noble—or nefarious—purpose," Kyger murmured. "I'd watch out for that jester, if I were you." The thought amused him, and it struck him suddenly that he and Lujan had become even fiercer adversaries, squaring off about a girl who was literally a nobody.

But two days later, he understood why.

The dressmaker had delivered Jancie's new dresses and there was a great deal of to-ing and fro-ing in and out of her room while Jancie tried them on. Adjustments were made, and she finally presented herself to Olivia in the first of her two workday dresses: a plain checked linen in shades of blue and taupe, with a suggestion of draped overskirt and a matching frill around the neck, wrist, and hem.

She felt as if she were walking a foot taller, wearing a dress like this; felt herself move with a grace she was not aware she had as she paraded before Olivia's critical eye.

"Yes, yes," Olivia said. "Just what we discussed—nothing too fancy, but still in fashion. Nothing too forthcoming. Exactly right. Now the other one, please."

The second dress was a beautiful shade of navy with a thin filet of red ribbon on the skirt, around the high neck, and at the wrists of the pared-down muttonchop sleeves.

Jancie liked this one even more. So did Olivia. The simplicity. The fit. Jancie in proper clothes was as elegant and desirable as any debutante in the whole of London, Olivia thought. And the lack of expensive ornamentation did not detract from the lines of Jancie's body, either. There was a full-bodied woman hiding under those dowdy clothes she had worn.

And those dresses could easily be made over, Olivia decided. They wanted but some taking in, a drape of the skirt, a ruffle, a piece of lace, a bow. The dressmaker could do that in a day.

She liked taking charge of Jancie like that, she thought; it was like having a daughter without all the fuss of having had to raise her. And any mother would adore a daughter like Jancie. Jancie could have *been* her daughter, if things had worked out differently.

Funny she'd never thought of that before.

So it was gratifying to see her family's response as she and Jancie came downstairs for lunch. *Dumbstruck* would be the word for it—Hugo calculating the cost in pounds even as he gaped, and Lujan and Kyger rushing to pull out a chair for Jancie and nearly colliding in the process.

Their reaction made Olivia catch her breath—the way they looked at Jancie—did she want—what she thought she was seeing?

What had she intended to accomplish, really? Not *that,* surely. Her boys would never think of looking at Jancie as anything but what she was—a paid companion. Someone whose meager compensation included some dresses from a generous employer. She could have just as easily had several of her own made over for Jancie if she had even thought for a moment that either of her sons would evince this kind of interest.

Maybe she ought to have. She didn't like the look in Lujan's eyes. But he was ever the wild card, playing his usual games and holding his aces close, ever the joker. And he was never serious. She could almost count on that.

It was just that he was bored, staying around, waiting for the end.

No, dressing Jancie had been a way to pass the time, she thought. A diversion. Something else to do other than watch the sun go up and down and watch the creeping grief over her illness insinuate itself into her life while she tried to pretend it wasn't there, and that what was inevitable would never happen.

That was all. Just a way to occupy time.

But in that warm moment, Jancie felt something shift inside her. The sensation was so strong, it was almost palpable. She felt as if Olivia had waved a magic wand and made her into a princess. Given her the glass slipper in the form of these beautiful clothes. Made her feel like Cinderella, just as Lujan had said. Up from the ashes and into the light—desirable, eligible, marriageable.

It felt so right, so exactly how things should always have been, as if now she had taken her proper place—a place where her father would have been at the head of the table, and her mother would still be alive.

And she felt her gratitude ebb away, and the truth of the hardships of her life came roaring back, and she felt something change, and more than that, that finally she was ready to do something about it.

*　　*　　*

Watching her, he felt something shift.

Had he thought this was a child? This was *not* a child. This was a woman, fully formed, with intelligence, wit, and opinions. Obedient and grateful, as she should be, but clear-sighted about the circumstances as well. So different from the tattered bundle of gratitude and obsequiousness they had expected. She was no fool, and everyone else around the table knew it.

But they didn't know that she knew it, too.

It was the way she looked in a fashionable, well-fitted dress, with her hair properly arranged, that had caught everyone off guard. Nobody had expected she would look like *this*.

It changed things. It was like a lightning bolt to his vitals. He saw it all clearly, in one soul-clarifying moment. And he saw what he needed to do, and what modifications he needed to make. And for the first time in a long time, he really felt as if he *could* make a change.

He would do it—he decided in that instant. It was the perfect answer, the perfect end of the story for someone who didn't believe in fairy tales.

But fate had dropped Jancie right in his lap. A man could do no less with that kind of temptation. It wouldn't be heroic at all. It would solve every problem, absolve every sin, wash away every stain.

It would be a blessing, really. For her. For him.

He couldn't keep his eyes off of her, which only cemented his resolve. He would do it—for himself first—but he'd be lying to himself if he didn't admit he was doing it *because* of her.

As any hot-blooded man would . . .

And then, Lujan decided to stay on at Waybury House for an indeterminate time. This was not happy news, for Hugo or for Kyger.

But it was especially bad news for Jancie.

There was something about those new dresses that made each one of them treat her differently, and she decided, after their first reaction, that she didn't like it. And then, when she thought to just put on her old shapeless dresses, she found they were gone.

She accosted the maid. "Where are my dresses?"

It was one of the tween maids, a girl who was pretty nearly

her own age, and scared witless of her. Jancie could almost see her trembling with fear that she thought the maid had stolen her dresses.

"The dresses, miss?" The voice quavered. "The madam had them taken to the dressmaker to be made over, miss. I hope that's all right."

Well, she couldn't be as ungracious as to demand that Olivia return them without alteration when Olivia's motives had been so kind.

Jancie sank onto the bed and looked at Emily, who was curled up on the pillow. Emily stared at her.

"What?"

That was nice of Olivia.

"That *was* nice of Olivia," she agreed, but she still felt disquieted. Olivia was making her into someone she was not.

Making you into the woman you really are.

Wise Emily. It wasn't the dresses being taken that bothered her. It was the woman part, the part that precipitated the reactions of Lujan and Kyger. The way they looked at her. Like an object of . . . someone they could . . . someone they might—

She brushed those disquieting thoughts away. That would never happen. Not ever. She was not nearly of their social class, she was not that kind of woman, not someone men like that married.

Hugo had stolen that away from her, anyway. She mustn't forget that. And he'd paid for it with a quid's worth of clothing that disguised what she would always be—a dirty girl.

That was what was driving her discomfort: they would never think of her as anything but a dirty girl—someone fit to be a companion, someone to be paid—*someone they would pay to bed*—but nothing else.

Still, it was hard to feel dirty wearing those new clothes. She was the equal of any girl she had ever known in that beautiful blue dress. Maybe that was all she had ever wanted: to be equal with them and not a charity girl, when she knew the truth was, she could have been as wealthy as they, but for fate—or Hugo Galliard.

If she let herself, she could really work up a full head of anger over that. She had tamped it down. Tried to forget it while she tended to Olivia's needs and tried to be honorable about the contract she'd made with Hugo.

But really—that was why she was here. To redress it somehow. She hadn't forgotten about that—and the beautiful dresses made it that much harder, being something she never could have afforded herself—but she still didn't know what to do.

Emily didn't blink once. *Wait and see.*

"What do you mean?" She thought about it a minute. Oh—exactly. Emily meant that some idea, some way would present itself. There was no rush, on her father's account; he wasn't coming to England, ever. But she would be with Olivia for an appreciable amount of time—Olivia was not flagging yet. She seemed still to have energy and interest in everything around her even though she tired easily, so there was time to figure out whatever it was her father expected her to do.

Meantime, she would deal the best way she could with Lujan and his knowing eyes, and his unholy appetites, and his propensity for scandal and disaster.

Emily got to her feet and stretched, the way only a cat can stretch—with every bone in her body and legs. *Hugo will make him leave.*

"Oh—of course he will. I should have thought of that. He doesn't want Lujan here any more than any of us do. Why am I so worried?"

Emily shook herself daintily. *I have no idea. I have mice to catch.* She jumped off the bed, and slid sinuously through the crack in the door.

When Jancie threw it open, she was gone. Obviously Emily knew her way around the house better than she did. Knew all the secret entryways. Knew every nook and cranny where she could hide from Olivia and sneak down to the kitchen without being seen.

Such a smart cat. But she felt better. Talking to Emily always made things better. This was her companion and her confidant, the one with whom she had conversations and commiserations, who mirrored back and agreed with everything she thought and felt. And somehow yet again, she had come up with the best advice.

She felt hungry now, ready to face Lujan and anything else. A way would present itself. And she would know in time what her father wanted her to do.

Dear Father,

All goes well here. It is no onerous chore to be Olivia's companion. She is charming, generous, thoughtful. She has provided me with a small wardrobe, and Hugo agreed to a modest remuneration for my time here. When I join you finally in Delhi, I will be a woman with means. I hope you enjoy that notion. It is a good feeling. Days pass slowly and quietly. We have a routine, part of which requires that Olivia have extensive rest. I am sad to tell you that the progression of her illness can only lead to one result. But her family is coping with it as they can. Both sons are in residence, and Lujan, surprisingly, is taking an interest in the running of the estate; everyone thought he would be spending the season in London as he always does . . .

He was spending the season *not* spending himself in every available body in the whorehouses of London. He was learning the business of the estate, learning to restrain his wicked nature, and watching Jancie.

He couldn't believe that he had willingly given up the fleshpots of London for the bucolic joys of tending to estate and family.

But something had shifted. Olivia seemed weaker and more distracted. Kyger was running things far too well. His father looked both weary and eager, in a way that didn't bode well for any of them.

And Jancie—well, the duck had turned into a swan and that was a very dangerous thing, if his father's covert interest was any indication.

He wondered if Jancie weren't a little too eager to serve, a little too comfortable in her circumstances, a little too cozy with his mother.

For all he knew, Olivia might leave Jancie everything she had, and then where would they all be?

Whose idea had it been for Jancie to come to Waybury anyway?

Shit. That was what cutting back on whores and wine did to you—it made your brain sharp and your inner eye clear. It made everything come into focus and suddenly, you saw what was under your nose that you had overlooked before.

Things like Kyger, so entrenched in the business of running things, the younger son who would never inherit, but harboring resentments, anger, bitterness—loath to relinquish what had been his domain for years to his feckless older brother who had never given a goddamn about his birthright.

Or his mother, fading before his very eyes, when no one else who was around her every day seemed to see it. Making busy-work for herself to keep herself going. Making Jancie into a living doll that she could dress and embellish to pass the time.

Or his father, hoarding passion, money, diamonds, and secrets, who played the country gentleman to perfection, but still was wary and uneasy somewhere in his soul.

And Jancie. She was the perfect companion—too perfect?—subsuming that spark of spirit she had shown the day she arrived into a more deferential posture, more fitting with what Hugo and Olivia expected of a companion?

To watch her, you would think her sole desire in life was to see to Olivia's comfort. She was very, very good at it. And his mother was very content to have her.

But he thought there was more to it than that. There had to be. Now that she was dressed up, now that her dowdy clothes had been made over, and she moved around the house in her elegant, economical way, taking care of Olivia, there had to be something more. She wasn't passive, for all she was young, and polite. She hadn't given in on the question of the cat. Or apparently on some remuneration for her time and trouble with his mother, if Kyger was to be believed.

Surely she was submerging her real feelings, her real desires, her real purpose. She had to be thinking all the time about the differences between her father's lot in life and life at Waybury House.

She had to be wondering—anyone would wonder—*had* all the diamonds been lost to those kidnappers and thieves all those years ago? *Everything* lost that her father and Hugo had gambled on, and almost given their lives for? Or had Hugo been able to hide one, or a handful, a cacheful of diamonds—enough to fuel a gentleman's life in a place where no one would ever question his wealth or think to look for him?

Even he wondered sometimes, especially because Olivia was always quick to tell anyone that Waybury and all that accrued from it had passed from her side of the family to her.

Too quick?

He never questioned it. Why had he never questioned it?

As for what really happened at Kaamberoo—well, he never questioned that, either. Nor was he one to invite confidences, and he had never been the kind of son to whom Hugo would want to impart them.

He was the rakehell son. The to-hell-and-gone son. The one to whom a father did not delegate responsibility, give money, or make plans for. The one about whom a father threw up his hands and said, *You know Lujan. You can't depend on him for anything.*

And so here he was, making believe he was dependable.

Or was it make-believe? Could a man change that much so soon?

He could if his mother was dying, if his younger brother was making himself too indispensable, if his father was really a thief, and if a stranger who could bear a grudge had insinuated herself into the fabric of his family's life.

Funny how clear it all seemed to him now. He had always thought drink was the fuel of clarity. It was like waking up to the bright sunlight and realizing the day had as much allure as the attractions of the night.

And that he had been asleep for far too long.

Everything was different now. It was in the air, in the way Kyger and Lujan looked at her. Those clothes had transformed her somehow. Made her into—what?

A woman. No longer a dirty girl. No longer a girl. Because suddenly she comprehended that she was feeling with a woman's intuition now, seeing with a woman's eyes, responding with a woman's interest to a man's presence, gaze, need, words.

It thrilled her. It scared her to death.

She wanted to grab hold of Emily, grab what was left of her meager possessions, and leave Waybury House this instant.

And then what?

Emily, ever practical.

Of course. There was still the hanging question of her father—what he wanted, what he expected.

And Olivia?

Exactly—she was honor bound to complete her contract—how could she leave Olivia? Especially now.

And Kyger.

And, a knowing little voice whispered, *Lujan?*

But it wasn't like that, it wasn't. She had no expectations, it was only that Kyger was so kind, so—exactly the opposite of Lujan—who looked at her as if he could see every inch of naked skin beneath her dress, who looked at her as if she were his equal, of his social status, and not a dirty girl.

And—he made her feel like a woman.

Made her feel—just by looking at her.

Made her start looking for him, made her miss his presence if he somehow on some pretext did not intercept her at some point during the course of the day.

She became aware, more aware of her body than she ever had been. And too aware of feelings and sensations that were a road map of pleasure if only she would follow it. Feelings that gave her deep, knowing pleasure just anticipating where any and all of this knowledge and play would lead.

She felt such guilt feeling these things while Olivia was so ill.

And so withal, she became even more attentive to Olivia. But no amount of time, no amount of good care, could prevent Olivia's illness from running its course.

Olivia was failing, it was clear. Everyone became more attentive to Olivia as the year wore on.

Even Emily. Emily slipped into her room whenever Olivia slept and curled up next to her, a coil of cat-heat and a reassuring presence that slipped past all the barriers that Olivia had created to give a dying woman comfort.

Jancie tried only once to lift Emily away from Olivia's quiescent body.

But Emily wasn't moving. She put out a restraining claw and looked up at her with those oh-so-wise golden eyes.

Olivia needs me.

If Olivia knew, she never protested.

It was only a matter of time. Jancie was constantly with her. And Emily.

And as Olivia's life force waned, something new and budding sprang to life, and one day, as she was tending to Olivia and watching Lujan ride out down the long shell driveway to the front gate, Jancie suddenly comprehended why she had been brought to Waybury House and exactly what she had to do.

Chapter Five

"So, Jancie . . ."

Lujan again, coming down the hallway as she checked on Olivia, as he had every day for the past year. It had gotten so she wanted to see him, looked for him, and was insanely disappointed if he missed a day.

"Lujan."

He came up right behind her, peering over her shoulder at Olivia. Touching her. Touching her arm, her shoulder.

"The cat is with her?"

"She won't move." Jancie didn't want to move. She was too aware of his hand, so warm, so large, on her shoulder. So aware of him, so tall and pulsating, beside her. "Somehow Emily always manages to slip out of there before Olivia awakens, but she's always with her when she sleeps. I wonder if she knows."

"Oh, I think she knows," Lujan whispered. "You take such good care of her, Cinderella. I wish you'd take that good care of me."

She ignored that, and wriggled out from under his hand. She knew exactly what he meant by that, but she wasn't biting. She was learning a lot about Lujan.

Taking on responsibility had not dampened his desire to play;

he expected women to fall into his arms, especially someone who was a *paid* companion, so that the more reluctant she appeared, the more persistent he became.

She wasn't reluctant at all. She had come to allow him liberties that gave her great pleasure, but she didn't know how far she wanted to take this game, how deep she wanted to play. She only knew his interest was a welcome respite from her time with Olivia and she needed it. Wanted it. Encouraged it for reasons of her own.

"A companion can't be too *care*ful, Lujan. But you know that, I'm certain."

"But I wonder all the time—what does Cinderella know?"

"She knows her place," Jancie said primly.

"But Mother is sleeping and your place is now with me. We can take a walk around the grounds for a while. Come . . . you need some time out of the house. It must be deadly, manufacturing things to talk about and things to do day after day."

"And how would it be different with you?" Jancie asked pertly. This was a set piece between them, with different dialogue every day, but today he surprised her.

"Oh, I think we can find things to talk about and things to do *naturally*," Lujan said lightly. "Come. I promise, Father won't deduct this hour from your wages."

He took her arm and pulled her toward the staircase. Down they went, exactly in step, and out the door into the crisp fall air.

It had been coming to this. Olivia was failing, but so slowly, oh so slowly. Sometimes she seemed revitalized, sometimes she could get out of bed and come down to breakfast, sometimes she had the energy to sit in the garden, and had the concentration to listen to Jancie read to her.

It gave them hope that things would get better; or they could pretend they would.

But still, for Jancie, it had been a wearing year and a half tending to her, and dodging Lujan's double-edged comments, and his restless hands, while trying at the same time to provoke his interest.

And too soon, she found she looked forward to crossing verbal swords with him, and that she craved the light touch of his fingers on her arm, her hand, her shoulder.

A caress across the cheek, once, which sent little darts flicking to her vitals every time she thought of it after. She took those moments to bed with her. She nurtured them.

And Lujan knew it. He knew it so well—he knew just how to create them, how to excite her, arouse her, and then withdraw, leaving her hungering for more.

There were kisses in the garden—light, sweet, luscious kisses. And his hands, as he wrapped his arms around her, and cupped her breasts, oh, his hands . . . Still, it had taken more than a year for her to acquiesce to his touching her in any sexual way. A year of his light, flirtatious coaxing, his expert kisses, his hunger for her, voiced in that seductive whisper in her ear.

A year to arouse him to a fever pitch.

"Watch out for him," Kyger said, ever her protector.

"Nonsense. I would have thought everyone would be delighted he was taking an interest in estate matters."

"Lujan is *only* interested in himself. He has never spent this amount of time at Waybury. Beware, Jancie. Remember, I warned you."

But perhaps, Jancie thought, Kyger had his own reasons for saying these things. Lujan had everything in hand now, things that had previously been solely Kyger's purview. He rode the estate, he monitored the accounts, he paid out the monies due, he saw to the planting and the harvest, all tasks that had heretofore been Kyger's domain.

What must Kyger be thinking of Lujan usurping all that had been his responsibility?

But it wouldn't be too long now. Olivia was fading. Slowly, inexorably, the disease was taking its toll. It was only a matter of time. She was bedridden, weak, listless. Emily kept her company night and day now, and she made no protest, because Emily's presence seemed to give her a certain kind of strength.

Sometimes Jancie came in and found her stroking Emily's head, or Emily curled in the crook of her arm as she slept.

"God, I hate this," Jancie fretted as they all sat in the library one cool evening. There was a blazing fire in the fireplace and the kerosene lamps flickered low as Hugo tried to read the paper, and Kyger sat watching Jancie as she attempted some embroidery just to keep busy. "I don't want to lose her."

"But it seems we must, Jancie, whatever we may want," Hugo said, and there was a note in his voice that made Jancie look at him curiously.

Kyger heard it, too, and instantly reached for her hand. What did his father mean by that? Resignation, perhaps? Trying to convince Jancie, and himself? Or was it that he was relieved things would soon be over?

He didn't like the look on his father's face. And as much as he tried to suppress it, there was something other than grief there when he looked at Jancie. Why?

His father was still staring at her. Jancie had lowered her gaze back to her embroidery hoop, so that she didn't see the brief flaring gleam in Hugo's eyes.

But Kyger saw it. And he didn't like it.

And Lujan, lounging across the room in a large leather chair, saw it, too. Hugo the Stoic, the martyr father, bearing the burden of a terminally ill wife, and terminally feuding sons. Hiding, watching, waiting—

For what?

Dear God, he didn't like the thought that slammed into him like a bullet. Jancie! But Jancie was *his,* just ripe for the plucking after all the time, all the energy and patience he had put into seducing her to this point—

—and here was his father thinking—what?

Oh, Hugo was a deep one. Wholly removed from any of them. Never a father, really. Just a figurehead full of demons and expectations that were impossible to meet.

Maybe that was why he had become the bad one—there had never been anything for him here—not a father, not a mother, just a perfect, willing, and *good* younger brother, and the ghost of another who haunted them all.

So what was *really* on his father's mind? He wondered what Kyger was thinking. He looked at Kyger, and he knew. Kyger thought nothing would change. Olivia would pass away and he, Lujan, would blast back to London like a cannon and never look back.

Kyger expected it, counted on it.

And Hugo would—

What would Hugo do? What would Jancie do, for that matter, once Olivia was gone?

Oh, here was a fanciful idea—she could marry Kyger. They got along all right, neither had any expectations, and they could rub along nicely at Waybury taking care of *his* inheritance.

He rather liked the idea, actually. After he got through with her, because, of course, she wasn't nearly the blueblood *his* wife must be.

Well, that solved that.

Except—Hugo. Hugo was eyeing Jancie like she was a morsel waiting to be devoured. And as Lujan stared at him, Hugo's eyes skewed away suddenly as if he had been caught peeking in the cookie jar.

Well, he had. Lujan could see it, he hadn't imagined it. He felt sick, he felt a rising fury.

Why had he never noticed before?

Hugo looked guilty because Hugo was having prurient thoughts about Jancie, and this wasn't the first time, either.

Oh, Jesus lord—the unthinkable was true: Hugo had to have been thinking for a long time now that right under his nose he had a convenient replacement for Olivia. Someone young, beautiful, nubile, and fertile. Someone still able to bear children. Able to have endless expendable sex. Someone he could root in and produce another half-dozen sons with . . .

Cutting his oldest son out and down.

Shit.

A whole other family to mold to his heart's content.

NO!

Goddamn his soul to hell. NO!

NO!

NOOOO!

Dear Father, Jancie wrote.

Things are coming to a head here. Olivia is that much more diminished. It is only a matter of time. The entire family is here— in fact, you will be surprised to hear that Lujan has spent the bet- ter part of two years here, attending to his mother's needs and taking an interest in his birthright. The family has been inordi- nately kind, and it is so hard to hold on to the reality that all

Hugo has should be half ours. I know not how to rectify this or even discover if his stories of thieves and kidnappers is true. I only know I am feeling bereft already at the thought of Olivia's passing, and that I may well be sailing for India sooner than ever I imagined—

The house was too quiet.

Olivia was asleep after having dined. Jancie had seen to it herself; as Olivia's appetite waned, she made sure that Olivia got the nourishment she had started denying she needed—or wanted.

But Jancie wasn't going to let her die of malnutrition.

And so, Olivia now ate earlier than the rest of the household, with Jancie spoon-feeding her, giving her her medicine, and making sure that Emily was tucked in by her side.

You see? I knew she needed me.

Jancie needed Emily, too, but she bowed to her cat's superior wisdom. Emily would come when her task of taking care of Olivia was done.

And truth to tell, this little thing that Jancie could do, feeding Olivia, was hardly anything in the scheme of things. Emily was doing much more for her now than Jancie could.

So she went, as she did every night now, and washed, brushed her hair, pinched her cheeks, then made her way down to the dining room.

As always, it struck her how quiet the house was. And yet there was something palpable in the air. She didn't know quite when she comprehended there were things bubbling beneath the surface that had not at first been obvious, but she was aware of it now.

Or maybe it was that she was so taken with Kyger, and so immersed in her ridiculous feelings for Lujan that she just wasn't paying attention.

Yes, that was it—she hadn't been paying attention, between Olivia's illness and her trying to keep the right balance between being a companion and being treated as a servant . . .

Perfectly understandable that she hadn't noticed Hugo watching her. Or Lujan watching Hugo. And Kyger keeping a skeptical eye on all of them.

"You are an innocent in a nest of snakes," Kyger had whispered to her one evening as they came down to dinner. "Look at Father."

It was the first time he had ever made such a comment. So she looked. Hugo was on the threshold of the dining room, looking up at the staircase, waiting for them.

But what did she see? An impatient old man waiting for two youngsters who were inexcusably late for dinner.

"Do you not see how he's looking at you?" Kyger whispered.

"No, he's looking at you, and wishing his more responsible younger son were the older one," she retorted.

"Oh, he's thinking of his mortality, all right, but it has nothing to do with me."

She hadn't liked the comment. She hadn't wanted to think about what it could mean, but as she came downstairs alone tonight, and Hugo suddenly appeared on the threshold, she saw what Kyger had seen—how Hugo's eyes lit up, how his gaze followed her as she descended and walked across the foyer, how he held out his hand to take hers as she crossed into the dining room, as if he were looking for any excuse to touch her.

All that she saw, and Kyger's knowing I-told-you look as she came into the room. She looked at Lujan, who was slouched at the far end of the table, and his burning gaze seared her.

Lujan knew. He knew what she felt, what she wanted, what his father was thinking, what Kyger was hoping, and there was nothing she could hide from him. And she didn't want to. Not now.

Dinner was quiet, too quiet, with all that emotion simmering under the surface. Lujan stared at Hugo; Hugo deliberately averted his eyes. Kyger grinned at Jancie, and Jancie wished she could take her meals up in her room altogether.

It was an effort to eat. No one attempted conversation—there really was nothing to say, with Olivia dying, and Hugo already thinking about his life after she was gone.

Oh, she hated him for that. But it was all of piece. If Hugo *was* the kind of man who wouldn't stop at attempted murder to steal a fortune in diamonds, then certainly he'd have no compunction about plotting a future before his wife was in her grave.

And who knew what other crimes he might have committed?

Because Jancie was certain he *was* that kind of man, and time

was running out and she was never going to find out how much
he had stolen from Edmund and her. When Olivia passed, she
would have no other choice but to leave, too.

Ow . . .

So there was no point making conversation. After the fact,
things would go on as they always had. She would have been
only a diversion for Lujan; she was smart enough to know that.
Something to amuse him, give him something to chase after,
something on which to focus his pent-up sensuality, something to
do.

Ow.

. . . But once Olivia died, she would revert to being a dirty girl
again. She would leave Waybury with some fancy dresses and a
nice number of pounds in her pocket. She would go to India. Live
like a queen, just as she'd always planned . . .

Ow.

She looked up then. Emily was sitting in the doorway.

Ooowww.

They all looked at each other.

"Olivia—" Jancie whispered, and bolted out of her chair.

Ow.

Emily was already in the hallway, at the base of the stairs,
waiting for them, and as they followed, she dashed up the stairs.

They pounded into Olivia's room, scared at what they would
find, and gathered around the bed. It wasn't the end. But soon,
soon.

Emily jumped up next to her. *I'm here* . . .

Olivia put out her hand and Emily ducked under it, so that
Olivia could hold onto her for security, for safety, in these last
minutes.

I won't leave you . . .

Olivia looked around at her sons, at Jancie, her vision dim-
ming, her fingers convulsing on Emily's neck. She took a deep
breath, as if she wanted to say something, and couldn't summon
the strength . . .

And then she turned her gaze on Hugo. Another breath, more
determined this time.

"Gaunt," she whispered on the exhale, and then, she was
gone.

* * *

All things must end.

That was the eulogy, the message of faith.

Jancie stood apart from the family at the gravesite of Olivia's ancestors, and listened to the vicar intoning the age-old words of comfort.

Ashes to ashes . . .

There weren't that many people there: three or four friends from church, a neighbor, the vicar's wife . . .

She had to leave.

. . . . give our beloved Olivia to God . . .

Today . . . this minute—she couldn't stand it; she was drowning in tears, in regrets, in guilt that she couldn't have done more for Olivia.

But there had never been any other possible outcome. It was just as Kyger had said: they had known the inevitable ending; they didn't want to believe it, they pretended it wasn't going to happen—and now . . .

All things must end. Reality always intruded. Her time at Waybury was over, and she had to get out of there, fast.

Kyger read her mind. Read her eyes, really, and the devastated expression on her face. "Don't do anything yet," he whispered.

"I have to go."

"Not today."

She gave him a mutinous look. "An unmarried woman alone in a house with three unattached men—are you crazy?"

"Stop it . . . just—"

"I'll go to the vicar."

. . . may she find her place in heaven . . .

"Stop it. You're not going yet . . ."

. . . I give you peace . . .

There would be no peace. She had to get out of there, away from her father's unmet expectations, Lujan's hot eyes, and Hugo's glimmering hope.

She had failed so miserably. At everything.

And then there was Kyger—dear Lord, Kyger . . .

Ow.

Emily, appearing out of nowhere, sinuously winding her body around a nearby tree.

Ow. Sitting on her haunches, watching the last moments of the service, before they all would turn away . . .

Amen.

Over, everything over.

Ow.

Maybe it was too easy to leave Olivia?

Emily stood up, arched her back, looked at Jancie. *I'll stay with her.*

Jancie turned away, tears streaming down her cheeks, and followed the mourners, keeping several respectful steps behind, through the grounds toward the village, where the vicar's wife would serve tea.

Mrow.

Emily, softly, saying her own good-bye.

Good-bye, good-bye, amen . . .

It was excruciating, sitting in the vicarage parlor, sipping tea she didn't want and being stared at by strangers. She could almost hear them whispering: *That one was the companion. Too young, too pretty for her own good. Who knows what really went on there? And she's going back to a household of men tonight, is she? And the lady not dead and in her grave a day . . .*

Even a dirty girl had more sense than that. All she had to do was ask the vicar's wife. There would be no problem, none. Everyone would understand. But no one would, if she elected to go back to Waybury House with Hugo, Lujan, and Kyger.

One death made all the difference. It wiped away lust and kisses, it washed away unholy expectations and irrational excuses. It made everything she'd thought possible the stuff of foolish dreams.

She'd had no idea what the impact of Olivia's death would be. Now she knew: death buried those dreams, as surely as if she herself had died.

Mrow.

Emily, at the parlor door, somehow having snuck in, and searching for Jancie, now that her vigil was over. *Ow,* as Jancie picked her up and carried her out of the house.

"We have to stay here," she whispered into Emily's neck. "We can't go back, and there isn't anywhere to go forward. I failed. At everything. I failed . . ."

Mrow . . . soft, consoling. *Wait till tomorrow.*

"Jancie, my dear." Here came the vicar's wife, to tell her, she was certain, that cats didn't belong in the parlor.

"Yes, ma'am?" She kept Emily firmly against her chest.

"You'll stay with us tonight, of course. Tomorrow we can decide what to do. I'll send someone for your things."

"Yes, thank you. I was thinking along those lines myself."

The vicar's wife smiled. "A cat is such a comfort, isn't it?" she murmured, running her hand along Emily's back. Emily purred. "We'll have a light dinner, and you can retire early. It will be for the best."

Jancie closed her eyes as a tremor ran through her. For the best?

For the best.

Emily again, slanting her golden gaze up at her, humming and purring against her heart. A solace for her—and for Olivia, in her final moments.

"You're right. It's for the best."

She bent over and set Emily on the floor; Emily promptly ducked under a table. Jancie rose and nearly elbowed Kyger in the belly. He grabbed her by the shoulders, held her close to his chest for a moment, and then released her.

"Keeping you prisoner here, are they?"

"It's for the best," she murmured, a little shaken by his nearness. Why not Kyger? Why couldn't she have those deep, fluttery, squirmy-dart feelings for Kyger?

"Because they're taking wagers which of us would bed you first if we took you back to the house?"

She felt heat wash her face. "Something like that."

"One of us would," Kyger said. "Maybe two of us."

"But not you."

He raised an eyebrow. "Don't be so certain I'm not one of those two."

"Kyger, don't. Not today."

"No," he said gently, feelingly, "not today."

She looked at his face closely. He'd cried for Olivia, she was absolutely certain, and she knew with the same certainty that neither Hugo nor Lujan had. *Why* couldn't she have feelings for him?

Those feelings, as opposed to other feelings—warmth, camaraderie, deep knowledge of who he was and what kind of person he was. That was what she should fall in love with, not the smug womanizer that was Lujan. Oh, dear heaven . . . why not Kyger? They were suited, they were equal, he cared about her . . . she could feel it, she would feel it forever. Kyger could love her, if only she would let him.

Why Lujan, and not Kyger? Why was she looking over his shoulder, and hoping that Lujan would come? It wasn't fair, it wasn't logical, it wasn't right . . . Kyger was the good brother, the moral brother, as handsome and raffish as ever Lujan was, and you knew he would never hurt you, never betray you—

And Lujan would.

And still, she yearned for Lujan. Wanted Lujan. Could never be satisfied with less than Lujan.

She watched Kyger move away to accept condolences from a neighbor. Lord, she must be out of her mind with grief for Olivia to be thinking like this; that had to be the reason, and in the morning she would see everything more clearly. Especially a mile away from Waybury House, where Lujan didn't suck up all the air and her every thought.

"Jancie."

Oh, good God. Hugo.

"Yes, Hugo?"

It was those glimmering eyes, skimming over her like she was something luscious and almost irresistibly desirable.

This soon—? Too soon, she thought.

"I'd like you to consider not leaving us," he said obliquely.

"But I must," she murmured. "I should."

"Even if there were a reason for you to stay . . . ?"

"Hugo, truly—"

"I am not at liberty to speak so soon, Jancie, but you must not leave us, not yet . . . Please consider—you must understand what I am hinting at."

"I do, and it distresses me no end."

"But it makes such perfect sense. Am I not still in need of . . . of all those things that must accrue to a man in a marriage? Does that die when his wife leaves him? Is every feeling, every need, every desire buried as well?"

"Hugo, I beg you . . ."

"I beg you think about it. I have stated my case as plainly as I can under the circumstances. There is so much for you to gain by not rushing off so precipitately. And I promise you, Jancie, you will *not* like India as much as you think you will."

Oh God—this could not be happening. Everything she feared, nothing she wanted. She *would* have to leave, and that had been the last measure of her plans.

But then, what did she know about stroking a rake and making him come to point? She knew nothing, she'd been playing with fire, she had no idea how to blow it into a conflagration, and so it had all turned to embers and ashes.

Sackcloth and ashes . . .

And yet—the offer was on the table. And there was nothing to stop her from accepting it. She could stay at Waybury forever, share his bed—how bad, truly, could it be?—bear him a child, perhaps, if that was his wont.

It would make Lujan very unhappy. Lujan looked murderous already, so he must have a very good idea what Hugo had said to her.

Perhaps all was not lost yet. Certainly if she married Hugo, she would be near Lujan, for however often he might grace Waybury with his presence.

Was that enough?

And would it be enough that she would finally have a way to investigate all the secrets of Waybury House? Especially the ones Hugo had buried himself in the country to protect and hide? The ones involving her father and the long-gone-missing diamonds?

Maybe it was enough. Maybe she hadn't failed, if Hugo was interested enough to hint at marriage. And Lujan was glowering. Maybe she hadn't failed in that regard, either: Lujan knew.

Good.

No, bad—*BAD* to even consider playing Lujan against his father. Against Kyger. Against her own better judgment.

Women in love were sorry doormats, she thought mordantly, as she made her way back into the vicarage parlor. Just waiting for someone to wipe their feet on them.

But she *wasn't* a doormat, she wasn't a dirty girl. She'd done everything she could for Olivia, and she'd foolishly allowed herself to nurture warm feelings for a man who consumed dirty girls like scones—one taste and then toss it away.

That was all anyone in their right mind had to know about Lujan Galliard. Except she wasn't in her right mind, and she was as overwhelmed with grief over Olivia's death as if she were a member of the family.

A night away from Waybury would be a very good thing. Emily would be with her and she could talk it out and get her thinking straight.

But it would also be a night that Hugo would continue to hope that she would see the sense of his plan.

She wished he wouldn't.

But—did it make sense? She could have been his daughter in another life. And Olivia had treated her almost like she was, anyway. She could not look at him as other than someone who could have been her father.

And he was so much older than she.

No, this was a plan that did not make sense.

But there he'd be tonight, thinking that she would consider his words in a favorable light. And Kyger would be there, thinking that in spite of the circumstances, she'd really rather not leave.

And Lujan would just be . . . irritated.

And maybe that was a good thing, too.

Why shouldn't she?

The question haunted Jancie as she tossed and turned in the spare bedroom at the vicarage.

The vicar's wife had been kind. She had put no pressure on her to be social beyond the necessities after the funeral. She had shown her to the room, which was comfortable, serviceable, and she had provided some soup and tea. And then she had left her alone.

Jancie wasn't sure she wanted to be alone. She couldn't sleep. She couldn't think. She wasn't hungry. Emily's presence was no solace.

Hugo's proposal had turned her world upside down. And it wasn't that Hugo's interest was wholly unexpected—it was just that she hadn't thought he would ever say anything.

And so unbelievably, indecently, soon.

It tipped her world; it was the last thing she had expected. She had thought to be leaving for London within the week, without having answered any of the questions that had plagued her father for the past thirty years.

There were no answers. Hugo had had much better luck than Edmund, and maybe that was the simplest explanation. And that the money that sustained his gentlemanly life had truly been inherited by Olivia and had nothing to do with a secret cache of diamonds he might have stolen all those years ago.

She had to believe that. There was nothing else.

Mrow. Emily, curled up on her stomach.

"Thank you, Emily. Let me amend that to 'nothing I've ever been able to find in my two years of trying to discover something.' "

Ow.

"Yes, I have been distracted."

Damn. The last six months . . .

And now, Hugo—

Why shouldn't I?

She blew out a hard breath and Emily shifted as her muscles contracted.

Mrowww.

"Yes, I know *you'd* like a permanent home. *I'd* like a permanent home—but—as Hugo's wife?"

And all that entailed besides? Her hands turned cold at the thought of Hugo touching her the way Lujan had touched her, kissing her, stroking her, murmuring arousing words in her ear . . .

Coming to her, naked, hot, pulsing with a man's needs . . . oh God . . . no—

But—

Still—

She wouldn't ever have to leave here.

Answers could still be discovered.

She would have her own home, her own life.

She would have Lujan . . .

. . . sometimes—

Her chest constricted. She had fallen too far if she were thinking of accepting a proposal in order to stay close to a reformed libertine who might well have been living a lie all these months.

No, *she* had been living the lie, presenting herself as a willing companion when actually she'd come to spy on them.

She was an inept spy, too, and she hadn't been much of a companion—to Olivia—in the past few months. Lujan had usurped her time, had filled her hours, had made her want things that weren't possible—with him.

But they are possible with Hugo . . .

She couldn't sleep.

How could she marry the father of the man she really wanted?

She could . . . she only had to think of him as a suitor, a man of substance. A man who wanted her.

Then it became an answer, a plan.

Women did it all the time. Married men for stability and status in exchange for sex and solace. There would be children, there would be other satisfactions. And if she were honest with herself, she would admit she would never have another offer like this.

Maybe she had no other choice. Maybe she wasn't thinking clearly—but as far as she could tell, there were no just impediments.

So . . . *Why shouldn't she?*

Chapter Six

Why shouldn't she?

The question kept Lujan awake all night, the unexpected shock of his overhearing Hugo's declaration reverberating through him like a bell.

To speak so disrespectfully soon. To speak at all, on the heels of Olivia's untimely death. The lecher ought to be in mourning a year at least instead of thinking about filling his bed with sleek, young, fertile flesh.

Why the hell should he care?

He hadn't thought he cared. That he had only stayed on at Waybury for his mother's sake.

But maybe there was something about the companion.

Except that, curse her soul, the butter-wouldn't-melt-on-her-soul little whore had cleverly seduced his unsuspecting father at the same time she was succumbing to *his* kisses and melting in *his* arms, and somehow she had pried this oblique proposal out of Hugo, and was now *pretending* to consider it.

Ha. She probably would've jumped on it like a frog if they hadn't been at a funeral.

Jesus. What a scheming little trull.

Just what he'd thought when she came here. She justified all his suspicions. After all, it had never been quite clear what use his family could possibly have for the indigent daughter of his father's worst enemy. Hugo could have hired anyone as a companion for Olivia, but no, he had to have *this* pound of flesh. He'd paid for the chit's education and he was the kind of man who made certain every debt was repaid in kind, no matter how long it took.

Well, he was paying for it now, because the companion had been using them in turn, trolling them both, hedging her bets so there was no way she could lose.

God, that made him furious.

She'd been so pliant in his arms. So willing, giving. Soft. Innocent. He'd been lured by that innocence; his head had been turned, just a little, by her unexpected beauty, her spirit, and the gift of her virginity, even as he was fully aware how dangerous it was to have such attractive female flesh in a houseful of men.

Still, the companion was *his*—Lujan was as certain of that as all his years of experience could make him, and no matter how many times Kyger had tried to prevent it, he had always won her back to him. He had begun to think she was starting to fall in love with him, and that had distracted him, too.

And so, he had lost all focus as his mother lay dying.

Well, he had it back now, sharp as a saber. Perfectly clear. The companion would not marry his father if he could help it, would not marry and give Hugo more sons to usurp *his* birthright, and cut him out.

And in turn, he would not allow Hugo the satisfaction of disinheriting him by marriage so he couldn't squander every cent of his legacy, as Hugo fully expected him to do.

What was to be his was going to be his, as it had been—father to son—since time immemorial. So he had only one recourse: to prevent this marriage somehow. The companion would not get a ha'penny of Hugo's money or the respectability of being his wife—even if he had to kill Hugo as a last resort.

What???

The thought was so shocking he bolted upright.

God, what was wrong with him?

Why not kill the companion, come to that . . . ?

Holy shit—

Or marry her.

What?

Marry her?

He felt the tension ease out of his soul. Ha. Of course. Marry her. His tension eased somewhat, it was so laughable. Give her exactly what she had been after all along? After she had proven she was just like every other predatory woman: ever an elusive virgin, and capitulating to pleasure before all that long.

He should have known what she was doing, seen through her from the start. That was what sobriety did to you—made you believe the impossible.

But everything was clear as a bell now: he would get his father out of her clutches and make it clear she would get no satisfaction from him. He wasn't going to marry anyone. No encumbrances, no heirs, no responsibility. Not for him.

He was wed to the coffers of money that he would expend on every secret pleasure in the future.

But—if you married her . . .

Don't even think about it. She's hardly your social equal, anyway. Just make sure that Hugo never proposes outright. Just . . . keep her busy and get her away from here as soon as possible.

She wanted to go to London. To book passage for India. Perfect. Take her there. Make sure she walks up that gangplank and disappears forever.

There. That was the answer. Satisfactory for everyone.

When she left, she'd be as good as dead anyway, and remembered no more.

But there would always be the possibility she'd come back, or her father would turn up on the doorstep—or make demands. They'd never be certain, never be secure. Hugo had secrets, Hugo was still wary of his former partner. And Hugo could still remarry.

Jesus.

There was no end to the complications because of the companion. Before the companion, everything had been so simple. Life had been one long, lovely dive into the hedonistic pleasure of the moment.

Now he had to worry about getting rid of the companion, Hugo becoming interested in still another fertile, young body after she left, the loss of his birthright, his too-righteous, do-gooder brother who would be only too happy to take over his legacy if he drowned in his drink, and some doddering old former partner making impossible demands for reparation in the future.

God, he needed a drink.

No, he needed a plan. Something that would circumvent all these potential disasters.

Some of the potential disasters. He couldn't think of *everything*.

Which led him right back to why the companion shouldn't accept his father's proposal. If she were half as smart as he thought, of course, she would. She would have every advantage, very little inconvenience, and nothing to lose.

A win on every side for her.

And should she ever conceive—

Inconceivable. Hugo wouldn't—

No, Hugo *would,* damn his corrupt and immoral soul . . .

And he and Kyger would be out on the streets faster than a whore achieved orgasm.

But if *he* married her . . .

. . . don't even whisper the thought—

But IF— . . . NO . . .

For *discussion's* sake, if—if he were to marry her—which took a long, hard moment to imagine—*if* he were to marry her . . . *if* he didn't factor in social considerations—*if* . . .

—it could—he thought with a flash of illumination—solve several problems with one master stroke—

—at the least, he would take her away from Hugo, and he would provide himself with the potential for an heir. He would secure his inheritance and cut out Kyger, which would give him leave to whore around all he desired because everyone would know he was married, so the pressure to make any choices would be over.

—and . . . marrying the companion would not only cover all those prime points but—her presence at Waybury would keep her mysterious father-partner at bay and out of sight forever.

Hmmm. Not a bad payoff for a ceremony and a song.

And the only other thing he had to worry about was Hugo flying off and finding some sweet, young thing who was willing to spread her legs for the price of a ring, and he could keep that under control by fucking whatever prime pieces Hugo trotted out as well.

Not a bad preventive measure, come to that . . .

. . . because, after all was said and done, his fastidious father wouldn't want used goods. He wouldn't want to be uncertain of the paternity of any child he might have fathered . . .

. . . and *that* would solve the problem of an unwanted half-brother inheriting anything in years to come . . .

By God—there was a way around everything, an answer to every problem, and in this case, the answers were all expedient for *him,* even if he had to marry a destitute little nobody to achieve the results.

Nice to be in that position.

So to speak.

The end justified the means, after all, and his mother had already started to make a Cinderella out of a sow's ear, anyway, so outwardly, the companion was no different from any other of the blueblood whores prowling the marriage mart.

And after all, she *was* the daughter of a gentleman—or at least as much a gentleman as his own father had been before he came into all that money. So he could forgo that requirement, given all that.

And that took care of that problem. It took care of almost every problem, this brainstorm of his to marry the companion, and it wouldn't be all that difficult to accomplish.

Well, he was a practical man. He was ready to take action. And the more he thought about marrying the companion to forestall Hugo, the more he liked the added recompense of having a body of his own at Waybury to fuck whenever he was there.

The meltingly innocent little companion, waiting, eager, writhing, yearning . . . It made such sense, he wondered why he hadn't installed a naked body in residence long before this.

And not only that, *he* didn't have to wait to make *his* proposal to the companion. He was ready now. He had only to say the word, and he'd cut out Hugo and be rooting between her legs by tomorrow noon.

* * *

Why shouldn't she?

By morning, Jancie was still wide awake, her eyes puffed from tears she had shed over Olivia.

And she still had no answers. There *was* no right answer. There were just advantages, too many to count and too few to resist.

How could she resist them? Did she even want to?

Mrroww, Emily said. *Can you be happy with that old man?*

Did it matter if she were not happy? She stroked Emily's head and Emily slanted a golden look up at her.

Was anyone happy, really?

And apart from the unseemly haste of Hugo's proposition—that she stay, that something more was in the offing after a proper mourning period was observed—there was truly no reason for her not to consider it.

It was the answer to everything.

Ow, Emily agreed.

Exactly—it was as simple as making comparisons. Marry Hugo and bury the dirty girl, have money to spare, manage a beautiful home, have servants, nice clothes, find out the truth about what happened at Kaamberoo, have a child, perhaps, sometime in the future. Lujan, whenever he might choose to appear . . .

It was the sticking point. Lujan.

Or—leave Waybury, leave Lujan, say good-bye forever to Kyger. And then have the adventure of your life. Go to India, be with Father, die an old maid. Never find out Hugo's secrets.

The scales were tilting.

She levered herself out of the bed and padded to the window. She was on the second floor of the rectory in a comfortably situated bedroom that overlooked the church grounds and the turnpike beyond.

Not too far down that road was Waybury. And Lujan. Was he tossing and turning in his bed as restlessly as she?

She didn't think so. Lujan didn't lose sleep over anything. She hadn't slept a wink. Because her decision would have as much to do with her father's expectations as her own desires. She was eighteen years old; did she really want to commit herself to a man almost three times her age? Let his old hands touch her young flesh, feel his old, flaccid body pump his seed into her young, fertile one?

Other women did. No small consolation, that. Women sold their bodies and souls for such a man, such a home, such a luxurious life. And all they needed to do was provide an heir.

But Hugo had his heirs, so what could he possibly want of her? The obvious was not so obvious. Besides, there were dirty girls to be had anywhere, and barring that, there were widows and women his own age available for his *needs*.

He didn't *need* her. The *her* that represented youth, vigor, fertility, and sons. He was long past that, anyway.

But she needed Lujan. Would she marry Hugo just to make him jealous, to make him desire what he had willingly relinquished?

Mrrroww . . . Emily, emphatic now, and utterly correct. She was no *femme fatale*. She was not one who inspired great passion in anyone. She knew she was too young, too inexperienced, too kitchen-wise, and too unused to the ways of the drawing room—and utterly confounded by the likes of Lujan and his vast sexual experience.

She was living in a bubble if she thought Lujan was top over tail over *her*. Lujan must marry a drawing room girl, simple as that. His position, his family's expectations, demanded it, and she would be utterly delusional not to recognize that and not agree with it. The rules of society applied, even in the depths of Hertfordshire.

So that was that: the decision was made and she needed only to choose whether she would marry Hugo for her own reasons, or leave altogether.

Suddenly India seemed impossibly far away.

Farther away than anything she could imagine down the road toward Waybury.

She didn't want to leave.

The sun was so bright, creeping up over the horizon, irresistibly warm, blinding her, heating her, beckoning her, seducing her down the road of least resistance toward Waybury.

Oh God, I can't.

But I want to.

Why shouldn't I?

* * *

Why shouldn't she?

The question had kept Kyger awake all night. Damn Hugo and his greed. All you had to do was dangle a fresh, young body in front of a man that age and he wanted to make it his. Hugo had been isolated in the countryside too damned long.

But then, so had he.

And if Hugo asked Jancie to marry him, he thought he might just do something drastic.

But then there would be no earthly reason for *him* to stay on at Waybury. Simple as that. He'd put in his time, he'd taken up his brother's slack, more to ease his mother's mind than to be the *heir pro temps,* in the hopes that Lujan would eventually go down from his own excesses, and he would inherit somehow.

He supposed that was how Hugo viewed it—that he was Lujan's understudy, just waiting for the moment that Lujan fucked up his life and *someone* would be there to take over.

Sometimes he was sick of the damned whole lot of them, sick of being the good son, the better son.

But then there was Jancie. Who could have predicted Jancie? Beautiful, tart Jancie with a backbone stiff as whalebone, and compassion to match. Dear God. Jancie.

The wonder was she had resisted Lujan for so long. But she had, and Lujan had been intrigued and Lujan had pursued her, and Lujan had won again. It was ever his lot in life to be the charmer, the rogue, the winner, and Kyger always turned up second best.

Even with the companion.

Even with their father, their mother . . .

Best not think about that—

He had not let himself mourn, not nearly. Because he knew Hugo wouldn't, Lujan couldn't, and it was only he and Jancie who had the well of emotion necessary for such a personal and compassionate act. She was mourning now, he was certain of it, and he only wanted to wipe the tears from her eyes and hold her.

So how was it then that they could not connect, and she and Lujan could—had?

Lujan had the touch, always had.

And so now their lives were up in the air, juggled by the hand of fate. Would Jancie stay? Would Lujan? Would Hugo ask her to marry him, this ungodly soon? And would *he* leave on that note, or suffer in silence?

Or—should *he* just go and ask Jancie to marry *him*?

By all the holy saints . . .

The thought stunned him.

Or had he been thinking that all along, under the skin, and just never acknowledging it? Were they not friends enough, companions enough, even attracted enough to make a go of marriage? Other couples had started up with far less between them—

Lord almighty . . .

Jancie in his arms—a wet dream come alive, as she yearned after Lujan and he lusted after her—could he bear to be cuckolded by the both of them in the end?

He felt the anger boiling up from somewhere at the thought of it. Lujan was a shit and he had suppressed his irritation far too long at Lujan's cavalier treatment of Jancie when it was quite obvious what was going on behind closed doors and in the garden.

Well, Jancie, for all her virginity, was no innocent. Not after her years in the kitchen at St. Bonny's. That had to have been an education in and of itself. Jancie knew what was what. Lujan could never have cajoled or convinced her to do anything if she didn't want it to happen.

It just might not have happened the way Lujan wanted. It might just be that Jancie was holding out for marriage.

Which Lujan would never do. He'd never marry anyone. It would spoil his fun. It would cage and corral him and make him feel responsible, which in turn would make him rebel. The satisfactions of that putative marriage would be very short-lived once his resentment at being tethered set in.

And perhaps that would be *his* chance, his time. The consoling younger brother—just like Lujan, only better.

Hadn't he heard *that* all his life?

The magnetism of Lujan was too powerful. The wealth and amenities his father could provide were too alluring. He had no chance at all against those two insurmountable walls—but suddenly he felt the absolute need and desire to scale them.

To upset the cart, to overset his brother, to show up his father—to win . . . for the first time in a long time, to win.

* * *

...shouldn't she...?

She absolutely should ... it was her mandate, her desire ...

There was a discreet knock at the door.

The vicar's wife, Mrs. Elsberry, edging over the threshold with tea, eggs, and toast.

It was eight o'clock. Just the right time, when a body needed a cup of tea and some sustenance, and Jancie said so. "You didn't have to go to this trouble, Mrs. Elsberry."

She waved it off. "Nice to have someone to pamper for a bit." She pulled a small table to the window and set down the tray. "My own are long gone and living in London just now—don't get down but once a year to see us. So this is a pleasure, especially in that Mrs. Galliard was so fond of you."

"Thank you," Jancie murmured, close to tears again. If only her allegiance to Olivia weren't a factor ... and Olivia's affection for her.

"There, there. You made her remaining time so much easier, I'm sure. Mr. Galliard has continually said he didn't know what they would have done without you."

Her tears spilled over. "So kind."

Mrs. Elsberry pulled back the curtains. "No need to rush. I'll have the girl come help you with your *toilette*. We took the liberty of freshening your dress. She'll bring it to you when she comes."

"So thoughtful ..."

"And you needn't think of leaving today, my dear. Maybe it's too soon? Grief doesn't evaporate the next day, you know. It will hit you now and again. Well, think about it, at least. Another day's respite couldn't hurt anything."

Exactly. Another few days to figure things out, to assess whether Hugo's veiled interest was for real, whether Lujan would step up and ask her to stay ...

She hated feeling at their mercy. She had done all she could, all Edmund could expect her to do, but for all she knew, Hugo had had second thoughts, and the Galliards were done with her altogether. It wanted only that she arrange for someone to retrieve her meager belongings, a mile out of sight, and far from anyone's mind.

The way it should be done. Discreet withdrawal. Never to

be seen or heard from again. As if she really were a dirty girl. Like a servant, pensioned off after long years of satisfactory service.

But Hugo and his family were no more aristocrats than she was. She'd do well not to forget that. But for the circumstances— and she must remember that, too—it could be her and her father in that house, cushioned in wealth and luxury.

And now, because Hugo had been so precipitate—for whatever reason—she had, in the palm of her hand, the entrée she wanted, the opportunity she needed, to find out Hugo's secrets.

And she knew, really, there was no other answer. She had been given her mandate the day she was born. She was going to say yes to Hugo.

The urgency he felt was totally out of proportion to the situation, but it didn't stop Kyger from racing out for the vicarage by nine that morning. Probably because the house felt too empty, because he couldn't find Lujan, because Hugo was nowhere in sight.

Damn them all.

Jancie . . .

The morning was cool, the road was hard, the sun barely topped the trees as he spurred his mount toward the vicarage— too late, too late . . .

. . . shit—someone there . . . God, he hoped it wasn't—who? Hugo?

He dove off the horse before he even pulled it to a halt—not too late—Jancie was probably asleep, they'd have to wake her, she'd have to dress . . . she might not want to see either Hugo or Lujan this morning . . .

Wishful thinking. She might not want to see *him*, either.

Sharp knock on the door; the maid opening, motioning him into the receiving parlor—breath let out—Lujan . . . *Lujan?*

"Well, old man—whatever can you be doing here at this hour?" Lujan asked lazily.

"Or you, you ballocker," Kyger growled, taking a combative stance in front of the chair where Lujan lounged by the fire, a cup of tea by his elbow. That was too cozy, too domestic for words. He hated Lujan at that moment with a ferocity that was almost murderous.

"Sit down, little brother. Don't get in a twist. We're all friends here."

"Not at nine in the morning, we're not. And I know exactly why you're here."

"Do you? Hmm. I don't even know why I'm here."

"God, you're such a son of a bitch. I'm not going to let you . . ."

"Let me? *Let* me. Who the hell cares what you'll *let* me, most righteous one. I do whatever I damned please. When have you ever stopped me from doing anything? *Let* me—" He shook his head wonderingly, and so did not catch the movement of Kyger bending toward him in one fluid motion until Kyger had grabbed his shirt, and yanked him to his feet.

"Well, here's what I'll *let* you do now, big brother. I'll *let* you walk out of this room with your head on your shoulders and your legs intact."

Lujan rammed his fist into Kyger's ribs. Kyger slammed him back against the wall. "Hands down, big brother—you are soft, you are sloppy, and you are no match for me."

"Think again, little boy—" Lujan grunted, hauling off a punch in his ribs on the opposite side.

"I'm still standing, brother bull, and you can't move," Kyger taunted him, but his voice was just a little hoarse. "It's all those years in the field, you know. Riding, baling hay, doing the dirty work, and knowing there's nothing in it for me. Makes a man real physically strong." He lifted his leg in a sharp movement that caught Lujan between his legs. "Makes a man able to meet all kinds of challenges."

Lujan crumpled, but Kyger wouldn't let him fall forward, and nurse the pain.

"Yes, I think I punctuated my concerns in the only way *you* can fully understand," Kyger murmured. "Just leave her alone. I'll wait till you leave."

"You bastard," Lujan croaked. "I want to marry her."

"The hell you do."

"I suppose you do, too."

Kyger thrust him back against the wall. "Let's put it this way—Father shouldn't."

"My thought exactly," Lujan wheezed, doubling over. God,

that hurt. Who knew Kyger had such passion under that contained surface?

"Fine. So you don't have to sully your reputation any more. I'll clean up your mess, just like I always do."

"Son of a bitch—" Lujan struggled upright and lunged toward Kyger.

Kyger fended him off easily and pushed him back into his chair. "Would you just stop it? You don't want to marry her, we both don't want Father to marry her, so who is really the likely candidate?"

"You don't understand, little brother. There are bigger issues here than just an available body."

"Issues, eh? Issues. Like Father getting another son on her?"

"Something like that."

"That doesn't diminish the fact that you're the oldest."

"He's brain-struck—I think there are things we don't know, secrets he's keeping. He could do anything, if he'd marry a nobody like Jancie."

"Really—?" Kyger drawled. "So why do you want to marry her?"

So the *father-new heir* argument wouldn't work, Lujan thought, slanting a look at his avenging fury of a brother. And Kyger's taking on the burden of marrying Jancie wouldn't solve anything, either. Nor could he leave Hugo on the loose, looking for fresh flesh, unless *he* had a possible heir in the offing.

So—his only choice was to lie.

"I love her," he said softly.

Kyger snorted. "You *love* her? That's rich, big brother. You love her. No, you love yourself. You love your irresponsible life. You love the money I generate. You love the fact that Waybury exists for you to come home to when your body is exhausted. But *love—a nobody like Jancie?* When the Countess of Cavell, with all her youth, wealth, position, and eligibility nearly killed herself over you . . . tell me another Banbury story, brother. That one won't fly."

Shit. "I love her," Lujan said again, injecting as much yearning and sincerity in his tone as he could.

Kyger laughed. "You are a bastard."

"Fine. I'm not leaving."

Kyger took a stance by the door. "Neither am I."

"This should be good. Mrs. Elsberry has gone to summon her."

"The *nobody*, you mean."

Lujan made a sound. "I'm going to ask her to marry me."

"*What??*"

"I'm going to marry her—if she'll have me."

"Marry the nobody . . ."

"God almighty, Kyger . . ."

Kyger shrugged. "It's a prank, right? Lift her up, throw her down, laugh your fool head off with your mates when you get back to London?"

"I can't believe you'd think that of me . . ."

Kyger snorted again. "But I do."

"I love her. I'm going to ask her to marry me. But I most assuredly can't do that with you standing there like a thundercloud. Go in the next room. Eavesdrop, if you don't believe me."

"I don't believe you. You don't love anyone but yourself." But Kyger's voice sounded distracted, and Lujan saw he was staring past him and out the window . "Oh shit—Hugo's on his way—"

Lujan bolted upright. "Head him off, damn it. Go *on*, man. Trust me—this time."

Kyger planted his feet. "I'm not leaving you alone with Jancie."

"Listen to me, man. He wants to marry her—in time. She has no reason to marry you. She cares about me. But she'll accept him because no woman in her position could refuse such an offer."

"I don't believe you."

Lujan pushed at him. "*Head him off before he gets here . . .* I promise you can believe I'm going to do what I said . . ."

"Believe him about what?" Jancie, in the doorway, slanted a curious look at them both.

Kyger stared at him uncertainly for a moment, his instincts warring with the truth of what Lujan was saying. But he was right: Jancie wouldn't have him, and it would be far more advantageous for her to marry Hugo, who could give her a comfortable life, and, eventually, children.

Dear God—half-brothers or -sisters from his father and Jancie? He'd rather she have Lujan, especially since she was *in love* with Lujan. Nothing he could do or say would change that. So the die was cast, and well before he'd ever entered the room.

"May the fates strike me dead if I'm wrong," he muttered as he brushed past Jancie out the door. "Trusting *you*, of all people—"

Jancie turned and stared after him as Lujan limped toward her, craning to see the last of Kyger's retreating form.

Jancie whirled around. "What's going on, Lujan? Why are you all here so early this morning? I couldn't believe it when Mrs. Elsberry told me you were waiting downstairs. And now Kyger— and, did I hear right?—your father as well?"

"No," Lujan said, his voice still a little rusty with pain, "they're just leaving, actually."

"I see," Jancie murmured. She didn't see anything at all, actually, not even why Lujan would come to see her this early. Probably they just wanted to remind her to get her things, probably Hugo had the last of her salary for her, and Kyger wanted to say good-bye.

But Lujan had the most sour expression on his face, and he was still gazing after Kyger, who was long gone outside, and whose voice they could hear remonstrating with Hugo.

Strange. Lujan was hovering, just a little unsteady still, and she didn't quite know what to do with her hands, or herself even, so after a moment she edged toward a chair and sank into it.

"So what's to do, Lujan? It's awfully early for a visit—"

"Well," Lujan sat down opposite her, "isn't there some expression about the early bird besting his rivals?"

"*Your* rivals?" Jancie's hands went cold. "Kyger? Your father . . . ?" *Surely he didn't mean . . . ? Dear heaven, please don't let him mean . . .*

"Well, we're all here, as you can see—and hear . . ." Lujan said with a touch of irony. Hugo was pretty adamant, actually; they could hear his voice, loud and irritated, from some far room on the other side of the rectory. "Why, do you suppose?"

Now what? One didn't leap into the lap of one's love with a declaration—even a dirty girl knew that. Nor would Jancie give him the satisfaction of acknowledging how much she had wanted to see him before she had to leave.

And surely that was all this was. She'd be a fool to hope for anything else. Hugo was her destiny, and she was prepared for it, ready to answer him in the affirmative, that she would stay, that she would wait, and after an appropriate time, she would marry him.

So she said, "Well, there is still some money to be paid, and I know I have yet to remove my things from Waybury. I was planning to—"

"Plan to marry me instead," Lujan said softly, leaning toward her, seizing her words, her hands, and the opportunity.

Her heart dropped. "I—*what??*"

"Marry *me.*"

She couldn't speak. This was beyond anything she had ever imagined—Lujan leaning toward her so beguilingly, his hands so warm, his proposal so seemingly heartfelt.

"My dear Jancie—surely you comprehend—"

"No, no—I don't. I don't understand. You're not a one who would choose to wed lightly . . . and not someone like me . . ." *What?* What was she saying? Trying to dissuade him from the thing she most wanted in the world? Oh, she was mad, out of her mind, wholly unprepared for this shocking proposal.

"Well, dear girl—here you have three who are avid to have your hand—if I hadn't come first, Kyger would be on his knees to you now, and you know full well that Hugo has already made his future intentions clear. What none of us knows is, who would *you* have? My father, who respects your tenacity and kindness? Kyger, with whom you already enjoy a warm friendship? Or me—the one you will have to tame? Whom would you choose, Jancie, which of us—assuming you would want to marry any of us . . . ?"

Her heart stopped. She stared into his eyes, his beautiful face, the face she had fallen in love with before she had even entered Waybury House, and she thought that here was the answer to everything. Even knowing what he was like, and what he would likely put her through . . . even with the choice of having none of them, or one—there had never been a question in her mind what she would do if her fairy tale could come true.

"You," she whispered. "Lujan Galliard—I would choose you."

Chapter Seven

Edmund couldn't come, but that was perfectly understandable, given the short amount of time between Lujan's proposal, the calling of the banns, and the actual wedding date. Mrs. Elsberry stood in his stead, both mother and father to the bride, helping her plan everything, while the vicar stood ready to perform the ceremony on the succeeding Sunday. Jancie stayed at the rectory, and together, she and Mrs. Elsberry worked out the minimal details.

She wanted to be married from the garden: she had no money or time even to have a dress made up, so she decided to wear the navy dress, which could be embellished with lace and ribbon trim. And she wanted flowers, lots of flowers, and a reception in the garden with tea and cakes. And she wanted everyone in the village invited, in the main because she had no kin.

It felt real. It didn't feel real. At any given moment, Jancie didn't know how she felt, except a certain relief that she was not going to have to marry Hugo. And much as she wanted her father, the time was too close, the trip too inconvenient, for him to come.

And Kyger stayed distant, which bothered her.

"Well, what did you expect?" Kyger asked her during one

short visit to see if there was anything she needed from the house. "Or did you conveniently discard the fact that I have feelings for you?"

She had never taken those into account, she thought remorsefully. Kyger was her friend, her confidant, someone she had wished she had feelings for, and now, of course, it would be harder for him to see her every day when he had had other hopes, and she would be sharing Lujan's bed.

Sharing . . .

Lujan wasn't quite ready to share; he had gone back to London instead, since the first banns had only just been read, and Jancie needed that time to get things ready.

"Just to wind up affairs," he had told her with not a small touch of irony. It was really to escape the suffocation of the wedding preparations; he actually didn't expect anything to change. The months he had isolated himself from his former life had only intensified his desire to have both the excitement of London and the convenience of a wife.

A wife in the country would hardly impact anything he might choose to do in London. It seemed like a good time to scout out what competition had emerged in the succeeding months. A whole year and half he had been off the scene, and a whole year's worth of juicy beauties he had yet to sample. He positively salivated at the thought.

And he'd bring Jancie back an expensive little trinket that would put paid to her questions and curiosity. She ought to be grateful that he wanted her, that she was marrying an heir, that she would have some pin money in the settlement, that she would be managing a sizable estate and living in wealth and comfort.

So maybe there wasn't some grand scheme after all; maybe she hadn't had any other reason for having come to Waybury House but that Hugo asked her to. Maybe the sole reason for her being here was to become his slave in residence, and ultimately the mother of his children.

There was something very just about that—the children of the partners coming together to create another whole.

Or—she had planned it that way.

But if that had been her intention, he would wager he'd never know. And he needed to have her bound to him sooner than later. The mourning obsequies could be observed by his father and Kyger.

At that moment, Lujan, ever the gambler, was hedging every bet.

They were married in the garden of the vicarage four weeks later, on a bright, early fall day when the leaves were still green and the air was cool and the sun hotly bright. There were vases of flowers everywhere, and more flowers tucked into the ribbons that cordoned off the seating area where the villagers awaited the moment of Jancie's appearance in a preternatural silence.

She was radiant as she came down the aisle, her dress remade with touches of lace and ribbon and Lujan's wedding gift, a single perfect diamond, around her neck. She touched it, thinking it was the symbol of everything: of her life before, as a kitchen girl; of her future life, as Lujan's wife. Everything about her life related to diamonds.

A diamond mined at Kaamberoo?

It didn't matter now. She was about to become the mistress of this house of secrets, as Hugo grudgingly gave her away. Kyger stood as best man, and Mrs. Elsberry attended her with beaming affection. And at Mrs. Elsberry's feet, Emily regally sat on her haunches, watching everything with a keen and eagle eye.

And Lujan, so handsome, so rakish in severe black frockcoat and vest. Jancie could see only him, no one else, as she stepped up onto the dais that had been built for the ceremony, and Hugo relinquished her arm.

The words were simple, the ceremony quick.

Keeping yourself only unto her . . .

Till death—

Do you take . . . ?

I do . . .

Words that echoed through time immemorial, no less profound because Lujan the libertine was making that promise to her. He meant it as he said it, and she believed their union would work.

The wedding ring had belonged to Olivia. More diamonds. Beautiful, sparkling, round-cut diamonds . . .

Do you take . . . ?
I do . . .
Owww, Emily said adamantly.
I do . . .
Till death us do part—
. . . I do—

Mrs. Elsberry's unexpected gift to her was a beautiful night-gown of the most delicate and translucent white lawn, which Lujan would remove about one minute after he joined her in the bedroom, Jancie thought, as she gazed at herself in the mirror.

The material felt like a feather against her skin, draping over her body and pooling around her bare feet.

In the mirror, she saw what Lujan would see—and it was a transforming moment: the dirty girl had turned into a swan, her neck encircled with a diamond, her eyes luminous with secrets, her long, dark hair curling wildly down over her shoulders and onto her breasts, her nipples protruding against the gauzy bosom of the gown, the spill of fabric over her hips and thighs, revealing and concealing both. Her heightened color, the sultry beat of her heart, her rising excitement as she anticipated the first moment he caught sight of her . . .

That ultimate moment . . . the waiting was the hardest and the best thing about it—she wanted, she didn't—that soaring moment of knowledge and culmination—

Her breathing felt constricted. But it wasn't as if she didn't know things. Dirty girls knew things. They gossiped, in great and graphic detail. They had spied on the tuition girls as they let their boys fondle and kiss and do other things to them. They knew what to expect, even if they had no idea about the mechanics of it.

They only knew the kissing and fondling felt good. *Really* good, to let the boys take such liberties.

Even she, dirty girl that she used to be, knew that.

And now she would know everything . . .

"And Lujan will be my teacher," she whispered to her reflection, shivering a little as she folded her arms under her breasts. The diamond shot color in the dim light.

The door opened behind her. Lujan, bare-chested, naked, easing his way in. Transfixed by her image in the mirror, as she was by his naked body, his jutting erection.

She couldn't stop staring at him; she dropped her arms almost involuntarily as he came up behind her. He slipped his arms around her, a gesture as familiar to her as his face.

She knew this. Day by day, on her walks, as she perused the bookcase in the library, he had come up behind her in just this way and slipped his arms around her—tight, hard, possessive, pressing against her, making no demands.

But never with his penis so real and hard, rubbing against her bottom.

"So—" he murmured in her ear, as he nipped it and swiped his tongue over the lobe. She felt good, she smelled sweet and hesitant, a hot, yearning, reluctant virgin, the kind he ate for breakfast in London.

But this one was now *his* wife, and his choice, and he must savor this once-in-a-lifetime delicacy.

And then teach her and train her to service him perfectly. A blank slate, his Jancie, willing, wanting, waiting to be filled with the knowledge of his preferences and pleasures.

That part especially would be so gratifying. He had already started the instruction in a most subtle way, in all the months he had touched her and aroused her in the garden, when he kissed her in the library, when he held her like this, moving his hands slowly, teasingly to her breasts, cupping and stroking them until her body felt boneless, and then letting them go.

He had taught her then to want him, to hunger for his touch, his kiss, his need. His expert stroking of her breasts. And now, he had come to the final step, the pleasure part: he had only to impart to his beautiful, willing virgin what would please him carnally, and then seduce her into doing whatever he wanted *when* he wanted, and she would be perfection.

The thought of it was enough to keep him hot, stiff, and pulsing for hours.

Maybe all night.

The challenge was irresistible.

"Do you like this?" he whispered, beginning his slow, sensual assault on her neck. "And this?" As he moved his mouth to her shoulder. "This—" Moving his fingers upward to touch one taut nipple. "This?" Tweaking it under the breath of material that covered it, and feeling her body jolt as sensation shot through the nipple tip right to her very vitals.

"I like it," she breathed as she tried to get control of her trembling body. This was familiar, this she knew from all their assignations all these months when he had finally come to touch her, to make love to her breasts and nipples. "I like . . . it—" as he cupped her breasts and began stroking each nipple with his thumbs. She watched him in the mirror, fascinated by every movement, every stroke, every subtle touch, and the glimmer of the diamond between her breasts.

This she knew, and she knew there was nothing to fear. He had touched her like this before, but never so close to the skin.

The pleasure was indescribable. The sensation was indefinable. She only knew she didn't want him to stop, but if he didn't, something was going to happen—she didn't know what.

She didn't know much. Except—and she hadn't been prepared for this part—she loved this . . . this unexpected thickening pearl of sensation that centered in her nipples but skirled downward between her legs, and the lofting feeling of pleasure coming from—where?

His fingers, her nipples so tight, so hard, so sensitive to his touch—? It took nothing at all for him to arouse her to a hardened peak. Her breathing grew shallow, thick. She knew this, but never so nakedly and her boneless body just melted against him, and she gave herself into his hands to do with whatever he would.

This was the moment of ultimate surrender. She felt the heat and heft of his penis pushing insistently against her bottom; she saw him easing away the material from her breasts, felt the first full force of skin against skin, watched as his fingers touched her naked nipples. Manipulated her nipples. Surrounded them, squeezed them expertly with his fingers, as she watched helplessly in the mirror, a slave to the pearling feeling, her body writhing and squirming with a sudden awful need to get away from his relentless stroking and tweaking.

Her hips gyrated wildly against his hard length, operating wholly on instinct, and she grabbed his thighs and gripped them hard to brace her body against his erotic thrusting.

But he wanted her nipples and only her nipples: he pulled at them gently, twisted them, squeezed them in incremental pulsations that made her knees go weak and stole her breath.

Who could have known such carnal sensations existed in that one small, hard, naked nub? Or that he would begin his maiden assault on her *there*—in such a familiar way, and with both of them watching every second of his handling of her breasts in a mirror . . . ?

This was so lusciously unexpected. This wasn't how she had envisioned their initial coupling, but as he massaged and caressed her nipples, she couldn't remember wanting anything more, couldn't feel anything other than the molten pleasure skeining irresistibly through her body.

And the excitement—he felt it, too; there was an urgency in the way he thrust and bumped against her buttocks. The way she answered in kind, writhing and rubbing against his heat and hardness. The greedy look in his eyes as he watched her in the mirror, watched her undulating body, her bouncing, naked breasts, the glittering diamond he'd bought her, his pumping fingers on her tight, hard, responsive nipples.

And the other wonder was how she affected him, how her body aroused him, the way her nipples elicited the most primitive sounds from him as if he couldn't get enough of feeling and fondling them.

She felt a mad, hot urgency to press something naked and hard between her legs. Something like—*him* . . .

She clawed at the skirt of the nightgown, she felt him ease back to give her purchase to spread her legs so he could poke his iron-hot penis between them, so she could just . . . shimmy . . . down onto his hard shaft—and position herself just so . . . God, he was so hot, thick, rigid—just right, between her legs . . .

Breathless, watching herself in the mirror, canting her body forward slightly so her breasts fell into his hands as he palpated her nipples, settling her slit on his poker-hard penis . . . she was beyond thought, immersed in sensation and moving wholly with her heart and her soul . . .

She caught her breath as her naked woman flesh grazed the heat and hardness of his penis. *Oh, yes yes yes yes yes . . . perfect, perfect fit, the heft of him enfolded by the naked heat of her . . .*

She ground her hips downward just as he squeezed her nipples one after the other, and thrust high, hard, and fast between her legs until she felt the sundering of the pearl, the crackling, crickling storm of culmination in his hands and on his penis, and she went down down down into the heat and storm of her orgasmic nipples.

He caught her as her body bucked and buckled, and kept her seated on his thick, pulsing shaft. Looked his fill of her in the mirror in the aftermath of her shattering culmination, of her straddling the thick heft of his penis, the thin lawn of her nightgown drifting over the tip, her body sentient, sated, and all because of him.

Perfect. The first lesson was over, and she had proved as apt a pupil as any whore. What man could want more?

He cupped her breast and sensitive left nipple and she shuddered and brushed his hand away.

Beautiful, luscious, succulent nipples, already so responsive with his many weeks of preparation for this moment; but he hadn't yet tasted them or suckled them. He'd left that pleasure for last, but he would have them in his mouth before another hour was gone. And she would let him gladly, because she had so loved the way he fingered them. Loved that little bit of roughness. Loved watching him in the mirror while he took them.

He had worked her body well all these months, making her yearn for him, making her hot for his touch, transforming her into a virgin to prize.

How many had he ever known like this one? Hot, naked, open, and willing, responsive to his little seductive tutorials all this time, trusting him now to teach her everything his *wife* needed to know. Which meant her utter submission to anything he wanted of her. *Anything.*

He hadn't even begun to teach her about that. Fondling her clothed in the garden was not even a prelude to naked nipple orgasms as she watched in the mirror . . . his carnal little virgin had come—come, indeed—very far, very fast from those chaste fondling sessions in the garden.

His body tensed and tightened as he held her and watched her recover from the storm of her first orgasm. She was soft and pliant against his chest, her eyes closed, her breasts thrust forward, her legs still straddling his jutting penis.

Only a saint could resist her now. She was his, and he wanted to root in her dark, moist womanhood and suck at her nipples; he wanted to taste them and devour them. He had never felt such an overwhelming hunger for virgin flesh; he wanted hers with a ravenous need that stunned him.

"You like watching us," he murmured as he stroked her body and kept his shaft firmly fixed between her legs. "You like looking in the mirror and seeing how I fondle you. You liked watching me feel and squeeze your nipples, didn't you?" He pulled her tight against his bare chest, so that her head was against his shoulder and her ear just at his mouth. "Tell me, Cinderella, didn't you—like the way I played with your naked nipples . . . ?"

"Yessss," she whispered. "Yes . . ."

"You want me to fondle them again, but I'm going to play with something else now." He raked his free hand into the folds of the nightgown and stripped it from her body. And made a subtle male sound as he gazed at her naked bush and his penis head poking out from her pubic hair.

"I could come right now," he breathed against her ear. "I could spew to the ceiling right now, but I want to make *you* come again first. You will come for me, Cinderella, you have no choice. And all you have to do is watch—"

She made a little helpless sound as he began to stroke her, inch by inch, down her body with his free hand, working his way toward her bush, toward her slit and the secrets of her woman's flesh. He was agonizingly slow as he massaged and felt her from her breast to her navel; her knees went weak as she watched, and he licked and sucked her lobe and whispered erotic nothings in her ear.

"Watch my hand, Cinderella. Down I go. Down down down, into your most private, secret places—I will know them like I know my own body . . . and you will know all the pleasure you are capable of and that I expect you to give in return . . . down—do you feel my finger in your slit? Do you?"

How could she not? He cupped her mound, then with one finger he stroked her slit, which, to her dismay, felt wet and creamy at his touch. All while she avidly watched where he put his hand, and avidly savored his every word.

Petal-soft stroking, softening her flesh, softening her body for the hard penetration of two of his fingers into her slit, and into her depths.

Depths she had no idea could accommodate a man's fingers, or a man's . . . thick, hard, pulsating—*that*. On which a little pearl of semen seeped from its head as his fingers rammed into her slit and her whole body jolted in stunning response.

And his fingers were unrelentingly there, in the hot, tight, wet, virgin heat of her, hard inside her, twisting and spreading insistently so she felt every movement—there.

"Take my cream," he whispered in her ear. "Take it on your finger, go on—" he thrust his fingers hard inside her and she gasped, as much at the sensation as the sight of him with his hand deep between her legs, his penis protruding beneath it, and the knowledge and feeling of his fingers penetrating her so intimately.

". . . my *cream* . . ." he growled again, deepening his invasion between her legs, pulling her bottom up tighter against the cradle of his hips to press his fingers deeper into her hole.

She felt stunned; she couldn't tear her eyes away from the vision of her nakedness draped around his penis and his fingers embedded so deep between her legs she couldn't see his hand.

This she didn't know. This was nakedness and man-fingers driving themselves into places that were not familiar with such a rampant penetration. This had nothing to do with that sensual, engulfing seduction with which he had led her on.

This was a kind of carnal reality she could never have imagined, and him commanding her to obey.

"Don't let it dry up . . ." his voice was hoarse, his fingers rooting and spreading inside her. But then he oozed yet another pearly drop of semen in response to his growing lust—but it was a lust for her, it was between them, as husband and wife, so how could it be distasteful to her?

He watched her swallow, meet his eyes in the mirror, and then skew her gaze downward to his thrusting, glistening penis head.

He watched as she hesitantly swiped the thick drop from him with a tentative finger, and looked at him inquisitively.

"Lick it."

She couldn't.

She must. She knew instinctively that if she refused, the balance between them would shift. This was the part of him she did not know—the part that was accustomed to commanding and getting everything he wanted, no matter what the cost.

And she knew somewhere deep inside, that he would walk away from her bed, her body, and their marriage if she did not obey, and find everything he desired with someone else.

This was the second hard lesson: he could see her assimilating it by the look in her eyes, and then she lifted her finger to her mouth and licked it.

Licked the essence of him. Sticky. Not that unpleasant . . . she shot a look at him, the essence, he thought, of Eve. And his penis head pearled again. The virgin was learning how to use her power—look at how just a look from those eyes made his penis ooze with thick, ripe, succulent semen.

He shifted her more tightly against him. "Now take that nice, fresh drop of my cream and rub it into your nipples."

Her eyes narrowed, but she didn't demur. Whatever he wanted, she would be willing. A good wife. The perfect wife. She swiped the pearly cream onto each finger and then touched each nipple.

"Massage my cream into your nipples," he whispered so softly she barely heard, and emphasizing his demand by massaging her deep in her hole with his fingers and spewing more cream.

She was feeling his fingers now, in a different way—not as an invasion, but in concert with her massaging her nipples, as a natural penetration—and suddenly, her senses focused, her burgeoning feelings of pleasure heightened, and she felt unbelievably avid for more of it, deeper, harder, endlessly there.

Wordlessly, she swiped two more fingers of his semen and brushed them against her nipples and then began lightly rubbing the taut tips.

He made a rough, growling sound against her ear—words, sensations, she didn't know, just that it escalated her excitement to watch herself massaging his semen into her nipples, and watch him embedding his fingers still deeper into her hot, wet core.

And suddenly she started shimmying against his fingers, riding them, pressing her body down on them—tight, hard, questing, seeking—that part of her she knew not, that part demanded surcease on his hard, pumping fingers, and her body answered the call. Her body knew, if she did not, how to move, how to seek, how to spread itself against those relentless fingers to find the hot spot that would erupt.

She held her breasts as she rode him, her head thrown back, every atom of her body focused on the pleasure—she did not need to watch, to see, to know. It was there, hovering, skirting the outside of her consciousness, teasing her, embedded in her nakedness, beckoning, waiting for her to find it there.

He rode with her, watching them in the mirror, his body pumping, her hips writhing on the hard bark of his penis, taking her down down down again, down until her body stiffened, electric with tension, heat, and the molten pleasure coursing through her every pore.

Down they went, hard and fast onto the floor, over they rolled; he spread her legs wide instantly, mounted her, and drove his shaft home.

The pain bolted through the swirling eddies of pleasure like lightning.

She stiffened again, pushed against his chest, tried to get out from under him and the jutting poker hardness that he had embedded so unceremoniously into her.

He felt the primitive triumph of possession.

There was nothing like a hot, squirming, virgin hole. So tight. So wet. So deep and unplumbed. So rare when it was coupled with such an unexpected carnal nature that loved a good nipple fuck, a good finger fuck.

Lord of the fates—to have given him such a succulent virgin for his house wife—he stopped his frantic pumping and lifted his body from the hips so he could feel the thick, deep connection of his possession, and he howled silently in exultation.

And then he looked down at Jancie, whose eyes were still wide with shock. "Cinderella . . ."

She barely had any breath left; she felt as if his huge, hot possession of her most intimate place had stolen everything from her. *Everything.* She wanted him out of her body and out of her life. She hated this. This, the ultimate dirty secret—that a man literally occupied your body . . .

And what was he doing? Spreading her legs wider still, and nuzzling her nipples and plucking at them with his lips and tongue. Licking them. Suckling the hot, hard tips.

Oh lord . . . there was something about her nipples—she was too susceptible to his fondling them. The pleasure was like a tickle at first, and then, as he began to suck harder, pulling the taut nipple deep into his wet mouth and swirling his eager tongue all around the engorged tip, wetting it, making it hot, succulent . . . then . . .

Suddenly, unexpectedly . . . the pleasure started mounting between her legs, her body of its own volition pressing down hard against his invasive, hot thickness.

Wait—wait. He lifted her legs and maneuvered them, one after the other, up and braced against his chest. Now she was closed more tightly around his long, hard length, and he undulated his hips to penetrate even deeper as he sucked and played with her nipple.

Her body arched involuntarily as the pleasure suffused her body from her nipple tip to where he canted his penis between her legs.

This now was perfect—all the pain had dissipated, and everything was hot and golden and slow and thick and ripe—her whole body was ripe . . .

. . . *she wanted his cream* . . .

The thought made her breathless. His surrendering to her, clotting her hole with the thick, visible evidence of his desire for her.

She wriggled a little, experimenting with how it felt to work her hips against the canting angle of his possession. It felt too good. It felt just like when she rode him before, only better, because he was rooted deep within her, crammed against her pleasure part, as deep as he could possibly go.

So deep . . . so wet . . . so hot . . . she began to move, her hips pumping and gyrating against that possessive hardness. She understood suddenly that all the pleasure their bodies generated was cohesive, and that this penetration was involved, and now the pain was over, she had nothing more to fear, nothing she could ever hide from him.

She had only to open herself and let it come.

"Lujan . . ." she murmured on a breath, and the pleasure came—it rolled through her body like thunder and broke over his heat and hardness, broke between her legs and gone.

He felt it; felt her body shuddering with the cataclysmic seizure of her orgasm, felt the pure, male victory of having conquered her and made her his slave.

He wanted more of her and more, before he would even allow himself to shoot his seed. In his mind, he imagined every way he would take her—on the bed, on the floor, on the chair, from behind, from below, from above, obverse, reverse—and then she would take him in her mouth and make him blow.

It wouldn't take two minutes with her sweet virgin mouth tasting the hard, hot length of him for the first time, her licky lady-tongue lapping at his shaft inch by inch, covering it with her hot saliva, biting into him, gnawing on his jutting bone, working her way slowly up toward the thick, ridged tip which she would take into her mouth and . . .

. . . *suck out all the cream* . . .

Noooooooo!!! . . . He came, spurting and spewing like a geyser—thrusting into her like a piston, a bottomless well of thick, potent semen . . . as she pumped his body and sucked out all his cream.

Chapter Eight

Lujan stretched like a cat, like a lion, a puma . . . he felt powerful, persuasive, perfect. His new wife was a revelation; the corrupting of virgin flesh was the most arousing thing in life.

He missed it. He should have taken a wife sooner. He should have fucked her sooner instead of wasting all this time courting and cajoling her.

But then again, she might have been that much more squeamish about the conjugal details if he hadn't. With all the other faceless virgin conquests, the pain was always a problem, and then having to coax and cosset her afterward to get her back to the matter at hand. And even then, his level of excitement would wane appreciably, and he would be overcome with the feeling that it just wasn't worth the effort.

But not the little companion. Not his *wife*. God, he ought to have gotten one of those sooner.

But lord, it required so much work. All those months he had invested in her; so clever to take the time to accustom her to his hands on her body. To make her yearn for his fondling her breasts, his teasing her nipples through her clothes.

By this tactic, he had created the perfect concubine: a virgin who was knowledgeable but innocent, hungry for his touch, submissive, and nakedly receptive to the heft and penetration of his penis when the moment was at hand.

And the end result was, he was avid to take her again—the ache hadn't nearly subsided with spending his seed. Thinking about her only increased his need to a much greater degree, and knowing she was mated with him legally for all time, and that no one else would ever dare touch that silky soft, naked skin, just made her capitulation that much sweeter.

She lay belly-down beside him. He stroked her back, all the way down to her buttocks crease, taking his time, sliding his hand all over her body, her curves. He cupped and fondled her buttocks for a long time, and then he insinuated his fingers between her butt cheeks and caressed her there, working his way downward, between her legs to her slit, still sticky with his residue.

The feel of his essence on her was so arousing, he started working his fingers between her still-moist labia, into that hot, tight hole that now belonged to him.

His penis, already at half-staff, stiffened like a pole as he plunged his fingers deeper and watched with satisfaction as she began undulating against the feeling of them, hard and insistent, inside her.

Such a sensual little virgin, his wife. No begging or importuning here. No tantrums or threats from his luscious piece of virgin tail. No coy refusals, no spiteful withholding of cunt.

No, the advantage of having a virgin wife was clear: she would always be naked for him and, as he educated her to accommodate his needs, she would never deny him anything he wanted.

Even him feeling up her bottom; even his fingers penetrating her slit as she tried to sleep.

Perfect. What man didn't want a wife like this, pliant and submissive, willing and open to his fondling her wherever and whenever he wished.

The ache to possess her again swamped his senses. He shoved his fingers deeper. By the saints, there was nothing tighter, more enfolding, more arousing than first-time virgin cunt.

He felt explosive. He needed to be embedded in that tightness, that heat, that wet.

He moved over her body, his fingers still inserted in her, he straddled her legs and he wound his free arm around her hips and lifted her body so that her buttocks were canted toward his ramrod penis.

The moment, his vision of that tableau, of him holding her, the shadowy curve of her bottom, his hand rammed up between her legs, and his rampaging need to penetrate her, almost sent him over the edge.

Aroused beyond all sense, he yanked out his fingers and jammed his penis into her, and stopped himself from pounding her further. *Wouldn't do to rush it. Delay the pleasure. Feeling your shaft slowly sink into her hot, moist hole. Push so slowly that she feels every thick, hard inch working into her. Don't come. Hold her bottom, perfect bottom, round bottom globes so perfectly curved for my hands . . .*

Holding them, flexing his hips, incrementally insinuating his engorged penis into her body, feeling her labia around his penis head, feeling her heat envelop his shaft, pushing deeper, harder, hearing her moan as he pulled back from letting her totally encompass him.

Not yet, not yet. There was a certain pleasure in withholding that moment of total penetration. But there was also the strain of keeping his penis wholly from her, and fighting the utter need to embed himself in her . . . Couldn't stop himself finally from grasping her hips and pulling her roughly against the cradle of his hips so that he was finally fully rooted in her.

If he moved, he'd explode, and yet he couldn't keep himself from moving, from pushing and pushing as if he could take one increment more, as if he weren't yet deep enough. He would never be deep enough, he thought hazily, as he pushed, rhythmically pushed, in time to her involuntary moans; he could push still deeper, she was so hot, so tight . . . all his, this untouched virgin cunt, all his . . . claiming it, deeper, deeper, pulling her bottom even more tightly against his hips, until she was jammed against him and immobilized.

Not enough, not enough . . . he felt almost dizzy with desire . . . stay this way, stay embedded in her forever like this . . . don't move . . . don't—

He had to, he did—just a fraction of a movement of his hips, pushing again, seeking her depths, and he fell—he gushed—a veritable geyser of semen erupting like a volcano before he could get control, so forceful all he could do was pump frenetically and just let it come.

And then he collapsed, covering her body with his own, still tightly joined with her, and so sapped he couldn't move.

He still wanted her. The realization hit minutes later, as he began to breathe again, as he became aware of her body beneath his, his still rock-hard penis embedded in her.

His body rippled with need. Or obsession—but he didn't know if he cared. If he could fuck her again, he would. She was soaked in his semen, so she couldn't be more ready.

And even if she weren't . . . She was his, to do with as he would.

He eased himself away from her, and cupped his hands between her legs to wipe up some of the soak. And then he smeared it on her buttocks, on her back, her legs, all over her skin, marked her with his essence, his scent, and then rolled her over, spread her legs, mounted her, and rammed himself inside her.

This was even better, her cunt rich with his come, hot and thickly moist. This was a man's place—a welcoming refuge where he could root and rest and live forever.

He spread her legs further apart and pushed himself tighter still.

She fit him like a glove, a made-to-measure glove, as deep and wide as he was thick and long.

Perfect.

He pinned her hips with his, and bent to nip at her nipples.

The little diamond necklace, askew on her neck, shot colors in the firelight. Perfect diamond for the perfect jewel of a hot and wanton virgin wife.

He swallowed her breast, as deep as he could take it, and rooted roughly at her nipple. She writhed and arched against him wildly, grabbing at his buttocks, moaning with pleasure.

No man could resist that—his body seized, and he unceremoniously blew. One blast, long and succulent, right dead center into her core.

Perfect.

And this—wife cunt—would be waiting for him every time he returned from London. A man could not get more delicious tail anywhere, even if he paid for it.

And he had ever so wisely decided to marry it.

He draped himself over her chest, burrowed his head in her shoulder, and he finally slept.

So now she knew the secrets. Perhaps not all of them, but the most important one—that a man would become a slave to a woman willing to give him all the sex he craved.

This was a good thing to know, a dirty-girl thing to know, but even better, she liked it, too—and she had a feeling she would grow to love it, once Lujan paid some attention to her.

But for now it was enough to let him have his way with her naked body so she could learn what to do to please him, and then . . .

He must be pleased now, she thought. Obviously pleased with how many times he had pummeled her into the bed. But she was not discontented. There was something very satisfying about wringing every drop of seed from his penis, and actually, once the dreaded battering of her maidenhead was over, the thing was very enjoyable.

She liked the feeling of his penis occupying her body. She liked how he filled her, once she got used to the idea that his penis was the instrument of pleasure.

And she loved him, and that was the most dangerous territory. But the die was cast now, and she had everything she needed to hand.

She stretched languorously beneath him, feeling his penis stiffen to attention at the movement.

She felt his body vibrate with carnal awareness as he came awake; she felt the subtle undulation of his hips as his penis lengthened and hardened and filled her more tightly.

He was coming for her again, and there was something dangerous in the way his body responded, as if he wanted to resist the lure of her body and the burgeoning ache in his penis. But he couldn't. And why should he?

Another secret.

She arched her body, and canted her hips up to meet his first rough thrust.

* * *

By the saints, would it ever be enough? He had managed, after this last endless humping, to extricate himself from her body, and to call for breakfast. It was too much, even for him. He was feeling a little whipsawed by his unruly penis, a little resentful that just the twitch of her hips could bring his jaded sex to the boiling point.

But as she levered herself up, bracing herself on her arms so that her breasts thrust forward, his body twitched and throbbed in response, and all he wanted for breakfast was her, naked and spread wide to receive him.

"Get over here." He was seated, naked, at a small table by the window, his penis rampant with desire yet again.

She eased out of the bed and padded over to him; he pulled her down on his lap so that her thighs pushed his penis downward and his right arm had purchase to snake around her hip.

His fingers itched, and he was salivating; her nipples were taut, hard, begging to be sucked.

"I know what I want for breakfast."

"Tell me."

"Nipples . . . hot, hard, succulent nipples."

It was simple to deduce exactly what to say. "Eat mine," she whispered, and he groaned.

He lifted her right breast to his mouth, eyeing her just as his moist tongue touched the nipple tip. Then he closed his lips around the nipple and pulled.

A bolt of pleasure shot right between her legs, followed by her awareness of his fingers encroaching downward between her legs, and pressing and pushing against her slit.

She arched her back and spread her legs. He sucked hard on her nipple, his fingers sliding easily into her moist, cream-clotted center. Two fingers at first, then three, spreading her labia wide, and wider still as he sucked avidly at her nipple, pulling it and covering it with his hot saliva.

She was both wide open and tightly enclosed when he inserted a fourth finger, and she gasped and dug her fingers hard into his shoulders.

His four fingers expertly spreading her labia and pumping into her. His tongue and lips expertly sucking and tugging at her nipple. His thumb suddenly at the hidden little pleasure point between her legs, rubbing and fondling it . . . His penis like an iron bar under her bottom . . . the two of them moving in unison as his fingers humped her and he sucked and soaked her nipple and wouldn't let her go . . . and the seductive pressure of his thumb fondling that elusive point of pleasure . . .

She stiffened, letting out a long moan before she shattered, her body convulsing in a rolling, crackling ride of pleasure that was both shocking and sumptuous.

She fought him then, fought his sucking mouth, his invasive fingers, so consumed with the orgasm breaking between her legs, she barely knew what she was doing. She only knew she had to get away.

And then the rills of feeling eddied away. He relinquished her breast, withdrew his fingers, which made her feel oddly bereft, moved her off his lap, and guided her to sit on his penis, straddling his thighs.

It happened so fast, she had no time to assess what he intended. But then the slow, slick slide of his penis into her depths aroused her to yet another pure pleasure not to be denied, containing his hardness from a sitting position.

And then they were face-to-face, and she wholly encompassed him.

For the first time, he felt he had finally plumbed her depths. He smoothed back her tangled hair and stared into her eyes. She was so young, so malleable. There was a virginal aspect to her still, in the faint blush on her cheeks as she stared back, all the while shimmying involuntarily on his distended shaft.

Just that—just that . . . and her nipple so pointed and hard and soaked with his saliva . . . his hips flexed and he clamped down on his lust. He had so much more fondling to do: her buttocks especially, so curvy and soft on his thighs. He hadn't nearly gotten enough of her buttocks or the luscious secrets in her enticing crease.

He explored her there, stroking, cupping, fingering, as she rocked gently on his shaft. She held his shoulders, held his eyes, as she moved, her hips shimmying and rocking, in response to his fingers fondling and invading those even more private parts of her.

Breathless—he made her breathless, and he had no less a response to her. It astounded him. It made him feel uncharacteristically possessive and unbelievably wary.

This kind of thing didn't happen to him. No one had ever breached the walls around his hard, cynical heart—ever. And neither would she, for all her beauty and innocence. He wouldn't allow it.

This was sex—convenient, conquering sex with a convenient, legal concubine. Who already was well versed in making the right movements as she saddled him, and those erotic little sounds as he had his way with her bottom and breasts.

There was nothing like a virgin wife, cradled on your lap and plumbed to the hilt. And her firm, young breasts with her pebble-hard nipples swinging enticingly in front of his mouth.

Nothing like eager virginal buttocks, so avid for his caresses. Nothing like it, no one like her.

He hadn't kissed her yet in this marathon of mastery over her body—but somehow he did not want to initiate that intimate contact. It would bring them too close; she would have some control, and he was not of a mind to give in to that yet.

Ever.

Rather, he nuzzled her breasts and spread her buttocks and took his fill of feeling her there while she wriggled and worked him still deeper into her core.

Suddenly he was at a moment of utter perfection—he stood on the precipice, with his fingers exploring her crease, his tongue lapping her nipples, her arms holding him close, his penis as rigid as a pole . . . hovering, hovering, his sharp point of pleasure almost at its peak, and then he fell, his orgasm shattering his control, erupting from his gut and pouring straight into her hot, enfolding woman flesh.

Pour—that was the right word for it, the wrenching, drenching emptying of his soul, and his semen seeping out from beneath her and all over his thighs so that she was seated, still rooted in the residue of his seed, her arms wrapped around him, his face buried between her breasts, her scent enveloping his senses.

She was a temptation of a siren and he was headed for disaster on the shoals of her subjugation . . .

No. Why did he think that? No woman owned him. He shook

off the disturbing thought as he became aware of an insistent knocking at the bedroom door.

"I did call for breakfast, didn't I?" he muttered. He didn't want to move. "Shit." He had to move, had to remove his engorged penis from its nesting place, had to move her back to the bed to cover herself so whatever servant was outside the door would not get even a glimpse of her naked flesh.

Shit. He pulled on a shirt, but there was no way to hide his still-vital erection. So be it. He pulled open the door.

Bingham, paper-thin and disapproving, stood there with a tray. "Mr. Lujan . . ."

Lujan took the tray. "That will be all." He kicked back the door and it slammed in the butler's face. He set the tray down on the table by the window. Tea, toast, jam, scones . . .

Her.

His erection just wouldn't subside.

He strode to the bed, pulled away the blanket, pulled her to the edge of the bed and in perfect alignment with the jut of his erection.

He pushed apart her thighs and nudged his way into her. She was still slick and coated with his come, creamy-rich and ready for penetration again.

He felt that welling howl of triumph in his breast. This was just how he liked his sex—separate but coupled, wearing her cunt like a girdle as he pulled her legs to hook around his hips, so that her lower torso was canted upward to receive him.

Perfect. Perfect. Her nipples tight, her diamond winking at him, her boneless body wholly given over to his pumping, humping pleasure.

He came swiftly, blasting into her almost involuntarily, short and sweet, no long song of an orgasm here. His body sought relief from the endless need of her, and took him there in one volcanic shot.

Soaked again. He would not have believed his penis was so full of juice. Or that he only wanted to stay nestled in her semen-coated snuggery.

She was Eve, reveling in his corruption of her innocence, knowing everything even when he thought she'd known nothing.

And he didn't care. He lay perfectly still, her legs wrapped around him, her arms outstretched, her hair in streaming disarray.

His.

Wife.

His cunt.

His convenience.

So why was he feeling so insanely possessive of her? She was the solution to a problem, period. She was his body in residence, surely enough of an exchange to make her happy. She didn't need anything else—just his penis and some pin money. The perfect arrangement.

He leaned over her. Her eyes were closed, her body sentient.

Wake up.

He started pumping almost involuntarily—there was something about her naked body that just drove him to own it, and his own body responded with a seemingly inexhaustible supply of spunk.

He was going a little crazy—he wanted to coat her nipples, her breasts, her body with his come. And next, he wanted her to swallow it . . . and next—he pumped himself ruthlessly, working his body into a lather . . . next—he would spew his thick cream all over her body, and in her mouth, with her virgin tongue lapping it up hungrily . . .

He felt the seizing moment of culmination—he yanked himself out of her at the very moment he peaked, and swooped the underside of his penis on her belly, rubbing, stroking, coming, coming—he helped it—oozing, spurting all over her belly, her midriff, her breasts . . .

Holy saints . . . he fell on the bed next to her, his penis utterly drained and sapped of life.

But not his body, or his imagination. He stroked the sticky residue of his come into the skin of her belly and her breasts, as she lay there like a living, breathing doll.

He felt the convulsive need to feel his juices slick and deep inside her. He stopped his insistent massage, and pushed her legs apart again, and pushed his fingers into her bush, into her slit, and into her mysteries.

And then, with his fingers insinuated deep inside her cream-coated core, he slept.

* * *

She slept, and he watched the slow, sated rise and fall of her breast with his questing hand anchored on her hip. Everything was quiescent now, including his penis—including, momentarily, his uncontrollable lust for her.

He had married the perfect willing wife. Someone teachable, touchable, and malleable. And she was beautiful on top of it.

Sometimes fate handed you the moon.

She was the perfect accessory to a man of his position. Background didn't have to matter. He could fabricate one, if necessary. But since she would be here, the chatelaine of Waybury, all the time, she would have no reason to come to London when he was there. He'd just go up and trot around for a time, muck and fuck a bit, and then come back to his cunt and ride it to a lather, and then do it all over again.

What a life. He never would have envisioned having such a plum fall into his hands . . .

He felt her tentative wakening movements and his penis spurted to life again, ready, able, urgent. He couldn't possibly let her off the bed before taking her again.

"May I not get up?" she murmured, as he pinned her there.

"No." He climbed over her, caging her body with his arms and legs, so that his penis was aligned with her bush, and nudging her slit insistently. "My penis needs to spend some cream right now, so spread your legs."

She made a sound—surely not resistence? She had no say in this, really. That was the exchange: Waybury and all its luxury and amenities for his bed. Of course, it had been a tacit understanding, and perhaps, innocent that she had been, she didn't quite comprehend what her end of the bargain really entailed.

For all he knew, she had some mad idea that she was in love with him. Best to rid her of that notion now. Let her not think it, let her not ever say it.

He drove himself into her, hard, masterfully, once, twice, three times, and he came in a long, drawn-out paroxysm of pleasure, his pleasure, just as it should be for what he was giving her in return . . .

He framed her face with his hands, still coupled with her, and panting in the aftermath.

"Learn this lesson well, wife of mine. When I need to ejaculate cream, you spread your legs, you open your cunt, and you swallow every ounce of me, is that clear?"

"Yes," she breathed, wondering how much more she could take. Or him, for that matter, after all these hours of coupling.

"We're not leaving this room until you wholly comprehend what that means."

"Yes . . ." *Anything, anything.*

"It means, I fuck you anytime, any way I can think of, and you will eat my penis and my cream and whatever else I can think of to fuck you with. Is that clear?"

"Yes . . ." *But it was easier than ever she'd thought to just lie beneath him and let him do what he would to her body—even if this was all there ever would be—for her . . .*

"So it cannot be that I heard you say you want to leave my bed."

". . . Oh no," she whispered, perfectly submissive, utterly coy. Another secret: men like Lujan liked their women obedient.

"You heard me say how fortunate I am you chose me to wed."

"Umm . . ." He undulated his hips, deep in her creamy cunt. "My penis really loves it when your cunt is clotted with my cream. It feels so good, Cinderella. It feels like I want to fuck it again. Spread your legs wider, let my penis root deeper . . . like that—" as she angled her legs and hooked her ankles behind his knees. "Just like that. Ummm . . ." as he pushed and worked his penis into her lustrous, rich heat . . . "feels good, good—" working his penis even deeper . . . "Ummm . . ."

The sound deepened, from the back his throat. He didn't move, but he didn't have to—his body crested the pleasure point and erupted into a galvanic pumping that shook the bed.

He couldn't have much more left in him, she thought hazily in the aftermath. And there was nothing hateful about his using her body to teach her what he wanted in this way.

But she loved him, the one thing he didn't want from her, and there would never be talk of that. There might never be anything more than his lustful possessiveness, and his frenetic desire to pump every ounce of his essence into her.

So be it. She could take some satisfaction in that, and her disappointment that he had no wish to pursue her pleasure could be set aside for a while. She was here, she was his, she loved him, and she would, eventually, make him love her, too.

"God, what are they doing up there?" Hugo muttered fretfully as he paced around the library after dinner. It had been three days since the wedding and three days and nights that Lujan and Jancie had remained in his bedroom, doing all the things that Hugo had ever hoped to do with a fresh, young, fecund bride.

"What do you think?" Kyger asked lazily from a chair by the fireplace. It was no less difficult for him, because he was more aware even than Hugo of Lujan's libertine nature and of Jancie's innocence. Lujan could be eating her alive up there, and they had no right to interfere.

And he didn't want to imagine any of it, anyway.

"I'll go up to London," Hugo said abruptly. "You can take care of things here."

"Going up to get it up?" Kyger murmured.

"Yes, well—a tween won't do in this situation. And Lujan just sucks the air out of everything. A man can't breathe but he's inhaling Lujan's debauchery. And in his own home, too. No, I'm better to be away from here. You deal with it."

"Hell." Kyger didn't want to have anything to do with Lujan and his unexpected desire to marry Jancie. There was something more to it, he was certain. Lujan always had a plan; he never did anything for the hell of it.

And as for Jancie—well, there wasn't a girl in the whole of England who wouldn't have married Lujan had he asked, no matter what her station.

But why did Lujan choose Jancie?

On the surface, she was more perfect for him. The daughter of the merchant class, as he was a son, no matter what airs and graces Hugo had adopted with his inherited wealth.

Perhaps inherited wealth—Kyger had never been quite sure what the story was there. Even so, neither he nor Jancie had any prospects in that regard, and they were linked by a common past, and an uncommon attraction.

But it hadn't been enough. Lujan had overwhelmed her. Lujan was the one who swept away everything in his sight. Used it, discarded it, and went on to the next distracting thing.

Well, he'd thought it before, and he considered it now: when Lujan was gone, he would still be around to pick up the pieces.

As he always was.

Although by that time, Lujan might well have broken Jancie into smithereens.

They lay exhausted, side by side, on his big four-poster bed in silence, that silence of satisfaction when the body was drained and sated and the mind was sentient and at rest.

Jancie slept once again, her body utterly wrung out from his pounding, and he lay on his back, staring at the opulent canopy, and reliving the last frenetic coupling in his mind. In his body.

His penis gave him no rest. It was in a state of permanent tumescence, it seemed. It couldn't get enough of Jancie's body. He couldn't stop the ache of wanting her.

He'd never experienced this with any other woman. This lust to own, to occupy, to mark her with his scent, his teeth, the imprint of his body.

And the fact that his innocent wife—whom he had only meant to be the solution to a problem—had turned out to be as compliant as any whore . . . Well, such uncommon surprises never happened to him. Usually.

But he deserved some credit for that because of how well and thoroughly he had taught her and accustomed her to his touch and his fondling, and familiarized her with how completely he could arouse her just by his sex play.

How farsighted of him, he thought smugly. But then, she had the only reasonable cunt around Waybury in all that time of Olivia's illness. The maids didn't count, and they were no challenge anyway. So of course he would try to play with her body to the extent she would allow.

He was reaping the end reward of all that now: her utter and complete submission to his sexual demands with a voluptuous obedience that was stunning. He was still reeling from it, he fed on it, he lusted for it, he couldn't get enough of it.

The perfect wife.

The perfect vessel for his cream.

A drop pearled at the rigid penis tip in tandem with the thought. His penis elongated still more, stiffening thickly beneath his hand. He was ready for penetration just like that, his scrotal sacs filled and taut, his whole body gathering, tightening, spiraling with lust.

He wanted something different this time—he wanted her to eat him.

He climbed over her quiescent body, straddling her chest, and nudging her lips with his penis.

"Wake up, Cinderella. He needs you."

She struggled to consciousness out of a deep, lustrous sleep, lifting her head to get a better look at him looming above her. Close. Too close. She wasn't ready for any sex play this morning, and here he was, with his insatiable iron bar of a penis ready to ram it—somewhere . . .

She levered herself up onto her elbows. "What—?"

"Open your mouth, now."

Oh . . . She parted her lips to protest, but protests weren't allowed, she remember foggily. Only what he wanted, what his penis wanted, wherever he wanted to spew his cream.

He inserted his penis head between her lips.

"Suck."

She sucked because there wasn't anything else she could do with him caging her like a tiger. She sucked tentatively at the succulent tip where that luscious little drop of semen pearled.

He pushed a little deeper, and she took the whole ridged tip— and deeper, more of his shaft, but he was conscious not to push too much of himself the first time—it did take some getting used to, having a penis poked down your throat; the head was the important part anyway, and the feeling of her virgin mouth taking him for the first time.

It was indescribable, the lush, inexperienced sucking of his penis head by his submissive wife. It was the most naked feeling in the world, her naïve sucking, her hot, hesitant tongue swirling over the tip, laving it, caressing it with an innocence that was still voluptuous and carnal.

Almost better than cunt, but not quite.

He couldn't work it deeper until she was more experienced, more accustomed, as she would be—soon. This was enough—her ingenuous rooting around his penis with her tongue and lips, learning it, licking it, trying it in her dovelike way.

He would have to teach her that, too—that his penis wasn't delicate, and she could pull on it and bite it with all the ferocity he knew she felt—she would come to feel—as she came to know his penis intimately in her mouth.

But for now, it was enough to feel her learning him, sucking him, nipping his very tip, making him crazy for penetration.

"Pull it," he growled. "Pull—*hard* . . ."

She pulled the whole ridged tip into the heat of her mouth and sucked him deeply right there, her tongue insinuating itself into that sweet, creamy place that instantly precipitated a long, slow spume of satiation deep into her throat.

And now her mouth was marked with his scent as well, as she swallowed the essence of him.

She valiantly swallowed as much as she could manage. He had penetrated her every which way but one now . . . and that was a moment to be savored for long in the future, even though the thought of it instantly made him rock-hard.

No, he had taught her enough for now.

He hadn't dismounted her body. He edged down toward her thighs, spreading them apart almost without thinking, and casually, because he was still so stiff and so ready, and because she was so nakedly compliant, and there, he stuffed his penis between her legs and made himself at home.

He felt a shuddering contentment. This—this was what having a wife and willing cunt was all about.

He lay heavy on her body, poled into her, not moving. He didn't need to move for all those sumptuous sensations to swamp him. Just being cradled between her widespread legs was enough. It kept the lust at bay because it was his penis nestling in her cunt. His cream clotting her hole.

The one thing he could be sure of at this moment.

No one else could have her.

Perfect.

He rocked his hips, just a little, in his never-ending need to root deeper. He didn't know why he needed to plumb her to the hilt like that, but he did. It was the lust, the obsessive possessiveness he felt, he hated feeling. He didn't know how he was going to go back to London at this rate. He wanted to occupy her cunt forever.

Whipsawed again—

Nonsense. He would go to London in due time. And she would be here waiting, begging him to come to her, to root in her, to fuck her.

As an obedient wife should.

He shimmied against her hips. His cunt in residence. Perfect. What an incredible idea. Enough to make a man cream five times over . . .

And he did, explosively, endlessly, one more time.

Her body felt syrupy, there was no other word for it: thick, heavy, treacly, dense—slow-moving as molasses, almost unable to move, utterly wrung out.

But this was a good thing—this was a measure of how possessive he felt toward her, and that her choice to marry him had been the right one.

She still could not quite believe it. Even after all these days and hours of fucking and fondling, it was still unbelievable. It was the stuff of penny-dreadful novels: the nobody and the gentleman's son.

Only, disaster usually followed before true love was found.

She shook off the feeling.

She'd known from the start she would have to tame him. Probably with a whip. But in these first hedonistic, bedridden days, it seemed possible he might tame himself, that he would buckle down, take control, and—love her.

He'd taken control all right—of her life, of her body, and her mind. . . . And in the aftermath of his strenuous sexual possession, it was too easy to shroud all his faults and negatives and veil the truth.

That, however, was not Lujan's way, and he could not have made more plain what his expectations were. She was his receptacle. It wasn't quite how she had envisioned it, but her feelings didn't enter into it, and she didn't matter at all, except as a vessel for his lust.

Did it matter? Men didn't marry for feelings, they married to get heirs. They married for love sometimes, if they were fortunate, or for fortunes if they were not. She had nothing to recommend her in either regard, and while she had nebulous reasons for wanting to marry him, Lujan's wanting to marry her, looked at in that light, seemed curious and strange. Not that he'd have any compunction about saying he loved someone to get what he wanted. But what did he really want of her?

Besides the convenience of a body to warm his bed . . .

Hugo would have been a better match, one that made sense, one that would have provided both of them with what they wanted.

In marrying Lujan, she had chosen to play with fire and it was already raging out of control.

But this was a good thing. Whether he loved her or she was his whore, he was for the moment so besotted with her body that he couldn't think straight.

Another secret . . .

Even now, though he had removed himself from her, his hand still cupped her mound, with one finger inserted in her slit. He did it deliberately, just so she'd be aware he was there, he was always there, always lusted to be there, between her legs.

It was arousing, that one expert finger tucked into her semen-soaked heat. Even as they lay side by side, both exhausted, he had to possess her, to ceaselessly remind her that he owned that part of her.

And then he inserted another finger, two fingers penetrating, stroking, arousing him, stoking her.

Soft, hard, she enclosed his fingers between her legs and felt the full force of their caress. Felt her creaminess. Felt her power. Let him stroke and pump between her legs just like that while she lay still and he came alive, his penis elongating upward the deeper into her he pushed and palpated his fingers.

She consciously kept still, even though her body clamored to move against the rhythmic pulsing. It was a battle of wills, wholly butting up against his edict of what her purpose truly was.

Conversely, he could withdraw his massaging fingers, but that would defeat his purpose, which was to exercise his complete marital right to possess any part of her naked body whenever he wanted it.

He was too infatuated with her creamy cunt. He was hard and

tight and thick with the obsessive need to stuff his penis into her, and cream inside her all over again.

What was it about this woman, this cunt, that made him feel so out of control? Three days with her, when another woman would have worn him out or bored him to tears, and he still wanted to fuck her into the floor, to finger fuck her hot, creamy hole, to make her come because of his fingers, his fucking, his penis.

He'd only just begun to teach her, apt pupil that she was. She was still and silent as he coaxed her cunt, but he could feel that little give in her hips as she pressed down on his fingers, exciting him, begging in her way for him to do more.

He insinuated another finger, pushing deeper, so aroused he was shaking with it. His penis spurted involuntarily, a waste of perfectly good cream. His scrotum ached with the need to spume even more.

"The hell with finger fucking," he muttered, withdrawing his fingers abruptly. "My penis wants cunt." He straddled her, mounted her, and poled himself forcefully between her legs.

This was more like it. There was nothing like the moment he felt his penis working deep into the residue of his hot cream in a whore's hole.

Nothing like watching his virgin wife wriggling and writhing to accommodate his thickness and length. Nothing like the sensation of being too big, too long, too thick for her, for any woman, and then finding that somehow she enfolded every inch of his thick, hard length right up to the root.

He grabbed her hands and pinned them above her streaming hair, levering his body so that he was only connected to her by the heft, the thickness and strength, of his penis.

Her body canted upward as he began to thrust, her legs spread outward, her back arched voluptuously, her nipples peaked into hard nubs as the pleasure rippled through her.

It was the perfect moment; she was wholly his, wholly submissive to his penis and his lust. And he was lost in her, in the creaminess of her, in her willing subjugation, in her innocence, in the knowledge that his was the only penis ever to penetrate her, the only penis ever to fuck her, the only penis that ever would occupy her cunt.

Only only only, waiting, begging for his penis only . . . hot for him, naked for him, his willing pupil in all things sexual, wanting only him, only his penis, only his cream . . . the perfect cunt, the perfect wife, the perfect naked, willing, penis-cream-clotted pupil . . .

". . . I love you . . ."

His penis exploded with a radiant, hot spume of long, slow, torturous come.

"I love you."

So much cream . . . he didn't know he had so much ejaculate in him. It wouldn't stop, it kept rhythmically exploding from his penis and pouring into her like gunbursts, sapping his life, sapping his energy, depleting his manhood—he had *not* heard what he thought he heard . . . she couldn't love him—that wasn't what this was about—shit shit shit . . .

STOP IT . . . shit—

He pulled himself out of her, hard and abrupt, and still his engorged penis erupted, shooting even more ejaculate all over her body, the bed, the floor.

He was out of breath, he was angry beyond rationality, his pleasure disrupted, his penis distended, his life upended, the swamping pleasure of possession doused like water on fire.

Damn damn damn shit.

He had to give her up. There was no other choice. Goddamn her, she was forcing him to give up that creamy cunt, those luscious tits, that insanely arousing body. Shit shit shit . . . he still wanted her, he wasn't nearly done plumbing her cunt, and he had to give it up . . .

Or had he misunderstood?

He drew in a deep, shuddering breath. "What did you say?"

"I love you," she whispered into a long, hard silence.

Shit.

"I hope not, Cinderella," he said finally, coldly. "Not wise. At all." He began searching for his clothes, even as his penis still convulsed and dripped ejaculate.

"I thought I made things very clear today. I made you no promises of love. I made you my wife and the vessel for my cream. There's nothing more. So if you really gambled you could play that game in my bed to bring me to heel, you lost."

He lost. And he had to let her go.
He sent her a cold, dousing look.
He had to go.
"Your black prince and his penis are leaving for London—tonight."

Chapter Nine

So now she was alone.

She couldn't cry; she wouldn't cry. Crying showed weakness, showed dependence. Nor would she lean on Kyger more than she had to. It wasn't as if she hadn't known what Lujan was really like. Or what to expect.

She had just hoped that his attention to her all those months had become meaningful to him as well as her. That something had happened between them that was real and blossoming.

Wilted, more like. Dead, from the lack of sun.

Lujan was the golden son, and without his presence, what was Waybury? She felt that loss so deeply; heretofore the house had been filled, the house had a family, a presence, Olivia.

But now—when she was nearly alone except for the servants, Waybury seemed intimidating, cavernous, without that presence. Without Lujan hovering in the bushes. Without Hugo counting ha'pennies in the library, Olivia waiting to be read to in her room.

She felt as if they had all abandoned her here, left her to flounder and figure things out for herself.

Wasn't that what she wanted—to figure things out? After all, she had had her own ulterior reasons for marrying Lujan; she had made her own devil's bargain.

The question was, what had Lujan given away?

The humiliating answer was, *nothing*. He was still free as a bird to pursue his debauched lifestyle wherever he chose. And when he returned, he would have his *receptacle* waiting for him, who, if she wanted to live in comfort and wealth—and what woman in her position wouldn't?—would accommodate him every time, and eventually give him an heir . . .

The thought stopped her cold.

. . . *of course—get an heir* . . . that had never entered into her calculations and she knew instantly why: because she had been the one besotted—by Lujan and the prospect of marrying him. Everything else, in her mind, was for the future.

But this—a child—Lujan's child . . . son—he'd want a son— the wonder was she hadn't considered the ramifications before— not that she hadn't fully expected to have children . . .

But to Lujan—her heart started pounding painfully—an heir could mean something else altogether. Because if he hadn't stepped in, she would have accepted Hugo. And *they* could have had a son together . . . thus precipitating a third cut of his inheritance.

A wave of horror washed over her. Of course, of course there was a reason Lujan married her—and it had been hastened by the fact that Hugo had declared his intentions, and she was considering marrying him *and* the possibility of a half-brother loomed.

For Lujan, it made no difference whom he married—he would never change, he would live his life exactly as he had before, but with the pressure to marry removed, *and* the freedom to do exactly as he wished until the day Hugo died.

He had been amusing himself with her all these two years, as he would have with any young, beautiful girl who took his fancy. He had no feelings for her; she was nothing more than a convenience, someone with whom a bored rake could dally while he waited for the inevitable conclusion to his mother's illness.

A wrenching anguish knifed through her body. She didn't expect it—not his defection or her cold, clear-sighted comprehension of their union in the aftermath.

Or the tears.

A gush of tears, welling up like a volcano, unexpected, undeniable. A keening pain tore through her body; she felt as if she would split in two.

She meant nothing to anyone, least of all Lujan; to him, she was a dirty girl for real despite fighting her destiny every inch of the way.

The tears wouldn't stop. The tears poured, her body heaved, the pain came from her gut.

All that obsessive sex. All that naked pleasure—meaningless to him, common for him. Nothing to him. A means to an end for him.

A woman surrendered too much of herself that had no meaning to a man. And what she had given Lujan, she realized sickly, was nothing he couldn't get from any willing woman anywhere, a woman on a street corner, the milkmaid down the road—

What, what had she done in the name of her own futile dreams and desires?

No!—Stop it!—Never cry over a man like Lujan. You knew what he was. You knew what the exchange would be. You had your own plan—he was a means to an end for you, too—

Stop it, stop . . . !

She couldn't stop. It seemed to her that he owned her body now and she could never get it back. She, who had basked in his attention in all the months she was caring for Olivia. She who stupidly, foolishly thought he could even care for her.

Everything had been subsumed to that. Her father's subtle pressure, her realization of what he had wanted all along, which her own growing feelings for Lujan merely enhanced. Her covert desire never to leave Waybury.

She couldn't stop. The sense of betrayal was almost crippling. She wasn't experienced enough to cope with this. She had naively expected some feeling for her to follow Lujan's expert seduction.

No more. Innocence was a precious thing, but when it was used and trampled on, the lesson was hard learned and never forgotten.

It wasn't Lujan's triumph, it was hers.

Another lesson, another secret.

The things tuition girls learned at their mothers' knees, and dirty girls had to discover for themselves. And usually too late.

Usually after they got a child, usually after their lovers abandoned them.

Hadn't Lujan abandoned her?

The truth was: men were dirty, they had no feelings, and the only way you could ever be safe was never to fall in love, and to use your body as an instrument to manipulate them.

Because otherwise, they would kill you—with their hands, with their kisses, with their promises of love.

A woman couldn't afford to be in love. She couldn't afford anything more than to be on guard and get what she wanted by virtue of surrendering her body.

And so Jancie would do from now on, as well. Tears were banished from this moment forward forever. No one would ever see her cry. And never again would she allow herself to feel anything at all for Lujan, except contempt.

But she couldn't run away from the fact that she had her own purpose in marrying him. She wasn't just another grateful dirty girl, even if he had treated her like one.

He probably thought she was stupid, easy, he probably thought his stamina and prowess enslaved her.

No. She was clear-eyed now, and ready to fight.

She would look at this as a blessing, his walking away so soon. Because otherwise, she might have fallen more deeply in love with him, which would have made his defection that much more devastating, and she would have been much more reluctant to do what she knew must be done.

She wiped the last vestiges of tears away.

It was time to fulfill her destiny, to claim what should have been hers and her father's all along. Time to lay bare the secrets of Waybury House, and uncover the source of Hugo's wealth and her father's penury.

Time to do what Edmund had always meant her to do: marry into the Galliards and root out the truth.

"So he's gone."

Kyger was already at the foot of the steps, already knew Lujan had gone, was waiting and witnessing her moment of humiliation as she stumbled downstairs alone the next morning so early she didn't think anyone would be around.

This was awful. She shot him a wary look, wondering what he thought. Except she didn't want to know what he thought at all.

Kyger motioned her toward the dining room and shrugged. "He shot out of here like a cannon early this morning."

"He got tired," Jancie muttered as she followed Kyger. Not tired—scared witless that he had unwittingly taught her to love him. But she didn't say that.

"You look tired," Kyger said. "Have something to eat. Things will look better after a cup of chocolate."

She shot him another look. She saw only sympathy there. But then, he had always been on her side from the first day, always the one she could talk to, and the one whose affection she had put aside as Lujan's attention became more blatant.

"I learned a hard lesson this morning," she said grimly. "You cannot love a Galliard."

Kyger snorted. "I could have told you that months ago and saved you the heartbreak. You should have married me, Jancie."

She made a distressed sound. "You didn't ask."

"You would have said no," Kyger said flatly and she looked at him again. "That's the way it is, when Lujan is around."

"I'm sorry." And she was, and comforted that he was here this morning with her. "I do feel affection for you, if that is any consolation. But it was Lujan, always, from the moment I arrived here." But Kyger knew that.

She wondered if he knew why Lujan had married her. If he had perceived the same thing she did. Or maybe he had some other idea, some other redeeming idea. "The question is," she added softly, "why was it me?"

Kyger held out her chair. "Why not?"

"Because there was every reason for me to say yes—I love him—but no reason at all for him to ask."

"Oh God—" Kyger muttered, as he took plates from the sideboard and began dishing eggs and cereal. "Don't tell me you love him. Don't believe you love him. You only think you do."

Jancie poured some tea. "I must be the only one who does," she murmured.

"So that's why he ran away," Kyger said, as if it were a given. Love Lujan, lose Lujan. He set her plate in front of her and sat down beside her. "Eat. It's the only sane thing to do when something like this happens."

She had no appetite but she swallowed two or three forkfuls of eggs and a spoonful of oatmeal.

"No matter how thoroughly he seduced you, you must have known you couldn't hold him," Kyger went on. "Look, this is the only piece of advice I'll ever give you—DON'T love him. And don't ever tell him . . ."

She made another anguished sound and he looked at her stricken face. "You told him."

She nodded.

He shook his head. "That was an awful mistake, Jancie. He may never come back."

Jancie blew out a breath. "Fine. But I'm still here and I'm still married to him."

"And he'll make certain everyone in town knows, and he'll go his usual reckless way and ignore you."

That made her feel even more cold and abandoned.

Mroowww . . . I'm here . . .

Emily, sitting haughtily on the threshold of the dining room, a warm knowing presence. She was not abandoned, she was still loved by Emily, and Emily was still there for her to love.

"Where is your father?" she asked idly, fully expecting to hear he was in his office going over accounts.

"Oh. He's to London as well—left shortly after Lujan, as it happens, with no excuse to break mourning like this," Kyger said sourly.

Even Hugo couldn't bear to be around her. None of them could stand the sight of her. Except Kyger, and she'd wager he wished he could leave, too.

"And you?"

"I clean up everyone's messes," Kyger said trenchantly. "And perhaps someday I can go to London, too."

She saw it was true. Kyger was more alone even than she, more responsible than either his father or Lujan, and all for no reward, really. He would marry sometime, someday, never an heiress because he had no prospects but the army, the church, or the life of a country farmer, and he would settle into the same life as he led here, finally master of his own domain.

And then Lujan would reign supreme—or Waybury would be let go to hell. And Kyger would rescue it once again.

But now there was something more in the picture—someone: her. And she was not going to let Waybury go. Or Lujan. No matter what happened, no matter what she found.

And soon, really soon, she would journey to London to retrieve what was hers. Not yet, though. She had too much to do, too much to learn about being Lujan's proper wife. After that, then she'd go. Then he'd see what love was all about.

"Don't feel sorry for me," she said.

"Nor will I say I could have told you he would leave. I think you knew that anyway . . ."

"You have no need to be so brutal."

"You've lived with us for two years. You've seen what he's like. I wouldn't have thought you were so susceptible."

But he wasn't seducing you, she thought. *He wasn't fondling and teasing you, working on your body so all you could do was yearn for his touch.* How could a man comprehend, when a woman's body was nothing to him but a vessel for his lust?

"Every woman is susceptible," she said.

"I must remember that."

"I would like to believe that so is every man."

"But not him," Kyger said. "He never has been susceptible to anything except his own will and whim. Any of us could have told you. You saw him up close for two years. You knew. I know you knew."

"Women don't want to believe it," she said. *She* didn't, she meant. It was so much easier to believe he wanted her, for real. And she wanted him, and Waybury, and an answer to the mysteries. "He was so—so . . ."

Kyger held up his hand. "Don't tell me. I know all about the so . . . I have work to do. I don't want to know."

She felt his impatience, and a prickly sense of him pushing her away. He had to. It would be too easy for him to succumb to something dangerous with them alone together in the house, with affection between them already, and her so vulnerable.

But he wasn't Lujan, who would have leapt to take advantage of the situation. Of her.

Not Kyger. He was too honorable, too respectful of a dirty girl. No matter what he felt.

He would go to the fields. To get away. To clean up everyone's mess.

Even hers.

He pushed out his chair abruptly, and left her there.

Where did one start? The tears were long over, and after the disappointment and the feeling of betrayal subsided in the maw of some mouthfuls of oatmeal and some tea, she felt stronger, more determined, less of a victim. The story wasn't over yet.

She was mistress of Waybury now.

She was where she had wanted so badly to be, placed to take her own revenge on Lujan merely by serving her father's needs. Loving Lujan had been the shock and surprise, and wholly unanticipated. Marrying him was *her* blessing. Making everything come right, her redemption.

Everything else she could learn, all those things that tuition girls had always known: how to manage a house and servants, how to dress, how to act like the lady of the manor, how to be a chatelaine.

After all, who was in charge now? Bingham, to all intents and purposes? Or the housekeeper—?

No, it was time for Lujan's *wife* to take charge, even if she had no idea what the chatelaine of a country manor house did.

At this moment, with Hugo and Lujan well away, Waybury was hers to do with as she would.

All she had to do was issue the command. Face Bingham and issue her orders . . . what orders?

She wasn't scared of that paper-thin, desiccated, disapproving old man . . . was she? No. How could she be scared of anything after these three days and nights with Lujan?

Thank you, Lujan.

She reached for the bell pull to summon the butler.

Ass. So what if she said she loves you. Women never mean what they say. You above anyone else know that. But you got so spooked, you just abandoned her.

You gave up the most luscious piece of tail you've fucked in years for the cold comfort of the road and a cold town house at the other end of it.

Jesus . . . fool. What's in a word—and what could it matter if your wife thinks she loves you? . . . that won't be true for long. You'll pound it out of her—into her . . . in no time—shit.

—Now look. A goddamned hard-on. Go away. Leave me alone. I don't even want to think about her . . . she'll be fine. She'll miss all that fucking. She'll welcome me with open arms whenever I feel like coming back. And that won't be soon. I'll make her want it so bad, she'll be walking around naked just hoping, yearning for my return . . .

No—wait—Kyger is there. Son of a bitch—if he lays one sympathetic finger on her, I'll kill him . . .

And my damned father, who, if he hadn't been so greedy for young cunt, wouldn't have said anything to her, and I wouldn't have had to marry her in the first place.

Shit . . . curse the bitch for chasing me out of my own house when I was ready for another week of hard-bore fucking.

Goddamn . . . I want cunt . . . and not a twat in sight anywhere around here . . .

Shit shit shit—I could be in bed wearing her cunt right now. And instead, I'm halfway between here and nowhere, and not an inn, not a farm in sight. I'd take a . . .

Forget that. Forget her. I can handle things just fine right here . . . that's why nature gave man the ability to jack off . . . like that—and I won't even think about her . . . not a thought—after I come—

Bingham was as intimidating as any headmistress at St. Boniface. It was the prim, disapproving look down his thin, knife-sharp nose, the crepey, downturned lips, the stiff bend of his body. The rusty way he said, "Yes, madam," to every one of her requests.

She knew nothing. That was obvious from his condescending tone of voice. Nevertheless, she pushed forward, making arbitrary decisions just to make the staff aware, through Bingham, that hers was the reigning hand.

"So, you will serve dinner at seven formally in the dining

room. You will tell Martin to come and attend me at seven
o'clock tomorrow morning. You will have Mrs. Ancrum take me
through the house this afternoon, prepared to give me everything
I will need to take over the running of Waybury. I'll have the mail
delivered to the parlor in the afternoon, and I want the bedrooms
cleaned and made up by eight in the morning. Have Trask serve
tea from now on at four o'clock in the library."

"Yes, madam. Yes, madam, yes, madam . . . yes . . ." He hated
saying *yes* to her. He knew she was making it up as she went
along . . . "Yes, madam . . ."

"And summon the dressmaker as well." That was inspired.
She needed to look the part of Lujan's wife. She didn't have to
mourn Olivia forever, did she?

"Yes, madam."

"I think that's all for now. Thank you, Bingham."

He withdrew, his expression still sour and stony, and she let
out a deep, relieved breath.

Now what?

Kyger was long gone out of the house, and she was alone except for the servants.

Mroww . . .

And Emily, of course.

She stooped down to pick her up, but Emily twisted and
pushed out of her arms and leapt to the floor. And sat, waiting.
Owww. And then she turned and daintily paced from the room.

Jancie followed her. Up the steps she ran, light as a feather,
and waited on the landing for Jancie to come.

Owww . . .

"This had better not turn out to be a mouse," Jancie scolded
as she made the landing and Emily ran down the hallway. Down
toward the opposite end of the house but stopping midway there,
and sitting on her haunches again, her golden eyes slanted up at
Jancie.

Mrrooww.

"Well, now what?"

"*Mrrrowww* . . ." Very insistent. *We search for diamonds.*

But it was not going to be that easy, Jancie thought. There
were so many rooms, too many hiding places, so many things

that could have happened to the diamonds and the money in the years since Hugo had abandoned her father at Kaamberoo.

The task she had set herself was daunting. She had no clue where to begin and in the time she had been here, she had been at Olivia's beck and call, and then Lujan's.

The only thing she had accomplished was to fulfill the first of her father's subtle, covert mandates: she had married into the Galliard family, she was living at Waybury.

She wondered fleetingly if he would have cared whether it was Hugo she married or Kyger. She could not imagine doing any of the things with Hugo she had done with Lujan.

But that was neither here nor there right now. This much she knew, she thought as she surveyed the upper hall: Hugo had lived a most comfortable life for the past thirty years and her father had not. Hugo had lost one son through misadventure—Edmund, a wife in childbirth. Hugo's sons had had every privilege, Edmund's daughter had not.

Where had Hugo got that money, if he had been beset by thieves and murderers at the pit in Kaamberoo? And how had he found the wherewithal to escape them and make his way back to England? How much of his wealth, if any, had come through Olivia's family?

What *was* Hugo's story, really?

The only diamond she had ever seen in the house in all those two years was the one around her neck. If Olivia owned any, they were not in evidence.

Or—she had never had any.

Or—they had been used solely to support this lifestyle for the past thirty years.

That made the most sense. And that maybe Hugo had gone up to London for precisely that reason: it was time to sell again. After all, he had buried his wife, he needed to make a gift to the church, there were expenses at Waybury, there was a profligate son whose debts he must pay.

Why would a man go out of mourning and go up to London unless there were such pressing matters weighing on him?

Ow, Emily said. *Why are you taking so long?*

Because she still wasn't sure her father's lifelong obsession had any validity? Or she was utterly mad, thinking there was more to this than appeared on the surface?

That was the most likely conclusion. The one she didn't want to make. Because she wanted to prove her father had been cheated and robbed. She wanted him to have a stake in whatever Hugo had smuggled out of South Africa. She wanted, finally, to take her place among the tuition girls.

To do that, she had to have no qualms about prying out Hugo's secrets, and she couldn't be squeamish about rooting around in the family's private places or possessions. She had to be as cold-blooded about it as Lujan had been about walking out the door.

Could she?

She owed him no loyalty, no love. And even though there was that little spark still simmering in the embers, she would not consciously fan that flame. Let it die of its own volition. It was dead anyway, trampled by Lujan's neglect. Better she was prepared for it, and on the offensive.

Better to have something to do than to molder away in an empty house pining for what she could not have.

Where to start? Where to even think about beginning a search?

Emily stared at her, long and hard. *Hugo's room.*

Hugo's room?

Emily paced down the hallway toward the door and sat down on her haunches, waiting. *Well?*

The hallway was dark, encroaching, even at this early hour of the morning, almost as if the walls were watching, looking for transgressions. The feeling was pervasive, heavy, and Jancie paused at the bedroom door for a moment, girding herself.

One step, one turn of the knob, and she committed herself wholly and fully to her father's purpose, acting as his instrument of revenge.

Oww, said Emily. *What are you waiting for?*

And Jancie thrust open the door.

Nothing was the same. London wasn't the same, the town house wasn't the same, and surely there were new faces threading their way through the dining room and bedroom, unobtrusive as mice.

His head was killing him, throbbing like a heartbeat as he rolled over in his commodious bed to the tune of a commotion in the hallway below.

He pulled the pillow over his head. *Never should have married the twittle—could've solved the fucking problem some other fucking way—didn't need to marry that virginhead—what the hell was I thinking?* . . .

. . . *never going back to Waybury—shit, she loves me, she loves me not—don't need love, don't need anything but wide-open cunt* . . .

. . . *Lord, she was so wide wide-open a man could drown in her* . . .

. . . *not like that little tart last night behind the pub, with her greedy, grasping hands and endless pumping hole* . . . *all the tricks, all the whore's hopes—Jesus, what a nightmare getting away from that one—and her not worth a dribble and a ducat* . . .

. . . *why am I thinking about HER* . . . *I am NOT cunt-struck* . . .

Shit—what the hell is going on down there?

. . . *need to find more well-bred cunt* . . . *that's it, that's what I need—tonight. Won't drink, go somewhere, get some good stiff-upper British grumble and grunt—the kind you can't buy for a crown. The kind that makes you feel like a king* . . . *God, I wish my head would stop pounding* . . .

No—that's the door—holy hell—stop the frigging pounding on the fucking door . . .

"Come . . ." he heard his voice thick and clogged with sleep and the fogginess of too much drink and too little release.

"Mr. Lujan, sir."

A servant—someone he'd never seen, no—maybe he'd seen him and hired him before he'd gone to Waybury to be with Olivia and seduce the—but he was never going to think about her or say her name again—*companion.*

"WHAT??" Oh God, too loud. Too . . .

"Mr. Hugo has arrived and sent me to see if you'd join him for dinner."

"Dinner?" Surely not. He had only just toppled into bed. Hadn't he? *Dinner?* He looked up bleary-eyed at the servant. "Hugo is here? Downstairs? In the house?"

"In the house, sir. Waiting your pleasure."

"Son of a bitch—Hugo shouldn't be here. He should be prostrate at the cemetery, begging Olivia's forgiveness for his transgressions. Goddamn it, a man can't even trust his own father with the hired help these—" He looked up abruptly at the servant, who was stony-faced at this diatribe. "What's your name?"

"March, sir," the man said reluctantly.

"March. March." He had to memorize it because he'd forget it in ten minutes. "March. Well, march right downstairs and tell Mr. Hugo that I will join him in a half-hour. And bring some hot water. And a tot of brandy."

"Yes, sir."

Was there a faint undercurrent of disapproval there? As if servants had opinions. Servants didn't have opinions, they had tasks . . .

It struck him suddenly that he was still prone, barking orders and having tirades. He must look like an ass. Not a position of power.

"You may go, March," he said, gathering some dignity together and easing himself into a sitting position. He held it until the door closed and then sank back down into his pillows.

Too dizzy. Jesus, how was he going to pull himself into shape to cope with Hugo? What the hell was he doing here, anyway?

Shit. He tried sitting up again. Everything started going in circles. *Where* had he been last night? Right, the pub. The whore. Not the companion, and his cock positively aching to blow off the companion. No, not the companion—his wife, his wide-open, naked vessel of a wife . . .

Lord in hell, what was he doing here?

Hiding from she loves me, she loves me not—right—only thing to do when a man's wife got sappy . . .

SHIT! He bolted upright. *His father had gone and left her alone at Waybury with Kyger?*

The fog lifted. Danger was imminent. His father was negligent, positively culpable, if anything happened between them.

He couldn't get out of bed fast enough. What the hell was his father thinking?

He didn't wait for the wash water; he stumbled downstairs in ten minutes, hanging onto the banister, furious as a lion.

"What the hell are you doing here?" he roared, careening into the dining room.

"The same as you, my boy. Looking for some cheap fig to console me. Why not? A widower still has feelings, needs, that old morning pride—"

"Why not? Why *not?* You left the companion alone with Kyger? The two of them alone, together, and him half head over tail about her—Jesus, old man—pride be damned. It's too soon. A man your age—goddamn it—you left her alone . . ."

"But *I'm* not the one who left her," Hugo said flatly. "You did. *You* left her. She's not *my* wife . . ."

"Goddamned *not,*" Lujan muttered. "Not dead yet . . ."

"Go to hell," Hugo shot back. "And whip your ass back to Waybury and start acting like a man . . ."

"No one more *man* than me and my *pride,*" Lujan mumbled, sinking into a chair. "Where's that brandy? Where's March? What the hell are you doing here? You should be on your knees in church, begging forgiveness. Confess you were lusting after a girl who could be your daughter, your daughter-in-law . . ."

"God," Hugo muttered. "Your *wife,* for Christ's sake."

Lujan banged on the table. "Exactly. My wife. Not yours. You go back to *your* wife, old man. Where's my BRANDY?"

Hugo got up. It was too late for talking, too late to drum any common sense into Lujan. Years too late. He was too drunk, too spoiled, too used to having his own way.

Beyond that, Hugo was tired. Not only from the journey, but tired of Lujan and his recklessness, irresponsibility, and his total disregard of anything but his own pleasure.

Fine. Jancie would wait—she'd known what Lujan was about before she'd agreed to marry him. Even if it was a bad decision—she'd have done better with him, but that was water down the drain now. And she'd get some value from this union. She had a life now she never would have had otherwise. Money. Position. A beautiful home. Children, eventually . . . always a consolation.

Sometimes.

As for him, he didn't give a damn about proprieties now; he would take his ease where he could, away from Waybury, the memories and the might-have-beens. Olivia would forgive him.

And at this moment, looking at Lujan laid to the bone, hanging limply over the table, banging his fist belligerently, his brain fogged and fuzzy, he didn't care if everything, all of it, went to hell.

Even him.

Chapter Ten

A man like Hugo—what had she expected? His bedclothes embroidered with diamonds? His room was neat as a pin and spare as a monk's cell. Not that there wasn't furniture—his bed was a massive four-poster set against the wall to the right. There was an armoire on the left wall, a chair and table by the window and one by the fireplace, and a thick Persian carpet on the floor. Kerosene lamps on the ceiling and sconced on the fireplace wall.

Nothing else.

Not a painting, not a decoration, not a piece of bric-a-brac, not a personal item anywhere.

Even Emily, prowling curiously around the room, found nothing.

In the armoire, there were several frock coats hanging; in the drawers, freshly laundered undergarments, an array of collars neat in a row.

In his dressing room, there was another cupboard with more suits, a selection of shoes, and a washstand with a hand-painted bowl.

Nothing more.

Jancie felt like a thief, skulking in his room, rooting through his clothes.

He had no jewelry—no diamond rings, no diamond watch fobs to be found.

She even stooped to looking under the rug for a secret hiding place in the floor, and to tapping the furniture for secret compartments.

Not that she'd know what she was hearing. She felt singularly incompetent. She was never meant to be a detective.

That she had gotten this far in carrying through her father's wishes was due solely to luck and fate. She could never say she manipulated events.

But here she was, getting nowhere. Whatever Hugo's secrets, he did not keep them cached anywhere in his room.

Ow, Emily said, seating herself in the very center of the room.

Emily knew something—what?

"There's nothing here."

Ow, Emily said, more emphatically.

Jancie turned around and around, trying to see the room from Emily's perspective. She saw nothing unusual or out of place. The plain furniture, the richly colored carpet, the bare walls, and the sun streaming in, making a halo around Emily's variegated fur.

Nothing glittered. Nothing seemed obviously out of place, nothing seemed any different from anything a man would have in his bedroom.

But then, Hugo didn't seem like one to leave anything to chance—or right out in the open.

It had been too many years since he'd returned, in any event, too many years to plan how he would hide and disperse the evidence of his betrayal. Still, there was always a chance that he had grown careless over those years. That since there was no one to question or constrain him, he had become less cautious.

But nothing in the room spoke to that except Emily, sitting patiently, waiting for her to deduce what she wanted her to know.

Mrroowww.

Well, that was pretty emphatic.

There was something in the room that she was missing, something Emily comprehended and she did not.

Ooowwww . . .

Emily was getting impatient. She rose up, arched her back, and stretched—and . . .

"Madam?"

And darted under the bed as Jancie whirled, her heart in her throat.

It was Mrs. Ancrum at the bedroom door.

Now what? This was a supreme humiliation, to be caught skulking in Hugo's room. It felt like a dirty-girl moment, not dissimilar to when one of them was caught sniffing an expensive perfume, or looking at the lustrous pearl necklace of some tuition girl.

She fought the feeling. She was the mistress of Waybury now. She was entitled to go where she wished, to look at what she wished.

"Good morning, Mrs. Ancrum," she said, still battling the moment and trying to maintain some composure.

She couldn't detect any nuance of disapproval in Mrs. Ancrum's voice, however. She was a tall, spare woman with iron-gray hair and a penchant for severe black. She ran the household with a smooth efficiency upon which Olivia had totally depended.

As Jancie planned to do. But she had never given it much thought in the months preceding her marriage. So for Mrs. Ancrum to have caught her like this was not a little embarrassing.

Perhaps it could be smoothed over—? Was she duplicitous enough to carry it off? The truth was, she was nervous as hell.

"I was just looking at what tasks each bedroom would entail, Mrs. Ancrum. Mr. Hugo seems scrupulously neat."

"Yes, madam."

No give there. "Shall we continue, as long as we're on the bedroom floor?"

"As you wish, madam."

How did one make her unbend? Where was Emily?

They went into the hallway.

"The maid has begun on your room, seeing as how Mr. Lujan has gone."

Jancie sent her a sharp look. What did she mean by that? Was there censure? Did she know that Lujan was gone for the foreseeable future?

Servants knew everything—she mustn't forget that, or that it was the mistress's business to act as if they didn't. "Excellent," she murmured.

"Now, as to Miss Olivia's room . . . I have had no specific instructions about that, whether to keep it closed, to clean it, to pack it up . . ."

They entered Olivia's room together, and Jancie immediately felt a surrounding sense of Olivia's presence. She couldn't kill Olivia this way—by clearing out the things that had meant the most to her; and besides, who would it hurt to keep the room intact for a while longer?

"Let's not touch it yet," she said, running her hand over the lowered slant top of Olivia's desk.

The wood was silky smooth; Olivia's pens and stationery had not been moved. The novels they had been reading were book-ended on the desktop.

The curtains were drawn, the bed was perfectly made, everything was neat and in order, as if Olivia had just gone downstairs for breakfast.

"The staff were so sorry . . ." Mrs. Ancrum murmured as the silence lengthened uncomfortably.

"I know she's missed," Jancie said. "You'd been with her for many years, had you not?"

Mrs. Ancrum nodded. "I came to Miss Olivia just before the last child . . ." She stopped abruptly.

"Yes. Gaunt. They told me—so sad, so tragic . . ."

"She never got over it, if I may say so, madam."

No. Not if that child had been the one thing in her heart and on her mind, the last word on her lips at the moment of her death.

She felt a shadow pass over her, as if Olivia were still in the room.

"How could she," Jancie said, "if the child was never found. One wonders, how could it not have been found?"

"If I may, madam—the search went on for months with not a trace of him anywhere. It was as if he'd been lifted up and away to no one knew where. They found nothing—and the conclusion they came to was that he had, for some reason, run away. Or alternately, that someone had kidnapped him. But there was no earthly reason . . . and since ultimately no demands were made . . ." her voice trailed off.

"Too tragic," Jancie said again, leading the way out of Olivia's room.

Mrs. Ancrum straightened her shoulders as if throwing off all the depressing thoughts of the missing child. "Mr. Kyger's room is this way."

Kyger's room. The private part of Kyger that no one knew except the maids and the housekeeper. And now her.

Mrs. Ancrum opened the door, and Jancie edged her way in. This was where Kyger slept, the secret part of his life that was not involved in the family business.

The first thing she saw was his massive desk, piled with papers and accounting books. The second, the bed, long and narrow— nothing fancy or opulent. The third, a big, comfortable chair by the window next to a rectangular table spread with books, and a kerosene lamp. The armoire, open and spilling with clothes, and his mud-crusted boots by the door.

A man lived here who was involved in his life, not like Lujan, who skimmed the surface, and Hugo, who had given up altogether.

"Mr. Kyger really doesn't prefer to have things moved. He wishes the bed to be made, the fireplace to be swept, the carpet to be kept clean."

"That's fine," Jancie said.

"And, of course, Mr. Lujan—yours and Mr. Lujan's room . . ."

That one was next, full to the brim with memories of the past three days. Needing a full and thorough dust and clean now that she was to occupy it alone, but that didn't enter into her instructions.

That settled, they made their way downstairs. Here, she was shown the kitchen, the gardens, and introduced to the gardeners and the cook, shown the menu book and where Mrs. Ancrum kept the stores.

Every morning, Mrs. Ancrum told Jancie, she was accustomed to consulting with Olivia about the day's menus. Generally, there was nothing going on—after the disappearance of the child, they had dispensed with entertaining altogether. After Olivia had come out of mourning, she'd gotten ill and hadn't been up to it, so things had become a day-to-day routine centered around that which didn't seem to change, even with the advent of Lujan's wife.

Lujan's wife.

The phrase still rang strangely in Jancie's ears. On top of that, for all her bluster and bravado about taking charge, there wasn't anything she really wanted to change.

"It will be myself and Mr. Kyger for dinner," she said finally. "Mr. Lujan had business in town."

The housekeeper bowed. "As you say, madam," and Jancie knew she knew exactly what Lujan was about.

Well, there was time enough to deal with that. First, she had to acclimate herself to Waybury. And—while Lujan and Hugo were so far away—she had *carte blanche* to search the house for all those long-ago answers.

She sat in the sun-warmed library and wrote to Edmund:

> *You have never made any overt demands upon me since I came to Waybury. And yet I feel it incumbent on me to represent your interests here because I have always thought this is what you most wanted: to find out the truth about Hugo and what happened that day so long ago. This is not an enviable task. There has never been anything obvious in the way Hugo has lived or any ostentation in the house that would speak to his having the reserves to sustain any sort of lavish living. And so I hoped I had made this clear to you over the last two years.*
>
> *Olivia always told me the house and what money they had came from her family, and I had no reason to disbelieve her. But the singular fact that all three of the Galliard men wished to marry me, a virtual nobody, gave me much to think about since my wedding. Apart from both Hugo and Lujan wishing for an heir, and Lujan's fierce determination to share nothing with anyone, there is no other clear reason for either of them to have wanted this union. And yet, here I am, married to Lujan and thinking that perhaps it is enough that I have attained the station and the comforts you have always wished for me, and any pursuit of the past would be of little value at this point.*

No, that wouldn't do. The truth was, Edmund would never rest until he knew everything, including what had happened to the Kaamberoo diamonds, and he had hung his scoundrel of an amoral partner by his boots.

She knew it. She tore up the letter in disgust. She had wanted everything settled, but when she had the first chance to really investigate the possibilities, she only wanted to worm her way out.

What was wrong with her? Her father's unspoken objective had always been hers, from the moment he had located Hugo and asked for his help, and his expectation had always been that Jancie would somehow descend upon Waybury, gain the trust of the Galliards, and find a way to insinuate herself into the family and somehow find out all their secrets.

Could he even have conceived of her marrying Lujan? That was a true roll of the dice. Even more so, Hugo's coming up with the idea of bringing her to Waybury to help Olivia.

Well, it mattered not. Lujan was out of the picture as of now. She wouldn't think about him for one minute more.

She had the perfect, longed-for opportunity: a near-empty house, and the authority to poke around as she would. Now that her senses weren't befuddled by Lujan. Now that she could see clearly. Now that she could think, and the trail was so cold it was frozen in time.

It didn't matter—her father's objective must be served and she had to take advantage of every moment she was alone in the house. And she would be alone—a lot. Kyger would stay as far away from her as possible as well.

There was only Emily, her one true companion. But where was Emily? Yes—she'd scooted under Hugo's bed when Mrs. Ancrum arrived. She didn't have to go find her—Emily would show up.

But Emily had been so insistent when they were searching Hugo's room. Why? Maybe it was time to find out.

Slowly Jancie mounted the steps to the bedroom floor. She hadn't intended to continue her search today, but she felt so restless, so alone. There was hardly anything for a body to do during the day—the house obviously would run smoothly without her direction. She had only to wait for the dressmaker, read a book, or take up embroidery, a tuition-girl talent she had never had the patience to learn.

She was excellent at peeling potatoes, however, but they had no need of an erstwhile kitchen girl in the kitchen.

Why did she still feel like a kitchen girl?

She opened the door to Hugo's room.

"Emily?"

Meuw . . . Emily was curled up on the bed. *Oww.* She stretched out a paw, and then rose up on all fours and jumped off the bed.

Mrooww. She looked at Jancie. *Well?*

"Show me," Jancie commanded.

M'owww. Not here.

"Where?"

Owww. Hungry.

Jancie felt deflated. Emily couldn't know all the secrets of the world, though sometimes Jancie thought she did. But all of it was really a function of her own loneliness and imagination.

There was nothing in Hugo's room.

Nothing anywhere. Lujan was gone, Kyger was hiding, and Emily was the only one in this world who loved her.

She spent the rest of the day in the library, reading. She waited for Kyger to return. For the dressmaker to arrive.

Nobody came. And in the end, she dined alone in the big dining room with the long shadows, and the even longer, empty table.

Emily sat at her feet, a warm, comforting presence, taking nips of meat from her hand.

She felt a fierce determination sweep through her like fire: she was not a dirty girl anymore—she couldn't ever let that sensibility overwhelm her again. She was mistress of Waybury, she was married and proper, and she had every right in this house, every right as Lujan's wife whether he was here or not.

She hated the fact that he had bolted at the first mention of love. Something like that killed love. It made other considerations come to the forefront. Their shared past. Why he had even married her. Hugo's secrets. Her curiosity about the long-missing third brother. And most of all, that she would have no hesitation at all in pursuing her secret desire to recover everything that Hugo had taken from her father and her.

* * *

Kyger made it a point to come down to breakfast early the next morning so he would not see Jancie.

It was too hard; her pain, her newlywed naivete, were too crushing to watch. He felt like a stranger witnessing her distress from outside the picture, unable to offer aid or succor.

But that feeling did not begin to mirror how he really felt. He would rather have taken her away in a grand, romantic gesture, even if she didn't want romance from him.

But she was Lujan's now. Untouchable. Unbearable even to envision her and Lujan in bed. So much simpler to step back, to take the easier choice of seeing her as little as possible so he didn't have to watch her slow disintegration from happy, confident bride to abused and abandoned wife.

It was time for him go, anyway. The advent of Jancie only emphasized the fact that this was not his home, his land, his responsibility, and he had allowed both Lujan and his father to take advantage of his desire to prove himself worthy.

But worthy of what? None of this could ever be his, and all he really had done was allow Lujan to follow his own heedless, dissolute course, and his father not to have to make any decisions while he pulled the purse strings and pulled the rug out from under him time and again on estate matters.

Time to go. Why should Lujan have all the fun whoring around London? Time for him to face his responsibilities.

Leave Jancie—to Lujan?

God, he couldn't. Lujan would never come here now that he'd shot his wad in Jancie. If there were a child, he'd consider that it was her problem—and that was about as much interest as he would take in it. If it were a girl—he'd never come home.

Hell. How could he leave Jancie to that?

Shit. He almost wished she'd never come.

He poured a cup of tea and went to the window where the long, sunny view across the front lawns almost always refreshed him. It was a beautiful piece of property, and how his father had come by it, he was never quite able to determine, just as he could never quite believe Olivia's declaration that Waybury had come to them through her family.

There were too many mysteries surrounding them, and it had

gotten worse after Gaunt had so mysteriously disappeared. Hugo became even more withdrawn, and Olivia was deep in grief for years.

He supposed that was when he had taken over, although the exact moment was lost in time—maybe when he was thirteen or so, and bit by bit offering to do this and that until, when he reached his majority, both Hugo and Lujan had been perfectly content to leave everything in his hands.

And he'd relished the role of family savior.

Only he hadn't been able to save Gaunt. Or Olivia. Or Jancie. And maybe not even himself . . .

"Good morning, Kyger."

He wheeled around at the sound of her voice. Her strong, brisk, take-charge voice.

He didn't know what to say to her. *I'm thinking of leaving. Lujan and the estate matters are all now in your hands . . . God . . .*

"Jancie. I had hoped not to disturb you."

"I am no longer disturbed," she said flatly, seating herself. Kyger shot her a look, poured the tea, and took the opposite seat. There was something in her voice, something dangerous and not to be trifled with.

"Jancie—"

"Truly, Kyger. I'm fine. I'm thinking life here without Lujan will be quite delightful." She emphatically bit into a piece of toast. "As a matter of fact, I'm expecting the dressmaker today."

He eyed her suspiciously. This was too fast a recovery from the humiliation of Lujan's leaving her. A too-easy coming-to-terms with Lujan's true nature. She ought to be more demanding, he thought; she ought not to let him do as he wished on his will-o-whim. She ought to send an armed guard after him. She ought not to cave in.

But that would not be his problem once he left.

"Tell me about Gaunt," she said suddenly.

Her question caught him off balance. "What about him?" he said sharply. "What brings this up now?"

"Mrs. Ancrum and I were taking stock in Olivia's room—it just came up in the course of conversation . . ."

"It was horrible. It was just as you were told. We were playing, he disappeared, he was never found. It went on for months until they couldn't think of another thing to do. Why?"

"I don't know. Had you always lived here?"

"I was born here. Why the questions, Jancie?"

Because I'm my father's daughter, she was tempted to say, but it occurred to her almost immediately that they didn't see her in that role anymore. That Edmund was a factor in their lives was wholly out of the picture once they had accepted her into the family, and she could have come from thin air like some guardian angel, for all they remembered she was Edmund's daughter.

She shrugged. "Just curious. Do you remember Gaunt at all?"

"Vaguely, now. I couldn't have been more than five or six when he went missing. There might be a photograph or a portrait somewhere—I think Mother put everything away after."

"Yet she was thinking of him at the very moment she died."

God, why was she after knowing about this? "Yes, she was. You're thinking she saw him as she left us?" It would just be the kind of insane, spiritualistic thing a woman would think.

"You don't believe that kind of thing, do you?" Jancie said, almost as if she had read his mind.

Kyger sighed. "Olivia *was* tempted to have a séance to try to contact him, but that would have meant admitting he was really gone—dead. Never to return. So who knows what happens at the last moment of one's life, anyway? She's at peace, and I hope she's with him just because I'd rather think that than that she—and he—are cold and alone."

"I see," Jancie murmured.

He didn't—it was just the most odd conversation to have, and he'd given her more than he'd ever said about Gaunt to his parents or to Lujan, of a time when he and Lujan had been as inseparable as twins.

When had that ended? When Lujan discovered what a boy's nether part was made for, and when Hugo let him run amok?

"I couldn't touch Olivia's room," Jancie whispered. "I felt her presence there yesterday. Do you ever go in there?"

"No. I don't want to. And I have too much work to do, and this is one day I'm thinking none of it is my responsibility. I'm strongly thinking that you should start looking around to hire someone to take my place. And that's all I'm thinking about right now."

He slammed his cup down, an unusually emotional gesture from him, and he didn't know quite why he was so irritated. All that talk of Gaunt. Gouging old wounds that had set the family off on divergent paths so they never became a cohesive whole again.

He tried not to think about it: how he'd missed Lujan; how they'd needed their father, who had wholly abrogated all responsibility toward his sons; Olivia's death. And now, Lujan's misplaced reasons for marrying Jancie. His unforgivable treatment of her.

Everything had escalated after she'd come—he'd never understood why Hugo had even wanted her here, or why she had chosen to stay. Why she'd married Lujan. Why she was picking at old wounds.

Except—hell, what else had she to do? Maybe she was pregnant.

Maybe he should just get the hell away.

He pushed away from the table without another word, and Jancie watched in perplexity as he stalked out of the room.

Just like yesterday, she thought with a curious and removed objectivity. This incursion into his past was instructive. None of them wanted to talk about it, and they utterly closeted themselves away when it was brought up. Witness how abruptly Kyger had answered her questions and then just stamped out of the room.

Why?

Ow. Emily jumped up onto the table. *We have work to do.*

"Indeed," Jancie murmured. Because it sounded to her like they did have something to hide.

* * *

. . . wife cunt . . .

The memory, the ache, pounded insistently in his head, his throbbing penis. . . . *wife cunt.* He needed it, he craved it—nothing else would do . . . he had only to reach across the bed . . .

Something was wrong. The bed was hard, Jancie wasn't there, his head felt like it was primed to explode, and there was bright light blaring behind his eyes.

Oh God—he groped around, trying to gauge where he was—and knocked over something that shattered. Glass. The brandy snifter. Shit . . . at the table. How many snifters of brandy had he topped off after Hugo left and before he'd fallen asleep? God, that meant Hugo really *was* in London, had really been here, really screwing around just as he'd said.

Damn. Fuck.

He lifted his head, and immediately swooned with dizziness. "HEY!! Servant!!" What was his name? "YOU—ATTENDANT—" He couldn't think. His erection was painful, needy. His head felt like a bomb . . . What was that son of a bitch's name?

Someone stepped into the room.

"I need wife cunt," Lujan muttered, his words slurred. "Get me wife cunt."

"Yes, sir."

"Gotta . . . gonna . . ." He couldn't even find a sense of himself in the words, in the hands that lifted him and pulled him to his feet. ". . . *Wife* cunt—nothing like it—virgin, you know—didn't have to marry her . . . now can't, don't want . . . wife . . ." And he slumped to the floor.

When he awakened again, it was because he was aware of a different scent, a lulling sway, and a forward motion.

He moved his hand, and immediately deduced he was prone against the leather squabs in his most comfortable carriage.

He inched open one eye. The servant—March, he remembered suddenly, because his head was finally clear and unfuddled—was seated across from him, gazing with marked attention at the countryside.

Brave man.

Smart man, not to look him in the eye.

He himself was dressed for travel, and he became quickly aware that the carriage was moving through the city streets at a brisk clip.

He opened his other eye. Yes, it was March, so his brain was still functioning after his bout with the brandy, and he had a good guess as to where the carriage was heading.

Stupid fool, he. Had he been rumbling on about HER? God, you couldn't even trust a servant to see to your best interests these days. The man had taken his drunken ravings literally.

The fool really thought he wanted the bitch . . .

Shit.

Except—this wasn't the road to Waybury—and after a moment he had a fairly good idea where they were headed—to the most exclusive brothel in the whole of England, where they catered to every taste, every perversion, every sex, every age, every size.

Bullhead Manor.

He shuddered with pleasure just anticipating what awaited him there. It wasn't a place you walked into out of hand. There were precautions. Secret passwords. Vows signed in blood. The open hidden secret of a closed aristocratic society.

He wasn't nearly wealthy enough to afford it, but it was just the thing he needed—he ached for—at the moment.

He should reward March for his acuity—

Nonsense. Any fool could have seen this was the right tack to have taken after last night. This was what your people were supposed to do—look after you, make decisions in your best interests. Remain unobtrusively in the background. Provide that which would assuage your every need.

"Very perceptive of you, March," he murmured, keeping his voice pitched almost too low to hear.

It was a test of March's awareness and investment in him. "My pleasure, sir," March said in kind.

Lujan allowed himself a slight smile and closed his eyes. *Exactly.*

Jancie began her search of the house. The most obvious places had to be looked at first, even though they *were* the most obvious: under tables, in sofas cushions, behind paintings, under carpets for under-the-floorboard secret stashes, in urns and vases for oilskin-wrapped packages.

She felt more and more like the heroine of a penny-dreadful novel, the one where the husband was gone, the brother was in love with her, the father was the villain, and a secret treasure was waiting to be discovered that would save them all.

But she found nothing like that, even though her imagination ran riot as she pursued her search item by item, piece by piece, starting first in the dining room, and moving on to the parlor.

That was about all she could do in the course of the morning, and before the dressmaker arrived, and she wasn't that reassured by the fact that nothing turned up.

She had expected that.

But it *was* imperative that something turn up somewhere.

Mroow. Emily, pacing by her side as she moved from sofa to table to paintings in the parlor. *Hugo is very clever.*

Or this is a fool's quest, Jancie thought, running her hand behind the painting which hung near a side chair. And she and Edmund were the only ones in the world who thought Hugo's sudden rise to wealth and status could be subject to conjecture.

God, it was so long ago—who would care, except her and Edmund?

She was fairly certain that he and Olivia had not yet been living at Waybury when Hugo set out for South Africa with her father. But that was all so deep in the past, it was becoming harder to remember what was the truth and what was her father's story.

Or what she'd embroidered all on her own.

Still, she was here now, living the life she should have led all along, and there was some justice in that. But there would be much more in the way of reparation if she could somehow make Hugo pay her father his fair share.

There was nothing behind the painting. Nothing under the chair.

She was on her knees, groping the underside of a drawer in a side table, when Bingham knocked loudly on the door, balefully announcing that the dressmaker was there.

Chapter Eleven

He lay naked and sprawled across an ermine bedspread that was drenched with his ejaculate, every inch of him limp, exhausted, and dissatisfied. The three naked women who had been coaxing, prodding, and jacking him off were still stroking and stoking him with all the expertise for which they were famous, but for some reason, his penis wasn't as responsive as it usually was, even after hours of fucking.

Ridiculous. These were some of the most beautiful courtesans in the world, trained specifically to pleasure a man with expert fingers and submissive bodies and the erotic arts of the ancients.

And still he was limp, unresponsive—too drunk, maybe . . . or too sober. He reached for the nearest breast and tongued the thick, round nipple.

Not quite as sweet, as succulent as . . . no—

What it was, was a well-used nipple nuzzled by many men in many rooms of this house. A nipple that had been fondled and suckled by a thousand different mouths and tongues, and thus his overture to the nipple was meaningless—to the whore, and to him.

She didn't care who sucked it, who fucked her. It was all of a piece—he could see it in her eyes. Fun for a while, but let's get on with it.

Maybe she sensed he perceived her ennui. Maybe someone was watching—most assuredly someone was watching, but whether it was the prurient voyeur who was always lurking behind walls and curtains, or the madam, she couldn't know, and she bent herself to arousing him all over again, doing her work, her task.

She took his penis in both hands and began stroking it in a rhythmic motion. The second whore immediately burrowed her head between his legs, her tongue rooting at his balls, pulling the flaccid sacs into her mouth. The third whore assaulted his mouth, shoving her tongue against his and working it slowly, waiting for his interest to heighten.

Being paid to make love with him. No interest in him, just in the money that would come after.

Hell. It was cunt. What did he care where he got it? One was the same as another, and he had three at his disposal whenever, however, he wanted them—one, two, or all three at a time: penis, fingers, mouth. A man could die happy with himself stuffed in three cunts like that.

They were all over him suddenly, his three naked whores, squirming, stroking, fondling, pulling, kissing . . . his penis stiffened, his body quickened.

There—it had nothing to do with wife cunt. He was just exhausted; whores were always ready and on. All they had to do was lie there.

One of them was on her back now, her legs lifted high and wide, waiting for his penis to penetrate her.

He obliged, jamming himself into her, pumping at her furiously, and going nowhere instantly. There was something about used-up cunt; even though it was wet and it was hot, it was also passive and jaded. It didn't enfold him and hold him because it was so wide-stretched, and he had to work hard to generate friction in its slick, slack depths.

A man shouldn't have to work for cunt. He should just slip right into a nice, tight tunnel and find repose there.

He found nothing in the whore's slack body. His penis agreed; his penis wanted wife cunt and it just wasn't there.

After three days—the equivalent three days he had sought to exorcise his craving for her—he had found no surcease. He was bored with the winding, grinding whores and their slippy, used cunts, and their practiced moans and groans, their perfunctory nipples, their pretense of pleasure.

Shit. He rolled over, away from them and their grasping bodies. They came after him, desperate to please now because it meant loss of money, loss of face if anyone who came to Bullhead Manor left dissatisfied.

Everything promised, nothing withheld, pleasure beyond reason, ecstasy beyond price.

Not for him. For three days now, with a variety of houris, odalisques, and whores, he had felt no bone-splitting lust, no saturating need, every orgasm nothing more than his will to sustain it.

Hell.

If a man couldn't find satisfaction at the Bullhead, there was nothing left for him anywhere. He might just as well die.

Or skulk home to be pussy-whipped by a wife.

God—go home to his . . . wife.

What was he thinking?

He pushed away their groping hands, their mechanical, questing hands, with no more feeling for the body they were fondling than a puppet. He pushed himself off the bed, noting abstractedly that his erection didn't notice the difference, and he wondered why he couldn't lose himself in his orgasm and subsume the rest.

For some reason, he couldn't. It was an odd, strained moment with three of the most beautiful Bullhead whores kneelng at his knees, mouthing his penis, stroking his buttocks. A man had to be dead not to want them, and he wasn't dead—he was quite alive and pulsing and hard, but he didn't want them.

He didn't want to fuck them.

They comprehended quickly and began vying for his attention; if he called for another cunt, they could lose their position, their luster as the most exclusive courtesans in London.

They were coming at him again, determined. They toppled him onto the bed again, and began ravaging his flailing body any way they could get at him.

"My lord, let me . . ."

"Oh, no—I have the secret . . ."

"Go away—I know just how to . . ."

They knew nothing—they who knew everything, which meant

he was going mad because he suddenly saw their lushly painted faces as caricatures, their bodies as empty shells, their skills as perfunctory and meaningless.

He couldn't wait to get away from them, but there was something else to be taken into consideration: the voyeurs, always present, having paid for their pleasure, who would whisper in the dark and spread rumors about his lassitude, his unwillingness, and the whores' inability to arouse him.

The thought of that exploded into a dozen scenarios, none of them favorable to him. And most injurious to this most elite secret club, which depended upon discretion and satisfaction.

Jesus. A man couldn't say no in this bedeviled place. He had no choice but to hand himself over to the whores and let them do what they would. As long as he could perform, whether he wanted it or not, everyone would be satisfied.

He felt as if he were outside himself, watching the mechanics of it. The whores devoted themselves to his penis, his scrotum, his mouth. They gave him their nipples; one after the other, they took turns massaging him top to bottom, while one of them straddled his head and lowered herself to just within reach of his tongue.

Caught, corralled, and saddled. The voyeurs were watching. What man wouldn't just give up and give in? *No choice. Pedestrian cunt. Take me away . . .*

She and Emily had now thoroughly searched the first floor. Had spent a whole day taking apart the library, book by book, looking for answers. A bankbook, a reckoning statement of some kind. A receipt. Things that could conceivably be hidden in a book or behind one on a high shelf where no one would ever think to look. Or maybe a family Bible.

But there wasn't a family Bible—why should there be when Hugo had invented himself out of whole cloth and a stash of diamonds that should have been half hers. And Edmund's.

There wasn't anything yet that she could point to and say, Hugo betrayed her father. And it was beginning to look as if that would never be, and that the only reparation she might be able to make was to bring Edmund to Waybury to live—which couldn't conceivably happen until Hugo passed away. Then, she could make her father's life comfortable and rich with all the things that Hugo had cheated him of, including a beautiful home and servants to attend his every need.

The thought pushed her on when she felt tired or discouraged, which was often; the temptation to just throw up her hands and say "enough" was overwhelming as the days passed and nothing came to her hand that remotely suggested that Hugo was living on ill-gotten gains.

Worse still, Kyger was as distant as the sun, and urging her to find someone to manage Waybury's tenants.

"Everyone's run away," he pointed out one morning at breakfast. "Perhaps you should run away. I'm planning to—why should I be saddled with Lujan's legacy when there's nothing in it for me?"

That was the kind of statement Lujan would make. Jancie was secretly horrified, but all she could say was, "Don't leave." What she meant was, *Don't leave me.* He was serious as stones about it. He was fed up with how Lujan was wrecking up his inheritance and his marriage, and he felt no just cause to save either.

"If you leave," Jancie said, a little desperate, "what will I do?"

"And if I stay, what will I do, being in love with you as I am."

"DON'T say that."

Kyger shrugged. "It's self-preservation on all sides, Jancie. This isn't my trust, and I took it on anyway, because I love this place as much as anyone. And it can never be mine until Hugo is gone and if Lujan ever should—" He didn't say the unthinkable, but he gave her a speculative look. "Would you marry me then, I wonder?"

"DON'T . . ."

"I have to go."

He always had to go. It seemed to her he never stayed. He was always out the door by nine o'clock and most days he didn't return until almost nine o'clock. Where he was until then, she couldn't fathom—certainly there wasn't enough of Waybury's business to occupy him all those hours.

But then, it wasn't her business, and that was the point. Her occupation was lady of the manor. The dressmaker came and they parsed out a half-dozen suitable dresses for a daughter-in-law in mourning to wear—grays and lavenders and deep blues.

And the rest of the time, after the half-hour she spent with Mrs. Ancrum discussing the meals no one was here to eat, and housekeeping duties, she spent alone—no, with Emily—using that precious time to finish her search of the main living rooms of Waybury.

She was meant to be the lady of the manor, she thought. She thought she did it with an ease and a grace that could have been inborn. The only one she couldn't charm was Bingham, the paper-thin butler, who looked at her with unceasing disapproval as if he could read her heart.

She ignored him, for the most part. He was one of all those who would be here until Hugo pensioned them off. And perhaps that ought to be soon. She didn't like him—he didn't like her.

Meantime, she and Emily could take their search up to the bedroom floor, secure in the knowledge that there was no one around to see what they were doing.

Except sometimes she had the feeling Bingham was lurking.

Was he?

She stood on the landing and surveyed the hallway, which stretched across the width of the house to the stairs that led to the attic.

Where, after all, had she not searched on this floor?

Oowww . . . Olivia's room.

"I can't—not yet . . ."

M'ow . . . do something.

She opened the door to Hugo's room instead. He'd been gone nearly a week, as had Lujan, and yet his room had the scent of fresh furniture polish, and his bed had been changed and smoothed as if he had slept in it last night.

Oowww. Emily, emphatic, pacing around the room.

Where would a thief conceal evidence of a cache of diamonds, and thirty years after the fact?

That was the sticking point—that she was counting on there being something left, something for reparation. Something that after this much time he would be careless about.

The man who bargained down your compensation and counted each shilling you spent on a dress?

Such a one could be parsimonious as a parson. And Jancie knew all about being prudent with money.

Eeeoww . . . A new sound, as Emily ducked under the bed.

Jancie stared after her for a moment, and then dropped to her knees to look under the bed.

Pristine as pearls. Nothing there but Emily crouching, her golden eyes fixed on her as if there were something she ought to be comprehending.

Eeooowww . . .

"There's nothing here . . ." Jancie whispered, feeling a zing of disappointment even though that was exactly what she had expected. So why was Emily so insistent?

"Beg pardon, madam . . ."

Oh God—Bingham.

She edged her way out from under the bed and sat on her haunches. No excuses. Servants weren't supposed to have opinions, anyway.

But he was looking down his nose, his lips pursed, waiting for some explanation.

Best not to move or to give him the satisfaction. "Yes, Bingham?" Was her tone haughty enough, lady-of-the-manor cool and supercilious?

"Beg pardon, madam." He paused a moment, waiting, and she cocked her head at him inquiringly. "A note from Mr. Lujan, madam."

She didn't move. "Let me see it." Which forced him to step toward her and hand it to her.

Returning Saturday. Just those brusque words in his slashing handwriting.

"Thank you," Jancie said dismissively, she hoped.

Owww, Emily said. Emily understood.

"Exactly," she whispered.

When a man's juice was drained like that, with the houris pulling and pushing on him for hours on end, he came to consciousness the succeeding morning with an unholy ache in his loins that was numbing. He felt rubbed out, sapped, distended to a point where he thought he'd never be tight and right again.

He couldn't wait to get out of there—anything was better than this charade. It wanted only to send word to Waybury and get his ass on the road.

It was all March's fault that he had drunk himself to a stupor and allowed this triadic sensory seduction that brought him no satisfasction whatsoever.

It wasn't wife cunt.

No, not thinking that way; whipsawed if I let that idea get the upper hand. A man just had to sometimes see to his responsibilities, make sure his brother wasn't being too responsible, too consoling. Too in bed with his wife . . . Cunt.

Christ.

His mouth was dry and coated with juices. His body was stiff and wracked, his penis at half-staff, wilting as he lay there, unable even to respond to the thought of . . .

He wasn't going to think it. Waste of time, this whole fuck festival. Gave him nothing but an ache in his balls and an abraded penis which wouldn't be good for anything for days.

Maybe he ought to hole up and recover before . . . hole up in his wife's hole . . .

Shit. There was no getting around it—his penis was hot for wife cunt. He could give in to that. Especially after these three days.

BUT—he would make it clear to her once again, he wasn't balling her because he loved her. Or because he wanted *her* sappy declarations of love. Fuck that. A man didn't marry for love. He married for heirs, and for a good, deep, uncomplicated, uncritical fucking hole. That was her purpose—that was the bargain. And in turn she got the luxuries in life she had been denied and a good, hard, regular fucking.

It was a good bargain, especially considering how their families' destinies were so interconnected. It was reparation in a way. She should be grateful, actually. He'd take gratitude and satisfaction over love any day.

So would his penis, now standing tall and looking a little more interested.

"A virgin takes the trick over a whore any day," he muttered. Time to go home. He raised himself to a sitting position. "MARCH!!!! We're going back to Waybury . . ."

She felt a compulsive need now to find something, anything that would point to Hugo's treachery.

She climbed to her feet after Bingham withdrew, thanking heaven Hugo had gone to London, and she didn't have to make excuses to him why she was poking around the house.

So much easier this way.

Even with Bingham silently watching her. Even back out in the hallway, she felt a sense of his presence.

Had he been watching her all along?

And now Lujan was coming back home. Another pair of eyes. Lord—*stay away*—she wasn't ready for a reckoning with him yet, nor did she want to examine her confused feelings about him. Or have him questioning just what she was doing all day long.

Why had she ever thought this would be simple? She didn't need Lujan's disturbing presence hampering her.

Not for long. He'd stay a night, get bored, and leave. Forget about him. He was of no consequence.

No? No! He would never get to her again, never humiliate her again, and certainly the news of his coming would not deter her from her search with what little time she had left this afternoon.

But where? She started walking down the hallway, toward the opposite side of the house and the attic stairwell, with Emily pacing just behind her.

Oww.

"I know," Jancie murmured. And she did—for some reason, this side of the house felt spooky, but there was nothing untoward anywhere. But somehow it seemed darker, colder, more mysterious.

Perhaps it was that the attic entrance was on this side of the house. And the chest under the window. Not a likely spot to conceal any secrets, really, because everyone had access to it.

Nevertheless, she couldn't discount the chest, and so she walked down the hallway, looking over her shoulder every step of the way, and with Emily trailing reluctantly behind her.

M'row. Emily, so soft, sounding so far away.

She stopped in front of the chest and turned to reassure her, but Emily was gone. She was all alone on the floor, all alone in the house for all she knew, with shadows all around her, and the feeling that eyes were watching, watching, judging . . .

Across the hallway . . . around some corner, hidden from sight.

She took a deep breath and bent to the chest, a wooden chest, as wide as a window, plain but incised with a pattern of lines and circles all over the sides.

She ran her fingers across the top, let out her breath, and wondered what she'd find—and did she want to find anything?

What would someone hide in a chest that was in such a public place?

The answer was *nothing*. She had to look. But she expected to find nothing.

She grasped the top and lifted it.

Heavy. And dark inside, with an overpowering musty odor seeping up into her face.

It was empty. She had had such hopes, given Emily's reaction. But the chest was empty. Her disappointment was acute.

She stood staring inside it for a long, anguished moment deepened by the still matte silence.

And then she heard a crickly, rolling sound behind her, as if a ghost were tossing dice. *Someone was there.*

She froze, she let down the chest top very, very slowly with icy hands, and she girded herself to turn around as she heard the sound again.

Emily, at the far end of the hallway, pouncing on something, batting it with her paws, and chasing it down the steps.

Where the hell was Hugo? Nowhere in the town house, and Lujan felt a great frustration that everything seemed to be spinning out of control.

His father on the loose in London, for God's sake, dishonoring Olivia's memory by making a fool of himself.

And him, disdaining the enticements of the most experienced whores in the country, and lusting after . . . don't say it—*don't think it* . . .

Jesus, what was happening to him?

He leaned over the upstairs railing. "March!!!!!!"

March appeared below, silent as a wraith. "Sir. Everything is in the carriage."

Of course it was. March was just that kind of servitor. A good man to have around. Discreet to the bone, knowing exactly what a man needed and when.

And the carriage was already waiting. He could be on the road imminently. On his way to—

No. That wasn't his purpose. He just needed some fresh country air.

Where the hell was Hugo? Hell, it didn't matter. Dispense with Hugo. Let him wallow in the cheap fleshpots of London. Let him choke on his spunk . . .

"All is at the ready, sir." March again, unobtrusive but answering the very question you were going to ask before you even framed it in your mind.

"I'll be downstairs in a moment."

"Very good, sir."

He was forgetting something—what?

He took stock of his disheveled room. God, did he even have clothes to take with him? No matter—there were closets full of clothes at Waybury.

Wait, there was something else—right . . . a trinket for the— *vessel.* Get that on the way. A little bauble. She liked the diamond he had given as his wedding present, but perhaps it might be better not to make it so obvious since both their lives had been steeped in them.

Why remind her of what she hadn't had, after all?

Hold on—was he considering the feelings of the vessel? She should be grateful for anything. Whatever struck him—he'd have the coachman take him to Bond Street for a quick, discreet purchase before they got on the turnpike.

Good. That was taken care of. He was lucid—he remembered. Everything. And his achiness was subsiding, which meant he would be ready for a good plow and tunnel when he got to Waybury. Also good.

Suddenly, he couldn't wait to be on his way.

He raced toward the stairwell, found his body stuttering, and pitched forward, head first, and tumbled down the steps.

Jancie took after Emily, racing across the hallway and barreling down the stairs.

No Emily. Emily had disappeared, but she could still hear the faint crickly sound as if Emily were playing tag with the object she'd found.

Which was probably a little pebble that had come from either Kyger's or Lujan's boots. Nothing mysterious. She didn't need to be chasing Emily like this over a random piece of rock she'd found in a bedroom.

Or was she running from something?

From the dissolution of her father's dreams now. From her own fallibility. From the inevitable reunion when Lujan returned.

She darted into the library and sank into one of the cushiony leather chairs. This room was usually a refuge for her, but right now it felt like a room in a haunted house—eerie and empty, and as if something awful were about to happen.

It was that chest—she could still smell that musty and empty scent—and this house, ghost-ridden and empty—empty of any heart, soul, or love.

She felt this way because Lujan was coming back, and with his return came all his mandated expectations: she would turn into his receptacle for as long as she kept her mouth shut and spread her legs. For as long as that much about her interested him—for about as long as a minute, she thought mordantly, and that felt oppressive as well.

Maybe it was all over for her here. Maybe it had been a fool's quest to begin with. She had given up more than her father would ever know in pursuit of justice for him.

And the best she could do was nothing.

Ow.

Emily was at the door, but whatever she had been chasing was nowhere in evidence. *Don't give up.*

"I'm tired," Jancie said to her. "Lujan will be here soon."

Oooww. That will be as it is.

As Jancie perfectly well knew. But why? Why did it have to be that way when he had pursued her so ardently, as if he really meant it, all the last year?

Not even Emily had the answer to that

But Emily was staring at her intently, as if she knew something.

"What?"

Owww, Emily said in answer, and Jancie rose up gracefully, and walked away.

Kyger found her there an hour or so later, staring at the door.

She looked up as she heard his step. "Lujan will be here soon," she said flatly.

"Excellent. Then I have leave to go."

"Don't."

"My dear Jancie, I'll tell you what—I'll sneak out in the dead of night, and Lujan will have no choice but to stay."

Jancie was silent.

"Do you want him to stay?"

"He'll always leave. You know that better than I," Jancie said heavily.

"So why do we let him?"

"I have no power over what Lujan does."

"Maybe you do. He's coming back after only a week. Normally, he'd sink into sin for months on end."

That only precipitated a sinking feeling in the pit of her stomach, hearing Kyger verify that it took nothing for him to just go off and sink himself into any lush body that enticed him.

Which was probably what he had been doing the past five days. Just left her and plunged into some anonymous body in some anonymous place that men went to do those things.

No power here. The exact opposite.

She wouldn't be at Waybury House much longer—no one, not even a dirty girl, should tolerate such behavior.

Especially from a husband.

Husband. It sat strange in her mind, in her mouth. It didn't register. Lujan was a cipher, a law unto himself, and she could sooner tame a tiger than make a dutiful *husband* out of him.

What *had* she thought, all last year when he was teasing and tempting her?

"So reassuring he got bored after only a week," she murmured, in answer to Kyger's comment.

"You had a choice," Kyger said ruthlessly. "You live with the consequences."

"Or not," Jancie whispered, the first time she had let that alien thought even cross her mind. She didn't have to stay, she thought suddenly. She'd done all she could for her father, and there was nothing she could do for Lujan. And she certainly hadn't envisioned a life where she would be immured in the country, waiting for him to notice her.

She'd rather be in India, she thought, alone in the heat, with a life that was her own. How much had she given away, between her father's expectations and Lujan's utter disregard?

Why had he married her?

"Ah, Jancie . . ."

"You know," Jancie said tiredly, "I might not be of Lujan's social status, I might still be a dirty girl, a kitchen girl, but I'm not a stupid girl. No one, least of all you and Hugo, should countenance what Lujan does. Nor should any wife stand for it. I won't stand for it. I'll leave."

"Haven't *you* grown up," Kyger said. "What happened to love, honor, and obey—or is it love, honor, and run away?"

"Exactly what *you* want to do, isn't it?" Jancie shot back. "There's something about this house and this family. No one wants to stay. You all take turns coming and going."

He couldn't much argue with that, although Hugo's defection so soon after Olivia's death had been wholly unexpected.

"And coming," he murmured. "Jancie—" He leaned toward her; she looked too vulnerable, sitting there sapped of her usual energy and liveliness. He wanted to take her in his arms and comfort her. He still wanted her, wanted her never to have married Lujan, could have told her the worst about Lujan, and didn't.

And now he was calling her into account for her decision, when he could have loved her so much better, so much stronger. So much more.

Could still love her and enfold her if only she would let him.

"Jancie—" he said again—it was a whisper, really, a breath of longing at a moment when this was the least thing she needed: another complication, a different kind of love.

But she was the reason he stayed, she was the reason he maintained the legacy that would never be his. He couldn't leave her— he wouldn't, and as hard as he'd tried to sever himself from Waybury, he couldn't walk away from *her.*

She looked up at him, her eyes blurry with unshed tears.

That was the worst—Jancie, so strong, so positive, so giving, reduced to tears by the thought of Lujan's return and what he had been doing in the interim.

He shouldn't have said a word. Sometimes a wife was better off not knowing. And if he'd been smart, he would have positioned himself to console her as things got worse and they became closer.

As it was, this might be the only time he could ever allow himself to get close to Jancie. Just lean into her, put out his hand, touch her to tell her he knew what she was going through, he knew better than anyone what Lujan was like—

—Tilt her face up to his—one tear, and he'd kiss her, he would . . .

It spilled, and he slanted his mouth over hers and touched her lips. Soft, a sigh—he pulled away just as—

"So predictable," a supercilious voice said behind him. Lujan. Of course—how could it not be that he would walk in on them like this?

Kyger moved away from Jancie to protect her and confront Lujan directly.

But he was acting so typically the way Lujan would act, sloughing it all off with sarcasm and disdain.

"So déclassé," he was saying, as he paced around both of them as if they were chained together. Or was he limping? "It's a French farce, is what it is. A man can't even trust his own brother. Or his wife. Or even his own father, who is nowhere to be found."

Kyger edged away from him to get a better look. Not that he noticed; he was too busy making his displeasure known.

"Well, what else can one expect? A man can't leave home and rest assured that all will be as it was on his return."

Definitely a limp, Kyger thought. And his face looked a little strained, his body a little wobbly.

But that didn't stop the venom. Lujan ignored him and turned to Jancie. "Well, my lovely darling, tell me everything that's happened between you and my brother. Tell me all the details. I'm sure there's a book full. I do like a good cuckold story. What a nice welcome home."

And then his legs gave out and he sank to the floor.

Chapter Twelve

"You son of a bitch." Lujan, groggy, lay on the floor with a cold compress on his head provided by the quick-thinking Mrs. Ancrum, who had also taken the liberty of chafing his hands.

"Bastard," Kyger retorted, but without rancor. "Finally brought down to your proper place, brother mine. You look good on your back, and helpless. What the hell happened?"

"Accident in Town. Thought it was nothing." Lujan struggled to a sitting position. "It *is* nothing. A stupid, unfortunate topple down the staircase just before we left . . . nothing to fuss about. I'm fine. Ready to kill you, as a matter of fact."

"As if you really care. You can go to hell, big brother, because things are this short of happening. You're damned lucky you came back today. Another twenty-four hours and I would have swept Jancie up and taken her to London with me because you're such a shit."

"It's MY wife."

"SHE'S your wife, you ass. And don't think it isn't possible I could still steal her away from you."

"You rate your charms too highly, dear brother." Lujan made it to his feet and sank onto the leather sofa, rubbing his head. "Jesus. Where is she, anyway?"

"She and March went for the doctor."

"Don't need it. Don't want it. Want wife—" He stopped himself before he said the nasty thing, stopped before he let himself feel again the foaming anger at seeing Kyger's mouth slanted across Jancie's.

His wife . . . shit . . . wives weren't supposed to cuckold a man. Wives were supposed to . . .

"And how many whores did *you* fuck this week?" Kyger murmured, his voice laced with censure.

"That's my business." Didn't admit to one's brother what a failure that was in the wake of the wedding night. "You should try it, baby brother, since there's nothing else in your life but my wife. In fact, it would be perfect if you'd just leave now."

"Finally—" Kyger breathed, "finally, the reprieve—I'm released from prison. I'd go this minute if I thought you'd treat Jancie the way a man is supposed to treat his wife. But no . . . you are the bastard of the earth, you can't be trusted not to get drunk or debauched, and I'm staying right here so I can rescue her when she comes to her senses."

"I will render her senseless with desire for ME," Lujan said grittily. "I don't need a doctor. I need my wife here—*now.*"

"Such emphasis, dear brother. Such unusual urgency. Those whores must have sucked every dime and every desire out of you, and given no value for the money."

"Bullhead whores, too," Lujan said a little peevishly. "Shouldn't have gone."

"I'm astonished to hear you say it," Kyger murmured. This was too forthcoming, even for Lujan; he had never, ever admitted such a thing. His dissolute reputation depended on his giving and getting satisfaction. And here he was, naysaying the best courtesans in the best brothel in the whole of England, *and* insistently calling for Jancie.

Very odd. Too odd.

"Nothing like . . ." Lujan stopped himself again. He sounded like a babbling idiot; the tumble had taken more out of him than he'd thought, which hadn't been obvious on the journey home because he had slept a good part of the way.

Bingham appeared. "The doctor has arrived."

"Send him in."

"Send him away. Where's Jancie?"

"She's coming," Kyger said.

Lujan leered at him as he levered himself up on his elbow. "Brother of mine, you can count on it."

Now he was in his own bed, he felt much better; it required only Jancie's presence, naked, to complete his cure. Potions and possets were useless. He needed a good, hot, creamy burrow between his wife's legs—

His penis poled to life at the thought. Exactly. All this nonsense about a perfectly ludicrous accident . . . medicine for headaches and binding his ribs just in case—just in case what? His body fell apart? That wouldn't keep *him* from fucking. Not when the sole reason he'd come back was to embed himself in his wife's enfolding heat.

He was supposed to be resting, but he was, deep in his mind, deep in her luscious body. The anticipation was exhilarating, painful almost, but in an arousing way, because he was acutely aware of his erection, his thickness, his length, the incremental hardening, the burgeoning excitement in the pit of his stomach—all in a way he had not been conscious of before.

A week seemed like a year, suddenly. And his week away seemed as if it had never happened. Everything in him, head to foot, was focused and centered on the moment when she—his wife—would walk in the door, when he would remove her clothes, when he would penetrate HER.

Where *was* she?

Stupid of him to accede to the doctor pushing him to bed and leaving her downstairs with Kyger, with all his dire threats and warnings.

As if Kyger could approach him in stamina and prowess.

Could he . . . ?

Shit—maybe he should get his ass downstairs before anything else happened between his brother and his wife . . .

How biblical. How trite. His brother and his wife—

But just the thought, just a flashing memory of the moment he'd walked in on her and Kyger leaning into each other this evening, not a touch away from a full, tongue-twining kiss, and he felt again that furious desire to just kill Kyger.

Shit. Enough of bed rest, even though he ached more than he would ever admit.

He swung his legs over the edge of the bed, feeling dizzy—and a sudden urgency to know where Jancie was and what she was doing and who she was doing it with.

Didn't have to think hard about that—there was only one obvious person in residence, and he was just waiting in the wings for him to fuck something up—

And it wasn't Jancie.

He cursed fate that he was so dizzy, so sapped right now. Where was Jancie? He grabbed the bell pull and yanked. March came running.

"Sir?"

"Where's my wife?"

"She and Mr. Kyger are dining, sir."

"Goddamn, they are not. Why didn't someone call me? Get downstairs, have them set a place for me. NOW."

He whipped out of bed, his mind churning with the gut-encompassing image of Kyger and Jancie holding hands, gazing into each other's eyes, wanting, needing, promising everything that he had already claimed when he married Jancie.

And he sat right down again, his head whirling. He couldn't claim anything right at this moment. Not even himself.

No matter. Another few hours and he'd be right and tight and ready to go. He fell back against the pillows and instantly fell asleep.

Jancie couldn't believe it—she actually felt some sympathy for Lujan. After the way he had used her, immured her at Waybury and abandoned her while he consorted with whores, she felt a ridiculous and out-of-place sympathy for the fact that he had returned, found her and Kyger together, and then collapsed.

She slipped into his room. He was sound asleep, and she pulled over a chair from the fireplace and sat down and contemplated him.

He was every bit as magnetic asleep as he was awake. She felt the same pull toward him as she had the very first time she'd seen him that first day she came to the house.

Before he had seduced her, when she was naïve enough to believe a dirty girl could become a queen.

Asleep, he was perfect; he was a disarmed satyr in his sleep, who could harm no one, make no woman cry, and he had all the potential for pleasure and pain encompassed in his beautiful body, his sculpted mouth.

But she was not there to forgive him. Nor would she defend that moment between Kyger and her.

It was hardly comparable to his betrayal. *Betrayals.* There had to be many more of which she was unaware. Because what could one expect? The Galliards had no honor whatsoever—and she ought to have known the deeds of the father would influence the son.

Her sympathy was wasted on the likes of him, because he would use it against her. She was certain as stones of that.

So why was she here?

Why *was* she here?

Oowww. Emily crept in, her *ow* low and almost piteous.

You're not leaving him yet.

Emily knew. No, she was not leaving him yet. And she wasn't going to let him seduce her again with that awful proviso that she be his receptacle and nothing more.

No, Lujan's dirty girl had learned some hard lessons in these first weeks of her marriage. No man was a prince, every man had a price, and women were chattel to be used at his will and whim.

They had all the power, men. The only thing a woman had was what was between her legs. And that had a price, too, wife or whore.

Better she should leave. She had accomplished nothing here, and the only thing in which she could take satisfaction was her affection for and her care of Olivia.

Maybe that was enough.

Lujan was too much, and she would never be sophisticated enough to play his kind of games.

She rose up to leave—and his hand shot out and grabbed her arm, startling her so she uttered an ineffective little shriek that scared Emily under the bed.

"Don't go."

She could almost believe the sincere note in his voice, the one he had used shamelessly when he was artfully seducing her all those months ago.

"Nonsense, Lujan. You have had more than enough coupling to satiate your need for company—or at least that's my understanding of what you do on your trips to London. You hardly need a wife to hamper your life of debauchery."

"Oh, but I found that I do," Lujan murmured silkily.

"I found that I don't," Jancie said, her sympathy evaporating like a cold breath. He would never change. Even when he had spent the past year here, with Olivia, and courting her, he had only been suppressing his true nature to please his mother, and to get at her.

But why?

Dreams did die hard.

"Of course you do," Lujan said. "That's the purpose of having a wife."

"No, I distinctly recall the purpose of having a wife is to have a ready receptacle at your beck and call. However, in your absence, I have found this is unacceptable to me."

"Nonsense. This is a fair exchange, Jancie. You have my home, my name, status, wealth, perhaps a child . . . what more does a respectable woman want?"

There was a question. She could think of a half-dozen things more she wanted: his father's confession; half of all he took from Kaamberoo; the eighteen years of poverty erased; her father living in England, a respectable country gentleman. What more could she want . . . ?

Lujan was watching her face—so beautiful, and yet something else there, he thought. There was something simmering below the surface that had nothing to do with him and her anger with him. And that was as much as he wanted to know about it right now. Because right now, he wanted wife cunt, and he'd be damned if she would deny him.

"Enough talking, Jancie. Just take off your clothes."

She bolted off the bed. "I will not."

He jacked himself off the bed to go after her. "Wife . . . " his tone was impatient as he cornered her at the door, caging her with his arms and body so that she could barely move, barely breathe at his constricting closeness. "I won't be denied, Jancie."

"I have no desire . . ." she murmured.

"I can make you have desire," he interrupted her. "You know I can. And let me tell you—wife—I resisted wanting you even more resolutely than you are resisting now. It just isn't *de rigueur* to be whipsawed by one's own wife—"

"As opposed—to someone else's wife?" Jancie inquired venomously. She couldn't move—he was pressing in too close, too tight. She could feel his heat, his elongating erection a long, thick bump against her thigh.

The erection that had spent the week nesting in other naked bodies, other naked women.

Her anger boiled over. "How many wives, Lujan? How many other women?"

His expression darkened. "You aren't permitted to know."

The words were a hammer. "What AM I permitted, then?"

"You are not permitted flirtations with your husband's brother."

"I see. While you ARE permitted to couple with anyone who takes your fancy? I think not, Lujan. I think that is not a good exchange. And I won't tolerate it."

There, she'd said it. She never thought she'd have a chance, or even have the guts to say it right this moment in the face of his sexual intimidation.

Not that it put a damper on his growing lust. It seemed, rather, to feed it.

"You tolerate me very well," he whispered insinuatingly. "You take me to the hilt, you enfold my penis and hold it so tight and hot . . . that's what I want from my wife, Jancie. That's what I need, what I came back for. What I want right now and an hour from now, and three days from now and a year from now—your cunt, hot and tight, wearing my penis."

She made a sound.

"I'll make you so wet, so hot, I'll just slip in and fill you. You remember how I felt inside you, Jancie. Thick. Hot. Necessary . . . I need your cunt, Jancie—"

She turned her head away, shaking it as if she were shaking off his words. Lujan Galliard needed no one, least of all a dirty girl with a little bit of pride that was slowly crumbling under his verbal onslaught.

He knew her dirty little secret, and he was exploiting it shamelessly.

And she was listening ... growing aroused by the words, by her own need, and her own pleasure in his possession.

She was not immune to his words. She still loved him.

"Let me penetrate you again ..." He began working the skirt of her dress upward. "Let me feel that lush heat, that tight, wet ..."

She didn't resist—for all her bravado, she had ached for sex with him, yearned to feel his hands caressing her again, seeking her, rooting in her—and he was almost there, his questing fingers pulling the delicate material of her undergarment, so conveniently split to accommodate a man's hand ...

She drew in a sharp breath as he cupped her mound, stroked her pubic hair, and ever gently began inserting his fingers between her legs.

"That's the way, that's the way—ease my way, spread your legs just slightly, just like that—give me your thick, wet, your heat—" He made a guttural sound as he penetrated her labia with his fingers, one two three, and she sagged against him and spread her thighs to ease the way for him to insert his fingers as deep as he could push them in.

And then the pleasure of feeling them pumping her, twisting and stretching her, his penis like a rock against her hip as he manipulated his fingers so expertly between her legs.

She couldn't help it—she moved her hips in the shimmering dance of an odalisque, undulating against his fingers in the eternal rhythm of sex.

"Saints—this is what I wanted, this body, this cunt ... mine ... mine—to fuck, to suck, to eat ..."

She heard him through the haze of molten pleasure, she heard him, heard the nearly uncontrollable lust in his hoarse, harsh whisper, felt it in the almost punishing pumping of his fingers.

Remembering his hot tongue licking and nuzzling her nakedenss between her legs, seeking her slit, inserting the hot tip between her labia, and rooting into her wetness.

Remembering—convulsions like little explosions rocketing through her body, uncontrollable, unfathomable, unending as he thrust and drove his fingers between her legs again and again and again . . .

And over. Done. Boneless. Sumptuous. If she could just sink into a puddle on the floor . . . it was too much, always too much, especially from him too much . . .

She froze.

WHAT HAD SHE DONE?

Stupid, stupid, stupid—no better than a dirty girl to let a man root his fingers between her legs when she was trying to take a stand with him.

But that was ever the way with dirty girls—they were always susceptible to gifts and guile in spite of all their resolve to resist and behave.

All he cared about was where he could put his penis.

And she wanted so much more.

It was just—oh, his words were so seductive, and the pleasure was the reason men went to war. And between those two things, he had destroyed her altogether. She couldn't resist either, and she had succumbed to both.

"To the bed, Jancie," he whispered close to her ear as he maneuvered her body to face forward, with his fingers still inserted between her legs.

There was no point to protest that statement. "I'm never removing my fingers from your cunt. So—let's get to the bed . . ."

It was less awkward than she thought, even with her watery legs. His fingers, urgently pressing against her clit, were insistent, ready to play within her again.

He toppled her onto the bed face forward, and covered her, his fingers working deeper inside her, even as they fell.

He lay on her, quiescent except for his throbbing penis pressed tightly against her buttocks, and his three fingers prodding and twisting in her cunt.

This way, his mouth was right at her ear, and he could whisper deliciously in her ear, grunt and groan in her ear as her body awakened again to his ferocious touch and began its ancient seductive gyrations.

"Oh God, I can't—" she breathed—she could barely breathe let alone speak.

"You can. You will. You need this fuck. I want this fuck."

"... Ohhhh ..." It was too much. She had to get away from the insistent stroking and manipulation. She started scrambling away from him, clawing the bedclothes, digging her feet into the mattress to give her purchase to move.

She couldn't get away; he was too strong, too encompassing. His weight pinned her right where he could reach her, and his roving fingers took her, rode her, and, as she heaved into her shattering climax, brought her home.

Silence. Nakedness. His fingers still enveloped by her, quiescent. His body shifting slightly on hers ... a moment's relief, but only so that he could lift her skirt, undress himself, and then hoist her up so he could nudge himself inside her from that obverse position.

She felt her body swallowing his penis, felt him burrowing into her full-bore, heard the low, guttural words of pleasure she couldn't understand, didn't want to understand as his release came so fast, so hard, so drenching that he barely had time for a half-dozen thrusts.

Once again, his weight imprisoned her, as he covered her, his penis still embedded, his fingers still enfolded, all in control of the most naked part of her.

All through the night, as she shifted and wriggled her canted hips to try to get more comfortable, she was supremely aware of the depth of his penetration, and that her every movement only served to pull him even deeper as he pushed to accommodate her.

And then there were her clothes. Too much bulky material in the way, and now her skirt and petticoats were bunched uncomfortably around her hips so that nothing impeded his possession.

Except her undergarments. And even she was getting a little impatient with the fact that she was not yet naked.

"The problem is," he whispered against her ear, "I'm loath to withdraw my penis when you're so hot and tight like this." He made an upward thrust, pressing her more tightly to his hips with his still-invasive fingers. "There." He rocked against her buttocks, fingering her clit, giving a driving thrust now and again to prolong his pleasure and the gathering impulse to release. Not yet, not yet. He wanted his penis, his fingers, to be the center of her world right now, the only conscious, tactile thing she could concentrate on, the only thing that mattered—he could tell by the

quality of her response, her moans, the eagerness of her movements in tandem with his . . . there was nothing like owning your
own cunt, nothing like wife cunt . . . nothing like owning the only
penis that ever had occupied it.

He felt the storm of possession overpower him; he couldn't
stop it if he wanted to—there was something about her, her sex,
and his response to it—his body seized tight, his penis poised on
the edge of forever—and with one wild drive into her, he blasted
free, spewing like a waterfall, heavy, foaming, drenching, life-
sapping, draining . . . a release like no whore had ever sucked
from him, pleasure beyond price, he thought hazily as he sank down
into her body once again, limp, exhausted—but with his fingers and
penis still in possession of her—and moments later, despite his
best effort, he was asleep and gone.

Well, she'd certainly made her feelings clear to him, Jancie
thought mordantly as she tried, under his weight and his controlling possessiveness, to sleep.

She was nothing more than a dirty girl—she talked a good
game but when it came to reality, she succumbed to sex as easily
as a whore in an alley.

And was getting paid a whole lot less, too.

She was horribly uncomfortable with her skirt bunched up
like that; it made her feel even more like a dirty girl. Mucking
around for a shilling in a carriage, or something like it, and keeping your clothes on because fifteen minutes later he'd have spewed
and gone.

There was a disrespect to it that was galling. Or at least it
seemed like that to her. He wanted one thing. All men wanted one
thing, and what she wanted mattered not. She was a body part, to
be gotten at whenever, wherever, however he could.

Stupid hopes, foolish dreams.

And he just wouldn't let go of her, no matter which way she
shifted her body or twisted and turned.

She needed a new strategy, because obviously trying to with-
hold anything from him hadn't worked worth a damn.

It really was a question of determining which, of all the com-
ponents involved, was the most important.

He thought the acquisition of status and wealth through mar-

riage was meaningful to her. She wanted her family's fair share—
and she hadn't cared whether marriage was involved or not. Until
that day when she realized just what her father's plans encompassed.

So that point was moot. Marriage was the means to the end.
Her mistake had been to fall in love with him. A dirty-girl thing
to do. The question she must answer this very night was whether
the exchange of his access to her body for her access to his house
and home was worth her condoning his cavalier treatment of her.

And the pleasure.

Hard questions. Hard penis. Hard to ignore, dismiss, or say
no to.

If only she were naked, maybe things would come clearer.
Only—too many buttons, undergarments, material, sleeves.

His fingers pressed tighter against her clit. His hips shimmied,
pushing him deeper. She spread her legs to accommodate his
movements.

She loved the feeling. She had her answer. And now, she could
sleep.

She woke up naked.

Sometime during the early hours of the morning, he had
awakened and undressed her so carefully, so tenderly, so lightly,
she'd had no awareness that he was even gone from her body.

He lay covering her now, one hand cupping her mound, his
penis hard, thick, and pulsing and pushing against her buttocks.
He hadn't tried to enter her or take possession again.

That showed some feeling, didn't it? Some respect?

The moment he sensed that she was sentient, he swooped his
fingers deep into her slit, and she gasped with pleasure.

"Ahh, need to hot you up again. Five fingers' worth this time.
Turn this way, angle your legs—that's exactly right. Four fingers
in—maybe . . . I haven't stretched you enough . . . let my fingers
work you . . . just . . . like that—feel them?"

She felt them, wriggling, stroking, pushing at her labia, easing
in, in in . . . his thumb at her clit—how did he do that at that impossible angle? It felt too good, comfortable, his fingers there,
spreading wide, spreading her . . . so naked this time, the pleasure

of his fondling so acute, she involuntarily ground her hips against the feeling, pumping the pleasure yet again.

How could she feel this much again so soon? This was more seductive than life, this mindless enslavement by his hand alone.

He was there, naked, behind her, and with every heave of her body, he pushed against her vulva, inching his way incrementally with minimal, meaningful thrusts—

She felt him, in a haze, as he slowly took possession of her with his penis, finger by finger, until he had penetrated her fully.

Now he was free to play with her clit while he stroked and tweaked her nipples with his other hand.

"I need three hands—four—" he growled. "I want every inch, all of your body, both nipples, lift your leg so I can get at your clit NOW . . ."

Now . . . her body felt like cream, whipped to a clotting consistency, the feelings of pleasure mounting one on top of the other, thick, luscious, pumping, pumping—settling on the hard point of . . . of—

She didn't shatter—she melted onto that point of pleasure, just let the sensation spread thick like treacle all over her body as she surrounded the point and surrendered to its power.

He seemed to like this obverse position because it gave him all the power. She couldn't wriggle him off, she couldn't push him off; he had all the strength and leverage of being on top of her and surrounding her, and he didn't have to see her face.

Consistent with his philosophy of her being his receptacle. The words were meaningless, just a way to set the scene, arouse her ardor, get her juices flowing.

It was too much sensation, too much pleasure. That part was simple. Investing emotion—that had to be put by the wayside. It must only be about the pleasure, for her just as it was for him.

Was it conceivable that she could use him in the same way?

How did a woman love a man and set that aside for the purely physical part of the marriage? It did have its advantages; she could see that clearly and suddenly it became easier to comprehend why a man might seek out a whore.

It made things that much simpler. No emotions. No involvement. Someone who, because she was paid for her time and her body, would not be critical. Someone who would pet and play and compliment, and then, a clutch of sovereigns in hand, just walk away.

It was a fairly seductive idea for a wife as well, whose recompense was in her home, hearth, and pin money.

Give him your body—remove your intelligence. A simple formula in which each of them got what they wanted. She kept access to Waybury, and this comfortable life, and he had his receptacle whenever he felt like it; they both enjoyed the sex, and they both walked away.

Hmmm.

Of course, lying here naked with him, with his legs pinning her, and his arms around her, one hand stroking and fondling her lazily between her legs, the other gently squeezing her nipples, she couldn't really think coherently. Probably that was why she thought all this pleasure without involvement was such a good idea.

Just put aside the loving-him part. Love the sex. Love how he learned how to fondle and fuck you. Forget the rest. Never even think about the rest . . .

He rooted himself in her for three long days and nights, endlessly, ceaselessly, never tiring, never diminishing in his lust for her or in his hard, vigorous presence ready to take her.

Just the pleasure, just the sex . . .

Food was hardly necessary, but it was delivered to the bedroom door nonetheless, affording Emily an unobtrusive way to go back and forth with each knock on the door. Jancie could sometimes hear the scratch of her nails, a soft *meuuw.* It comforted her to know Emily was there.

Lujan would bring the tray to the bed, in those rare moments of quiescence, and they would dine on whatever Mrs. Ancrum saw fit to send up to them.

Or he would dine on her, slathering her body with sauces, jellies, creams, anything he could lick and suck from her nipples, her belly, her mound.

Just the pleasure, just the sex.

He mounted her again and again. He couldn't stop, couldn't let up; it was as if some voluptuary passion outside himself moved him. He reveled in the endless seeking of her depths, in her pleasure, her passion, and the knowledge that he and only he could bring her to this mindless, soaring surrender.

She wanted it, too—just the pleasure, just the sex.

But for her, it was like being in a prison, wholly at the mercy of Lujan's lust, and deliberately sloughing off the feelings and immersing herself in a bottomless pool of pleasure.

She had become exactly what Lujan most desired: the depthless receptacle of his lust.

And—quite unexpectedly—her own.

Just concentrate on the feelings, the sensation, the satisfaction of coming to climax in his hands, with his penis, at his words.

She was concentrating . . . to the utmost, although she was rubbed raw and worn out by the time, deep in the night, he rolled off of her for one last time and fell into his usual deep sleep.

Then, she heard the light scratch that signified Emily's presence, and a faint, ghostly, crickling sound.

Emily at play. Emily here, a presence under the bed when she needed her, consoling her yet again.

The marbley, rolling sound went on and on, as if Emily were chasing whatever it was under the bed. It sounded so loud in the silence of night. She kept listening for it, concentrating on the sound as Emily scrabbled under the bed.

So now you know Emily is there. Now you feel better. Now concentrate on Lujan's unsatiated lust for your body—nothing else . . . just the pleasure, just the sex . . .

She didn't want to. She hated it.

It was more than a lot of wives had.

It was too little—

. . . and it was too much . . .

Chapter Thirteen

In the morning, after toast and tea, he mounted her yet again, tunneling into her, cradling himself against her hips and rocking gently, almost dispassionately, as he considered her face.

"Don't look at me," she murmured, avoiding his gaze. "That isn't the point, is it?"

He shifted, thrust. *"That's* the point."

"Get on with it, then."

He was surprised to find that her matter-of-factness irritated him. "Jancie . . ."

"These are not my terms, Lujan. This is what you said you wanted. A receptacle, wasn't it? No need to search for any emotion, any feeling on my part. I've come to be completely amenable to looking at it just the way you do. It's all about the the pleasure, correct?"

That wasn't quite what he was looking for after three days of unparalleled coupling with her. Three days of finding in her what had been lacking in all the others. He didn't want to hear his words parroted back to him, that their union meant no more to her than his banging a whore.

He wanted something else. Maybe not quite that rash, unmentionable declaration she had made a week ago—but what, then?

Get on with it?

"Ah, Jancie." He moved, just a little, pushing, prodding.

"That feels lovely," she said, her voice devoid of feeling. *Just the pleasure, just the sex.*

"Nothing else?"

She opened her eyes wide. *Breathe.* "What else is there?"

He didn't know, but her cavalier attitude was making him queasy. It meant her loyalty to him hung by a thread, and anything could snap it—another man, more money, better sex. It meant he didn't have the power over her that he had thought, that his sexual prowess was not the center of her world.

It was rather stunning to comprehend that Jancie could just up and walk away from him, and it wouldn't take too much to push her in that direction.

Well, he would just stop wanting her that much. He pulled back suddenly and withdrew from her, just to see what she would say, what she would do.

She did nothing—she just lay there, swinging her legs to the left so her hips and body were slightly turned away from him.

What?

Why was he feeling so bereft? And so off balance. Sweating. His penis lowering to half-staff.

"Why did you do that?" Jancie's voice, soft, impersonal, coming to him from a distance, as if she were on the opposite side of the room.

"Do what?" Yes, that was coherent, but he wasn't feeling coherent suddenly. No, mustn't go on about feelings.

"Why did you . . . stop?"

You stopped. No, that wasn't what he meant. He had stopped her, so that didn't make sense, except that he didn't want her to stop now. He wanted . . . what did he want? Not to stop.

But he had stopped. And flopped. He levered himself up on one elbow, and the room tilted.

Holy hell. He fell back on the pillow. *Don't stop.*

"Lujan?" Her voice was even farther away.

"Here. Don't stop . . ." He felt boneless, suddenly. Couldn't move. Don't stop—call Kyger . . . he couldn't get the words out. He felt Jancie shake him, call to him, and then jump out of the bed, heard her blurry voice calling down the hallway, heard pounding feet and voices . . .

. . . heard nothing more as he slipped into unconsciousness.

He swam up through the darkness and the tentacles reaching out for him.

"Jancie . . . ?"

"I'm here."

"What happened?"

"Something you ate. The doctor doesn't know which meal, which food. Just that something you ate reacted in your system. You've been sleeping for two days."

Two days? TWO days? Forty-eight hours that Jancie was alone with Kyger in his house with him as good as dead to the world?

Jesus. God. And they put him in pajamas, too. Wait—was he remembering correctly—had someone, Kyger, induced him to . . . heave all over the bedroom that night? Before he passed out?

That, too?

Jesus.

He struggled to sit up and a firm hand pushed him back against the pillows. "Not yet, big brother." Kyger, damn his soul. Enjoying himself immensely, too. "Bed rest for you. Gruel and barley water for the rest of the week."

"You'd love that," Lujan growled. "But I'm not down and out yet, little man. Out of my—our room, *now*. Just go away."

Kyger shrugged. "Sure. I'll just let you take over right now, and I'll be on my way."

With Jancie, no doubt, Lujan thought mordantly. Damn it to hell. How had this happened to him? When had he lost control— of his life, his wife, his brother's feelings of responsibility? His father's lenient hand . . . And where the hell was Hugo mucking around, anyway?

He felt soggy, soft, deflated. Useless in the face of Kyger's vigor and Jancie's detachment. "Go away."

"My pleasure," Kyger murmured. "Jancie?"

"You should rest," Jancie said.

Lujan hated her at that moment, hated that neutral tone, hated that she didn't seem to care one way or another, and maybe she'd just as soon be in Kyger's bed than his. Hated his brother for being so hatefully helpful and generous and looking so virile and strong next to him, so weak and helpless in his bed.

How had he come to this?

"Fine, I'll rest. Both of you, get out."

He wanted Jancie to protest, to say she'd stay, but off she went with his brother, and he felt a murderous urge to jump out of bed and follow them, to spy on them, to catch them doing what he suspected they wanted to do, what they were planning to do, while he was so incapacitated.

He wasn't quite able. Still dizzy, still weak. He lay back on the pillows, fuming.

Mrooww. Emily jumped up on the bed.

Damned cat.

She rubbed against his arm. *Oww.*

She was no comfort whatsoever.

"Go away." He lifted her—he barely had the strength to lift her—and dropped her on the floor.

Immediately he heard her scrabbling across the room, and the sound of something rolling and her chasing it, pouncing on it.

He was too tired to look, to care, even to sleep. What was Jancie doing?

The rolling sound filled his head.

Stupid cat. And Jancie so attached to it. And Kyger. And not to him . . .

He was getting delirious. The crickling sound felt like it was rolling around in his head, a marble on a table, rolling inexorably toward the edge . . .

Falling . . . off the edge . . . falling . . . down the steps . . . falling . . . into oblivion—

. . . if he fell . . . he thought fuzzily, grasping for sentience and failing . . .

If he fell forever—his last thought . . . Jancie would be free . . .

She had never thought Lujan would return home this soon. She felt frantic, as if she were missing something, but she didn't know what it was.

The two points of her life were about to intersect: Lujan's presence meant more of his claiming her time, and her body. What if he stayed on for the foreseeable future?

Not likely. He'd miss the fleshpots of London soon enough. He'd get tired of her sooner than later and off he'd go. Thank God, she'd clamped down on her feelings before she'd made more of a fool of herself. This way was better. Then she wouldn't be so devastated when he left, and she could continue on her quest.

She couldn't do much now. The servants were hovering everywhere, in deep concern for Mr. Lujan. Kyger closeted himself in the library and worked the house accounts instead of riding the fields.

Bingham was ever-present, cementing her feeling that he was always watching her now. Mrs. Ancrum kept preparing broth and oatmeal for Lujan, who pushed it away, and kept asking for Jancie.

But there wasn't much she could do for him. He needed bed rest, and a few days of letting his system regulate itself and get rid of the toxins was about all that could be done generally.

"Well, then, rest with me," he coaxed her.

"My company can have no restorative powers that I can conceive of," Jancie told him primly, "and besides, you're in no shape to do anything but lie flat on your back."

"Well, then—I'll do that, and you sit on my penis, and do all the work. That will be amazingly curative, I think."

"I think not," Jancie said, removed and detached once again.

He hated that. She could just as well have gotten naked and saddled him. But the emotion wasn't there. However, the minute *he* conceived of the idea, his body had gone haywire with emotion, rigid and upright, and he felt powerful, virile, and in control.

The next day he felt even better—he felt like himself, he felt clearheaded and ready to tackle the problem of Jancie.

He wanted her with him again. So he needed a strategy— somehow, he needed to captivate her all over again. Needed to seduce and enthrall her and make her . . . *don't mention that word* . . . what? Want him? Submit to him? Care for him?

Care—that was a good word. Care. Willing she was, and involved in the physical process. But she had become disengaged on a level that was truly disconcerting. As if she didn't care.

Get on with it. That was all she wanted of him.

No—that was all he'd said he wanted of *her.*

All right, then. Maybe that had been a mistake. Maybe he hadn't known just how enthralled he would become with *her.*

Yes, because he knew it might not last, so why give it too much credence? Exactly—in his experience, nothing lasted. Everything was of the moment, done on impulse.

There were no good women. There were women with certain hopes, concrete dreams, greedy schemes, digging for money, status, and marriage.

What had been Jancie's motive?

Forget that—he tended to forget exactly how things had gone; but she was no mercenary—he had pursued her those two years, and she'd been halfway out the door to her father after Olivia's death.

They had come after her, all the Galliard men, seeking a convenient vessel who happened to be young, beautiful, available, and alone.

She had done nothing to try to seduce them. He had bullied her into marrying him, using her growing love for him, and then he had quelled her ardor, and demanded that she withdraw her emotions.

Who was he to complain that she was aloof, when he'd invited it by his treatment of her?

That was about to change.

He needed a strategy. He needed Jancie. Now.

Ooowww. Emily appeared on the threshold of the library and Jancie leaned down and scooped her up and held her close against her chest.

"This is a madhouse," she whispered into Emily's most receptive ear. "I don't know what I'm doing here."

Mrrooww. Don't lose sight of what you want.

She knew, she knew, and she tried to keep the purpose of her presence at Waybury constantly in mind. But she felt so discouraged. She'd come again to the library to go through the books on the highest shelves, but the prospect was so daunting, she had just stood there staring up and around the room, doing nothing.

And nothing was what she had found after having gone through the rest of the house, she had no idea what her next step should be.

Ooww. There is an answer.

Emily was purring. Jancie hugged her tightly. Emily was always right. There *was* an answer to be found—she just hadn't looked in the right place. The upper bookcase shelves, for one, where no human hand had handled a book in years.

She set Emily down resignedly and pulled the ladder around to the far side of the room.

She was doing something. It felt good to do *something*.

But then, and she ought not discount this, she'd also made a decision—the absolutely correct decision—not to love Lujan. Although love was not a faucet, to be turned on and off at will.

But a woman *could* choose to set those feelings aside, and fall in love instead with the sex and the pleasure.

The startling thing to her was how easy it was. She'd had several days to come to grips with it, and she had concluded that, for her, there were no negatives, and that not loving Lujan would save her a lot of heartache in the end.

And she also found that she was feeling a certain urgency to couple with him again. As if she, too, could separate the desires of her body from the emotions in her heart and her mind.

Just like men did.

So that conceivably she could couple with any number of men, and still come back to Lujan with that same obsessive need and desire that he had brought to her after his week of London debauchery.

That was a liberating thought. It struck her that it meant she never had to be a hostage to needing love or the need to give love, ever again.

She didn't have to love Lujan, she just had to spread her legs for him, and be perfectly willing to service him and thereby pleasure herself.

She was on the rolling ladder, propped up against the far bookcase, painstakingly examining every book on the uppermost shelf when she heard a crusty sound that could have been, "Ahhemmm."

She nearly dropped the book; her hands started shaking and she felt heat suffuse her cheeks. Bingham did that to her. Made her feel less than the mistress of the house, made her feel like a dirty girl caught in a tuition girl's room.

But there was no reason she shouldn't be perusing the more inaccessible volumes in the library, no reason she shouldn't be curious about them or climb the steps to explore the upper shelves . . . no reason, except—

Never give away anything. Especially to a servant. So she hoped her tone was cool and dismissive. "Yes, Bingham?"

Bingham seemed even more paper-thin and disapproving from up above. "Mr. Lujan is asking for you, madam."

"Thank you." She waited, he didn't move. "Is there something else?"

He took a step. "No, madam."

"Thank you, Bingham."

He moved, reluctantly, out of the room, looking as if he wanted to say more.

Oooowww. That was a most emphatic wail. Emily did not like Bingham any more than she did. Jancie climbed slowly down the ladder, the random volume still in her hand, and set it on a nearby table in order to scoop up Emily.

Mrroow. Emily's body was stiff in her arms, her back arched. She didn't want to be held; she pushed off with her hind legs, jumped to the table, knocked the book onto the floor, which scattered a handful of photographs on the carpet, and disappeared under the sofa.

Photographs. Of a child. No more time to wonder who— Bingham could be watching. Jancie swooped down and gathered them up quickly . . . shoved them into the book. Looked around. Everything silent. No sound. Everyone off doing something else. She could examine the photographs here, but . . . what if someone walked in?

She tucked the book under her arm and walked casually to the staircase, driven by a certain cautious urgency.

Lujan was waiting . . .

Just get up the steps, and decide what to do after that. Simple, and not. Because she was intent on listening for Bingham's slow step, she didn't even see Kyger until she felt him grasp her free arm.

She almost jumped out of her skin. He turned her face-to-face with him, which meant he was standing three steps below her, and he was staring at her as if he could see into her innermost thoughts.

Thank God, he was so focused on her, he didn't even see the book tucked under her arm. How many more things could trip her up?

"Are you sure?"

She knew what he meant even if she didn't dignify it with a response. Lujan had called and she was going to him, and it was her choice, and Kyger knew it.

She didn't answer him; she pulled her arm away, clutched the book, and continued up the steps, aware of him watching her. Aware of his frustration with her.

She was Lujan's wife, committed to Lujan and the course she had set. And now, with the unexpected discovery of the photographs, it was more imperative than ever that she firmly establish her place at Waybury.

But what was most interesting to her was the wash of mounting desire as she climbed the steps.

This was something she hadn't expected so soon, that her decision to focus on the pleasure and the sex would trigger this shuddering excitement at Lujan's summons.

But the book with the photographs was the most important thing right now—she ran upstairs, intensely aware of Kyger's gaze, her excitement warring with her need to look at the photographs and put them someplace secure.

God—now what? Hide the book. Look at it tomorrow. Lujan was waiting.

No. Too curious. It would just take a minute to look at it, to hide it.

Olivia's room . . . she darted inside.

It was dark in there—still a shrine, still full of the sense of Olivia's presence. She pulled back the curtain, and sank into the chair that Olivia had always occupied when she used to read to her.

At least there was still some light. She examined the album, which had been made to look like a book with its rich blue binding and scrolled gold decoration.

Inside, there were five loose photographs, each of which showed a very small boy posed in five different scenes: dressed in a sailor suit; with a pony; with a much younger Hugo stiffly posed in the parlor; with two boys who had to be Lujan and Kyger, very young; and one with Olivia, so beautiful and serene.

Gaunt. Sweet baby, mischievous face.

Still intact in the hinges, there was a photograph of his christening; of his first birthday, as detailed in Olivia's perfect Spenserian script; his communion; and one more of the family stiffly posed all together.

Nothing more.

Gaunt. Four or five years old and mysteriously gone, only living on in this photographic memorial that had gone to dust in the uppermost shelves of the library where nobody could find him.

Closer to heaven?

They couldn't bear to bury him for real.

Olivia couldn't.

This was all anyone would ever know of Gaunt. By now, not even his brothers remembered him all that well, just the circumstances of his disappearance and the aftermath.

Jancie wondered if they knew of the existence of the album.

Maybe Olivia saved it and hid it up there when Hugo would have obliterated all traces of his missing son.

Or Hugo had, against the time when the wounds would not be so fresh, and Olivia might want to see all that was left of her last and youngest child.

Who could fathom the reasoning of the human heart?

Lujan was waiting.

What to do? This was something she never should have seen, never should have found. It was too personal, too hurtful to Olivia's memory to be prying into what was left of her missing, probably deceased, son.

But she couldn't stop examining the photographs, couldn't stop searching for the minutest detail that might give her a clue as to why this child had vanished off the face of the earth.

And what she had neglected to do, she thought suddenly with a twinge of terror, was arrange the shelf downstairs so that the missing book was not obvious. And she would hide the album in here, give Olivia back her son, let her help find the answers.

She tucked the photographs carefully back into the hinges, and then looked around. There were so many places in this room she could just tuck a book and no one would be the wiser. No one ever came in here.

Not even Hugo, himself missing now for over a week, drowning his sorrows in the sin pots of London. A peculiar kind of mourning, one that hardly honored his wife, or even his honorable proposal to her.

But what did one expect? Like son, like father. And it took only something catastrophic to bring out the worst in him, and in Lujan.

Don't think about that; you've come to terms with what you need to do about Lujan, at least.

Where to hide the album?

Quickest, least likely place to be searched? Under the bed.

Dusk had fallen. The room was steeped in shadow. She didn't want to turn up the light, so she knelt at the foot of the bed, and slipped the album just under the footboard, where no one could see, no one would think to look.

I'll find some answers, she thought. For Olivia. For my father. For Gaunt.

Lujan was waiting . . .

She knew what he was waiting for.

For myself.

When a man was down, a woman would always step all over him.

Where was Jancie?

Lujan had prepared himself for her; he sat naked, propped up against the headboard, flexing his rigid shaft which grew tighter and harder the longer it took Jancie to come.

It had been too long since Jancie had come. The curtains were drawn, the fire banked, the lamps had been turned down to a sensual, flickering glow—and whatever it had been that had laid him low, it was well over, and he wanted Jancie. Now . . .

This was the last day he was going to stay in bed unless Jancie was naked with him. It was part of the strategy. Maybe the only part he had really thought out. Jancie, naked in bed with him forever. It sounded good. It sounded possible.

The grandfather clock in the lower hallway struck nine. She was taking too long. He'd sent Bingham an hour ago, more. Damn. Bedtime already, and his wife was nowhere to be found.

He yanked the bell cord. "BINGHAM!!!!"

A moment later, Bingham opened the door, oblivious to his nudity—or pretending to be. "Sir?"

"Miss Jancie."

"I told her, sir."

"Where is she, then, with my brother?"

"No, sir. Mr. Kyger has gone out."

"Where—is—Jancie?" Lujan asked painstakingly.

"I will find her and remind her," Bingham said carefully.

"Remind her???"

The door swung shut on his indignation.

Damn it all to hell. If Kyger had gone out, it was reasonable and possible Jancie had gone with him. Which meant she was gone for the evening. Gone forever?

Then what would he do?

His imagination was running riot. This was inconceivable that he was so besotted, so top over tail about Jancie.

Well, then, he wasn't. He was infatuated with her innocence, her beauty, her tight, hot cunt, her fresh, unused virgin's body, and her submissiveness in bed.

A man couldn't buy such a partner for a thousand pounds, even at the Bullhead. Couldn't purchase that kind of virgin flesh in the most exclusive catered sex clubs in London. Wouldn't be sitting here, in a sweat, wondering if she'd chosen someone else.

What a career she would have if she ever left him. But she wasn't going to leave, ever. That was what marriage was for—to bind that luscious, lubricious naked flesh to a man whenever he was fortunate enough to find it.

Where is she??

He felt ridiculous suddenly, sitting there naked like that and Jancie nowhere around.

. . . Jancie would be free . . .

What?

The door opened slowly and she was there, her body clad in a diaphanous nightgown, limned by the soft hallway light.

Finally.

"I'm here—"

"So am I," he said, with a soft break in his voice that was just a small intimation of his excitement, but he wasn't sure he didn't want to inflict some punishment before pleasure because she had kept him tantalized and waiting.

He grasped his shaft. "I need you right here—right now . . ."

Fascinating to watch a naked man handle himself. She inched toward the bed, transfixed by the sight, her excitement escalating.

"Jancie—"

"I'm here . . ." What could she say?

"*I'm* here . . ." He flexed his penis. "Get over *here.*"

Just the pleasure, just the sex . . . There was something different about him now—a shift—as if he were both master and supplicant. It suited him. It suited her. It made her even more eager for the pleasure to come.

She climbed onto the bed, and settled herself between his knees. Bent over his penis. Enclosed the head in her mouth. Heard his hard-suppressed groan. Squeezed the tip hard between her teeth and lips. Tasted a spurt of his come, and began the serious work of manipulating him to climax.

It came so soon. It took no time at all, as if he'd been poised on the brink for hours. A pull and tug, a suck and squeeze, a long, drawn-out groan of pure release, and he filled her mouth with buttermilk until it dribbled down her chin.

He reached for her mindlessly, for it, to rub the thick ejaculate into her bare skin. He tore off the thin nightgown and stripped it from her body.

"You will never again put anything between your naked body and me," he growled into her ear, bending over her, as she hung onto his bulging penis head with her lips and tongue. "I'm always naked for you, you will always be naked for me."

She made a guttural sound and pulled hard on his penis tip, hard, harder, grasping his shaft, pulling the last spurt of ejaculate from his shuddering body.

"Come . . ."

She made a sound that sounded like, "not letting go . . ."

He fell back against the pillows, watching her. No more ravishing sight than a naked woman hanging onto a man's penis with her mouth. Positively succulent. Utterly enslaving.

Made a man hard, thick, tight with voluptuous need.

Need her. Can't wait one minute longer to soak her with my cream . . .

"Jancie—"

She couldn't deny the note in his voice, the urgency of his hands as he grasped and pulled her mouth away from his penis.

"Mount my penis, *now*—"

He was so long, so thick, it took a little maneuvering to center herself over him at just the right angle for penetration. And then, inch by inch, with his hands on her hips guiding her, she slowly seated herself on his thrusting hardness until she enfolded him entirely and her mound pressed tight against the girdle of his hips.

Breathless, taking him this way. Face-to-face, where Lujan had never wanted to be, staring at the rapt expression on his face which must mirror her own. Feeling his hands cupping her breasts, flipping her nipples with one finger, knowing he had the total freedom to caress them however he wanted . . .

Just the pleasure . . . beyond words, beyond description . . .

She shifted her body as her nipples responded to his play and a tingling sensation coursed through her.

"God, I wish I had five hands," he muttered, moving those provoking hands to her hips again to ease her movement.

"What would you do with them?"

"You know."

"Tell me anyway." Now she was moving in a rhythm, tutored by his hands stroking her hips and thighs.

"One hand each for your breasts to finger your nipples, one hand each on your hips to feel you move, one hand deep between your legs, feeling you up there . . ."

She bucked at the sensuous words.

"Just like that." Her breasts, bouncing in tandem to her movements, fascinated him. He caught one in his mouth, and ground her hips down more tightly on his shaft. Pulled at her tantalizingly hard, naked nipple. Licked it, covered it with saliva and pulled at it again, felt her body straining, shifting, undulating like a belly dancer trying to get away from the almost unbearable pleasure swirling inexorably downward between her legs.

Just like that, just like that . . . he wanted every inch of her, he couldn't put his hands enough places to feel her every movement—her grinding hips, her pumping thighs, into her crease, all over her lush, writhing buttocks, all the while they moved in tandem to his hard, tight, incremental thrusts.

She was coming. Coming. He felt it, felt her body seizing up, felt her careening toward her orgasm. Another thrust. Another pull of her nipple. She felt creamy in his hands, creamy between her legs.

Just like that, just like that . . . she sank down on his penis one last time and erupted, her body pumping, humping his penis, and pitching her into orgasmic oblivion.

He caught her as she fell, spewing into the eddies of pleasure that engulfed her, and drowning in his turn.

He lay flat on his back, with Jancie faceup between his legs, her head on his chest, her thighs draped over his, his hands cupping her breasts gently, asexually.

It was a moment of pure repletion, almost too much pleasure. Or maybe not enough. He wasn't sure. He didn't want to define it, or analyze it. Except he did.

It was Jancie. From this angle, his head raised slightly because of the pile of pillows, he could admire the long, lean line of Jancie's naked body, and the seductive tuft of hair that curtained her secrets, that now was drenched with his cream.

Instantly he had the voluptuous desire to dip his fingers between her legs, to feel his cream co-mingled with hers. To stroke and feel those cunt lips that were so enveloping and snug around his shaft. To pull apart her secrets and know every inch of her inside and out.

He maneuvered himself upright against the headboard, and pulled her up higher against his chest, keeping her legs draped around his thighs.

So much better. This way, he could see everything, he could stroke her arms, play with her nipples, or slide his hands down between her legs.

Not quite yet. Anticipation was everything. She was utterly boneless in his arms, completely sated in sex; she wasn't going anywhere, and he wanted to prolong this deep desire to intimately explore her cunt.

Her nipples occupied him nicely for a while. Deliciously hard, pointed nipples, perfect for thumbing, rubbing, and squeezing. And she felt every sensual caress. He wouldn't let her move, wouldn't let her shift her legs to press down where all the sensual feeling crystallized, sharp, bright, fractured.

Put his hand there instead, slinking his fingers neatly into her labia and into the thick residue of his clotted cream mixed with hers.

Her body arched and bucked, and he pulled against her hips to keep her legs spread and his questing fingers in her slippery, hot slit.

He was consumed with voluptuous excitement. His penis hardened to iron. She stopped fighting him as her body responded to his penetrating fingers. Her hips canted upward, inviting more.

He slipped his free hand between her legs, and pulled gently at one side of her slit. He slipped his invasive fingers out of her heat, and pulled at the other side, so that her cunt lips were spread and she was open to his fingers probing her.

Her body writhed as his fingers kept incrementally spreading her wider and wider, his fingers stroking, pressing, caressing the lush, wet inner flesh of her cunt—so wet, so pink, so perfect—opening her still farther to expose her pleasure point, and stroking it lightly as he whispered in her ear, "Whenever you're naked, I want you spread open like this."

She fought him as he caressed her; she couldn't take the unbearable pleasure, the feeling of being wholly exposed and open to him, and they rocked together in a combative sensual dance even as he pushed her legs still farther apart.

"I want you always to feel my fingers spreading you—when you're dressed, when you're naked, when you sleep—I want you to feel me working you wide open like this, wet and creamy like this, before I take you . . . I want . . ."

He exploded. A man could only take so much. Her body could only take so much.

As the pressure of his fingers eased, she scrambled away from him, to the other side of the bed, as she was smeared by his spuming orgasm, as she watched him helpless in the grip of his pleasure.

Pleasure she had given him, that her body provoked. All those secret pleasures. Pleasure for her, too. Leave all emotions at the door.

It made things so much easier.

Just the sex. Just the pleasure.

Chapter Fourteen

Lujan was right. She felt it, just as he'd said, as he wanted, felt him down between her legs, spreading her wide, even though she was fully dressed and intending to take breakfast in the dining room.

"Stay with me." He had pulled her close, reached under her skirt for her mound, his fingers seeking her nakedness through the open slit of her undergarments. Finding her. Prodding her.

Her knees went weak.

"Reason enough to stay in bed."

She pulled away. "You stay. I'll have Mrs. Ancrum send breakfast to you."

"Come here."

"I have things to do."

"Nothing more important than taking care of my penis."

She wavered for a moment. He was at full, hard staff, primed and ready, and her body was shooting off little darts of desire. If she stayed, he would undress her, caress her, spread her again.

Oh lord—her breathing grew heavy as her body remembered and recreated all the sensations from the night before.

Last night, in his hands, pressed, caressed, and detonated. And he hadn't even begun to explore how much she was capable of feeling—there.

It almost scared her, how much pleasure her body was capable of. Thank God she had decided not to love him. If he ever did this with some other woman, it would have killed her.

"I think I took very nice care of your penis all night."

"It's not enough. Come back, Jancie. I shouldn't have let you even get out of bed."

He held onto her arm, pulled her onto the bed. "I'll have nipples for breakfast, thank you."

"Lujan . . ."

"You need to be in bed with me. I need to feed on you. All of you. Now." His voice was thick with lust and desire, and she felt her body respond in a corresponding way.

"Lujan," she whispered, knowing already she was helpless to resist. She wanted it, too. She felt drugged with power and pleasure. It took nothing at all for a woman's body to acclimate, to want what a man wanted, to give him what he needed to see.

He had her naked in moments. "Yesss—" nuzzling her ear, her neck, and slowly working his way down to her breasts. Pushing her back so that he was over her, taking one nipple into his mouth while he insinuated his hand between her legs. "Can't get enough . . ." A growl of words around his sucking her nipple and rubbing her slit, warming her up for his fingers first, and then for his penis.

She angled her legs and arched her back. He worked his way down from her breast to her navel and further down between her legs. It was daylight now; she had unwittingly pulled the curtains, and sun flooded the room, the bed, pouring heat over her body in tandem with the heat he generated as he gazed his fill of her mound, as he began working her labia apart to reveal her glistening nub.

And then he bent and kissed it, and began sucking at it, and the sun spun away, and the dark and the light, and everything she knew, she felt, she thought, was absorbed into him, his body, his tongue, and that one explosive pleasure point at the center of her world.

He had never had sex like this, ever. God, it was all he could do not to let Jancie walk out the door. She could barely walk as it was, he had plumbed her so deeply and thoroughly.

But after this morning's round of coupling, she still protested that she had things to do.

The only thing she had to do was keep his penis busy and satisfied, damn it. Oh, hell, he *was* satisfied, in a way he hadn't experienced before. He knew why, too—this was his cunt, his woman, his wife, all for him, and no other man would try her out or try her on.

And he wasn't scared of Kyger's attraction to her, either. There was nothing Kyger could do that could equal what they had experienced together last night and this morning.

He still hadn't had enough. Just thinking about it . . . he'd never been with a woman who gave him such an incessant hard-on, a woman he wanted so much and so often. He wasn't fit to be in company right now, and he had meant to join her downstairs for breakfast.

The hell with breakfast. He wanted to eat something else. Something ineffably feminine and only Jancie's.

He had to get a grip on jack lance. He couldn't walk around primed and poked all the time.

Well, maybe he could. He had. But this was different.

How was it different? This wasn't a grand love affair. This was his wife, available to him in all the ways he could conceive of, when he wanted her. He wanted her now. That was the difference. He kept wanting her, and each time they coupled, it still seemed like it wasn't enough.

Why didn't she feel that? He wondered what she wanted.

She wanted breakfast. She had things to do. The lure of unremitting sex was not enough to keep her by his side.

He found that curious suddenly. Why? Was it not enough? Was he not enough? *Was* it Kyger?

Shit. He bolted out of bed. Kyger had to go. Kyger had been running things and living off Waybury for far too many years. He couldn't have Kyger around as a temptation, anyway. Waybury was his, and if he had to, he'd take the reins as he should have done years ago.

He had made a massive mistake leaving everything to his righteous brother. Respectable women loved men like Kyger—so solid, steady, serious, faithful, dependable—

Son of a bitch—dependable—something he wasn't. Never

wanted to be. Too many willing women in the world just waiting to be fucked.

But they weren't Jancie. Who was willing, but she wasn't waiting. She wasn't dazzled, by him, by his prowess, his stamina, his unending desire for her. Why wasn't that enough for her? Why wasn't she still in bed with him instead of downstairs having breakfast, and probably with Kyger.

Shit. Kyger. Every time he turned around, there was Kyger.

Goddamned Kyger. When did everything around Waybury come under Kyger's control?

He couldn't get dressed fast enough. Kyger was done for. Kyger would be gone from Waybury before the end of this day, he swore it. No more temptations for Jancie. He'd teach Jancie to wait—for him, his need, his lust, his desire.

His penis. Thick and hard, and deep inside her.

He pounded down the steps and raced into the dining room.

It was empty. He didn't expect that. He expected to see his so-dependable brother dependably holding Jancie's hand, and feeding her bacon or a biscuit. Sipping hot chocolate from her lips.

Damn him. Damn her.

If they had been there, their plates and cutlery had already been removed, and all that remained was the array of covered dishes on the sideboard, the usual morning fare: eggs, sausage, herring, toast, scones, oatmeal, brioche, a fruit compote.

Enough to feed a small army. Which made him lose his appetite.

Waste. And who was responsible for such waste?

Why, his wife. Did she not go over the menus and choose what would be served?

Damn it, where was she?

There was no one downstairs except for a maid dusting the parlor, and the boy who cleaned the ashes from the fireplaces.

Was Waybury always this empty? It seemed to him that it had not been, that Olivia's presence had filled it and made it home, and now that she was gone, it felt emptier than ever.

Or was it that Jancie was nowhere to be found?

Oh, he had a good suspicion where Jancie was.

Damn damn damn damn—he stamped back into the parlor and yanked the bell pull.

Bingham appeared as paper-thin and disapproving as ever. "Sir?"

"Where is my wife?"

Bingham's eyebrow arched. "Riding with Mr. Kyger, sir."

"Is she?" Lujan murmured through gritted teeth. "Well, well, well. She had things to do, did she? So she did. Thank you, Bingham. I'll find them."

"As you will, sir." Bingham withdrew, discreet as a cloud.

And now what? He put a rein on his temper, on his fury. He couldn't go off half-cocked looking for them because he would kill Kyger. No doubt about that. And he didn't know what he would do to Jancie.

Did it matter? All he wanted was Jancie, waiting for him. It goddamned wasn't too much to ask, was it? After yesterday? And this morning?

All right, then. He would just calm down. He didn't need morning sustenance, so he would just calmly walk to the stables, saddle up, and he would take a calm, leisurely ride out because, well, it was a beautiful day. He wouldn't be looking for them, necessarily, but if he happened to find them together, he would kill them.

As any rational man would.

Simple as that.

Thank God, Hugo was nowhere around, Lujan was still in bed, and Kyger had left the house. For sure, with her luck, any one of them could come walking through the door just as she was extracting the album from under Olivia's bed, and how would she explain that?

All right then, that was done. Only the book was now covered with the dust that no one was cleaning from under the bed. Better that they shouldn't, actually. Let them leave this room as Olivia's shrine, for now.

She settled herself in the chair by the window. She had brought a magnifying glass she'd found in the library, where she'd gone immediately after she came downstairs to straighten out that row of books.

Even then, tottering on a ladder first thing in the morning had been something sure to raise questions, if anyone had walked in. Kyger could have found her—or Bingham. Oh God, the thought of Bingham finding her had rattled her badly.

And she still couldn't shake the feeling Bingham was watching her.

So she was already feeling fairly jittery. Really, she didn't have much time before Lujan came looking for her. And she had no idea what she was looking for.

Seven pictures. A small boy. A family stiffly posed in studio settings. They'd probably gone up to London for the photographs, or the photographer had come with props. So there was nothing personal there.

Hugo so stern. Olivia with a loving hand around her long-gone child. The three boys lined up by height. So alike, so different. Lujan could never have been that innocent. Kyger was always that severe, already in charge and responsible at that young age.

And Gaunt, impossibly young forever, in his smile a hint of the mischievous child he must have been.

What was she looking for?

She didn't know.

How could such a little boy vanish off the face the earth?

The same way a fortune in diamonds disappeared.

Somebody took them and made up a story to fit the facts.

Somebody took the child and made up a story to fit the facts.

She was fooling herself if she thought that no one, back then, had come up with that solution. Kyger had told her they'd done everything they could think of, but the end result was, the child was gone. And there were no remains, which meant the child could be a grown man living anywhere on earth.

Maybe even South Africa. Maybe Kaamberoo.

Maybe she was delusional; maybe she was desperate to find some kind of clue to explain how Hugo survived his captivity at the hands of those putative murderers and thieves, and why they had not killed him.

Because there he was, in the family portrait, his face as stolid as always, looking much younger than he did now, with the fruit of his homecoming at his feet.

Oh Father, I'm failing you again. I don't see a thing except a comfortably circumstanced family with a child who subsequently disappeared.

Wait—how long after these photographs were taken had Gaunt gone missing?

The boy looked to be four or five years old. *What* had Kyger said?

Maybe not too long after . . .

Which meant what?

She didn't know. She just didn't know.

Did her father know?

What did her father know, really?

In all those years, after he regained his memory and set out to discover what had happened to Hugo and the diamonds, what *had* her father found out about Hugo's family?

And what more did he know apart from the stories he had always told her about the disaster at Kaamberoo?

Had he known about Gaunt?

She needed to piece the story together again and add the missing pieces to what she already knew: Olivia's claim that the money had come from her side of the family; Hugo agreeing to support his erstwhile partner's daughter all those years in boarding school and then making his claim on her for Olivia's sake; her father's motives in even begging this *largesse* from him; why he hadn't demanded reparation altogether.

And then, Olivia's death. Her hard-to-conceal feelings for Lujan. The three Galliard men each seeking to marry her. Her accepting Lujan. Her decision never to love him. Her sworn purpose to search for something that would prove Hugo had stolen Edmund's share of the diamond strike all those years ago. The long-missing, and probably deceased, child . . .

Nothing connected—quite.

The pictures told her nothing, except that Hugo could afford a photographer, and the young Gaunt had a fey smile, a glint in his baby eyes, and a possible propensity for mischief.

She closed the album and secreted it under the footboard.

Nothing.

And she was spinning flax into dross. It was quite possible that everything was just as it appeared. That there had been no intent to steal from Edmund, that Hugo had really thought he was dead when he left Kaamberoo with his fortune, that his child had fallen down a well and that was why no one had ever been able to find him, that the house and the money *had* come from Olivia's family . . .

That Lujan could come to love her.

Fairy tales, all.

She closed the door to Olivia's room, closing the door, for the moment, on all her futile speculations.

She heard a sound behind her, that rolling, crickly sound of whatever it was that Emily had been playing with.

But Emily was nowhere in sight, and there was no one around, at least on the bedroom floor. So the sound seemed magnified, ghostly, portentous in the silence, and Jancie froze.

It had to be Emily. The sound persisted. Somewhere in this hallway, Emily was chasing the object just as she had before.

Whatever it was. It just sounded so eerie. So strange, coming after all the time she'd spent in Olivia's room. Stranger still, because Emily had been pursuing it when she'd brought the album to hide it there.

If she were superstitious, if she believed in ghosts, she could almost believe it was Olivia generating the sound somehow, trying to send her some kind of message.

Nonsense.

The rolling sound stopped suddenly, and then she heard a faint sound.

Owww.

Emily—and she wasn't in Olivia's room, as Jancie would have supposed.

Mrowww—more emphatic this time.

From hers and Lujan's room. How . . . ?

She threw open the door and Emily stalked out, slanting an exasperated look at her.

Owww.

It wasn't Emily. Shocked, Jancie looked down the hallway. All was silence. The sound was gone.

Here it was, spread out before him, that which would be his legacy—the rolling fields, the orchards, the gardens, the neat little farms that rimmed the outskirts of his holdings. Everything that

Kyger had been caring for and keeping in good order for the moment when his feckless older brother would come to his senses.

The man was a goddamned saint.

What did he gain from plowing another man's furrow?

It was so clear: the differences between him and Kyger were like night and day. Kyger was the better man. The upright man. The pillar. The saint.

No wonder Jancie was drawn to him.

It wasn't wholly about sex.

It was a stunning thought. Everything was about sex. His brother's attempt to seduce Jancie . . . No, that was rivalry. That was to prove he could and would, because Lujan was such a whoring bastard.

The son of a bitch always had the upper hand just because he was so *good. Good* men should die. They made life impossible for the rest of humanity. No one could live up to the standards of a good man . . .

And besides, a good man could be corrupted, too, come to think of it. Maybe *he'd* been a good man before he'd gone to profligate London and discovered free, untrammeled, heedless, wanton fucking.

God, what was better than that?

Jancie.

Exactly. The reason he was out here riding his brains out instead of in bed fucking her.

Where the hell was the saint? Burning at the stake, he hoped—he wished.

Nowhere to be found for miles around.

Probably in the hayloft, screwing Jancie.

God almighty—could a man not even have his own wife without his brother getting in the middle of it?

He turned and headed back toward the house, taking the riding track that led to the stables.

And there he saw Kyger, hefting bales into the hayloft.

Where the hell was Jancie? Probably sitting in the wagon, admiring his strength, his power.

Shit.

He spurred his mount into a gallop. Faster, faster—Jancie was there, he was certain of it. And he was going to get to her before something happened between them.

Something happened: he felt something give, felt his body slipping to one side, and he fell onto the track—hard, gritty, jaw-crunching—while his horse raced frantically down to the stable.

Flat out in bed again, every muscle aching, with severe bruising to his arms and back so it was too painful to move. Goddamn.

And it was Kyger who'd found him. Kyger who was alone, doing the work he had always done, the work he, Lujan, did not wish to dirty his hands doing . . . Always the righteous position. Always the credible brother. The ethical one. The praiseworthy one. Admired, valued, esteemed . . .

As opposed to him—discounted, discredited, and disdained . . .

And now this—over and above the stomach upset—it made him look like a weakling, a fool, especially beside Kyger, so tall, strapping, imposing.

Damn damn and damn—

And then Jancie, a shadow floating around the room, offering sympathy and compassion, her cool hands and even cooler words—meaningless, he couldn't comprehend her, he couldn't stand it. To be helpless again. At the mercy of piety and protection . . . and those cool, consoling hands . . .

What was happening here?

He needed to think . . . his head hurt.

Kyger filled the room, pushing everyone and everything else out of the way. Pretending to be concerned. Pretending he even cared about his older brother.

Maybe he was pretending something else to hide what he was really feeling, what he'd always felt: that his feckless older brother was useless, erratic, volatile, unstable, and altogether in the way.

In the way of—what?

Kyger's long-held and deeply buried desire to be the master of Waybury? It wasn't something his brother would ever admit, but Lujan had seen the way Kyger looked at him when he came back home drunk and spent his time at Waybury hung over, in bed, or chasing the maids, or coddling and cuddling up to Jancie for the past year.

Kyger hated him. Hated that he was older, that he was to inherit, that he would get everything and Kyger would get nothing.

This accident was tailor-made for Kyger. Maybe he was hoping it would prove life-altering . . .

Or—

. . . *No, no, no—don't let that thought even sneak into your mind . . .*

It came anyway: . . . *life-threatening? . . .*

Lujan felt like all the air had been expunged from his body. And his head—it felt like a huge stone ball with a hammer pounding against it.

He had to be delirious to be thinking like this. He wanted to sleep. He wanted someone to just knock him unconscious so he could sleep.

He felt Jancie's hand on his shoulder. "Take this." Her soft, soft voice, her soft, compliant hands, her soft, succulent nether flesh—he wanted it, he wanted to be coherent enough, well enough, to want it . . .

He obediently drank the potion Jancie gave him. Somehow, in concert with that, she and Kyger left the room, left him to his thoughts, his delirium, his own devices . . .

Left together—always together—

He wasn't imagining it. Right now, they were together. Did they really want that badly to be together?

Enough to—hoping it would . . . ?

. . . *and then Jancie would be free . . .*

But then there was Jancie—so cool, so hot, so aloof, so involved, and yet not. Never another utterance of *that word.* The *word* that had sent him haring off to London.

Jancie. What about Jancie? She would be free . . . Did she? Want to be free of him? After all that succulent sex, all they had shared?

It was inconceivable to him. But—here he was again, beaten down, bedridden, and Jancie and Kyger were together some other where in the house.

He started drifting off into that shadowy world where everything was blurred, dark, moving, shifting, becoming something else. Jancie—was she in the room, testing him to see if he were oblivious enough for her to spend the night with Kyger?

God, was he that jealous of Kyger? You never found *Kyger* flat on his back, ever—yet this was the second incident that laid *him* low.

No—wait: the third time . . .

The *third* . . . The first being the day he'd returned from London, after that stupid topple down the steps. On his back, woozy, stupefied . . .

Jancie beside him. In and out of Jancie.

What was happening here?

And who would be stupid enough to engineer these attacks on him and think he wouldn't be caught out?

Jancie? Sick to death of him after three weeks, now she was privy to what he was really like? Wishing she'd accepted Kyger?

But Kyger couldn't offer her what he could, and God help him, the sex couldn't be that spectacular, either.

Could it?

His head whirled. He wouldn't want to wager on anything today. Even that Jancie still . . . *not that word*—desired was better—him; she was too disengaged, and somewhat removed, in spite of her heat and all-enveloping sensuality in bed.

Did she have regrets? Did she wish now she'd married Hugo?

Hell and hounds—Hugo. He hadn't thought for two minutes about his father since he'd returned from London.

Where the hell was Hugo, and why wasn't he back at Waybury?

He could be anywhere, doing awful things to dishonor Mother—anything he wanted, out of sight of family and the constraints of his world.

Anything.

Out of sight, and thinking that no one would take his absence into consideration? Still lusting after Jancie behind the scenes? Whoring and fucking over every woman in sight while he still had his eye on that ultimate prize? And plotting to remove his worthless older son from the picture?

God, he was delusional. This was beyond insanity—it had to be whatever drug he'd been given to soothe his headache. He couldn't be rational, thinking like this about his father and his brother.

And his wife.

. . . This creeping mistrust—it was the drugs, whatever they'd given him, that was making everything fuzzy and threatening.

They weren't all against him, separately or together. No one was plotting his demise. No one was trying to kill him.

There wasn't any reason. They all had to see: he had willingly come back home, he was completely sober, he felt more satisfied in these early days of his hastily concocted marriage than he ever could have imagined; he intended to be faithful, and he was almost ready to become a staunch country gentleman with a half-dozen children hanging from his coattails.

All of this, because of Jancie. All of this, Jancie made him want, Jancie made him feel.

It could not be that no one had noticed.

And yet—he'd toppled down the steps, eaten something that near poisoned his system, taken a bad fall from his horse. His brother and wife were continually thrown together, and Hugo had gone missing somewhere in London, or, for all he knew, he was at the local inn, holing up and plotting and planning to take Jancie away through nefarious means.

. . . God, he was going crazy. If anyone could read his mind right now, with him thinking everyone was plotting against him . . .

He sounded like a lunatic, even in his own mind.

His head was pounding. The medication wasn't helping except to magnify every one of his vague apprehensions. They felt real, they felt as if danger was imminent and he could die . . .

. . . three seemingly innocent incidents . . . so close together, too.

And three seemingly innocent explanations: a small rug on a slippery floor near a staircase, a spoiled piece of meat that somehow had been served to him, a loose cinch on his saddle . . .

. . . how—who? . . . Anyone in his family, if someone meant him harm. It was too easy to do . . . and while Kyger and Jancie did not have access to the town house, it wasn't inconceivable that someone there could be helping them, or that Hugo had planned that little incident on the stairs.

IF he believed—really—that someone wished him ill . . .

He was ill, broken by that fall. Everything broken, including his common sense, and his rational mind.

He needed desperately to fall asleep. Sleep would heal everything. He felt as if he could sleep forever . . .

They want me to . . .

That insidious little voice inside his head just wouldn't let go.

Kyger would inherit, and Jancie could choose between the *better* Galliard men. So any of them could be orchestrating this, or two of them together.

It made so much sense.

They'd always wished he'd go away like a bad dream, his father and Kyger.

Only Olivia had had faith. And Jancie. Once. Enough to marry him. Enough to have the guts to say *that word* to him.

And what had he given her in return? Scorn, contempt, disrespect . . .

Not how Kyger would have treated her.

Or his father, who would have been so grateful that this nubile, fertile beautiful young woman—wanted—him that . . .

. . . that . . .

He was drenched in sweat. The room was whirling. Jancie came to him. The daughter of the long-thought-dead partner . . . who had found Hugo somehow and made him feel indebted enough so that Jancie, in gratitude, was now the center of their lives . . .

Really—you thought I was grateful for all your father had done? Grateful to be his paid servant?

What? Wait—he reached out to touch that thought and it evaporated. Of course she was grateful—what else had she had? That stupid old man who was her father? Useless old bastard insinuating himself into their lives again.

There was nothing for him here, if that had been his thought. Nothing. It was all Olivia's, all Hugo's now, soon to be his unless—unless . . .

Grateful . . .

Not even that he'd married her—to keep her father satisfied, keep things the way they always had been . . . ?

Wait—wait—there was something there and he couldn't quite get hold of it . . .

Yes . . . yes—Jancie. What was it?

". . . grateful he came up alive . . ."

Voices, standing over him. Familiar. The vicar? Last rites—?
What? Grateful he was alive? Were they?

He tried to open his eyes. Fuzzy. Dizzy. Damn it all . . . they
were all there, surrounding him, come together to finish what
they had started.

". . . he was much more feverish . . . better now . . ."

Jancie's voice, something cold on his forehead. Another couple
of inches and she could smother him.

He took a deep breath, planning his strategy . . .

*Strategy—hadn't he been planning a strategy . . . was he losing
his mind or his memory?*

". . . another day—" Kyger now, ". . . he'll be fine . . ."

I'll be dead . . .

". . . that's a relief then . . ."

Oh Jesus—he knew that voice.

Hugo. The conspirators all together now. The danger was
real.

Hugo had come back.

Chapter Fifteen

Oh dear lord, Hugo was home, Lujan had had yet another accident, and now what was she going to do?

Jancie felt a moment of pure panic. With Hugo in the house, and Lujan suspiciously incapacitated, she would be constrained at every turn.

Owww. What are you thinking?

Oh, ever-practical Emily, roundly scolding her and rightly so. Her first concern should be for Lujan, who looked frail and diminished, lying there with his eyes closed and his senses whirling.

She wasn't yet ready to say this accident was suspicious—but it was certainly strange there had been three incidents following one upon the other in the three weeks since he'd returned from London.

She hated seeing him like this, but the vulnerable Lujan was infinitely preferable to the arrogant one. It made all her loving instincts come to the fore. When he was like this, he needed her, he leaned on her, and it could be that he loved her a little bit, too.

But none of that solved her dilemma: Hugo was in the house and it made everything that much more difficult.

She should just concentrate on Lujan. Make sure that no one

could harm him further. Investigate that loose cinch—see if it was a careless mistake or if someone had meant for him to take a fall.

She probably should talk with him, and see what he was feeling about the accident, but he had been in no condition to talk at all for the past two days.

He kept chasing everyone out, barely taking any food unless it was hand-fed by Mrs. Ancrum, and not before she tasted it first.

How odd that was. He was so insistent. But then, he'd had that bout with something in his food last week.

Surely a coincidence?

What now?

She sat beside his bed that evening, waiting for him to awaken. Emily was curled up by his side, not unlike the way she had comforted Olivia, *mrowing* softly.

He wasn't so awful, if Emily wanted to be by his side.

But that solved nothing for her. When he awakened, she would have to hide her devotion, her anxiety. Pretend everything was perfectly normal.

And she would have to find secret moments to pursue her search. Her dual search, now. The mystery of Gaunt was suddenly running in a parallel line in her mind.

Kyger came to the door. "How is he?"

"No change, still sleeping."

"Rank carelessness," he murmured. "But whose?"

She waved away the comment. "Don't—"

"No, I won't. Come downstairs, then. Let him sleep."

She didn't want to, but there was no reason for her to stay, and no reason to refuse either Hugo's company or Kyger's.

She rose reluctantly to follow Kyger out of the room, turning back to look at Emily

But Emily wasn't there.

She went out into the hallway. Kyger was halfway down the stairs.

And from somewhere far away, Jancie heard that hard crickling sound rolling down the hallway floor.

Pretending again. Everyone in this house was pretending, and Lujan felt so constricted he didn't know what he was going to do.

Even Mrs. Ancrum, seated by his side and feeding him broth after she had taken her own healthy swallow of the steaming liquid, even she was pretending that this was something anyone would do on any given night, and not something she'd been ordered to do.

Humor him, Hugo had said, and she did, but he was starting to feel somewhat ridiculous—ten years old—at her babyish urging of him to eat.

God, enough of this.

He sat up abruptly. "Mrs. Ancrum."

"Sir."

"We're done here."

"Yes, sir."

She began cleaning up, piling everything neatly on her tray, folding napkins around the utensils she had used, and finally withdrawing without a further word.

There. That was better, more normal—he felt much more himself today. He felt a clarity in his thinking, and a sense of being in control that he hadn't felt in days.

The solution had come to him this morning, elegant and simple: he'd just go back to London, and he would never be alone in this house ever again . . . or at least until he had unmasked his enemy

At this point, much as he hated to believe it, he had to count Jancie among those who might want to do him ill.

The only answer was to leave—now—no, after a bath and a shave. Go back to London and sort all of this out with a clear mind, clear head; go somewhere he could see it all objectively.

No drinking. No whores. No distractions so he could figure out why he was being attacked, why it was so critical that one of his family get him out of the way now.

It struck him, too, how Jancie seemed to be at the center of it. If she hadn't come to Waybury, if he hadn't married her, if she weren't Edmund Renbrook's daughter—

And why *had* he married her? The reasons seemed so specious now: so Kyger wouldn't have her; to keep her from marrying Hugo; and to stave off her father. All decisions borne of the passion of the moment, and now his uncontrollable passion for her.

His own fault. He had started the flirtation with her out of boredom, to add some edge and excitement to the endless days preceding Olivia's death.

In those days, he had wanted both to be the son Olivia thought he was, and to get away with seducing Jancie in his family's sight without the consequences.

Just to prove he could.

But the end result was, he rushed the consequences, and now, conceivably, she wanted him dead.

Or Kyger did. Or Hugo.

His reckless life of dissipation had finally led down the road to this. His family dead set against him, and the one who owed him the most loyalty and gratitude was probably the instigator of it all.

Well, enough thinking about it. He knew what he had to do, and that was to get out and get away.

The ever-discreet March would help him. And no one would know until they were long gone.

The house was eerily quiet. No one had come down for dinner except Jancie, and now everything had gotten cold on the sideboard.

She picked at her food, wondering why Lujan hadn't rung for dinner, wondering where Kyger was, and not a little shaken by that ghostly, rolling, marbley sound that seemed to follow her down the stairs.

Emily was among the missing, too.

Maybe she ought to just go upstairs and check on Lujan. She'd rather have gone and examined the photographs again, but Hugo's unexpected presence in the house was a constraint.

For all she knew, he was in Olivia's room right now, on his knees, begging her forgiveness in heaven. But not, please Lord, searching under the footboard of the bed where *her* secret was hidden.

She didn't know why those photographs haunted her. Maybe it was because Gaunt seemed to her to be almost a symbol of the missing diamonds ... and her father's missing life—and that if she could solve the mystery of his disappearance, she would finally find out all the other truths, and they would not be Hugo's truths then.

Or Olivia's.

Do you really want to know the truth—about everything?

There were times she wasn't so sure, because she cared for Lujan too much, and hadn't loved Kyger enough.

But they had nothing to do with Hugo's betrayals. She was certain of that. And to this minute, she still believed that marrying Lujan had been the only way she could stay on at Waybury and try to discover what had really happened all those years ago.

That she had fallen in love with him was inconsequential to that. If he ever discovered the real reason why she had married him, he would never forgive her, and her odyssey here, and her marriage to him, would be over.

She had been very canny to comprehend that she should not let herself love him, but not for the obvious reasons; her own treachery had always been reason enough, and she'd be lying to herself otherwise.

She had been walking a very thin line here, convincing herself that the one had nothing to do with the other, and whatever she found would not impact Lujan—or her.

She'd been wrong.

Just the photographs of Gaunt and the way they had seized hold of her imagination . . . she hadn't expected that. Hadn't prepared her for feeling that she wanted to find justice for Gaunt as well as for her father.

She could do nothing about that tonight, much as she wanted to. Her first two close and hurried examinations of the photographs had proved nothing; there was nothing in those poses that was not usual in photographs of that sort.

Which made her feel an urgency to pore over them again.

But not with Hugo wandering around the house, not with Lujan falling off horses and tumbling down stairs. Not with that rolling, marbley sound haunting her.

That had to be Emily. Somewhere in the house, Emily had found a marble or a stone that so intrigued her that she was endlessly batting it up and down the hallway.

But it seemed otherworldly sometimes, the way she heard it rolling when she least expected it. And that Emily seemed nowhere in sight.

Strange, disparate things.

She felt vaguely discomfited suddenly, as if, at any moment, Hugo would find her out.

It always came back to Hugo.

She wondered if she weren't a little scared of Hugo.

She was probably right to be. He still held the power. He still could remarry. There could be other sons, other heirs. He could cut Lujan off and out. He could banish Kyger altogether.

He could have . . .

But why would he? What would either he or Kyger gain by hurting Lujan?

It made no sense. These incidents had to be random accidents. Lujan was not that careless. He had a fine sense of self-preservation, if any of his gossiped-about exploits in London were true.

Lujan would always land on his feet, she thought. She was the one in danger. She was the one prying into Hugo's past, trying to dig up buried secrets, opening all the closed doors.

The house was a little spooky when no one was around. And it didn't seem likely that Kyger or Hugo would come keep her company. She finally decided to go upstairs and check on Lujan. See if he wanted dinner. See if he were finally awake.

All the doors on the bedroom floor were closed, making the hallway, dimly lit by gas sconces, seem a little spooky.

She stepped onto the landing a little reluctantly, pausing for a moment to listen for that rolling sound.

The silence was like a thick, woolen blanket. Like fog. Opaque, dense, creeping into her bones. The way she felt the first time she'd walked in the door.

No cats . . . she shivered as she remembered Olivia's dictum. And Emily howling, mourning her death . . .

Best not think about that. Better to think about Lujan awake and waiting, and wanting . . .

For the first time in days, she thought about the wanting and the sex, and the way he had handled her and spread her and taken her.

A different kind of urgency possessed her suddenly, burgeoning instantly from memory and desire, and the thought that perhaps this was why she had come to him tonight, and nothing else.

And now she couldn't wait. *Lujan . . . !*
She pushed open the door, and stepped inside their room.
Their empty room.

She raced unthinkingly down the hallway to Kyger's room. No
answer to her imperious knocking. Where? Where? Kyger would
know what to do, why he'd left.
Or maybe something had happened to him? What?
Out into the hallway, feeling panicked, feeling a presence, eyes
watching, again.
And the rolling sound . . . coming out of the shadows somewhere down the hallway, distant, ghostly, something rolling, rolling . . .
She ran down the stairs, calling, "Kyger! Hugo!" their names
echoing eerily under the pounding sound of her feet. Where were
they? How could she suddenly be so alone?
"Jancie!" Kyger appeared like a ghost near the library at the
opposite end of the downstairs hallway. "What's wrong?"
She ran into his arms. "He's gone."
"He's gone? Who's gone? Lujan? Why are you so surprised?"
She was taken aback by his cavalier answer, and she pushed
his arms away. "Why aren't you?"
"My dear Jancie, this is what Lujan does. When things get
tight, when emotions are involved, when any prospect of his taking on some responsibility comes to the fore, Lujan ducks and
runs."
"And when he thinks someone is trying to hurt him?" Jancie
demanded, prickling up. Defending Lujan? Really? Or just wanting to be contrary in the face of Kyger's indifference.
"They were accidents—coincidences. Honestly, Jancie, who
would want to hurt him?"
"You?" she murmured without thinking.
"That's a hell of a thing to say," Kyger said with a hint of
anger in his voice. "Lujan's done what he always does—he disappears. He's probably gone to the town house, and right now, he's
probably at a whorehouse. That, in sum, is Lujan."
And that was brutal, Jancie thought; he didn't have to put it
that way on the heels of her terror at Lujan's disappearance.

"Well then, I'm going after him," she said. "I'm going to get him."

"You don't want to do that."

"I don't? Why don't I?"

"Because you'll have to haul him out from between some other woman's legs, and you don't want to do that."

She hated him then. He hadn't needed to parse out the bald reality. He just really didn't have to say that. "You do it, then."

"He'll come back. He always does."

She refused to back down. "I'll get Hugo to go."

"Jancie, this is Lujan's way. Didn't he walk away the day after you were married? There's no difference. When anything or anyone gets too close to him, he reacts by running away, whether it's a woman or a possible enemy. He never stays around to find out which is which. So don't interfere, don't go. You'll be happier in the long run."

He sounded so matter-of-fact about it. He was shrugging it off as usual behavior, as if he really didn't care. He had his place, his work that he would shoulder for as long as Lujan relinquished it to him.

And he had the superior moral stance: he was here, Lujan was not, and if something happened to Lujan, so much the better—he didn't even have to step up to become, in essence, Lujan.

Lujan—only better—she remembered she had thought that the moment she met him. What had she sensed then that was a reality now?

"You hate him," she said softly.

"I don't hate him. He's my brother. I have no feelings about him whatsoever after all these years. I'm rather sorry you do. This is not unusual behavior—it's nothing to get upset about. So take my advice, Jancie. Don't go after him. You're better off not knowing anything more."

She stared at him a long minute and then whirled away. He was wrong. Something was wrong, and this *was* the time to go after him.

. . . Or was it?

She felt baffled, her initial panic seeping away at Kyger's certainty that there was nothing mysterious in his disappearance.

But for Lujan not to tell anyone, just to sneak away like that . . .

Maybe it *was* just possible that Lujan was being childish and irresponsible and not wanting to deal with things.

Her wedding night was proof of that.

And now she didn't know what to do.

It was easier to do nothing. Lujan would return eventually. Kyger was certain of it. Hugo reassured her about it the next morning.

And then off they went to spend their day, leaving her to her own devices.

Even with Hugo back at Waybury, the house seemed preternaturally silent and empty after they'd gone.

Maybe that was a good thing. She felt so off balance, she needed time to think, to plan. She felt crowded, as if events were piling up one after the other and coming too close to the bone.

She felt as if Kyger had gone over to the side of total disinterest in Lujan's affairs altogether. She did not need an enemy in this house if Lujan already believed he had one.

And last night—she'd been half scared out of her wits last night—between Lujan's defection and the sentient feel of the house.

It had to be all her feelings of guilt. Her sense of being watched, her ongoing searches, and the ethics of filching the family album for her own purposeful prying.

She hadn't ever felt that way before. In all the years she had been here, she had had no qualms about pursuing her course, once she understood what it was.

But now, there were more layers: her marriage to Lujan, his coincidental accidents. The mystery of Gaunt. The discovery of the photographs. The sense of being watched. That haunting, rolling sound.

Lord, she wished she could talk all this over with her father. There was no one else, and he was so far away. She had lost Kyger just when she most needed his helping hand. No, she had depended on having his help, his approval, and she had ignored his perspective, and his ingrained loyalty to his family, in the process.

Hiding her own true purpose, thinking that everyone saw Hugo as the traitor she did.

The truth was, she was the interloper, she was the one they ought to have been suspicious of, and yet somehow, everything that had transpired was centered around her. And all the while she was busy infiltrating their family and their lives so successfully that she had married the putative heir.

It was this, when she thought about it, that was so confusing. She had accomplished what she'd set out to do, and she had the rest of her married life to pursue the rest. *If* Lujan ever returned, *if* he never discovered she'd had other motives for marrying him.

So why did she feel this growing sense of urgency now? She wished she hadn't come to love him, because that meant nothing to him, and it meant she had not an ally in this house, and she was feeling very, very wary.

Owww.

Emily stalked into the hallway, with an indignant expression on her cat-face.

No friends?

Emily, as always, her friend, her companion, her guide. How could she forget Emily?

What do I do?

Oowww. The house is empty. You know what you want to do.

Go after Lujan.

Mrroowww. No. Find Gaunt.

Show me how.

Oww. Why not now?

Why not? She looked up and down the hallway as if she expected a maid or possibly Bingham to appear out of thin air. Especially Bingham, seemingly always there.

There was no one. And Kyger and Hugo were not in the house. So she could just get the album, take it to her room, and really examine it. Take all the time she needed with Lujan gone.

It was a step, a plan. Something to do, at a moment when she felt helpless to do anything.

She ran upstairs, with Emily following close behind. Quickly down the hallway to Olivia's room, slipping in like a shadow, as if ghosts were looking over her shoulder, as if eyes were watching her.

Emily jumped up on the bed to watch Jancie as she groped under the footboard, *mrowing* as she pulled out the dust-covered book and magnifying glass she had had the forethought not to return to the library.

She lifted her skirt and tucked the book under her waistband, and the magnifying glass in a pocket.

A precaution only—if anyone should see her.

Carefully to the door now as Emily jumped down and started scrabbling under the bed.

Into the hallway quickly—and suddenly she heard the rolling sound—from behind her, or from down the hallway or, in her mind, she didn't know.

Just the sustained, scary, marbley, rolling sound . . .

Where was Emily?

She thrust open the door to Olivia's bedroom. Emily was right on the threshold.

Mrroww. What took you so long?

She stalked out of the room, sat emphatically on her haunches, and slanted a considering look up at Jancie.

Well?

The curious thing was the sudden silence—so stunning, complete. No more marbley, rolling sound. No sound at all.

Just Emily's golden eyes watching her as intently as if she were a mouse.

Emily's eyes only?

Fear clutched at her vitals.

The sensation of being watched was as palpable as a touch.

She pulled the door to Olivia's bedroom shut and ran for her room, slamming the door behind her.

For the first time since she'd come to Waybury House, she felt utterly and completely alone, and consumed with fear. As if there were unseen forces operating against her.

It was utterly irrational, she knew. No one had the slightest idea that she was acting as an agent for her father. No one knew how obsessed she'd become about Gaunt's disappearance.

No one cared. Now that she was married to Lujan, she had fulfilled a purpose: she was his vessel, potentially the mother of his children. No need to care or worry about her, or her motives, or her father.

She was responsible for all of that, and now, for prying into family circumstances that were better left untouched.

She had no idea what she would do beyond five minutes from now.

But for now—she had the photograph album, she had the magnifying glass. And she had hours in which no one might come looking for her.

And daylight, pouring through the windows.

She didn't know why, but she was shaking. She didn't know what she was searching for.

Maybe it didn't matter. She pulled a chair up to the window, opened the album, and began again to scrutinize the details.

Lujan was stunned that he did not feel any more secure in London. If anything, he felt as if he had abandoned Waybury.

What an odd thing to feel.

In the town house, with all the servants around, and the solid mahogany doors protecting him, he felt no safer than if he were at Waybury.

Strange.

He felt alone.

Even stranger.

Even March, hardly a stranger, had thought his flight precipitous, and that he ought not to have left Jancie alone at Waybury.

He couldn't think clearly. He felt as if his whole world had turned upside down with just the notion that Jancie could possibly want to harm him. Could conceivably want a better choice of husband and was plotting to kill him.

Or his brother, acting on twenty years of festering anger at him.

Oh, he had made enemies in his family, all right. Treating Kyger like his indentured servant. Treating Jancie like a whore. Discounting Hugo's hopes and wishes altogether . . .

Wait—that sounded like he was having regrets . . . he never regretted anything. What was done was done—he couldn't go back, he wouldn't make amends, it was against his philosophy in general to apologize for anything.

So when had he developed a conscience?

He hadn't—he wouldn't . . .

But something was very different—these coincidental little accidents had scared him. Jancie's dispassion irritated him. His obsessive desire to root himself in her appalled him. She cared too little, and that gave her too much power.

He couldn't give that up. He would not be whipsawed by a chit he'd given status and money to by marrying her. He'd divorce her first, but he couldn't stop thinking about their last coupling, his last thorough, naked exploration of her hole. The way she had willingly spread herself for him. The way she had come for him.

Goddamn . . .

He would not be a slave to it, but goddamn, he couldn't stop wanting more of it. Couldn't stop thinking about it.

Even with the possibility that Jancie wanted someone else, something else, he couldn't quell his raging need to plant himself in her.

He knew the answer to that—head to the docks, get a tart's worth of pussy and shoot his wad. Except it wasn't the answer anymore.

There were no answers, either to who wished to harm him or why no woman's cunt would do for his penis but his wife's.

Now he was in London, he couldn't have her cunt. If he were back at Waybury, he'd have to watch his back.

He had to stay away. He needed the distance to sit down and figure out just what was going on, and who was really his enemy.

But more than that, he needed a drink and he needed a good humping, mindless fucking.

No—

He needed his wife.

Here now, in this strong, undiluted morning light of the bedroom window, with the magnifying glass, Jancie could see things in the photographs that she hadn't noticed before: the pattern on the carpet, the lace insets on Olivia's dress, the handkerchief tucked in her hand, the carved leather of the saddle on the pony, the pinstripe in Hugo's suit, the rose motif on the back rail of the sofa on which he was posed with his son.

Nothing nothing nothing . . .

But what had she thought, that something would jump out at

her? As if she were more aware of the nuances, the intricacies than Hugo or Olivia? As if they themselves hadn't pored over the pictures in the aftermath of Gaunt's disappearance?

And then buried them in the library?

Actually, when she thought about it, that seemed odd. Why hide the book rather than just throw it away, if the memories inside were so painful? And they must have been.

Nowhere in the house was there any sign, any memento, any other picture of Gaunt. Only this album, covertly placed among a hundred other books to look no different, raise no eyebrows, evoke no curiosity.

Olivia would not want to forget her missing son. Jancie was as certain of that as she was that it was daylight. It was entirely possible Olivia might hide a book of photographs in an inconspicuous place where she could surreptitiously take them out and look at them.

But Hugo wouldn't. He'd want to obliterate a bad memory. Pretend it had never existed.

She turned back to the photographs.

Gaunt in his sailor suit, the sailor's hat cocked jauntily to one side, one hand in an insouciant salute. A scrape on his knee unnoticeable except in this bright light and with the magnifying glass. One untied shoelace. A slightly rumpled tie.

No clues.

Gaunt with Hugo. Hugo so stiff, unbending, years younger, as he must have looked when her father had known him. Handsome, though—she could see vestiges of both Kyger and Lujan in those youthful features. Gaunt's face, however, was as yet unformed. Baby cheeks. Mischievous eyes. Grubby hands clutching some small pebbles.

And Hugo almost at once removed from him, as if he didn't want to soil himself with the excesses of childhood. Hugo, who had groveled in the dirty diamond mines of Kaamberoo, now the picture of a pristine gentleman with a dirty, boisterous child.

Gaunt's christening photograph, Olivia holding him delicately in her lap. Gaunt at one year—holding someone's hand, as if he had just started walking.

Gaunt standing beside his pony, one hand holding the reins.

The family photograph. The boys standing behind the sofa on which Hugo had posed with Gaunt, and Gaunt between his seated parents. No hint here of any family emotion, either. The boys looked uncomfortable, and Olivia looked as if she were restraining Gaunt.

Only the look in her eyes gave away her affection. And Hugo was staring at her as if he disapproved altogether.

Nothing else.

She felt a keening disappointment that she had found nothing more, that the mystery would never be solved, not by her, not in this life.

It had been an unholy waste of time to try to pluck a clue from thin air. Gaunt was gone forever, and the only thing she could do was close the book on him, too.

Chapter Sixteen

She sat for a long time, she didn't know how long, her arms wound around the album, Emily curled at her feet.

She didn't know what to do. For some reason she was finding it hard to relinquish the album, even though it wasn't hers to keep. It had given up no secrets, and yet she couldn't bear to put it back up on that upmost library shelf where nobody would find it again, ever.

She would kill Gaunt all over again if she did that . . .

. . . why did she think of it as *killing* him?

It would be the same as if Hugo deemed it time to dismantle Olivia's bedroom. It would be like losing her all over again.

Yet—it might be time. Time to put all of that behind them, time for her to stop acting like a Gothic heroine and start being Lujan's wife.

Time to acknowledge that Hugo had not cheated her father, and that his good fortune was all due to luck and a fortuitous marriage. Had her father been that much more aggressive, he might have had Olivia as his wife and Waybury as his domain.

It was just fate, nothing more, that had put her father at the explosion site, and Hugo at the mercy of the kidnapping thieves.

She had to believe that. Truly, to close the book, she had to believe that.

It was time to stop all this skulking around and thinking there were plots and betrayals everywhere. And Gaunt had to have run away. Or been kidnapped. By the same thieves who'd almost killed Hugo? A fanciful idea, not out of the realm of possibility, but more likely to be a plot point in a penny-dreadful than to have any basis in reality.

And perhaps Gaunt *was* alive somewhere, if indeed he had been taken, and had no memory of Waybury, his parents, or his brothers.

It didn't matter now. Olivia was dead and presumably with him in heaven, and Hugo had come to terms with it years ago.

Only she, prying into things that were none of her business, cared about any of this at all.

She'd have to write and tell her father—she was at the end of the road, and there was nothing more she could do.

Mrrrrowwww. You won't.

Emily was right, she wouldn't. She felt inside herself—she couldn't yet let go. Even Olivia . . .

She rose slowly and, with Emily following, went across the hall to Olivia's room.

The air inside was suffused with a stale odor compounded of illness, lavender, and disuse, something Jancie hadn't particularly noticed in her urgency to conceal the album.

It was shadowy in there—no lamps had been lit, no shrine had been erected. And dusty—the minuscule motes floating in the beam of sunlight that infiltrated between the curtain panels.

The carpet had gotten dirty, too—Emily, scrambling at her feet, raised little puffs as she leapt on a drift of dust and chased it under the bed.

And it was cold. No fires had been lit since Olivia's death, and Jancie could easily believe she had been the only one even to come into the room since the funeral.

Thus we die and we're forgotten, she thought. But she hadn't forgotten Olivia. She would never forget Olivia. She had never known her own mother, who had died in childbirth. How could she forget Olivia, who had been so kind?

Except to the cat. And yet she'd tacitly welcomed Emily's comfort in her last days. How strange that had been, and wonderful, in a way.

She heard Emily under the bed, scratching at something, and then a few minutes later she appeared from under the bed, puffs of dust on her whiskers.

Oooowww.

"I think you're right," Jancie said. "It's time to stop this."

Ow. A blunt assessment to say the least.

She'd keep the album, too. Tuck it right back under the footboard and leave it there for the time being.

"Emily?"

Emily had gone back under the bed. *Scratch, scratch, scratch . . .*

"Emily!"

She darted out from the footboard, batting something with her paws.

Enough. If she left, Emily would follow.

She was just at the door when she heard it—the rolling sound, in the hallway, faint, hard—like a marble or a pebble rolling across the hallway floor.

She whirled back into the room. Slammed the door. Stepped on something as she impatiently scooped up Emily. Picked up the dust drift, tucked it in her pocket, and opened the door.

Her heart pounded, her hands went ice cold. The sound was there, constant, rolling, rolling, closer to her and closer.

Or it was in her mind. At that moment, she didn't know . . . she couldn't see the object. But she knew it wasn't big, it wasn't loud, it just *was*—elusive, illusory, phantasmic—a constant, ghostly sound—that followed her as she eased shakily out of Olivia's room, and crossed on tiptoes to her bedroom door.

It took a half-hour for her to calm down. And she spent a part of that time brushing the dust off Emily's whiskers and fur.

Aarrrowww. Emily did not like to be handled like that. But lord, she was filthy with little picks of something that looked like sawdust under her claws. One scramble under the bed, and she had gotten this dirty?

It was good to have something mindless to do while she considered why that mysterious rolling sound so scared her.

She didn't believe in ghosts. It was conceivable a spiritualist might think it was Olivia trying to send her a message, but it had sounded too real to her.

And it wasn't Emily at play, either.

Some unseen hand, then. Which she couldn't believe, either. It wasn't any more an explanation than thinking it was ghosts.

MRRRRROOWWWW—Emily kicked off and twisted out of her arms and jumped onto the bed. *Owww.* She rubbed against Jancie's arm, and slanted a look at her. *Scare you.*

No. Who? Why? Forget that. Her own too-inventive imagination overreacting to everything.

She pulled at a puff on Emily's ear. So much dust. But then, the album had been covered every time she extracted it from under the footboard. The room hadn't been cleaned in months.

Maybe it was time to clear it out and clean it up.

Not her decision, though.

She broached Hugo about it at dinner, on a night that Kyger was absent and they were dining alone.

He stared at her coldly. "I'm sorry? You want to dismantle Olivia's room? Whyever would you? Have you been going in there?"

"I—" What to tell him? She didn't expect this reaction from him, this frostiness at what would be a common ritual two months after someone passed away. "I've gone in several times just to—"

To what? Make certain everything was in order? What could be out of order? To pray? She wasn't a praying person. To feel closer to Olivia? A woman who was her employer? No reason for her to want that in the general course of things.

"—because I miss her," she said finally. "I miss her, and her presence still fills that room."

"That's all well and good, Jancie, but I would appreciate it if we left Olivia's room untouched and unvisited."

She took a deep breath. "All right, if that's your wish."

"It is, and I hope I don't have to lock the room."

She shook her head. "No. I'll respect your wishes." And Gaunt could repose there then, close to Olivia, with no one disturbing him. Maybe it was the best decision. "I apologize that I haven't been more sensitive."

He stared at her for another minute and then bent to his oxtail soup. "I appreciate the fact that you miss her, Jancie."

But he didn't say that he missed her, too. They finished the meal in silence, and she went, alone as always, to her room.

She was ready for bed; she had laid her dress on the bed to smooth it out before hanging it in the armoire. It was one of her mourning dresses, and everything showed on it, especially cat hair and dust.

But she was a little shocked at what a nest of dust drifts were ruffled around the hem. From Olivia's room, she supposed. That dusty.

She started brushing it all off when she felt a little lump in the pocket. She extracted it and its puff of dust, remembering she had stepped on it as she had grabbed Emily when she left Olivia's room.

She brushed away the dust. It was a small stone, irregular in shape, and pointed on one end. It looked like a pebble or a piece of broken glass.

Like the object that might make that ghostly, rolling sound in the hallway.

She turned it over in her fingers. There was one way to find out.

She knelt on the floor and flicked it with her middle finger and thumb. It caromed across the floor for a second and wedged up on one of the irregular edges.

But perhaps that wasn't a fair test. Her room was carpeted, furnished, didn't have an echo.

She picked the object up and opened her bedroom door. Knelt again and flicked the stone toward Olivia's room. Again, it rolled crazily and stopped. Slight crickling, rolling sound. Nothing sustained. Nothing proved.

And then Emily came from nowhere to jump the stone.

She watched in fascination as Emily batted it all the way down the hallway and back.

Maybe the ghost sound. Maybe she shouldn't be chasing a piece of rock down the hallway at this hour. She swiped it up as Emily made another pass down the hallway.

Ooooowww. Emily didn't like that—she was having too much fun. *She* wasn't disappointed, Jancie thought. She hadn't been abandoned or threatened . . .

Was that a threat? What Hugo had said about locking the bedroom door if she continued to go in there?

She felt like going into Olivia's room right this minute. Instead, she climbed in bed, shoved the stone under her pillow, and sat considering her unexpected feeling that Hugo had issued her a warning.

Emily jumped up beside her. *Owww. It was.*

Was it? Had he taken it for granted that no one visited the room? Did *he?*

She rubbed Emily's ears. She was imagining things. The room was dirty, and needed a thorough cleaning. If Hugo wanted it to molder into dust, fine.

But why would he *lock* it?

Forget it—he was just irritated with her for taking the liberty of even entering Olivia's room. Although why—when he knew how fond she had been of Olivia—

. . . *locking* the room to keep her out?

She was making too much of it.

Mrrooww. Are you?

She didn't know what to make of it, actually.

Maybe Hugo's intensity about it seemed really overstated under the circumstances, even if he felt he wanted to keep Olivia's room sacrosanct for the foreseeable future.

No. No. It was perfectly understandable. Olivia hadn't been gone all that long. Of course he wouldn't want anything to change. Not for a while yet. No matter how much dust and dirt accumulated.

It was her own perception: she was still seeing plots everywhere just when she had decided it was time to stop pursuing this course.

Maybe she ought to take just one more look around Olivia's room . . . ?

Mrrroww. I'll come.

Penny-dreadful. Emily was such a loyal companion, perfectly willing to play the intelligent, perceptive shadow to the bumbling Gothic heroine.

What did she think she'd find in the dark, anyway?

Well, the one thing she could do was retrieve the album. If Hugo truly meant to keep the room closed up, the album would, in effect, be buried. And she wasn't sure she was finished with it yet.

So there was one reason to circumvent Hugo's request. And the other was that he conceivably *could* have a lock put on the room as early as tomorrow—if he truly believed that she would not respect his wishes.

Ah, it was only a bluff. It was just too odd that he'd want to lock up the room just because she went into it now and again.

And since he felt so strongly about it, of course she would do as he wished.

But only because she was going to pay her last visit, her last respects tonight.

Silence so thick it felt like cotton wool. Deep in the night, when no one was about, and the hallway was lit with one low-burning kerosene sconce that threw long shadows like dust drifts across the floor, Jancie found it easy to believe there were ghosts afoot.

The clock had struck one, and sometime after that, she tiptoed out of the bedroom, a lamp in hand, and across the hallway to Olivia's room, with Emily trailing behind her.

The door was closed, as it always was. It could even be locked, a thought that only occurred to her as she was about to turn the knob.

Her hand froze.

Suddenly, out of the thick silence, she heard the rolling, marbley sound. Her heart stopped—she turned the knob convulsively and was stunned to find it moved and the door fell open.

She ducked inside the room, pulling Emily with her, her breath constricted, her heart pounding like a hammer.

Dear heaven. The sound. The everlasting sound of something rolling across a bare wood floor was more frightening than seeing a ghost.

She had to get hold of herself. She'd be useless in the very little time she had to canvas the room. She felt a paralyzing urgency to just get out and leave everything—her suspicions, her fears, her resistance—moldering in the dust.

The album first.

She set the lamp on a nearby table as Emily nosed around the bed, and got down on her hands and knees at the footboard. Yes, thank heaven, it was still there. And the magnifying glass, which she'd tucked into the cover.

Good. Now she should just get out.

There was something in the atmosphere of the room: a flat, black stillness, unnatural, chilling. Breath-catching. *Go.*

Owwww.

She jumped, almost dropping the album.

Emily darted out from under the bed, suddenly, chasing something with her paws.

This was too scary. She felt utterly numb and immobile. She couldn't find the pulse even to begin a search. This was a stupid idea. Hugo was right—she should just let Olivia rest in peace.

There was nothing to find in here; she'd just skulk back to her bedroom and forget all her grandiose notions of solving mysteries . . .

. . . And what was Emily after, racing around like that?

Emily pounced at her feet, and she was certain for one shuddering moment that it was a mouse. But it was too small for a mouse—a piece of mouse maybe . . . no, it was hard, Emily was scratching at it, and she stooped and pulled it out of Emily's paws.

Emily's dirt-encrusted paws.

It was another stone, only much bigger, in a similar rough, irregular shape, covered with dirt and dust, nosed out from under the bed by Emily.

Under the bed.

There were always monsters under the bed, waiting to jump on you, kill you, dismember and bury you.

She took a long, deep breath. Time was wasting. She had to get out of there. She rolled the stone around between her fingers. One of two that Emily had batted out from under the bed.

So? Maybe it was a bigger-than-usual mouse dropping.

Time time time . . .

She took the lamp, pulled up the carpet, and set the lamp on the floor away from her, but close enough so it shed some light downward. This was dicey, she knew it; there would be very little light under the bed, but probably enough so she could see the accumulation of dust drifts.

And a handful of stones scattered underneath, very close to where she lay. And blackness. As if there were something else stored under the bed.

Oh, now she needed light. And she'd never been more frightened in her life. All those funny-shaped stones. All that dust.

She reached for the blackness, which she thought was limitless under the bed, and her hand touched wood. Lightweight wood. Crumbling wood. Sawdust or something dirt-like at the base of it. More stones.

Oh God . . .

Her first instinct was to run. And to try to extricate whatever it was from under the bed. But it was too scary. Someone might come, someone might see. Someone might be checking whether she was in her room.

She couldn't do this tonight. She needed daylight and sanity, she needed not to feel this creeping sense of vulnerability, of danger.

Time to get out of the room. She grabbed a handful of the stones and eased her way out from under the bed—

—and into the sudden, complete darkness of nothingness.

The sun woke her, pouring in through the window and across her face, an irritation when she was trying so hard to stay asleep, to keep her mind a blank; if she woke up, she would have to parse out what had happened last night, and she really didn't want to think about it.

Besides which, she was feeling dazed, as if her head was stuffed with cotton batting, and as if her mind was a sieve.

All right, she'd just stay in the bed then. It was probably the safest course until she could ascertain that Hugo was gone.

For certain, some other things were gone: the album, the stones, her credibility.

Her head hurt. She didn't want to move. She didn't want to see any of them, not even Kyger.

What had happened?

Owww. Emily, at the foot of the bed, curled up against her ankles.

Let's figure it out.

Oh, the last thing she wanted to do. The last she remembered, she was poking around under Olivia's bed, she'd found the stones, and the wood dust, and something else . . .

And had planned to go back this morning to explore further.

But she'd woken up in her own bed. And she didn't remember coming back here.

Had someone else been in the room?

She couldn't remember anything after touching the wood particles.

She looked at Emily. Emily stared back at her. *Yes.*

Yes what? Someone else was there?

Emily's gaze was steady, unwavering.

Yes.

Oh God—someone was there? Someone saw her?

Someone stopped her.

She bolted up from the pillows, her whole body bathed in ice and sweat. Fought to stay rational and not panic. Swallowed the fear in her mouth, her gut.

She couldn't do it. Her whole body convulsed with terror. Someone had been there. Someone had stopped her.

Hugo? Kyger? Who else?

What was under that bed that Hugo did not think anyone would ever find?

She had to get out of the house. NOW.

No—no—what she had to do was act as if nothing had happened.

Really? In her state of utter, abject fear?

She swallowed hard, took a deep breath, grabbed hold of the covers, and held on hard as she expelled it. Beat back the horror. The fear.

She had to.

Mroww. You will.

Emily had such faith. All right. For the both of them, she had to calm down and think clearly, if she were going to be able to negotiate this treacherous territory.

First. Act on the assumption that someone had found her, made certain that she would not continue her exploration of Olivia's room, took away everything she had found, and brought her to her room.

Unconscious.

She had to have been—she had no memory of anything past the moment she'd started to back out from under Olivia's bed.

First item—check Olivia's room. In daylight. If it was even accessible. Hugo had probably locked it up forever.

Second—get out of the house.

She would tell Hugo she was tired of waiting for Lujan to come around and come home, and she was going after him.

Good. That made sense; it sounded rational, and she didn't have to pretend to be a bored and annoyed wife. She was—she'd waited long enough for him to come back home.

She could convince Hugo of that and then she and Emily—surely Hugo could spare a driver—would go to London.

All right. Now she had to get dressed, simply as possible.

It was hard even to move a muscle to get out of bed. She forced herself, as Emily watched her every move curiously; she washed up perfunctorily, and grabbed the first shirtwaist and skirt she found.

Grabbed a brush—knocked over the stone she'd picked up in Olivia's room, picked that up, tucked it in her pocket again, went back to brushing her hair, and finally pinned it up.

Anything to keep busy, not to think.

Soon she'd have to think, to act. Now. She had to start, now.

She moved to the door, grasped the knob.

First step, and she felt panicked. What if it was locked from the outside? What if Hugo were waiting for her to open the door?

Oh God—she squeezed the doorknob and turned it. Pulled open the door.

No ghosts. No monsters waiting. Just silence in the hallway. The discreet sound of the maids starting their morning duties on the floor below. Sun pouring in from the stairwell window, making a square-paned pattern on the floor.

Nothing threatening. Nothing frightening.

No lock on Olivia's door.

That stopped her. She was certain as stones that Hugo would have already put a lock on the door.

. . . Did she dare—?

Was she crazy?

She had to know. She touched the stone in her pocket. There had been a dozen of them under the bed. Maybe a dozen more to be found . . .

Oww. Emily led the way, pacing across the hall and sitting on her haunches, waiting with a patient stare.

What did Emily know?

Mrowww. Secrets.

And Emily would never tell. Jancie was shaking as she wrapped her fingers around the knob.

. . . Or she could just walk away, and forget everything she'd ever thought.

She turned the knob. The door opened easily—too easily?

She stepped into the room and closed the door behind her.

Nothing was different. Nothing had changed between her last clear memory of last night, and this morning.

Oww. Are you sure?

Emily slithered under the bed, a clear signal that she must go down on her knees again. What did Emily know? What?

She was so loath to get down on her hands and knees again. She would be too vulnerable that way, too defenseless.

Owww. Most emphatic Emily.

She supposed she could lie flat on the opposite side of the bed, but then she'd be facing the door, and she had been counting on the light from the window to reveal whatever was under the bed.

All right. A quick five minutes on her hands and knees, and all her questions would be answered.

Or not.

She got down on her knees and pushed herself flat on the floor, and under the bed, where fingers of sunlight dimly illuminated . . .

Nothing.

No stones, no wood dust, no wood.

No dust drifts.

No mistake.

Everything—gone.

"Good morning, Hugo."

Her tone was icy cool as Jancie marched into the dining room for breakfast, knowing that Hugo, if not Kyger, would probably be there.

More security in numbers, she thought. And she was now more angry than afraid. She was seeing for herself that Hugo was the master planner, always several moves ahead. No wonder he had so easily swindled her father.

He had done it to her. Last night. And now, he could accuse her of having an overwrought imagination if she ever broached the idea that he had hidden something under Olivia's bed.

He'd say her mind was playing tricks on her. That she dramatized everything, and was looking to make someone pay attention to her in Lujan's absence.

But she knew the truth. There *had* been something hidden under the bed. And she had the one lone, glassy stone to prove it.

Well, she wouldn't play into Hugo's hands by making outrageous emotional claims. Calm, strong, and icy cold, that was her tack. She wouldn't lose her temper, wouldn't let him manipulate her.

Couldn't lose the minuscule advantage of knowing what she'd seen, what she'd touched.

"Good morning, Jancie," he answered in kind. "Did you sleep well?"

Clever Hugo with his double-edged question.

"Excessively well, for some reason," she said, as she filled her plate with the usual eggs—shirred this time—brioche, a dish of fruit compote, and tea.

She took a seat opposite him and exaggeratedly went through the motions of salting and buttering her food and sugaring her tea. "I think the time has come for me to go to London."

"Do you? Why is that?"

She slanted a look at him. "Do you not think that Lujan has avoided me and his responsibilities long enough?"

Hugo shrugged. "I hadn't thought about it."

"Well, I'm extremely upset about it. This is the second time he's abandoned me, and that is no way to start a marriage." Yes, that sounded good. Just the right indignation for an ignored and ill-used bride.

Hugo opened his newspaper. "I'll send someone."

Oh no. Checkmate. And this was a man who had wanted to marry her.

She stolidly tackled her eggs. There had to be an argument that would hold weight with him. "I was also thinking that were I with him in London, a change of scene might be beneficial for us both."

"Were you? I assure you, Jancie, you would not want to be in London with Lujan. He'd ignore you even more than he has here. Too many temptations for a man of his bent."

Oh lord. "His *bent?*"

"Dear Jancie, you know what Lujan is like. Everything is about . . . what it's about . . . and it's no different in London than it is here, except there are hundreds more women willing to take him on. You don't want to witness that."

Just what Kyger had told her, she thought, fuming. They had the same stories, the same answers, the two of them.

"And you do have the distinct advantage in his having married you. Rest easy with that." Hugo set aside his paper and rose from the table. "He will return, I can promise you that."

He paused at the door. "Someday."

Her appetite fled. She'd been checked and mated. Now what? *Kyger.*

She took a deep breath. Not Kyger. Kyger had become his father, and even though he'd said he wanted to marry her, he'd never been her friend.

She had to depend on her own very limited resources. Except she had no resources. Damn Lujan. Damn his family. She had no one—not even her father. She had Emily.

God, she had to get out of there . . .

How?

She took out the little odd-shaped stone that she had stepped on right by the side of Olivia's bed. She wasn't crazy. There *had* been more stones. At least that.

"Madam." Bingham, his voice rusty and paper-thin as ever, at the door.

She shoved the stone in her pocket. "Yes, Bingham?"

"Is madam done?"

"I am." She pushed away from the table as a thought occurred to her. "Bingham?"

"Yes, madam?"

Bingham had always wanted to get rid of her. All she had to do was ask. "I wish to go to London, to Mr. Lujan. Today."

Did his expression change? "Yes, madam. At what time shall I have the carriage waiting?"

Ask for what you want. "Within the hour, please."

Bingham couldn't wait for her to leave; his face gave nothing away, but she knew. "As you wish."

That simple.

Why was it that simple? After Hugo's explicit refusal.

But Bingham couldn't know about that. Why was she so suspicious?

Don't look for plots, intrigues, complicity.

Hugo didn't even have to know for some hours, unless Bingham told him. And by that time, she would be long away.

Chapter Seventeen

He'd been hiding for days. Didn't want to visit his usual haunts. Didn't want to eat. Didn't want to drink. Didn't want to fuck any other woman but the one he thought wanted him dead.

He was feeling totally unlike himself, and fighting a great urgency to go back to Waybury House. Which, in and of itself, should have been enough to send him to drown himself at the nearest pub.

It was too unlike him not to steep himself in sex, sin, and stimulants when he was in Town. And God help him if he ever had a thought for Waybury, his brother, or his life.

So the fact that he was holed up in the house, watching the street and watching his back, was worrisome.

Doing nothing accomplished nothing. It got him no further in uncovering who was behind his coincidental accidents.

It kept him from Jancie's . . .

. . . and if it was Jancie . . .

Maybe that was the staggering thing—that it could be Jancie. He could hear her repudiation of any accusation now. He'd told her he wanted a body, a vessel. He'd told her that was her function as his wife: to spread her legs whenever he was home, whenever he wanted. He'd as much as told her not to love him.

He'd been irritated when she'd become distant. A perfect setup for revenge—a woman scorned by the man she'd told she loved him.

There.

Except she couldn't have engineered his fall down the steps at the town house. . . . Unless she was in collusion with someone . . .

But they hadn't been married long enough for her to make any alliances with the servants. And certainly not anyone in the town house.

At Waybury, however—she could well have slipped something in his food, easily could have loosened his cinch. But so could anyone—Hugo, Kyger—the ever-devoted March, even.

So instead of going around in circles trying to figure out everyone's motive and where they were when, he ought to just go back to Waybury and confront them all.

However, he wasn't quite ready to do that. He was still reeling from the realization that one of them might want to kill him. For some reason, he had taken everyone's loyalty to his interests for granted. Even as he was whoring around in London, he'd been perfectly certain that Kyger was tending his interests, and that his father was there, in the background, with his usual help and support.

That was a naïve assumption—past childish, in light of the accidents. And with the advent of Jancie, and the fact that all three of them had wanted her so badly. Of course he had won. He had all the gifts and skills to attract and seduce any woman.

Jancie was a lovely, lush piece of clay, waiting to be molded. Too easy to twist this way and that. The reward had been beyond price: his own living sex toy.

Who had exercised her right to remove her feelings and emotions and to become exactly what he had meant her to be.

Except—he didn't.

The realization was shocking.

He wanted *her*, wholly and completely, with every emotion, feeling, and nuance intact.

And she wanted him dead.

Maybe.

Except it was too easy to believe. Jancie wasn't immune from feeling rage and jealousy, and she had told him his behavior was unacceptable. So it was all right there: a woman scorned, with two handsome, respectable, dependable men right in the house to comfort and cosset her.

God almighty—what the hell was he doing in London? And what was Kyger doing with—to—his wife . . . *right now?*

Jesus. And that was even with considering his father, still in his prime, three years into abstinence because of Olivia's illness, and lusting to get at some firm, young flesh.

His wife's flesh.

Her luscious, lickable, pink flesh . . .

Lord almighty—just the thought—he craved it . . . *now* . . . with a mad, red lust that he couldn't control. His body spasmed and spurted and there he was, hot, hard, and ready to go.

He slammed into the parlor. He had to get some resolution to this or *he* would go mad. Staying away didn't solve anything. Rather, it made the feelings he didn't want to acknowledge that much stronger.

And if it proved that Jancie was the perpetrator of this insane scheme, it would be that much more devastating.

Maybe some part of him didn't really want to know.

Well, he'd immured himself long enough. Life went on outside this house. He could see it clearly from behind the curtains of the front window: carriages passing by; people on their way to somewhere; friends in conversation, strolling down the wayside.

No one hiding because someone wanted to kill them.

But then again, their putative murderer wasn't walking baldly and boldly up to their front door, holding a cat in her arms . . .

He went very, very still as the doorbell pealed, as his butler, Poole, answered it and let her in. Turned slowly as he heard her step outside the parlor door.

Saw Emily first at her feet, trailing her as she came slowly into the room as if even she were uncertain how he would receive her.

And then, she was in his arms, and for the first time since their wedding, he kissed her.

The kiss. The intimate, mouth-to-mouth, tongue-to-tongue kiss. A kiss that went long, wet, sweet, deep, deeper than even Lujan wished to go, but he couldn't help himself. Jancie was here, in his arms, flesh and blood, and he wanted no words, no excuses, explanations, or declarations.

He just wanted her body, pure and simple, and he was aroused enough to take her on the parlor floor.

Or on the table . . . or on the sofa . . .

Oh God . . . when had he last kissed her? Didn't he used to kiss her when he was trying to seduce her? Why did she feel so new, luscious, delicious, virginal?

He couldn't let himself be seduced by her. He pulled away abruptly, even though it cost him; her dismay could not have been more obvious.

Or the deep breath with which she reordered her emotions and consciously removed herself from him.

And wiped away the kiss.

"Well," he said, because he didn't know quite what to say, and he disliked that his kiss might have been that distasteful—or that she was being spiteful.

Her eyes grew cool, her stance more combative. "I'm actually shocked to find you here."

"Why is that?" he asked, ringing for the butler and motioning for him to bring tea. As if he were entertaining some society doyenne for an hour, and not his own wife.

God, he was all turned inside out by this whole situation. And Jancie, *here?* And that kiss. Which now was as if it had never been.

"You will not like to hear this, as I didn't like to hear it, but your father and Kyger both thought I ought not to come because I would have to pry you out from between some whore's legs."

Oh Jesus. Damn his father and Kyger to hell. To hear those words from his *wife's* genteel mouth, the mouth he had just been devouring as if she were the only woman in the world—

She is the only woman in the world . . .

Not that once—six months ago, even—it would not have been true—

He swore mightily just as the butler rolled in the tea cart.

"Thank you, Poole."

"Sir. Shall I pour?"

"No, my lady will do the honor. Jancie?"

She lifted the teapot and poured, and then looked at him expectantly.

"Well, what should I say, Jancie? Can a man not change his philosophy and act accordingly?"

She was fascinated. This was the rueful Lujan, open and beguiling, and as seductive as a kiss. "Truly, can he?"

He picked up his cup, wondering how much to say. But she was here, and not likely to initiate an attack in this house, surrounded by servants and security.

In fact, her presence was a possible answer to his quandary about confronting all of them.

He would challenge her first. "I won't lie to you. I don't know. I think so. I've had no great yearning to go out and about since I've been here. No pubs. No brothels. No—other women—"

She sent him a skeptical look.

"But the circumstances are such that—"

Circumstances? Ah, she thought, now they would get to the nub, the reason why he'd left. "Oh, are there circumstances?

"The accidents . . . see it from my perspective. All of a sudden, three in a row, all after we wed, and after I laid down the parameters of our marriage . . . after which I left."

She laughed, a short derisive bark of a laugh. "You fairly bolted out of the house."

"I left," he said dryly, "and as I see it, it isn't inconceivable that you might have wanted both revenge and a way out . . ."

"Oh." She was dumbfounded. Lujan thought her capable of such violence . . . ?

Lujan went on inexorably: "Not inconceivable you could have wanted to choose another husband from the two who had already evinced an interest in marrying you, two who would most assuredly treat you more respectfully . . ."

"And who would stay?" she interpolated sarcastically. She was nearly speechless at his theory. "You think I would attack you, I would *kill* you—so I could marry either Kyger or your father?? Are you insane??"

"Am I?"

She made a snorting sound. No help here. On top of the fact that he really didn't want a wife, the man thought she could be a murderer. These Galliard men had no qualms about the method of their kill—they stole from you, stripped away your emotions, or they figuratively put a gun to your head.

The only way to get away from them was to go away altogether, out of their sight, out of their minds, and out of their circle of power.

"You're deranged, Lujan." She put her cup down emphatically. "I'm sorry I came." She stood up, her back ramrod with anger. "Emily and I will leave in the morning."

She had a secondary plan: she'd go to India. She'd always meant to. And now, she could find out what she needed to do to go to India, to go to her father. She needed him now, needed the balm of his forgiveness for all she'd been through, and for the fact that she'd found no reparation for him.

That was what she needed—not Lujan, not sex, not surmises, not secrets.

But her leaving was the last thing Lujan wanted. He watched all the emotions play out on her face—the most important of which was her stupefaction at his suspicions.

She was magnificent in her fury. He wanted to stoke it, use it, possess it, devour it. "Deny it, then."

"I can't—because it's too tempting to contemplate right at this moment."

"Jancie . . ." He grasped her elbow and turned her around to face him.

"No, I'm immune to that, Luujan." But she wasn't. The heat of his hand fairly burned through the sleeve of her morning dress, the dress she had not changed from this morning in her haste to get away from Waybury House before Hugo became aware that she was gone.

"Why did you come?"

She didn't want to answer that. It was hardly worth mentioning after his draconian accusations. He had instantly negated everything by his suspicions of her.

"It doesn't matter now, does it? If you think I'm capable of wanting to harm you."

His voice dropped, husky and hot. "And yet I still want you."

She didn't doubt it. Lujan wanted anyone with nipples and a cunt.

"So?"

That—*that*—she just didn't care what he wanted, and he hated that, despised that tone of voice, that insolent disinterest. *That* . . . he didn't know what it was, but it made him wild to subjugate her and make her beg. For him. For his penis. For his sex.

He was furious. He dropped her arm roughly, and stalked to the window. *So?* He wanted to retaliate against that disdainful *so.*

"Well, that says something, doesn't it? You couldn't care less if you fuck me, Kyger, or my father, could you? Or was that the original intent of your coming to Waybury, to seduce one of us to get something back for your father?"

She froze, shocked that he would think it, hot with guilt because she had succumbed to it, and she couldn't deny reparation *had* played a part in it.

"Your father requested my services," she said through stiff lips. "It was not my intent to come to Waybury—ever."

"And yet, there you were. One wonders who put the idea into my father's head. Knowing what a penurious sort he is. Knowing he'd be resenting all those years of supporting someone else's child in a posh boarding school."

A red fury took hold of her. "Oh, he did, he did—such support, such luxury. Yes, let me tell you about the attic suite, the mice, the vermin, the cold, the wind, the five girls who slept in one bed, huddling together when the snow poured in the broken windows. No heat, no water, no blankets. No boots, no coats . . ." She had wrapped her arms around her midriff as she raged around the room, almost as if she could feel the cold, the loneliness, the destitution.

". . . The classes in the finer points of slicing potatoes and onions and how to serve the wealthy tuition girls. Very posh that was. And then there were the classes in dancing around, letting a duke's son seduce you and get you *enceinte.* Yes, I did learn some French there, Lujan. It *was* an education, all right. As elegant as ever a girl could want. But who would want it? For what?"

He couldn't bear to look at her stormy face. There were other forces at work, and she might well have been a pawn, but his father had had a purpose every bit as obdurate as hers. "For your gratitude, Jancie, so you'd do whatever he needed you to do whenever he requested it of you."

She wanted to disabuse him of that notion. "I felt no gratitude at all."

It made no impression. "Nevertheless . . ."

"It was not my doing."

"It was your father."

That stopped her in her tracks. Did he mean that? *"No."*

"Your father suggested it."

She denied again. "No." But she saw it could be so—Hugo would not have dreamt up the idea on his own. She wished she could remember the details, but it was too long ago to remember the fine points. Just that Hugo had sent her a letter and asked her to accommodate him after all he'd done for her.

She'd thought it was a way out of St. Boniface, finally. She remembered that her father had encouraged her to take the position, that he thought she would be better off at Waybury than coming to India at that time.

She remembered the moment when she realized just what he hoped might happen. A year or two later, she thought, as she cast her mind back. But never had she thought he engineered her presence there for just that purpose.

Dear heaven.

But why should that surprise her, really? Her father had been feeding her the fairy tale of his dealings with Hugo from the time she was old enough to listen to his stories, and always about all he'd lost, all that Hugo had taken from him, all he was owed.

And in the end, all he'd asked of his former partner was tuition for Jancie's schooling. It had never made any sense to her until she had finally comprehended his true intention.

And by then, she was that far gone with deeper feelings for Lujan and he was hot in pursuit of her.

More secrets.

She couldn't bear any more secrets. She knew too many herself. And Lujan knew too many of hers.

It was useless going any further.

"Maybe he did," she said finally. "Maybe he planned everything, just as you said, all those years ago—" But dear lord, that was such a long road to vengeance—even given the years Edmund had lost his memory.

"And so here you are—the cat among the pigeons, and all you have to do is marry them and kill them off slowly, one by one, until Waybury is finally yours, and your father's revenge is complete."

"No." She put up her hands as if to ward off his words. *"NO!"* But her denials were sounding weaker and weaker. Edmund had demanded so little in return for everything Hugo had allegedly made him suffer.

So if she could find a way to insinuate herself into his family . . . to marry one of his sons—a marriage was forever.

And Edmund would triumph by proxy.

"And he never got his hands dirty."

No, he never did, she thought dully. And all of it made too much sense, and made her feel like nothing less than a pawn in a game she didn't know she was playing.

It knocked the fight out of her. She wished she hadn't come. Wished she'd never acceded to Hugo's wish that she come to Waybury. Wished she hadn't become so fond of Olivia, hadn't felt the responsibility of trying to make reparations to her father, because she hadn't known she had already claimed the reward he had always wanted: her marriage to Lujan.

If he had known all three of them wanted her . . . ? Would that have trebled his triumph?

She felt sick to her stomach.

Why *had* they all simultaneously wanted her?

Did she really want to know?

"There's nothing more to say," she said stiffly. "I'll leave tomorrow. And I won't return to Waybury."

Lujan stepped toward her. "Jancie—"

"I think we've both said enough. Poole can show me to my room."

His wife was in the house. His WIFE was not two rooms away, down the hall from him, and in his anger, he'd managed to alienate her within an hour after she had voluntarily come to him.

He didn't know where that argument arose from. Maybe it had always been under the surface, waiting to bubble up, and his frustration, his need, and his distance from Waybury had brought it to the fore. As if the further he got from there, the clearer everything seemed to become.

Because it all meshed, it all made sense in a way that none of it had made sense before. Had no one in his family ever considered that Edmund Renbrook had instigated Jancie's presence at Waybury as a means to settle his score with Hugo?

Even he, with all his initial suspicion of her, had never guessed the depth of her father's desire to exact satisfaction for all he had lost.

And, by the look on her face—if it was real—neither had she.

So the woman he'd been craving, missing, yearning for was not only the one person who had the perfect reason for wishing him harm, but she was also the perfect instrument of her father's revenge.

That alone ought to have sent him running.

Instead he lay in bed, thinking of her, erect as a pole and perfectly willing to submerge all his clamoring distrust and suspicion of her in the depths of her naked body.

God. He had no scruples at all. He hadn't changed—he'd just sloughed everything off onto something else, as usual.

And meantime, he thought, Jancie was down the hallway, lying in bed, probably sleepless, angry, regretting she'd come, furious at her father for the way he had manipulated her. And unforgiving of him for parsing out the exact details.

But in the middle of the night, steeped in secrets and silence, none of that seemed to matter. There was something about being removed from one's normal circumstances that made critical things seem less crucial.

Everything could wait till tomorrow—till next week. Forever.

He wanted Jancie. It seemed like the only critical thing at the moment. And that the night was forgiving, enfolding, warm and enveloping—like the endless reaches of her body.

He'd never thought she would come to London.

Why *had* she come to London? Not to kill him. She had looked utterly stunned at the idea. Not to hear him rail about her father's covert plan for revenge, either. Obviously, that had appalled her, too.

Why *had* she come?

Maybe he didn't want to know. Maybe she was best left alone.

But after nearly a week of self-imposed exile from her, that hardly seemed the solution.

He was a man who never could leave anything alone. And certainly not Jancie. She'd had a purpose in coming, and he wanted to know what it was.

And obviously, there was only one way to find out . . .

She didn't know why she had thought anything would be different. Everything was, in fact, worse. The awful things Lujan had said. It sounded worse coming from him than her belated realization that her marrying into the family was Edmund's true desire. Finding proof of how viciously Hugo had cheated him and treated him really had gone secondary to that.

But she'd never thought of it as revenge—just reparation for her family by virtue of her marriage to Lujan.

Now that she'd heard it from Lujan's perspective, it sounded horribly, irreversibly wrong. Lujan didn't want her love—he had no sense his family owed Edmund any justice. He was perfectly content pursuing his usual course, and getting his own way.

Only now he was saddled with her.

What if he didn't wish to have a wife anymore? What if he were tired of her, disgusted by her father's schemes, and screwing around with some other woman he'd met since he'd come to Town?

What if he wanted to get rid of her?

Lujan was not the kind of man to settle down and marry. He might, at some future time, step up to his responsibilities at Waybury, but he was not a man to be leg-shackled to one woman forever.

Innocent as she was, in her heart, she'd always known it. He was one who wanted constant variety, stimulation, and entertainment. There wasn't a woman in the world who could provide that. So he would buzz around like a bee and spray his pollen everywhere, strutting his power and prowess, and that was all that Lujan was about.

And not for the likes of her.

Tomorrow, she would leave, go to a hotel, a travel agent, and start the process to go to India. Lujan would be rid of her forever. Hugo could keep his secrets, his money, his empty rooms.

M'euuww. Emily, soft, padding over to the chair where Jancie sat, dressed in her gauzy lawn nightgown, with her legs pulled up so she could rest her chin on her knees.

She was never going to sleep this night. How was she going to tell Edmund she had failed in all quarters—that she was leaving the marriage, leaving Waybury, and coming to India? And that she'd found nothing, not a shred of proof that Hugo was living off their unlawfully gotten gains.

Just a mysteriously missing child, a handful of stones, and something wooden under a bed, something that had subsequently disappeared.

Nothing. She had nothing. She'd alienated Hugo, denied Kyger, and now that Lujan comprehended the depth of her treachery, and thought her capable of murder, she'd lost him, too.

She had no money, save the pittance Hugo had paid her; she'd brought one change of clothes, but no jewelry except her wedding band. And, as a souvenir of this whole disgraceful episode in her life, that odd little stone she'd found in Olivia's room.

If only she hadn't been so curious, if she'd just not pursued it so obsessively, if she'd not gotten so besotted by the idea of solving the mystery of Gaunt's disappearance, she'd still be at Waybury, waiting for Lujan's return.

Which was preferable? Waiting for him forever, or losing him altogether?

Euuwww. Emily understood; the tone and tenor of her voice said as much. She jumped up onto the table right by Jancie's chair, and rubbed her head against Jancie's shoulder. *It will work itself out.*

Jancie wasn't so certain. And she was tired. And the whole idea of returning to her father empty-handed was abhorrent to her. But she had no other choice. She couldn't stay. She had to go. She'd have to send word to him tomorrow. It would take time to arrange things, in any event.

And it solved nothing . . .

She wished Olivia were still here.

Eooowwww . . . Don't forget me—oh, Emily for sure didn't like the notion of being supplanted by memories of Olivia.

"All right," Jancie whispered, her eyes stinging with tears. Oh, no—she wasn't one to cry over something like this. Not this. Not when years at St. Bonny's had taught her to be stoic about everything.

No tears . . . "You're right. You're my very best friend, and I'm still just a blundering dirty girl." The tears came then, anyway.

And I don't know how to make anything right.

Was she crying?

There wasn't a man alive who could cope with a woman's tears. He himself could be brutal about that sort of thing, had been on occasion, but this was Jancie, in his house, sobbing so quietly that no one, unless he were within three steps of her bedroom door, would have ever known it.

Jancie had backbone—it would take a lot to dissolve her into tears. Nothing at all for her to dissolve in his arms.

She wasn't skulking down the hallway with a weapon, intent on harming him. He had to let go of that idea. She wasn't his enemy. He didn't *feel* as if she were his enemy, but when had he ever relied on *feelings?*

Those feelings had propelled him down the hallway to her room, and now he stood uncertainly outside the door, effectively dissuaded from high-handedly walking in and throwing her on the bed.

Not a good tack when she was so distraught.

He knocked instead. "Jancie . . ."

"Go *away* . . ."

No sane man would go *away.* He eased the door open. His whole body shot to attention at the sight of her, curled on the chair, facing away from the door, so that her hair tumbled all over her shoulders and legs, her shoulders shaking with those subdued and anguished sobs.

"Jancie . . ." His voice was soft, low, compassionate, and so unlike him, he wondered if some entity had taken over his body and was speaking for him.

"Don't come in." Her voice was muffled, tear-sodden. He came in anyway, and she was aware of his approach, his kneeling down next to the chair, of him extending his hand to Emily and her nuzzling and rubbing against it.

Emily was a traitor.

"I'm in." Not as *in* as he wanted to be, the desire rising instantly in him like fire, searing him, stunning him.

This wasn't a sexual foray—or was it? He thought he had purer motives, but maybe anything like that went by the wayside where she was concerned. The safest thing was not to move. Not to touch her. Just to ask the question he'd come to ask.

She said nothing, but her suppressed sobs seemed to have subsided; she seemed calmer, and more accepting of his presence.

Good. "Tell me why you came."

"It's nothing." She lifted her head, her eyes still liquid with tears. "I'll be leaving in the morning."

Tears destroyed him. No, *Jancie's* tears destroyed him. And her leaving was out of the question. "We'll talk about that in the morning. Tell me why you came."

"It's nothing in light of the larger picture—you never wished to marry me, you abandoned me twice, you subsequently demolished my life, and you think I'm capable of murder. Anything else pales next to this litany of ills. I'm done."

"Yet there was some reason you came."

"It was time for you to return to Waybury."

"No, it's my father's or Kyger's task to wrest me from the clutches of the demimonde. A wife wouldn't go within ten miles of that tall tale. Tell me, Jancie. It can't be worse than anything I deduced today about your father."

But her sin *was* worse. She'd been spying and plotting against Hugo, all on her own. And to admit that on top of Lujan's pinning her about her father would put the cap on the bottle. She'd be out of there like a hound after a fox and to the nearest hotel before she could catch her breath.

And there was no excusing it, no rational reason for it. And it defined her so completely as her father's daughter, she almost couldn't bear to think about it.

There was no difference between her searching for clues to Gaunt's disappearance, and her searching for clues to the putative cache of diamonds that Hugo had allegedly stolen. None whatsoever.

"Jancie . . ."

She stiffened. "All right. Why not? I'll say this—you were fairly dead-on in your assessment of how everything came to pass, with this exception—I had no notion that your father would offer me the position here. I fully expected to join my father in Delhi directly after I completed my studies at St. Bonny's. It's also true he encouraged my taking the position, but I can't speak to whether he also encouraged Hugo to offer it to me. But Father was adamant that he didn't want me in India just yet. Too much disease, too hot—I don't know—he had a variety of excuses, all of them reasonable, none of them questionable, and so I came.

"Only two years later did it come to me why he wanted me here. I never expected to have feelings for you. To me, coming here was a way to discover concrete evidence of whether Hugo had betrayed my father. It seemed the least I could do for him. He'd lost years, he'd lost Olivia, he'd lost my mother, he'd lost the comfortable life he might have had from his share in the profits from their strike.

"Nor was it easy for me to see just what our life might have been like had fate not intervened . . ."

Her voice trailed off. It didn't seem necessary to round out the picture. That was enough—she'd confirmed nearly everything he'd surmised, and more. What more was there that didn't redound badly on her? And by her own account, her own purpose in coming to Waybury was every bit as nefarious as her father's in sending her there.

"I was not grateful," she added.

"And so what happened yesterday?"

She could fall in love all over again with this Lujan, this patience, this warmth, this unusual kindness when his wont was to be merciless.

". . . I've been looking for evidence that Hugo's wealth derived from the strike at Kaamberoo. About a week ago, I was searching the upper shelves in the library when I came upon a book that turned out to be an album of photographs . . ."

"Oh?" Now he stiffened, all his sympathy gone, the face of the pitiless Lujan back in place.

"Of Gaunt. There were eight or nine altogether. Two of them portraits of you, Kyger, and him. He haunted me. I wanted so badly to discover what had happened to him. I kept the album in Olivia's room, under the footboard of her bed. I don't know—it made sense somehow. It felt as if he were buried in the library where no one could ever find him. And in Olivia's room, at least, he could be with her . . ."

It sounded insane, and not her decision to make at all. Someone had done that. Banished Gaunt for all time on the library shelf.

She swallowed hard. "Anyway, after I finished looking at the photographs with a magnifying glass one morning, I stepped on something on the carpet. Emily had been under the bed, and I thought she had been playing with a pebble or something. But that it was so odd to find a pebble in Olivia's bedroom—

"Well, I suggested to Hugo that perhaps it was time to dismantle her bedroom. He was adamant that it be left as it was, and that I not intrude by going in there anymore. He said he would lock it up if I did not respect his wishes."

"Let me guess," Lujan said coldly. "You didn't."

"I didn't." The words sat heavily in the air. "It felt as if she were being buried all over again. I went back that night to look under the bed."

Again her words sounded deranged. Who would go contrary to a husband's wishes and poke and pry under his deceased wife's bed?

"And you found—what?" If his voice went any colder, she'd freeze.

"More pebbles. A lot more of them. I grabbed a handful. And sawdust. Dust drifts. I couldn't see, it was dark—but there was something there, under the bed, something hard, wooden, something Emily could have been scratching at . . . and—suddenly there was nothing more because I woke up the next morning in my own bed."

"Walking in your sleep." He sounded relieved—but still cool, removed, a little wary of her.

"Or—not. One more thing—I went back to Olivia's room the next morning to look and see in daylight what I felt the night before. And there was nothing there. Not the album, the pebbles, the wooden object, whatever it was. Nothing."

"You dreamt it. It was a dream, Jancie. You just wanted to find the boy."

"I didn't dream it. Someone stopped me from exploring Olivia's room any further. Someone tried to scare me. Someone removed everything that was under the bed because his ideal hiding place had been found out."

"Don't say it, Jancie."

"Fine. And one more thing. I have the original pebble. That's how I know it wasn't a dream."

"Where?" His voice was clipped, angry. He didn't believe her. It sounded awful, even to her. It sounded like the most base betrayal—of him, of Olivia, of whatever there was of their marriage.

"I have it."

"Show me."

She unwound herself from the chair, moved to the dresser, and rummaged in the top drawer for a moment.

"Here."

He turned the stone every which way in his fingers, and held it up to the dim light of the table lamp. "You *saw* more of these? Under the bed?"

"Yes. I think I picked up about a dozen all together, and they were all gone the next day."

"Jancie . . ." His voice had changed, lowered, warmed. "This is a diamond."

A chill shot right through her body like an arrow. "How do you know?"

"He taught us about them many years ago."

"Oh my God—" Everything she'd been looking for had been right in plain sight, under that sacred shrine, Olivia's bed.

And she hadn't even told him about the ghostly, crickling, rolling sound in the hallway . . .

"That's why I came to London," she whispered. "I didn't know it was a diamond. I just thought he would come after me anyway."

Chapter Eighteen

Suddenly everything was turned upside down.

"*My* father??" Lujan murmured in disbelief. He kept rolling the stone around in his fingers, seeing in it Hugo hiding his secrets under Olivia's bed, more secrets buried with Edmund Renbrook in the explosion at Kaamberoo all those years ago.

Hugo consorting with murderers and thieves, in the familiar family history, but not because he'd been kidnapped—but no, these had been hirelings who'd helped him bring out a cache of rough diamonds he would never have to share with anyone but his ghosts.

Every story, every justification a lie?

Hugo the potential killer—not Jancie?

Who else could Hugo have killed to protect that secret?

Jesus God. And then his father living all those years on the knife-edge of wondering if Edmund had even survived, and terrified he might return from the dead to blackmail him.

And the ghost *had* come back. After all those years, there was Edmund, hovering in the background. Asking for nothing. Just making certain that Hugo was aware. Aware of what he could ask for, aware of what he had the potential to do.

It was monumental. He had the power to ruin Hugo. It must

have always been in the air—that he would do it, under certain circumstances, even if he never saw a shilling from his share of the diamonds.

His father, Lujan supposed, was a reasonable man, but how nerve-wracking must it have been, waiting for Edmund's ultimate demand?

How little it must have seemed when it finally came.

Support Edmund's daughter at boarding school? Happy to comply. Ask her to Waybury to care for Olivia? Surely Hugo knew how much Edmund had cared about Olivia. Let his daughter stand in his stead and help her through her final days.

The perfect solution to a thorny situation.

Hugo must have been relieved beyond the moon.

And when Olivia passed away—

Another solution to another prickly situation instantly presented itself: propose to marry Edmund's daughter, and by doing so, avert the threat of Edmund ruining him altogether.

And here it was—the father *and* his profligate son plotting to keep Edmund and his potential for blackmail at bay.

He bore just as much guilt as Jancie . . . for everything. Plots and schemes. They were all guilty—Jancie had been the one caught in the middle.

It *was* a diamond.

And if there had been a stash of them under his mother's bed—which meant Hugo *had* brought them out of South Africa in the rough—he had done more than just swindle Edmund out of his share; he had also lied egregiously to his family about his past history and what had really happened at Kaamberoo. And had taken Olivia's money without qualm into the bargain.

"Lujan?" Jancie was back in her chair, her knees drawn up, her eyes grave.

"I'm still putting it all together in my mind."

But the obvious *was* obvious, Jancie thought. "He lied about the diamonds."

Lujan didn't want to condemn Hugo quite yet. "So this suggests."

"They could have been under her bed all the years since he returned from South Africa."

Lujan shook his head. "I wouldn't think so. Mother was a stickler for turning out the rugs and cleaning out the rooms every season."

"All right—then hidden . . ."

"We can infer that—" Lujan agreed impatiently, still reluctant to believe even a part of what sounded so utterly unbelievable, and indefensible, even, "*if* you saw all those stones under the bed . . ."

"I saw them. I had them in my hand. I wish Emily could tell you—she was always under the bed, she was obviously scratching at something. I found sawdust in her claws both times we were there, and she batted that stone—that diamond—out from under the bed. That's how I found it—I stepped on it . . . I—"

She broke off abruptly because even to her own ears, she sounded incoherent now, and he still wavered, still wanting to believe that the world that Hugo had created for his family was still intact, and that his father was not an out-and-out liar.

And that those stones were not the mythical diamonds that had been stolen by the long-ago kidnappers. And that Hugo was not a thief.

Emily said, *owww*, as if to punctuate Jancie's testimony.

He stared at the stone. It was so long ago. How could anyone make reparations for a life not lived? Only Jancie had even a chance at reclaiming the past, but only because Edmund had schemed to put her in the one place she *could* take it back.

God. Had they all been just pawns in the games their fathers played?

A cache of diamonds hidden under Olivia's bed. He shook his head. How was it possible? But of course, she had been ill in those years, and things had not been done to her usual precise specifications.

And the cat hadn't ever gone in there, except in the last days as she was dying. Possibly the cache had been moved there after her death? Sawdust presupposed some kind of wooden box or container.

The perfect hiding place, then. A dying woman. Her indigent companion linked to her by a mutual history that was secreted under her bed.

Had Hugo been drunk, mad, or just plain arrogant?

Or was it just that under Olivia's bed was the last place anyone would look for anything at that point?

He was too tired to sift through all the details any further. He hadn't expected this stunning revelation, and he still couldn't quite grasp the enormity of Hugo's duplicity and Edmund's guile.

He didn't want to. Not tonight.

Far easier to bury himself in Jancie's enfolding heat, as he had fully intended, and just rock and root there forever.

He still wanted it. Above and beyond his suspicions, his anger, his desire to keep her at arm's length, he still only wanted her.

Jancie's deceptions were nothing to his own—he was no saint. But he was not roaming the streets looking for easy cunt, either, as he might have done two months ago.

And his father's sins were not his. He felt as if Hugo's life were a piece of fiction, and he had come to the resolution of the story, and put it down because he didn't want to read the rest.

He felt removed from his father, and closer to her. He didn't want to move, didn't want to leave her. He wanted to stop this moment before any further disastrous revelations destroyed it.

Something had changed.

And it wasn't whether this irregular, dirt-encrusted, glassy piece of rock represented the truth.

It was just that his wanting her was a constant ache that couldn't be assuaged by any other woman anywhere.

Whatever that meant in terms of his past, or for his future.

But he wasn't struggling with it any more fiercely than she was, Jancie thought. Because the diamond proved that everything Edmund had ever told her was true.

But then that made Hugo the villain.

There was no good outcome to this.

She wished she could make time stand still, that anything beyond this moment could be lost forever in history.

They would have to go back to Waybury. To confront Hugo. To find the diamonds and whatever it had been that contained them. And to finally have the answers to all her questions.

But maybe not today, not yet. It seemed too soon after these suppositions that had such a ring of truth. He was as shocked as she was by them, and wholly uncertain how to proceed. Didn't even want to think about how to proceed.

And in spite of them, he didn't want to leave her as much as she wanted him to stay.

She felt uncommon tenderness well up into her heart; he was on the floor, just by her chair. She could touch him. She could push him away. Emily was sitting on her haunches on the table, a posture that was stiff with portent, as if she were waiting, too, to see what his decision would be.

The air was close, tight, the flame in the lamp on the table flickering as the kerosene burned low. There were shadows everywhere, hiding in corners, behind the furniture, under the bed . . .

"Jancie . . ."

There was such sweetness in his voice that she completely understood. In that one word, he encompassed all the uncertainties they faced tomorrow. They didn't know what would happen tomorrow—it would be the culmination, the resolution, the thing that could rip everything, every assumption, wide apart.

They only had tonight, and the burden of equal culpability of deceit and desire.

And something *had* changed—she felt it, just in the way he said her name. The way he had listened tonight. His willingness to consider her perspective and deny his own.

And the way he touched her, his hand on hers now . . .

"Jancie . . ."

There was nothing more than tonight and no more shadows and secrets between them.

Even Emily appreciated that. She jumped from the table and scurried under the bed as Jancie lifted her nightgown and parted her legs.

And he was there, where she needed him, wanted him, between her legs, spreading her labia, exploring her secrets, stroking and feeling the inmost tender flesh of her body.

This was what she couldn't live without—his spreading her vulva so gently, masterfully, so that she could only submit to his thorough erotic exploration of every inch of her there with his fingers, and his hot, stroking tongue.

The way he nuzzled and sucked her delicate flesh, and teased her erect pleasure point, the way he kissed it and pulled on it, all the while spreading her labia wide open so nothing could be withheld from him . . . this was unbearable, explosive pleasure beyond words, beyond the orgasmic culmination of it. This was his pure ownership of the most private part of her body, his possession of her soul.

She loved it, loved it, loved it—and missed it, missed the feeling of his expert fingers spreading her, pulling at her, missed the naked feeling of being utterly open to him, missed his questing tongue tasting her, eating her.

All of that, she had missed, and she ground her hips and sought his tongue and his lust to devour her between her legs, and when he finally thrust his tongue into her hole, she shattered—fragile as glass, hard as diamonds, she came on his tongue, naked, open, and his this way forever.

They lay side by side on the bed, his hand possessively between her legs, his fingers deep within her, spreading her still, lightly, meaningfully, erotically, so that even in the aftermath of that earth-shaking orgasm, she still felt breathless with erotic anticipation at feeling his fingers there.

It was totally dark now, but dawn was coming, inexorably, and nothing would hold it back. But until then, he held *her*, inexorably his, hard between her legs, aroused by every incremental movement of her body as she involuntarily responded to being so firmly and unrelentingly spread.

"No matter what happens . . ." he whispered on a breath, "no matter what . . . this—"

"Yes—"

She didn't need the words—she had his unyielding fingers, his towering penis, his hot, naked body, his avid mouth . . . her body arched and undulated in subtle enticing movements as he aroused her to a fever pitch merely by his fingers constantly pushing and prodding between her legs.

And when she was at the boiling point, he held her labia wide for his penetration, mounted her, and forcefully drove his penis home.

She sheathed him tight and deep in an immeasurable pocket of sensual heat. It was barely enough. He wanted more . . . a hundred ways more . . . He felt as if he'd never plumb the depths of her, and just that thought and the pumping gyrations of her hips sent him flying—spewing to the sky—and deep inside as far as he could go.

She made him come so easily, so effortlessly; the way she responded to him made him pour out his seed, which made him ache for more of her body, and the more she gave him, the more he craved her.

All of her.

It was such a tight, sensual circle of need. And different from anything he had experienced before.

He just couldn't get enough of her cunt. He would die with his fingers penetrating and spreading her cunt. He wanted more already, and he wasn't even a half-hour past his own bone-melting culmination.

She moved restlessly against his fingers splayed between her legs, enticing him to stretch her wider, to fully lay open every inch of her luscious inner flesh.

She loved his baring all of her nakedness; her body bucked as she felt his fingers firmly manipulating her in that most private place, opening her wider still. He held her there with a relentless mercilessness that was so arousing she almost came. Her body shuddered with excitement and agitation, because it was too much and it was exactly what she craved.

And if he even touched her clit, she would dissolve and explode.

Not yet, not yet. She wanted to float forever in this hazy cloud of erotic anticipation. This was the best part . . . the moment before, because her mind knew exactly what was to come. Her body knew. Her arousal was so complete she was shaking with it, and staving it off.

She never wanted to come. It would break her, fracture her into smithereens. If she didn't come, she could carry this feeling with her forever. She would always be aroused, always steeped in yearning, always on the brink.

So much better to be on the brink where such incredible, inexpressible pleasure was possible.

Not yet not yet not yet . . .

She rolled her hips, pressing against his splayed fingers even more tightly. She could barely breathe for the voluptuous excitement of it. Not yet not yet . . .

She felt him at her clit, she felt herself throbbing, seeking, her body reaching for the one explosive touch that would demolish her.

Not yet not yet not yet . . .

She grabbed his rock of a penis, grabbing for sanity, for safety, for forever . . .

And he touched her, his one finger pressing against her distended clit, and her clamoring body burst into a thousand spangling points of molten light, glittering and cascading all over her, him, the bed, the darkness, and sizzling into nothingness in the morning light.

They stayed in bed another day, another night. An endless day and night, wholly immersed in each other, apart only long enough to let Emily in and out as was her wont. Fending off the darkness connected to each other. Seeking that indelible surcease only as one. Naked and open, together as one.

It was Poole who finally discreetly knocked on the door the succeeding morning. "Mr. Lujan? Mr. Lujan!"

He was deep in sleep, entwined with Jancie and barely able to move, because he was drained to the root, and he jolted to consciousness at the insistent knocking. "What? What is it? What?"

Not coherent. He pulled himself out of the bed and went to open the door a crack to see who had the nerve to disturb him.

Poole inserted an envelope. "This just came from Mr. Kyger, most urgent."

He ripped it open. *Father in an accident, serious, possibly critical. Get back here.*

It didn't quite register, but he wasn't quite awake. "Tea, Poole. In five minutes. Have the carriage ready in a half-hour. Jancie— wake up! We're going home."

They arrived at dinnertime. Kyger was waiting, and by the looks of it, he'd been pacing in the front hallway the whole day, as if he thought the trip would take an hour instead of four or five.

He greeted them by saying, "He's not dead yet."

"Oh, excellent news," Lujan snapped, instantly irritated by Kyger's anger and unwarranted bluntness. "What's wrong with you?"

"What's wrong? I'm damned tired of cleaning up after you is what's wrong. Why the hell weren't you here? You goddamned abandoned Jancie, and you goddamned abandoned him, and the hell with you . . ."

"Go to hell. What happened?"

"Horse bucked him off as he was saddling up yesterday."

"Jesus."

"He fell straight down, broke his back, hit his head. Doctor doesn't know the extent of the internal injuries yet. Or if there's internal bleeding. Or whether there's any spinal damage. We're in a waiting situation."

Jancie grabbed Lujan's arm; she was exhausted, both from the past two days in bed, and from the trip, and now this.

"Is he conscious?"

"Yes. Sleeping a lot. Medication for the pain. The prognosis isn't good."

"Can I see him?"

"Go right ahead."

Lujan took the steps two at time with Jancie following as best she could, and Emily right behind her. She didn't want to see Hugo like that. She didn't want to see him at all.

Lujan entered the room first, fearing the worst. Hugo was swathed in blankets, with no bandages in evidence, flat on his back, being fed some broth by a local woman who'd come in to nurse him.

"About time," he muttered around the spoon. "This is bloody hell."

Lujan drew up a chair. Jancie hovered just inside the door, suddenly aware, just by Lujan's tenderness, how much he really cared about his father.

Hugo was not a villain to him. And she saw immediately how much more complicated that made everything.

"What do you know?"

"It was Gunshot. He shied. Don't know why." Hugo took another sip of the hot broth, nearly choked because he swallowed so fast. "Fast. Up, down, hard on the ground, couldn't move.

Couldn't *move* . . . anything—arms, legs, body. Just mouth, eyes. Voice. I can breathe—barely . . ."

"God almighty," Lujan swore. "No one in the stables?"

"Didn't notice. That's enough, woman. I'm nearly dead anyway."

"No—*NO,*" Lujan contradicted him passionately. "Don't say that. Don't think that."

Hugo shook his head. "Nothing left. Not good."

"I'll make it good. Listen to me . . ."

But Hugo had drifted off into some drug-induced cloud. "Jancie . . ."

She nodded. He took her arm as they went back downstairs.

He was so quiet. Jancie didn't dare say anything, but it felt suddenly as if the past two passion-steeped days had never happened, and he had abandoned her once again.

It felt as if he was a stranger, suddenly—wholly on his father's side now, and Hugo's sins would be washed away, no matter what events might prove later on.

And where was she in this scenario? She was the interloper, still hovering on the threshold, prevented from entering and unable to leave.

Emily comforted her a little; now she could take her rest, and let her body relax its grinding and urgent need for Lujan and sex. There would be no sex for a long time, as long, and beyond, as it took for Hugo to recover or for him to . . .

But she must not think that way. For Lujan's sake, she had to believe that Hugo would recover.

But then what?

Would one then confront a desperately ill man with the evidence of his treachery? Or would she let all that fade into history, and just stay content with her marriage to Lujan, the comforts at Waybury, and her mistress-of-the-manor life?

She sat in the library at the desk, staring at the book-lined walls, wishing desperately she could talk to her father. If he were aware that Hugo was injured so seriously, he wouldn't wish her to pursue her desire to confront him. He'd tell her to ease up and slow down and forget about it altogether until Hugo recovered.

Wouldn't he? Perhaps that wasn't a fair question. She didn't think anything would stop Edmund from wanting the truth to come out, but surely he'd agree this was a dire situation. And that it wouldn't do anyone any good to pose the questions and demand the answers she needed when Hugo seemed so near death.

Still, she wished there were someone in the house on *her* side—besides Emily—and maybe that was all her desire to talk with her father really meant.

Where *was* Emily, anyway?

"Madam."

Bingham, scaring her to death as usual. Wanting what?

Cool and calm. She must not let him discomfit her. It was her ongoing prayer. He still unnerved her just by his presence.

"Yes, Bingham?"

"Most happy you and Mr. Lujan are back at Waybury, madam."

"Thank you, Bingham." Cool, calm, aloof, removed.

"Does madam wish to have some tea?"

"That would be very nice." But she wondered why *he* was being so nice as she watched his paper-thin body slither out of the room.

Slither was the word. Bingham was a snake, striking in silence, never shedding his skin.

She felt surrounded by enemies. There was nowhere to go in this house, and even this room, in which she had found some comfort, seemed alien after several days away.

This room. Where, high above her head, on the topmost shelf in the most obscure corner, she had found that album of photographs.

How did one forget about that? Or the stone . . . the diamond . . . which she had wrapped up and tucked securely in her bodice. This was the proof, this was the one thing with which she could confront Hugo and know she stood on firm ground.

Except the ground was shaky, it was quicksand, and she might well get sucked into the mire of forgiving and forgetting.

Especially if Hugo—

But no. Not to think of that. Too easy to think that would happen.

"Madam."

"On the desk, please."

"As you wish." Bingham set down the tray, bowed, withdrew.

A serpent in *her* garden. Watching her again, with his squinty, reptilian eyes. Still spying for Hugo, even now.

Even now. So Hugo was sentient enough for that . . .

And she still saw plots everywhere.

"Ah, the happy bride . . ."

Kyger. Angry and popping off at anyone in his path.

Cool, calm. Forget he's Hugo's son, and that he had said sometime in the too-recent past that he loved her. "Have some tea."

"The ready remedy," he said caustically, but he didn't refuse it. "Madam Galliard, collected and ready for anything. Anyone. How do you do it, Jancie? How do you continually wind up in Lujan's arms after he's treated you like so much refuse?"

"I married him," she said carefully.

"You married Waybury, you mean. You married him, my father, me, the house, the farm. You don't need Lujan, actually. You have everything you ever wanted just as things are. So of course it's easy to take him back time after time. It has nothing to do with him, your marriage."

Too brutal, too honest. She couldn't deny some of it was true, but she wouldn't give him the satisfaction of giving any credence to his cold-blooded assessment.

And she loved Lujan. She had fallen in love with him all over again these past two days at the town house.

"Let me refresh your cup," she said instead.

He grasped her wrist as she reached for it. "I'm leaving."

"Perhaps it's time," she said, disengaging her hand and topping off his tea. He hadn't even taken a sip, and she poured too much and it splashed over into the saucer.

"You don't want to know why?"

"What do I know? You know everything, Kyger. I know nothing, not even why I married Lujan."

He jacked himself up from his seat, and banged the cup and saucer down on the desktop, spilling tea everywhere.

She yanked the bell pull. "It's a beautiful desk—I would hate to see it ruined." A maid appeared. "Some cotton cloth, please— I'm afraid I spilled my tea."

"Yes, madam."

She looked up at Kyger. "I think you're right. It's time for you to go."

"As I said—you married the house, and the life." He turned on his heel and left her just as the maid came in. She wiped down the desktop, she took Kyger's cup, and she withdrew.

Out the window, Jancie saw Kyger, mounted and riding furiously toward the village.

In her hand, she held a cold cup of tea. Cold comfort, at that. She didn't have Lujan now.

Hugo had him, held tight, by virtue of the almost certain possibility of his death.

Chapter Nineteen

She was exactly back where she had started—abandoned by Lujan, and searching for the truth.

Still.

Or did any of it matter anymore?

If Hugo died, everything would die with him. There would be no reparation, no answers, only the hanging, thirty-year-old question of whether Hugo had stolen a fortune in diamonds from her father.

And not having the satisfaction of knowing would kill her father. He had pushed too far for too long to have Hugo's secrets die with him.

To have had all this patience all this time, and ultimately come away with nothing . . . all those years sweltering in the hot Indian sun for this one revelatory moment which might never come.

She couldn't let go of it. She had to know. And she had to convince Lujan all over again that it was her right, and her father's, to know.

He had identified a clue that could prove it.

He had believed it was possible. In London, in the swamping heat of their bone-melting sex, Lujan had conceded that his father could be a thief.

But here, in the cool, clinical bedroom of a dying man, he would not accuse or judge him.

It was an impossible barrier. He wouldn't breach it, and if she wanted to preserve what she had, she could not cross it.

There had to be some other way . . .

. . . *if she found the album, or the cache of diamonds . . . ?*

Not realistic. She'd been singularly unsuccessful before. She wouldn't even know where to look. Every possibility would be closed to her anyway, with those mysterious unseen eyes— Bingham's eyes?—watching her every movement, everywhere.

And on top of all that, Kyger threatening to leave . . . She felt as if she had unleashed a monster.

She ought to just get out and go to her father.

Instead, she girded herself and went up to Hugo's room.

There, it was cold and quiet as a tomb. The local woman, whose name was Charlotte, was sitting in a corner, quiet as a mouse. As Jancie entered, she tiptoed to the door and whispered, "He's asleep, ma'am. Mr. Lujan just left."

"Thank you." Jancie moved to the bedside. Hugo looked pale as death, his skin like marble, unmoving as a stone.

She straightened his blanket because she didn't know what else to do.

It was time to give over, she thought. She couldn't bear the burden of her father's desire for retribution any longer, not with Hugo like this, and her marriage a function of her need to serve Edmund rather than her own needs.

It was over. There was nothing more that she could do for Edmund. Or that she wanted to do, in these circumstances.

A weight rolled off her shoulders that she hadn't known she was carrying.

That easy. Just make the decision and shrug off years of purpose in the service of maintaining some peace while a man was dying.

Just let it go.

The room felt like a crypt. It wouldn't be long now.

She would write to her father. Let him know that after all this time, he would have to let go of it, too.

Father—
Things have come to an unexpected head. Hugo

has been grievously injured and is possibly near death.
There is nothing more I can do for you here. It wouldn't
be right, nor would I feel right pursuing any other course
but to wait until nature and God decree his recovery
or his death. The latter seems most likely.

I am so sorry. I feel as if I have failed you when I
truthfully believe I've done everything I could to this
date, everything you would have wanted and more.

Tell me what you think I should do now, and I will
follow your express wishes to the letter . . .

Now *she* had lied. She hadn't failed Edmund to that extent, really. And while she had something tangible with which to confront Hugo, it just wasn't enough, and it was years too late.

And if Lujan hadn't identified what it was, she would never
have known that funny little stone was a diamond anyway. So it
was the same as if she had found nothing, and therefore, not a
flagrant misrepresentation of the facts, and just enough to excuse
the fact that she didn't tell Edmund about it at all.

How tangled was the web they were all weaving—someone
was certain to get caught in all the lies . . .

But at the moment, it didn't seem important.

She didn't care.

And she didn't know what else to do.

She came downstairs to hear Lujan's raised voice coming from
the dining room.

"Someone wants to destroy this family. Someone tried to kill
me—and then went after Hugo in my stead, and I swear to you—"

There was a low, conciliating voice in answer to that statement—and then Lujan again: "No. *No.* It's not possible, I don't
believe it. I won't believe it."

Another comment.

Lujan: "Shit."

She edged closer to hear with whom he was arguing.

"Well—" it was Kyger—damn it—"you just parse it out, big
brother. See what's on either side of the ledger. Make a count—
who is your enemy, really? Some woman you knocked up in

Town? Or the man who has always felt cheated by your family? Who has more reason to come after you? And who has he sent as his agent? And who does he really want dead?"

Lujan was silent for a moment.

He couldn't refute a thing Kyger said. Jancie knew it, he knew it, and he knew the truth because she had told him. How much was he willing to share with Kyger?

"Jancie found something in Mother's room."

"And what was she doing in Mother's room?"

"Well, that's the thing, although maybe it's beside the point to what she found."

"Which was?"

"A diamond, rough, uncut."

"No . . . impossible . . ."

"And she claims there were many more under Olivia's bed."

Kyger laughed—a short, derisive bark. "Did she? How cunning of her."

"She said she had a handful of them, she touched them . . ."

"And where are they now?"

Lujan was silent again.

Jancie couldn't blame him. Listening to Kyger's skeptical response would have made anyone doubtful. It sounded false, desperate—everything she was and felt. A cold feeling washed over her as she comprehended what next he would say.

"Gone."

"Umm-hmm—except just the very one Jancie happened to have . . ."

Another silence.

"That she probably had all along, you idiot. That she probably planted under Mother's bed, though God knows why she would even be in Mother's room. Well, brother mine, you've been gulled by the mistress of misdirection. She finds a stone, you identify it as the one thing that will prove that your own father is guilty of everything she says he is, and—oh, by the way, he's on the edge of death suddenly. How coincidental. Just like all your accidents. All of a sudden. And who is in the middle of each and every incident? Who benefits if you die? What happens if Hugo dies? What's left?"

A long, hard silence.

"You and Jancie, as it happens," Lujan said finally, coldly. "So maybe the story is that *you* are in collusion with her."

Jancie fled. If she could have left the house then, she would have, but calling a carriage to go back to London would have been a stupid move right now. They'd chase her to London, she thought. They'd chase her around the world for what she'd done.

All she wanted was to make herself inconspicuous, to reduce herself into a speck of dust so no one could ever find her.

There was nothing left, *nothing*.

Lujan believed her no longer, and thought it was possible that she had not only wanted to kill him, but also his father—all in the name of avenging her own father . . .

She was the one caught in the web of lies, and she had murdered everything she ever wanted in the process.

She just did not know where to go, what to do that someone wouldn't see her.

"Madam?"

She jumped. Turned. Mrs. Ancrum.

"Is there anything madam wishes?"

As if she were still the mistress of anything except deceit.

She swallowed her panic. "Thank you, Mrs. Ancrum. No. Except that everything is being done for Mr. Hugo."

"Indeed, madam. Charlotte is not to leave his side, and notify myself or Mr. Lujan if anything should change. The doctor will be by once again tomorrow morning."

Make it seem like everything was normal. "We'll dine informally tonight."

"Yes, so Mr. Lujan said. Thank you, madam."

Oh God . . . She sagged against the wall as Mrs. Ancrum disappeared down the hallway. What else? Her nerves were stretched to the breaking point. She was shaking and icy cold, and she wanted nothing more than to go upstairs and just burrow under the covers in their bedroom.

Except it was no longer *their* bedroom. She was no longer mistress of the house, and there was no safe haven here. No place to hide anywhere.

If she could sink through the floor. Or run away. Or become invisible so she could bury her shame, sneak away, and never return to Waybury again . . .

She would never send that *mea culpa* letter to her father. Never wanted to see him ever again. Never, as long as she lived, forgive him for manipulating her all these years.

Lujan would divorce her. Quickly.

She would lose herself on another continent, a woman without a country.

She had no future, and her past was a lie. Where did a person go to escape the consequences of her actions?

No one ever used the parlor—she could slip in there and it was possible no one would find her for days. For years. Forever.

At least she could take a moment's respite from the pounding guilt she felt for all the years of betrayals, both her father's and hers.

The parlor was dark. She felt her way to one of the sofas by the fireplace and sank down in the farthest corner.

No lights here, but she still felt as if unseen eyes were watching her, judging her. She buried her head against the sofa arm.

Dear God, what was she going to do?

And then she heard it—or maybe she was dreaming it—that crickling, marbley sound rolling inexorably across the parlor floor.

Son of a bitch—where was Jancie?

No one had seen her since—not since Mrs. Ancrum had seen her in the hallway earlier. Since she'd visited Hugo's room this evening for a couple of minutes after he had been there.

Since they'd come back this afternoon.

She hadn't come to dinner.

She seemed to have totally disappeared. But she hadn't left the house, that anyone noticed. Hadn't called for the carriage. Wasn't in their room. Or the library.

She had a lot to answer for, he thought. It was too much—between her story of the diamond and his father's accident, and all the grim possibilities in between.

He felt split in three different directions, three different loyalties. To his father and Kyger. To Jancie.

Maybe not to Jancie, because this whole notion of Edmund taking his revenge through her was enough to shake what little faith he had in the veracity of her version of her story.

But there were so many different stories, so many different perspectives. Kyger had shaken him to the core with his, so of course he'd struck back. But every permutation made so much sense; any one of them could be the truth.

And every point led back to Edmund. And, if he looked clearly through the fog of his explosive orgasms, to Jancie as his proxy.

It was the worst possible scenario. He had believed her story about finding the diamond until Kyger shot it down. But that didn't mean it couldn't be true. It was as true as her conspiring with Kyger, as true as her having been insinuated at Waybury for the sole purpose of marrying him.

There was a little bit of truth in each of those accounts, and no one truth in any of them. And until he knew the truth about the diamonds, nothing could be resolved, and the master teller of these tales would go scot-free.

He had to find Jancie. She had to be somewhere in the house.

"You still want to believe her," Kyger drawled, watching him over the dinner *en buffet* as they picked at their vegetables.

"As much as I want to believe you."

"Listen, big brother—Jancie was a siren insinuated in our midst. I don't know how her father engineered it, but somehow he did. She's been taught since the day she was born to hate the Galliards. She came here to wreak havoc on us, and she has. Just the fact that all three of us wanted to marry her—you don't call that destructive? How did she do that?"

"I can tell you," Lujan said, "but it will kill all your theories."

"I'll listen, but I won't say I'll agree with you."

Lujan shrugged. "It was as simple as this—Hugo wanted to silence Edmund. He thought that by marrying Jancie he'd keep Edmund's demands in line because Jancie would have the kind of life Edmund had always wanted for her and status as the mistress of Waybury. Hugo thought Edmund wouldn't make outrageous demands or blackmail him if his daughter were his wife. And, as a further inducement—he'd have all that fertile, young flesh . . ."

Dear heaven—even now, thinking about Hugo's hands on Jancie . . . it made him prickle. *Never.*

He went on, "Which was the first of my reasons for asking Jancie to marry me? You know I didn't want Father getting more heirs on her. And he damned well would have, with a woman like her. There could have been a half-dozen more brothers and sisters—not a pleasant prospect in the scheme of things.

"And second to that, I, too, wanted to keep Edmund at bay. The threat from him was never overt—it was always hovering in the background. After he contacted us, he made certain Father always knew that he was there, waiting to pounce. Marrying Jancie seemed like an elegant solution to both problems.

"You, of course, were merely in love with her."

Kyger leapt on him. "And you're out of your mind. She's tried to kill you three times now, and who knows how she got to Hugo, but she did. She's picking us off one by one until there's no one left but her and Edmund. Or are you too whipsawed to see it?"

"I see it—but is it the truth?" Lujan said. "I don't know."

"It fits like a puzzle," Kyger growled. "Which will never be solved because you'll be dead."

"Jesus, baby brother—you sound too damned bloodthirsty for my comfort. Let's take first things first. You check on Hugo again. I have to find Jancie."

"Oh—she fled the scene of the crime already?"

"God, for someone who was in love with her, you're sure not in love with her."

"Well, she chose you, in spite of my best efforts. But all these coincidences can't be overlooked."

"But they could be rearranged to form another picture."

"God, you're besotted. You can't *see* the whole picture for the fog in your brain. And by the time you do, you'll be goddamned dead."

"Hell, I hope not. We'll just have to be more careful. It's us against Jancie. If she's really the instigator, she has no chance at all."

She was frozen in place. The rolling sound had stopped and she could hear their footsteps, back and forth up and down, Kyger calling to Lujan that Hugo was about the same. Lujan calling to Kyger to check out the stables to make sure Jancie wasn't hiding there.

Oh? They were searching for her? She'd have thought they would never want to see her again, would be happy if she just up and disappeared.

Or she might just go insane from that ghostly sound. It held her in place for the length of time she heard it. She felt as if those ghostly eyes were watching, and knew her every move.

It was strange to be huddled in that dark netherworld of an empty, little-used room, to hear everything going on in the house around her, and to comprehend that it all centered on her, and on Hugo.

The house pulsed around her as if it were a living thing; the house had a story, too. Of Olivia, who had inherited it, and welcomed her husband home from his allegedly unsuccessful foray in South Africa.

Of a family and three sons. A child gone missing. A partner coming back from the dead. An ill and dying wife. A stranger in their midst . . . one who was there by design and desire . . .

She had gone over and over it in her mind, and there was no getting away from it: Edmund had instigated her presence at Waybury, had wanted to deliberately put her in proximity to Lujan—or Kyger—and so that nature would take its course, and he would be one step closer to taking his revenge.

Nothing about it was precise. It was all plots and dreams, manipulation and prayers. How had Edmund lived like that all those years while he schemed and hoped, and couldn't even know if anything he planned would come to fruition?

It was beyond her, and she thanked God her mother hadn't lived to witness all this happening. It was enough that Jancie had been his pawn, his willing accomplice. Had known, without his spelling it out, precisely what he wanted her to do.

She was haunted by the knowledge of that. Haunted by the spooky, rolling sound which she solely associated with the child who'd gone missing. It was as if Gaunt were watching her. Gaunt knew her secrets. He lived in the album, and he would, eventually, show her where.

But for the moment, she sat like a statue, listening to Lujan and Kyger racing around, gratified they were even looking for her, because right now, in the dark environs of the cold and empty parlor, she felt as if she were really lost.

* * *

Meuuuww . . .

From where she sat hunched up on the sofa, Jancie could hear Emily. Emily was close, and looking for her.

She had almost forgotten about Emily.

Meuw. Her cat call was soft, as if she knew Jancie was hiding, and wanted only a sense of where she was, so her cat sense was guiding her.

Reuww. Suddenly she was there, landing lightly on Jancie's lap and rubbing against her elbow. *Owww.*

Jancie brushed her away. Emily came right back up onto her lap. *Owww.*

Insistent, this time.

Jancie ignored her. *Can't you see I don't want to move?*

Mrrooww. Emily didn't see that at all, obviously.

And her voice was getting louder.

How did you tell a cat to lower her meow? It was such a ridiculous notion that Jancie blinked away her tears.

Emily made sense—the only thing in her life that did. Emily didn't hate her, didn't judge her, use her, or manipulate her. Emily was her only family. She had always thought so at St. Bonny's; it was no less true now.

Emily was the best part of her life. The one that kept her sane, and kept her going.

She reached out her hand and Emily fit her head right up under her palm. She stroked Emily's soft, pointy ears, and listened to her soft, deep-throated purr.

Instantly she felt better. Her tears stopped. She felt warm, she felt as if things weren't hopeless and that there *was* a solution somewhere.

That much Emily knew, and that much her reassuring presence told her. With Emily here, she didn't feel haunted, and the shadows simply fell away. Emily knew her, understood her . . . everything about her, warts and all.

She gathered the bundle of warm, pulsating cat fur into her arms. God, what would she ever have done without Emily?

Meuw. A tiny little protest, hardly enough to take note of. She needed this contact, she thought; Emily was the only one who could assure her that everything would be all right.

Emily broke loose suddenly and jumped down on the floor. *Ooww.*

Now what?

She sat on her haunches, facing the door. *Ooowww. Listen . . .*

What? *What?*

Oooowww . . .

Oh God, she knew that chilling howl. It meant *come now.*

I'm coming.

She jumped up, her heart pounding with fear. Lujan . . . ?

Emily ran out of the parlor. She followed cautiously, careful to make sure the hallway was clear.

Up the steps, no one coming . . . down the upper hallway, so suspiciously empty—her knees shaking, her hands boneless.

Owww. Emily sat right down in front of Hugo's door and looked at Jancie over her shoulder.

I can't.

Mrooww. You have to . . .

But Charlotte would be there. And it wouldn't take thirty seconds for her to reach for the bell pull and summon everyone else, and Lujan would surmise the worst reason why she had come.

Ooowww. You have to go in.

She knew it; she had a strong feeling of foreboding, heightened by the ghostly, rolling marble that had paralyzed her, and all the accusations leveled against her tonight.

And Emily was so adamant—what if that woman Charlotte weren't there?

Mrrroow—NOW . . .

She reached out her hand, tentatively grasping the doorknob as if it were burning hot. Turned it. Let herself into the crypt-cold room.

The cold *empty* room. Charlotte wasn't there.

But something else was: a pillow, over Hugo's face—

Dear God—no, no, NO . . .

Owwww . . .

"NOOOOOO . . ." She cried out, she screamed it in concert with Emily's mournful howl. She grabbed the pillow off his face, but even she, in her anguish, could see that Hugo was dead, his face blue, his body stone-cold.

Thundering footsteps, that she heard as if in the distance. A moment later, Lujan and Kyger burst into the room, followed by March, Bingham, and Mrs. Ancrum.

And there she stood, by Hugo's bed, the pillow still in her hand, and tears streaming from her eyes.

Everyone stopped in shock. It was like a tableau, everyone poised in motion, no one knowing quite what to do.

And when she finally looked up at Lujan, she knew it was really the end of everything—there was just nothing else to be said.

Emily moved first, leaping up onto the bed and throwing herself, claws first, at Lujan.

Jancie reacted instinctively, throwing the pillow in Kyger's face, and wheeling toward the door made a mad dash out of the room, not even thinking she would get farther than the stairs.

She heard Lujan's voice shouting after her, heard March and Kyger arguing.

She turned toward a light flickering down the hallway, not thinking—just seeking safety anyplace where she could close a room and lock it.

—Olivia's room?

How could this be?

The door was ajar—lamplight flickered from within, a shadow moving on the walls. The ghost? Who stole the album and diamonds, who was stalking the family, and who watched her all the time?

She pushed open the door with icy cold hands.

"... Father ... ?"

Chapter Twenty

He was searching the room. Things had been tossed on the bed, on the floor, he had rifled Olivia's desk, gone through her papers, the few books she had on a shelf, torn down the curtains, ripped apart her bed, and at the sound of Jancie's voice, he stopped, turned, and said, just as casually as if they had met on the street, "Hello, daughter. I got tired of waiting."

She was so shocked to see him, she couldn't move, couldn't speak. She hadn't seen him in years, and she was stunned at how he had aged—his features were sunken, his body was thin and slack, and he was slightly hunched over. If his face were not so familiar, she wasn't sure she would have recognized him at all.

Except for the eyes. The eyes were still there, hot, glittery, greedy with the lust to get what he wanted. His face was flushed as well, from his exertions, and he straightened slightly as he heard footsteps pounding down the hall.

"Hmph. The gathering of the clan."

"What—?" Her lips were stiff, her life was over—what was her father doing here, and in Olivia's room, of all places? Or had he gone to another room first?

Her heart stopped. Time stopped. Edmund's patience had finally worn thin. He had come to take his own revenge in the only way he knew how, and the diamonds be damned.

"What are—" her voice sounded rusty in her own ears, "you doing here?"

He shrugged. "Doing your job, daughter. Getting to the bottom of things, finally. You made me wait too long, I'm afraid. Had to take things into my own hands. Thought you might be too—preoccupied . . . Ah—the progeny . . . Lujan, I take it?"

Jancie shot Lujan a terrified look. He motioned for her not to speak.

"Edmund?"

"The one and same, my boy. So sorry about your father."

"Are you?"

"Oh, absolutely. He was my dearest friend once upon a time. It was my greatest gift to help him find peace."

Shock reverberated through the room.

Edmund? On the premises, on the grounds, stalking Hugo, making more plans, plans that didn't include Jancie . . . plans to take over Waybury one murder at time?

Jancie felt sick. Edmund—how long had he been in England? In Hertfordshire?

"Well," Edmund said, "isn't this cozy? I'm meeting my son-in-law for the first time, and we're here in Olivia's place—Olivia, the love of my life—did you know, my boy? Oh, and is that Kyger behind you, there?"

It was March, actually, but he nodded yes at a signal from Lujan.

"You look nothing like him—or her. But—Hugo was ever one to sow wild oats. Now, me—I was always focused on one thing only—working the mines, making our fortune. But do you know what? The son of a bitch married Olivia before we even got on the ship. Married her, got sons with her, got us to Kaamberoo, got all those stones from the pipes, and then he tried to kill me . . ." He trailed off for a moment, comprehending that this was as familiar a story to Lujan as it was to Jancie.

"Well, be that as it may, here I am, Hugo is dead, Jancie is married to you, and eventually all this will be mine. That was the plan, that was my scheme—Jancie and I would take it back, bit by bit, piece by piece, and somewhere, in the process, find the fortune your father stole from me.

"So . . . if you gentlemen will excuse me . . ."

He was deranged. Jancie saw it in his eyes, heard it in his voice. The waiting was over for Edmund. The moment he pressed that pillow down on Hugo's face, his reason had snapped, and everything he had done in innocence and revenge turned to murder and madness.

Jancie didn't know where to begin. Lujan kept motioning for her not to move. The silence in the room expanded and grew deafening. Edmund stood there, as if he were waiting for them all to leave so he could continue his search.

Time stopped. Edmund shrugged and turned to Olivia's armoire. Lujan took a step forward, which must have sounded like a gunshot to Edmund, because he whirled, a gun in his hand, and aimed it right at Lujan.

"My dear boy. You could have been my boy, you know? My poor deceased wife could only get a girl. She died in childbirth, you know. I hope Jancie produces sons—if not with you, with . . . someone. Your brother, perhaps? Yes, I think so—since I'm about to kill you."

"Don't add this to the litany of sins you've committed," Lujan said. His voice was cool, calm, neutral. "It *was* you, wasn't it? At the town house? Poisoning my food? Loosening the cinch? Spooking the horse?"

"Subtle, wasn't it? I really liked the symmetry of both you and Hugo dying by virtue of being thrown from your horses. But I never get what I want. I wanted my diamonds and I never got them. I know he had them. I know he hid them. I know he never could have spent all of them. Jancie?"

"I never found them," she said shakily, another lie.

"Hugo knows."

"No. His secrets died with him, Edmund, and you are the one who killed them."

Edmund let off a shot that blasted into the ceiling. "*NO!* No. That son of a bitch left me for dead. Do you think a man ever forgets that? So I left him for dead. An eye for an eye—finally. Jancie couldn't do it. A son would've done it. A son wouldn't have left me burning up in India all these years."

He was crazy—absolutely crazy. How could she not have known? "Father—" Even though she knew it was no use.

"Useless. Making me wait all these years . . ."

"Three years, Father."

"Nineteen years, *daughter*. From the day you were born, you were meant to give me back my life. And what did you do? Frittered time away at that stupid boarding school, came here and played la-di-dah companion to Olivia, as if you were some kind of daughter to her, married the son of my enemy—fit right into the life at Waybury and couldn't find a place for me—couldn't find anything I wanted, I needed. Always excuses. Couldn't find anything here, there's nothing there . . . suggesting what?—maybe I was wrong, I *imagined* he tried to blow me up? I imagined the loss of memory, the loss of a fortune?

"No, my girl—you got too comfortable, too fast with these thieves, and the end result was what I should have done at the first—come here myself, wrested the truth from Hugo, and killed the lot of you. Which I will make up for now. Lujan first . . ."

He lifted the gun. Lujan tried to rush him, but Edmund was prepared: he sidestepped Lujan's hurtling body, and grabbed Jancie and pulled her in front of him.

"Now we find out what a daughter is good for," Edmund said. He pressed the barrel of the gun against Jancie's neck. "There we go—that's a more docile Lujan. You—Kyger—" Speaking to March, who looked terrified. "Step in the room. You're next, you know. Then Jancie. Yes, my dear. Even you. Blood will not save you."

Time froze again as March edged his way into the room, his eyes on Lujan only. Tailing him came Emily, silent as fog, but only Jancie noticed her slipping in and curling around March's feet and into the shadows.

Everyone was focused on Edmund, on the gun, on the awful realization that Edmund was mad and perfectly willing to kill them all.

Except that Lujan was unnaturally calm, and—where *was* Kyger?

"Father—" she tried again, knowing it was futile. This had been a plan, too, a long-conceived plan he had carried out in stages, probably from the time she married Lujan. He'd gotten tired of waiting. He thought she had betrayed him, and been seduced by his enemies. "—I would have given this all up and come to India to be with you," she whispered brokenly.

"Who wanted you there? What else were you good for but that for which Lujan used you? Don't place so much importance on your role in this, Jancie. You won the golden ring. I hope you enjoyed these few months of your misbegotten marriage, when you totally forgot about me."

But she'd never forgotten about him. Everything she had done was motivated by him, by her desire to find justice for him.

She shot a desperate glance at Lujan. She hadn't told the whole truth about the diamonds, she thought. Maybe that—

But no, Lujan shook his head. One stone would not make up for all the lost years and his lost mind.

Jancie felt the gun barrel move to her head, felt her father's arm tighten around her midriff. Saw Lujan's stance shift slightly, saw March move subtly to one side, saw Emily out of the corner of her eye, felt that pulsating moment of portent just before something was about to happen.

She heard the ominous click by her ear, felt Edmund's unsatiated fury, saw Lujan incrementally move again, saw Emily crouched just by Lujan's feet, saw a shadow just outside the bedroom door, felt her mortality, her madness, her utter defeat . . .

And in that instant, several things happened simultaneously— Kyger crashed in through the window, Emily jumped, digging her claws into Edmund's leg, March fell on the floor, Lujan wrenched her away from Edmund, and a shot rang out from the doorway.

"You!" Edmund's last words as he fell, his eyes on the doorway, the smoking gun, and Bingham, paper-thin, disapproving, his unexpected angel of death.

"God, what a mess," Lujan muttered. It was worse than that because he had so maligned Jancie, had been so suspicious of her, could readily believe that she was a liar and a cheat because she was Edmund's daughter, the man in the background, the threat, the unseen menace, the danger to them all.

And what was he? The scheming son of his traitorous father. The only one whose hands were wholly clean was Kyger. He was a goddamned saint.

And Kyger was in love with Jancie still.

And in spite of everything that had happened, so was he.

What?

He looked across the dining room table at Jancie. She look drawn, haggard; her face was paper white, her hands shaking still.

They were waiting for Kyger, who, with March, had taken on the task of removing Edmund's body from Olivia's room.

In love with Jancie . . . this was not the time to be ruminating on love and life. And certainly in his life, he never, ever allowed that word to intrude in his consciousness.

They had more important things to deal with, anyway. Where to bury Edmund, for one thing. Although it would be a just irony to inter him on the grounds of the house he had coveted for most of his life.

Maybe he'd rest easy then.

"Why did Father say that?" Jancie said suddenly. "As if he recognized Bingham?"

"Didn't you think Bingham was about the last person to be our family's avenger?"

"I don't know. I don't know anything."

He made a decision. "We'll bury him here, Jancie. Maybe he'll rest in peace."

Tears stung her eyes. "Thank you." And he'd banish her. Nothing could expiate her sins, not even her father dying for them.

"Jancie . . ." His voice was low. "It's not your fault." He could forgive anything at this point. His stalker was dead, could threaten his family no more.

His family. Jancie.

"All right. I'd like to believe that. I'm not so certain that's so."

"We'll start over. We'll . . ."

Kyger burst into the room. "The deed is done. We laid him out in the tack room rather than in the house. It seemed right."

"That's fine. We'll bury him here."

"What!! Have you gone mad?"

"I don't know. It seems fitting somehow."

"Jesus. Fine. It's too late to start an argument with you. We should get some sleep."

"All right. We'll figure out the rest in the morning. Jancie?"

300 / Thea Devine

"I can sleep on the sofa," she said dully. She didn't know quite where she fit in now, the daughter of a man who was a murderer.

"Come upstairs with me," Lujan said. She was so obviously glazed wlith shock; she couldn't know what she was saying, or even what she thought. It was too much to take in tonight and no time to try to analyze what it was about.

Even he felt a little dazed by it all. "Come . . ." He held out his hand. "Come to bed."

It was a house of shadows that late at night. And of spirits and retribution. And still-unsolved mysteries.

Edmund was the key to some of them. But Edmund was dead now. Dead. She kept saying that to herself as Lujan made her lie down, clothed, and covered her over, and then settled himself in a chair to keep watch over her.

Edmund was gone, but had she ever had Edmund—a father—really? Or had she always been this puppet, her strings pulled from thousands of miles away while she willingly believed in the innocence of her quest?

The questions were imponderable. Her culpability would drive her mad, and then there was no question but that Lujan would divorce her.

Cold comfort there, but a fitting ending to her betrayals and lies.

Edmund is dead.

Had she imagined the rest?

Somehow in the netherworld of sleep, she was back in Olivia's room, scrabbling under the bed. She could feel the stones in her hand, the warmth of Emily by her side, *meuwing* and scratching.

The album was under the bed just where she'd left it under the footboard. Good. She had them both now—the stones and the photographs. She could show everything to Lujan and then he would believe her, and they could start all over again.

She wriggled out from under the bed, and sat with her back against the footboard. She had to make sure the pictures were there. With her free hand, she opened the album. Yes, yes. All the photographs—eight, maybe in all. Just as she remembered. Baby Gaunt. One-year-old Gaunt. Older Gaunt, older brothers, younger Hugo, Gaunt streaked with dirt and clutching pebbles in his hand . . .

And there it was—the crickling, marbley sound of something rolling down the hallway.

Awake or asleep—?

Rolling, rolling, in her consciousness forever, she would hear that hard marble sound of something rolling down the hallway.

Another one dropped, rolling. Stopped—no, that was real, what she was hearing—not a dream . . .

No, a dream . . .

She didn't know if she was awake or asleep, but that stone kept rolling in her head, in her brain, on the floor—in the room, maybe—

Or she was going mad. Maybe she had inherited the madness, and she would hear that marbley sound in her head forever . . .

No. She was awake. Distinctly awake, and she could hear the heavy tread of someone walking down the hallway.

At this hour of the night?

No—a dream. She swung out of bed, certain she was in the midst of a dream, and padded out into the hallway without her shoes.

A large, hulking shadow moved down the dimly lit hallway, bearing an oblong box on one shoulder, from which something small kept dropping, and rolling.

Absolutely a dream.

She followed after the shadow, because what was the worst that could happen in a dream? She'd wake up. She'd die.

Click, roll, stop. Click, roll, stop.

She bent over and picked up the object.

A stone. Small, more rounded, glassy. Many stones, littering the hallway as the shadow came to Hugo's room, and pushed open the door.

Light blared out—candles, lamps were lit within, and she could see clearly that it was Bingham at the door.

Of course. In a dream, it would always be the person you least expected to see.

And he was carrying that oblong box that looked like . . .

Like . . .

It's a dream . . .

. . . a coffin . . .

She edged her way down the hall, picking up stones as she

stepped on them and putting them in her pocket, until she reached the doorway.

She was afraid to look in the room.

Of course she was. This was a dream, and something horrible was in that room.

I have to know.

Where was Lujan?

No, Lujan was sleeping—it was all up to her. That was what dreams were about—the symbols and the things you suppressed, that you feared.

Like a room with a body in it. And a disapproving old butler who was carrying a strange, oblong box. And stones on the floor, which could have been the very ones she had found under Olivia's bed.

She had to go in that room, and she was scared to death of what she would find.

She peered around the casing. Bingham had set the box down on a table he'd drawn up by the bed. And she could see clearly that the box was old, rotting, and the corners had been gnawed and scratched until there was nothing there but hanging shards of wood, sawdust, and holes.

Sawdust under Emily's claws . . .

This was the perfect dream—she'd finally discover the answers to every question . . .

"Come in, madam."

So he'd seen her, the disapproving, paper-thin Bingham. Or heard her. Well, that was fine—for a dream.

She eased into the room, the whole scene—Hugo a stone-dead presence on the bed, the rotting little coffin, the paper-thin butler with a righteous expression on his disapproving face—a grotesque nightmare . . .

She gestured to the coffin. "That's Gaunt, isn't it?"

"Gaunt's bones, madam. I've brought them to Mr. Hugo. He would want them here."

So Hugo had always known what had happened to Gaunt. Terror coursed through her.

She stood riveted, unable to move. She had to ask, but the words stuck in her throat. She didn't know if she wanted to know. She didn't know how she couldn't ask.

It was a dream, after all. The answer might not be the truth. Or it might be the clue she had always wanted to find.

"How did he die?" Her question was barely above a whisper.

"He found the diamonds, you see. He wanted to show his mama and brothers all the funny stones . . ."

The funny stones—

. . . the pebbles in the picture in his hand? And Hugo had seen that and thought he had no other choice—?

"And Mr. Hugo never could convince him that the stones had to be a secret between them. So . . . we did what needed to be done."

We.

"And you kept the funny stones in the coffin under Olivia's bed . . ."

"It got moved now and again when she went into a fit of cleaning the house, you see, but yes, Gaunt was always with her, and our secret was always safe. I made certain of it."

Our.

"Until *you* came." The tone changed, grew ominous, his paper-thin face implacable. This was a man with no scruples; he had killed her father, aided and abetted Hugo in his quest to keep his secrets, had no qualms at all about killing a child—or killing her, for that matter.

A murderer to the bone. A thief.

Murderers and thieves.

From the jungles and mine pits of Kaamberoo he had come, the one who had made it possible for Hugo to return to Waybury with a fortune in diamonds, who possibly had set the explosives intended to kill her father, who'd stayed on at Waybury all these years, a comfortable pensioner always certain of his place.

And now Hugo was gone—

He'd take the diamonds and disappear.

It was a dream. It couldn't possibly be true.

"And so, madam, when you pry where it isn't meant for you to pry, you must take the consequences."

Gaunt's bones and a coffin full of diamonds—rough and uncut, like the thirty years of secrets and betrayals it had taken to conceal them . . .

"You watched me . . ." she whispered.

"Yes, madam."

"That ghostly, rolling sound in the hallway . . . ?"

"Myself, madam, to scare you away . . ."

To terrorize her, he meant. And he had . . .

No—it was a dream—it *had* to be a dream. Everything she'd sensed, everything she'd felt, heard—all of it Bingham, in service of his master . . .

A dream—

Except that Bingham was pointing that gun at her, the same one with which he'd shot Edmund.

You—of course Edmund had known him—from the fields at Kaamberoo. Hugo's ally, working side by side to swindle his partner.

What a nightmare. Every piece of the puzzle shifting right into place. Now she only had to wake up, before he killed her.

"Madam . . ."

"It's a dream," she murmured.

"Oh, it is very real, madam. You will die."

Ooowww. Oh God, Emily—Emily was in her dream, sitting in the doorway, staring at Bingham. Staring like she was putting a spell on him or something, with the intensity and hatred of a predator.

"I hate cats," Bingham said, aiming the gun at Emily and firing. Emily bolted. The bullet hit the floor. And then he had no choice—he had to try for Jancie—he had to fulfill Hugo's dying wishes . . .

He aimed again as Lujan shouted her name. She whirled—the bullet whizzed by her into the opposite wall, and Lujan raced into the room.

It was real—*real!*

Bingham froze, and then he threw down the gun and dove out the window to his most certain death.

They buried Gaunt with Olivia. Those fragile bones, hiding all those secrets. That rotting coffin, lined with valuable stones. Whose fortune, whose diamonds? And the album. Hugo had put the album with the bones, fleshing out the boy who had been, and burying once again the one clue to his disappearance that no one ever would have deduced: the handful of pebbles in the photograph.

Not unlike the handful of pebbles Jancie had culled from under the bed. She wept for Gaunt, for his little lost life, for his curiosity, for his misfortune to have found Hugo's fortune, with which action he had sealed his fate.

What an adorable, sweet, mischievous child he must have been. How Olivia must have mourned him. She must never have gotten over that. And she had never known he was buried all those years under her bed, the scent of death bleached from his bones by then.

The tangled web.

What a monster Hugo had been. Two fathers, two monsters, each in his own way. How did the children of such monsters live with that?

They buried Hugo and Edmund side by side, partners in life, partners in death, both equally sharing the wealth of Waybury.

They buried Bingham in the village cemetery.

And they came back to Waybury and they counted the stones. A fortune in small, filthy, irregularly shaped, uncut stones.

"We'll divide them," Lujan decreed. "There's no way to determine equality—it will have to by count. And in this way, we'll be free."

But were they? They were tethered to the past by the stones. By the greed and lust for diamonds and wealth. What would the possession of those diamonds, uncut, worth much, do to them?

Were they their fathers' children, the strain of madness and greed running through their veins?

They agreed to go back to London that day, all of them together.

March made it possible—they went on ahead, and he packed for all of them and joined them later the next day, bringing Emily with him as well.

Kyger would stay with them for perhaps a week.

"I told you—I'm leaving," he said over dinner in the town house dining room. Poole hovered. They wondered about Poole as they would wonder about every servant now who had worked for any length of time in Hugo's service.

There was so much to do—announcements to be sent to the newspapers, a period of mourning to be observed, discreet inquiries into how one disposed of such a valuable treasure trove.

Lujan already planned to allocate his share to enhancing and refurbishing Waybury. And they wouldn't return there until every vestige of what had happened there was painted and plastered over and gone.

And Kyger was leaving. "It's all yours, brother mine. Everything that should have been yours all these years. Welcome to the world that I will be so happy to leave."

"You weren't unhappy," Lujan said.

"No. Just waiting in the wings, dear brother. Always the understudy for you, Lujan, only better. Except you've changed. And so it will be Kyger on his own now. No understudies for me."

Kyger was right. Something had changed. The burden of guilt for the sins of his father, and for his own sins, had turned Lujan around.

That, and having a wife.

Jancie, still pale, drawn, as guilt-ridden as he. Diamonds wouldn't buy Jancie any happiness. If he loved her—perhaps that would.

"Get a child," Kyger said to him later. "Name it after Gaunt. Let him live again."

"Yes." A child. With Jancie. A most hopeful prospect—sons, to carry on, to make a man walk tall, make a man proud.

Had his father ever been proud of him?

In all his years of screwing around, how could his father ever have been proud of him?

Did he care, in light of everything else Hugo had done? Nothing he had ever done could compare.

But he wanted any son of his to be proud of him. He wanted Jancie to be proud to bear his sons.

They bid Kyger good-bye a week later. He had converted a good part of his share of the diamonds to cash; the rest he left on deposit in the bank and he was going off into the sunset, with no destination in mind.

He held Jancie longer, perhaps, than he should have. "I do love you," he whispered for her ears only. "Don't blame yourself for any of this."

It was a handsome admission after everything he'd thought, everything he'd surmised. Her brother-in-law, about to go. Oh God, she would miss him horribly.

"I love you, too," she whispered in return. "Good-bye, good-bye."

And then it was the two of them, and everything in between.

Lust, greed, secrets, monster fathers, hidden treasure, his dying mother, the missing Gaunt . . . God—the almost insurmountable barrier of the past, crushing Jancie like a stone.

Lujan saw it, he felt it, and he felt helpless in the face of it.

He had gone past it. He had, in the way of men, put it aside, not to be reckoned with for one moment longer than was necessary. Yes, it would always be part of his past, but it didn't have to be part of his future.

And he had to make Jancie see that.

He wanted Jancie with a gnawing ache that was killing. She had to understand: their love would banish the monsters.

Love.

He wondered about the evanescent nature of love—what it was, how it snuck up on you, enhanced you, made you tall and proud and eager to conquer the world. That was how he felt right now.

How he felt about her.

He could move the stone that crushed Jancie. He could move mountains in her name.

They didn't even have to go back to Waybury. He could hire people to run the estate. He could lease out the house, they could stay in London. Every action he took pushed him one step further away from the recent disasters and one step closer to all that was good.

They could have a baby. Do exactly what Kyger suggested: give it Gaunt's name and let him live again.

Hope—he felt hope and the courage to take on the future.

Jancie was feeling it herself, the pressure to bury the past and move away from the sorrow. It was too depressing, repining over all that had happened. It pulled her down, made her feel morose when she should feel a measure of contentment that it was over, and that everything was explained.

None of it would ever alter any of the facts.

Fate had been kind, if she would but admit it, and dealt her and Lujan an equal hand: both fathers had paid for their greed, lust, and cupidity, and his long-missing brother had finally been found.

Surely that was enough on which to build a future with Lujan.

Because something *had* changed. Something vital—in him. In her. She loved him still, and all the more.

Lujan meantime had been busy taking care of those social obligations that were necessary when a family member died. The notice to the newspapers, the reading of the will, the execution of Hugo's wishes, which were simple in the extreme: a portion for Kyger, deposited immediately with his diamonds, the rest to him with the proviso that he take on his responsibilities, or the estate would devolve on Kyger.

He also arranged the complete renovation of Waybury House, and for Mrs. Ancrum to come to London to do for them.

He was careful and gentle with Jancie, making no demands, even sleeping in a separate bedroom, while she came to terms with her father's death.

Once they were apart like that for the several weeks since they'd returned to London, Jancie found she was ready, even eager, to come together with him. She missed him. She missed their sex. She missed everything about their explosive coupling. *Everything*.

But how did a wife tell a husband she missed *everything* in the aftermath of all they'd been through?

She hoped. She flirted. She touched. She waited . . .

And one night, about two weeks after Kyger left, Lujan and Mrs. Ancrum plotted and planned a special dinner for Jancie to be served in her bedroom. Lujan would deliver it on the tea cart at an appropriate hour.

It would be the first time he'd been in her bedroom since they came to London, the first time there would be any hope of sex since she had come to him here over a month ago.

The time had come. He was ready, but he didn't know if she was ready. He deliberately came early, when she would, in all probability, still be dressing.

He hoped she'd be dressing, and not sitting around dressed, in her stays.

She opened the door in her dressing gown, unaware of the fact, as was he, that Emily had trailed him to the room and slipped into the bedroom unnoticed from beneath the tea cart.

"So early, Lujan?"

"Umm," he murmured, pushing the cart into the bedroom. Jancie's room, redolent of Jancie's scent, presence, sex. "I'm hungry." He didn't mean for food.

Jancie closed the door. "I am, too." Nor did she mean for food.

He wheeled the cart to the window, pulled up the drop leaves, and set two chairs on either side.

She sat down, she sniffed . . . the smells were delicious, appetizing. Him opposite her in her bedroom was appetizing. Emily winding herself around her ankles was utterly familiar and comforting.

"What's first?"

"That small covered dish to your right."

She lifted the cover, and found a bulbous, oval glass egg nestled in a warm water bath. "What's this?"

His voice was husky as he asked, "Will you wear that for me?"

She knew exactly where he meant her to wear it, and what it was intended for—to keep her labia spread and her body open for him all the time. The thought of it made her body go boneless. To always have the sensation of him spreading her . . . to know that he wanted her ready for him all the time, anywhere, everywhere . . .

Everything she had ever wanted of him, spread out before her now, more tempting, more appetizing, more filling than any meal could be.

Her answer would set the course of their lives.

She looked at him a long time. Everything had changed. He had changed. He had changed her. And now things were changing once again, and she needed to know the most important thing before she allowed him to insert the warm, bulbous, oval glass between her legs, because it would make all the difference in the world.

"First I have to ask you something."

Emily immediately jumped up beside her with an approving

mrooow. Her best companion, the one who loved her most in the world. Except maybe now, Lujan could . . .

He patted Emily's head absently as she rubbed against his shoulder. "Ask me anything."

She had to know. She said it. "Could you love me?"

Could he? He already did. It had snuck up on him, inch by inch, until she was all he ever thought about, all he could ever want. And he'd never told her. He'd taken her, and used her, and he had been cavalier with her feelings and her love from the moment they'd met.

But that Lujan was gone forever.

This Lujan wanted more—he wanted what she wanted: a home, a life, children—sons—and he wanted all of that with her. He wanted desperately to claim her now—to insert the smooth silky glass egg between her legs and begin a new sexual odyssey with her.

She wanted it, too. She was shaking with it, just imagining it— imagining lying back on the bed, feeling him spread her cunt lips, and gently burrowing the bulbous glass egg just where it would keep her spread wide apart. Imagined wearing it, walking with it, dressed with it, going about her daily chores with it, her body primed, hot, explosive all the time.

She was minutes away from it now, and the only sustenance she needed was that one satisfaction, those three important words.

All he had to do was say it, and she would lie down for him and part her legs and welcome him home.

He reached across the tabletop and took her hand. Took her in marriage one more time for better or worse, took her to the place where the past and present were wholly redeemed and nothing could ever stand in their way.

It wasn't a question of *could* he love her—he had, for longer than he had been aware; he did.

Emily pushed at him gently. *Owwwwww. Me too.*

And he said, "I love you. I do."

Please turn the page for a sneak peek at
Good With His Hands
by Lori Foster from
BAD BOYS IN BLACK TIE
Coming from Brava in May 2004.

Pete was up with the sun. After hearing that disturbing moan—disturbing on too many levels—he'd tried turning in early. But sleep had been impossible and he'd spent hours tossing and turning, thinking of Cassidy over there with someone else while his muscles cramped and protested. He'd tried to block the awful images from his mind, but they remained, prodding at him like a sore tooth: Cassidy with some suit-wearing jerk; Cassidy getting excited; Cassidy twisting and moaning.

Cassidy climaxing.

He couldn't stand it.

By seven, he was showered, standing at his closet and staring at the lack of professional clothes. Oh, he had a suit, the one he'd worn for his brothers' marriages. Gil had fussed, trying to insist that he buy a new, more expensive one, but Pete refused. He hated the idea of shopping for the thing, trying them on, getting fitted. Then he'd have to pick out a shirt, and a tie, maybe cufflinks . . . He *hated* suits.

But Cassidy loved them.

Stiff and fuming, Pete jerked on khaki shorts and a navy pullover, then paced until it got late enough to go to her place. She generally slept in on Saturday mornings. He knew her schedule as well as he knew his own. Right now she'd be curled in bed, all warm and soft and . . . He couldn't wait a minute more.

He went out his back door and stomped across the rain-wet grass to her patio. He pressed his nose against the glass doors, but it was dark inside, silent. Daunted, Pete looked around, and discovered that her bedroom window was still open.

Shit. What if the guy was still in there? What if he'd spent the night? What if, right this very moment, he was spooned up against her soft backside?

A feral growl rose from Pete's throat, startling him with the viciousness of it. No woman had ever made him growl. He left that type of behavior to his brother, Sam, who was more animal than man.

Now Gil, he was the type of man Cassidy professed to want. A suit, serious, a mover and shaker. A great guy, his brother Gil. So what would Gil do?

He'd be noble for sure, Pete decided. Gil would wait and see if she did have company, and if so, he'd give them privacy.

That thought was so repugnant, Pete started shaking.

To hell with it. His fist rapped sharply on Cassidy's glass door.

A second later, her bedroom curtain moved and Cassidy peered out. "Pete?" she groused in a sleep-froggy voice. "What are you doing?"

"Open up." Pete tried to emulate Gil, to present himself in a calm, civilized manner. "You alone in there?" he snarled.

Her eyes were huge and round in the early morning light. "No, I have the Dallas Cowboys all tucked into my bed. It's a squeeze, but we're managing."

Pete sucked in a breath. "*Cassidy* . . ."

"Of course I'm alone, you idiot." Her frowning gaze darted around the yard in confusion. "What time is it?"

She was alone. The tension eased out of Pete, making his knees weak. "I dunno, seven or so." The chill morning air frosted his breath and prickled his skin into goose bumps. "Time to get up and keep your neighbor company."

"Seven!"

He took five steps and looked at her through the screen. She had a bad case of bedhead and her eyes were puffy, still vague with sleep. She looked tumbled and tired and his heart softened with a strange, deep thump. "Open up, Cassidy."

Still confused, not that he blamed her, she rubbed her eyes, pushed her hair out of her face. "Yeah, all right. Keep your pants on." She started to turn away.

"What fun will that be?"

Her head snapped back around. Seconds ticked by before she said, "Get away from my window, you perv. I have to get dressed."

The thump turned into a hard, steady pulse. "Don't bother on my account."

Please turn the page for a sizzling preview of
RETURN TO ME
by Shannon McKenna.
Available next month from Brava.

"Excuse me, miss. I'm looking for El Kent." The low, quiet voice came from the swinging door that led to the dining room.

Ellen spun around with a gasp. The eggs flew into the air, and splattered on the floor. No one called her El. No one except for—

The sight of Simon knocked her back. God. So tall. So big. All over. The long, skinny body she remembered was filled out with hard, lean muscle. His white T-shirt showed off broad shoulders, sinewy arms. Faded jeans clung with careless grace to the perfect lines of his narrow hips, his long legs. She looked up into the focused intensity of his dark eyes, and a rush of hot and cold shivered through her body.

The exotic perfection of his face was harder now. Seasoned by sun and wind and time. She drank in the details: golden skin, narrow hawk nose, hollows beneath his prominent cheekbones, the sharp angle of his jaw, shaded with a few days' growth of dark beard stubble. A silvery scar sliced through the dark slash of his left eyebrow. His gleaming hair was wet, combed straight back from his square forehead into a ponytail. Tightly leashed power hummed around him.

The hairs on her arms lifted in response.

His eyes flicked over her body. His teeth flashed white against his tan. "Damn. I'll run to the store to replace those eggs for you, miss."

Miss? He didn't even recognize her. Her face was starting to shake again. Seventeen years of worrying about him, and he just checked out her body, like he might scope any woman he saw on the street.

He waited patiently for her to respond to his apology. She peeked up at his face again. One eyebrow was tilted up in a gesture so achingly familiar, it brought tears to her eyes. She clapped her hand over her trembling lips. She would not cry. She would not.

"I'm real sorry I startled you," he tried again. "I was wondering if you could tell me where I might find—" His voice trailed off. His smile faded. He sucked in a gulp of air. "Holy shit," he whispered. "El?"

The gesture tipped him off. He recognized her the instant she covered her mouth and peeked over her hand, but he had to struggle to superimpose his memories of El onto the knockout blonde in the kitchen. He remembered a skinny girl with big, startled eyes peeking up from beneath heavy bangs. A mouth too big for her bit of a face.

This woman was nothing like that awkward girl. She'd filled out, with a fine, round ass that had immediately caught his eye as she bent into the fridge. And what she had down there was nicely balanced by what she had up top. High, full tits, bouncing and soft. A tender, lavish mouthful and then some, just how he liked them.

Her hand dropped, and revealed her wide, soft mouth. Her dark eyebrows no longer met across the bridge of her nose. Spots of pink stained her delicate cheekbones. She'd grown into her eyes and mouth. Her hair was a wavy curtain of gold-streaked bronze that reached down to her ass. El Kent had turned beautiful. Mouth-falling-open, mind-going-blank beautiful. The images locked seamlessly together, and he wondered how he could've not recognized her, even for an instant. He wanted to hug her, but something buzzing in the air held him back.

The silence deepened. The air was heavy with it. She didn't exclaim, or look surprised, or pleased. In fact, she looked almost scared.

"El?" He took a hesitant step forward. "Do you recognize me?"

Her soft mouth thinned. "Of course I recognize you. You haven't changed at all. I was just, ah, surprised that you didn't recognize me."

"I didn't remember you being so pretty." The words came out before he could vet them and decide if they were stupid or rude.

Based on her reaction, he concluded that they were. She grabbed a wad of paper towels from the roll on the counter, wiped up the eggs and dropped the mess into the garbage pail. She dampened another paper towel. Her hair dangled down like a veil. She was hiding.

"What's wrong, El?" he asked cautiously. "What did I do?"

She knelt down, sponging off the floor tiles. "Nothing's wrong."

"But you won't look at me," he said.

She flung the soggy towel into the garbage. "I'm called Ellen these days. And what do you expect? You disappear for seventeen years, no letter, no phone call, not so much as a postcard to let me know you weren't dead, and expect me to run into your arms squealing for joy?"

So she hadn't forgotten him. His mood shot up, in spite of her anger. "I'm, uh, sorry I didn't write," he offered.

She turned her back on him. "I'm sorry you didn't, too." She made a show of drying some teacups.

"My life was really crazy for a while. I was scrambling just to survive. Then I joined the Marines, and they sent me all over the map for a few years while I figured out what I wanted to do with myself—"

"Which was?" Her voice was sharp and challenging.

"Photojournalist," he told her. "Freelance, at the moment. I travel all the time, mostly war zones. By the time I got things in my life more or less straightened out, I was afraid . . ." His voice trailed off.

"Yes?" Her head swiveled around. "You were afraid of what?"

"That you might have forgotten me," he said.

And we think you'll enjoy an excerpt from
My Thief
by MaryJanice Davidson from
PERFECT FOR THE BEACH
Coming from Brava in June 2004.

As he slipped his key card into the slot, the door was thrown open and an arm snaked out and dragged him inside.

He dropped his suit bag, ready to rumble, then realized the arm was attached to a woman. A stunning, redheaded, blue-eyed woman with prodigious freckles.

"Strip," she ordered.

He thought that over. Naw. He must have misunderstood. She'd probably said something like, "You're in the wrong room, dicklick," and in his shock he'd misheard her, which was perfectly understandable because—

"Dude! My lips are moving, can't you see 'em? I said strip."

"What?"

"Strip. Undress. Take. Off. Your. Clothes." He noticed with surprise bordering on alarm that her own clothes were flying off her as she spoke. "Do I have to write it on my forehead?"

As more and more creamy skin was exposed, alarm changed to something else. And speaking of something else, she certainly was. Her hair was shoulder-length and curly, bouncing around with a life of its own. The shades were drawn and the lights were out, and her glorious hair was the brightest thing in the room. It looked like coals banked for the night. Her limbs were long and slender, and she had the cutest little belly, which rounded out slightly above the darker red thatch between her—

"Jeez, all right, I'll help you," she said, clearly annoyed at his slothfulness. "Don't take this the wrong way, but did you take a special bus to high school? A *short* bus?"

"What?"

"Never mind." Then her hands were on him, pulling his jacket off, loosening his tie with nimble fingers, tugging his shirt.

"All right, all right," he said mildly, but he didn't feel mild. She was stunning. It wasn't so much her looks, which were very fine. He had never met a woman who possessed more natural charisma in his entire life. She fairly vibrated with life. And impatience.

Clearly pleased to see he was finally getting with the program, she bounded over to the bed, yanked the covers back—he was treated to a flash of a creamy white bottom—and then was as snug in his bed as a redheaded bug.

Nude, he followed her, sliding between the sheets and wondering exactly what the hell to do now. "They really take this hospitality suite thing seriously," he said.

Then he said, "Mmmff!" because she had grabbed him by the ears and was kissing his socks off. If he had still been wearing any. Which he certainly wasn't.

His arms slipped around her, drawing her closer, relishing the silky skin of her back. Her breasts flattened against his chest and his hands slid lower, caressing the fine globes of her butt. Her tongue snaked inside his mouth and he nearly groaned.

Bam! Bam! Bam!

"Oh, here we go," she mumbled into his mouth.

"That's the spirit," he mumbled back.

Bam! Bam! Bam!

"Go away!" they shouted in unison.

"Hotel security! Open up in there!"